AN EXTRAORDINARY NOVEL
THAT GOES RIGHT TO THE
HEART OF FATHERHOOD AND
FAMILY LIFE—THE CRISES
AND DREAMS, FAILURES AND
TRIUMPHS WE ALL SHARE.

"As touching and honest a first novel as any in
a long, long time. It has some wise and wonderful things to say about being a husband and a
father, a wife longing for an identity of her
own . . . There is not a member of the family
with whom you do not sympathize . . . as the
song says, 'You gotta have heart,' and this one
has it all the way—heart and hope."
Publishers Weekly

"A HUMDINGER . . . VERY HUMAN,
HEARTWARMING AND TOTALLY CON-
VINCING."
John Barkham Reviews

STEALING HOME

a novel by

Philip F. O'Connor

BALLANTINE BOOKS • NEW YORK

Library of Congress Catalog Card Number: 78-13791

ISBN 0-345-28478-X

This edition published by arrangement with
Alfred A. Knopf, Inc.

Manufactured in the United States of America

First Ballantine Books Edition: April 1981

For
STEPHEN FARNSWORTH
MAXINE GROFFSKY
SUSAN KAYLOR

AND

JAMES O'CONNOR

ONE

"Quit before it's too late," she says from under a fury of black hair.

He's already backing the four-year-old Plymouth station wagon out of the driveway, knowing he can no more change his mind now than a base runner can come to a halt in mid-slide.

"Well?"

"Too late," he calls as he swings the car into the street.

Bobo is beside him, a finger in each ear. The equipment and what's left of last year's uniforms are in the back seat. A faded baseball shirt hangs partly out over Bobo's ragged jeans, and his cleated shoes are scarred.

"We've got to be there on time," says Benjamin, marking the obvious. "I'm the coach."

As they turn onto Main, he sees Bobo still holding his ears.

He reaches over and nudges him. "Did you hear what I said?"

The fingers slide away. "Don't remind me."

Yesterday on the front steps Bobo's friend, Tim, asked Bobo what his dad knew about baseball. "Hardly anything," Bobo said falsely, without taking even a moment to think about it. Benjamin would have called Bobo in and given him hell had he not felt guilty about eavesdropping.

Today he'll have a chance to show them both what he knows.

I'll give them all a few surprises, he thinks.

They turn into Pee Wee Park. Bobo has the door open before they reach the parking space in front of the fence. "Don't embarrass me, okay, Dad?" he says as he darts from the car.

Benjamin thinks of ordering him back to help with the equipment, but he pictures his son hissing out a refusal in front of the other players.

A tubby kid comes up and offers to help Benjamin drag the equipment to the side of the dugout.

Good parents, Benjamin thinks, sure that that's what he and Marilyn aren't.

The tubby kid is puffing by the time they get the bag to the dugout. "I want, *phwoo,* to be a pitcher," he says. "Everyone looks at me, *phwooo,* and thinks I'm a catcher. I don't want to catch. I want to, *phwooo,* pitch."

"I'll give everyone a chance at whatever position he wants." He thinks of fat pitchers he's heard of or seen, like Eddie Lopat and Mickey Lolich. "You may be pitcher," he says.

The tubby boy, soothed, waddles toward a knot of sullen-looking players around home plate. "I might be the pitcher," he tells them.

Bobo is among the sullen. His expressions are transparent. The look he now gives his father says, "You have just embarrassed me, turkey!"

Benjamin used to feel guilty about wanting to put an end to Bobo. Not anymore. He pictures both of his hands becoming a tight collar around his son's throat. He hopes baseball will help change things between them. No sign of it up to now.

Bobo is only one of his frustrations.

The bookstore he bought five years ago because of his love of books has turned into a T-shirt store. Not quite, but close. A month ago he gave in to his assistant's suggestion and purchased a letter-stamping machine. Now the store offers T-shirts with messages on them. "These days," he told Marilyn, "people read clothes, not books." She didn't see his problem: "You sell a lot of T-shirts, don't you?"

Lately he's had daydreams of going down to the Greyhound bus depot and buying a ticket for some far place: Waco, Texas.

Long Beach, California.

Burlington, Vermont.

He wouldn't bring a suitcase, only the clothes on his back, plus a few dollars to get him settled. *Crazy,* he thinks as he begins arranging equipment in front of the dugout.

He tells his players to go into the outfield and start throwing balls back and forth. He plans to look them over to see if he can match talent to positions. In this league, twelve- and thirteen-year-olds, he's sure a good set of infielders will make a big difference. And one good pitcher. At the draft meeting he picked a kid the other coaches said could pitch. Now he can't remember the kid's name. It doesn't matter. He'll watch, find him. He himself was a catcher in college and knows something about spotting pitchers.

They're still hanging around home plate.

He waves them away: "Get moving!"

"You *got* to have *base*balls to *play* this game, *Dad!*" The remark oozes with sarcasm.

Benjamin goes angrily to the equipment bag. A few years back the only ones who spoke in Bobo's smart-ass tone were hard types, fifteen and sixteen years old. *It's changing too fast,* he thinks.

"Hurry *up!*" Bobo again.

He starts flinging balls toward home plate.

As the players sluggishly move toward the outfield, one of them says, "God, these balls are filthy."

Another says, "You should see the uniforms."

They move like old men. Where's the spunk? At this age he'd have grabbed a ball out of the bag right away and found someone to toss to. He feels like yelling the way he did when he was in the army and served briefly as his battalion's playing coach. He'd better not. Some parent will complain: "My kid loved baseball 'til this clown scared it out of him." Sooner or later he'd yell the way he used to. Not on the first day, not during the first hour.

"Hustle, boys," he says. "Hustle!"

Hustle? Bobo in short right field turns with that pained look he saves for Benjamin's most out-of-date words and phrases. An accusing look. *Hustle? God!*

Deliberately, eyes on Bobo, he says, "Fire those apples straight."

3

He waits for Bobo to bend in agony over the remark. This time Bobo ignores him.

"Let's see you guys get those butts down and scoop up those one-hoppers."

"Coach?" It's the tubby kid, calling from second base. "What?"

"Your shoes are untied." He points.

Bobo, in the outfield, hears, looks, and shakes his head, as if Benjamin had just dropped his pants.

Benjamin bends, ties his shoes.

When he gets up he counts his players: eleven, not fifteen.

Where are the others?

They're probably lazy, like Bobo, he thinks. Bobo had to be dragged away from cartoons and his bowl of cereal this morning. The others are still trying to find their socks. He assures himself that getting kids away from cartoons was reason enough to take this job. Did others resist their parents like Bobo? If not, why not? He'll try to notice the kids who act civilized and later ask their fathers useful questions:

"Ever hit him?" Things like that.

A blond boy raises a ball toward Benjamin. "Look. You can stick your finger right under the cover of this one."

"It's still round," Benjamin calls back. "Keep throwing."

He has to admit it: The equipment is in bad shape.

Late yesterday afternoon he picked it up in the driveway of Herman Block, last year's manager: three of fifteen uniforms only, no catcher's mask, only one shin guard, two of the five bats cracked, and a handful of balls as brown as cooked meatballs. Block had a tic in his eye which operated slowly except when he talked; then it looked like tap dancing. "You got to do it all by yourself," he told Benjamin. "No one helps." Tickety-tic-tic. He wanted to know if Benjamin had taken the job for sure. Yes, he had. Block immediately started throwing the equipment into the back of the station wagon. "Do the best you can," he said. "They can't expect more." Tickety-tic. From the living room window Herman's wife, pale, with a hanging face, watched, nodding, nodding, as if she could hear what her husband was saying, and ap-

4

proved. When the uniforms and equipment were in the wagon, Herman slammed the lid shut, removed the keys, and handed them to Benjamin. "What do you want this job for?" Tic-tic-tickety-tic. Benjamin looked from Herman to his wife, who was still nodding, then back to the manager. "I've been asking myself the same question," he said, expecting Herman to laugh. He didn't. "I have personal reasons," Benjamin told him seriously. Herman merely patted the back fender of the wagon and started toward the house, toward his wife, whose hands were gesturing him on as if he were in a cross-country race and might not make the finish line.

The air was full of warnings.

Earlier he'd called the Pee Wee League commissioner, a Mr. Francis, and offered to serve. Francis said, "It's not much of a team. You don't have to feel obligated." Didn't they need someone now? "We need someone. Yes. But some of these men don't know what's involved." Saying *he* knew, Benjamin took the job.

After his meeting with Block, Benjamin suspected he might be in charge of a Pee Wee League version of the original New York Mets, a team that had lost nine straight games at the beginning of its first dismal season. Casey Stengel, then manager, had said, "This sets up the possibility of losing a hundred sixty-two straight." Casey was referring to the number of games in a major league season. But in the Pee Wee League nine games was most of the season.

Nevertheless, at supper he told Marilyn it was definite. He struggled for reasons after she began stubbornly shaking her head. He muttered some platitudes about helping Bobo and other boys stay off the street. She kept shaking her head. He didn't dare mention the equipment problem or other problems he'd begun to foresee. She said, "You hardly ever throw the baseball with him in the backyard anymore. Now this sudden interest." Before the meal ended Bobo was nodding to some of his mother's observations. Benjamin held firm.

Bobo, before leaving the table, said, "Want to help, Dad?"

Benjamin said of course he did.

"Then have me traded."

5

He'll earn his son's respect. And his wife's.

It won't be easy.

A foul ball turns above the sparsely occupied stands, begins to fall.

In more than a decade of watching games at the Mud Hens' park he's once touched but never hung onto one. It's been bad luck: Some people come to one game only and get a ball.

It's descending toward him.

He hurries to the aisle so as to be able to move up or down, depending on which row it gets into. Little chance it'll land just where he's standing.

Crack! It's hit the top of a seat two rows down, ricochets almost straight up.

He looks around, sees no one else waiting for it. There are three young women a few rows below, the nearest people, but they're not interested, don't even seem to know that the ball is above them.

Now kids are beginning to charge from distant rows.

He looks up, calculates the likely destination of the ball, and like a kid himself, rushes downward, toward the row where the girls are sitting.

Phwomp! It hits the arm of a seat, goes up, striking the middle girl on the side of the head, bounces along her row, away from Benjamin.

By hurrying down the row behind the girls he can jump over a seat and snatch the ball before any of the kids reach it. He starts, stumbles once, recovers. He's about to leap over a chair near the girls when he sees the one who's been hit turning, her face pained, hand rising to her head. Her companions, one of them waving her own hands helplessly over her friend, give Benjamin supplicating looks.

He stops: a critical hesitation, for three boys now fly past in the row in front of the girls, dive into the girls' row, and go crawling toward the ball.

The injured girl raises her squeezed-up face toward him.

"I think you'll be all right," *he says, not knowing whether or not she will, wanting to comfort her.* "An ice bag. You need an ice bag."

The injured girl gives him a soft and grateful look.

6

"I'll take you." He reaches out, catches the hand that's not holding her head, guides her to the aisle.

On the way downstairs he says, *"My name is Benjamin. What's yours?"*

"Muh . . . Marilyn."

The soda pop lady gives him crushed ice in a plastic bag. The girl holds it against her head and says she feels wobbly. He leads her to the waiting bench between the men's and ladies' rest rooms. He offers to take her to the first-aid station.

"No. It'll be all right in a few minutes. I think."

When the Mud Hens' right fielder sent the foul ball up, there were runners on first and second bases with the Hens losing 2–0. Now he hears the crowd cheering and wonders if the right fielder has straightened one out for a hit, maybe some runs.

"It's just an accident that we're here," she says.

"Huh?"

She and her friends filled out a ticket at a pizza restaurant near Central State University and won several tickets. They'd been trying for first prize, a hi-fi record player, but won third. This is the first professional baseball game she's ever seen.

Good, he thinks. He'd enjoy sitting with her in the stands and pointing out some of the less obvious aspects of the game.

Is she a student at the university?

"Yes. Majoring in psychology. Are you?"

He nods. *"Economics, with a minor in English."*

Now the crowd is groaning. The inning has probably ended with runners left on base. Or maybe the runners are still on the bases. He likes talking to her, but he wants to see what's happening up there. It's the kind of game, he's sure, where there will be only a few important plays.

"How's the head?"

"Fine."

"Want a cup of coffee?"

"No, thanks. When do you graduate?"

"Um." His eyes glide anxiously toward the stairway. *"Next year."*

She sinks down a little, seems pleased.

He's been taking a course in creative writing and last

7

week had an idea for a story about two people, male and female, who meet at a ball game when they both end up with tickets for the same seat. He considers telling her that and remarking on the coincidence, or near-coincidence. It would no doubt lead to a conversation, however. He wants to return to the game. He won't tell her until they're back in the stands.

A wild cheer plunges down the stairway.

"I think I'll take that cup of coffee, after all," she says.

"Okay." He gets up quickly. "We can, um, drink it in the stands."

She's shaking her head. "I don't want to go back there. I'll just stay here and wait for my friends."

"Oh."

"Will you tell them I'll be waiting here when they come out?"

"Is it your head, being afraid to get hit again?"

"No."

He hoped she'd say yes. He could have assured her the odds were enormous against her ever again getting struck by a foul ball.

He waits.

She doesn't explain.

He goes for coffee.

A roar seeps muffled through the concrete above, and the fans begin to stamp their feet. The coffee lady has a small transistor radio on a shelf behind her. Faintly he can hear the Mud Hens' announcer but can't tell what he's saying. "What's happening?" he asks as he pays for the coffees. "Don't know," the coffee lady says. "I'm not listenin'." She reaches up and turns off the radio.

After he returns and hands Marilyn her coffee, she says, "You want to go back there, don't you?"

He shrugs. "Mox nix." But can't resist adding, "The best part is probably over anyway."

"Please go back if you want to."

He does, but doesn't. He could go up and return to her between innings. No. That would be more insulting, somehow, than going back and remaining there. "I'll stay here," he says.

"Are you sure you want to?"

"No real problem."

They sip coffee and give each other warm looks.

"Is it the crowd or something?" he says finally, groping for the reason she won't go back.

"No," she says. *"It's a lot simpler than that."*

"Oh."

"I can't stand baseball. It's always seemed to me such a . . . silly sport. I came because we won the tickets." She shakes her head. *"Men acting like boys by hitting a ball with a stick. It's just one of a lot of things I don't understand about people. Maybe that's why I'm majoring in psychology."*

He sits down beside her, closing his ears to the angry chant now coming from the stands, certain, at least this moment, that for every truth, no matter how indelible, there's an opposite counter-truth, perhaps as valid, perhaps as deep.

He notices a boy sitting on top of the right field fence. He's playing catch with two others on the field, one of them Bobo.

"Hey," Benjamin shouts, "you don't play ball on fences. Get down."

The boy nods, as if appreciating the information.

The others keep throwing to him; he keeps catching.

Do I or do I not run this team? Benjamin asks himself as he starts toward right field.

"Mr. Dunne?"

He looks down. The fat kid is at his side.

"You got to write a note to my mom."

"Huh?"

"She doesn't want me to be humiliated again this year. She says if you don't write her a note saying I won't get humiliated I can't play."

This unexpected demand stirs a thought. "Life itself is humiliating," he says, "at least a lot of the time."

"I know," says the fat kid, as if he actually does. "But you don't have to have people holding you down and others jumping on your stomach and stuff like that." His lower lip is quivering now. "Especially when they're . . . players on your own team."

"You're right," says Benjamin. He's pictured Bobo using the boy's stomach as a trampoline. "I'll put a stop to that."

"And . . . and write my mother a note?"

"Tell her I'll take care of you."

He looks toward right again.

"What the hell?" The team has vanished. There are a few mitts, a couple of balls, but no players. He turns around, sees the fat kid walking around the backstop toward the drinking fountain. "Where are the others?" he yells.

The fat kid looks to the outfield, shrugs, says, "Maybe they quit."

Benjamin turns back.

There's movement. A foot. Wiggling in the narrow space between two boards at the top of the fence. And now a thumping sound. Voices? Yes, voices, excited boys' voices. Then a yell:

"Helllllppp!"

Benjamin runs toward, along, around the fence.

They're all standing in the tall grass on the other side, all but the boy whose foot is caught. He's hanging upside down, banging his fist against the fence and groaning.

Benjamin rushes over, with much effort raises him— "Aaack!"—and lays him on the ground in front of the others. The boy cries out.

Benjamin turns to the others. "Why didn't you get him down?"

"We didn't know how," someone says.

Or maybe, Benjamin thinks, *it was fun to watch him dangling there helplessly.*

"It hurts!" says the boy on the ground. He's taller than most of the players and, like Bobo and one or two others, well-proportioned. His intense eyes are locked on the ankle.

Benjamin kneels, starts to undo the shoe on the foot that was caught. "You probably just stretched something while you were hanging there."

"No," says the boy, moaning. "It was . . . okay then. It got hurt when you . . . lifted me off."

From behind him Benjamin hears a knowing grunt from a grunter he knows.

"No, it didn't," says Benjamin to the injured boy, sure it can't be true.

"Yes, you did," says the familiar grunter.

It seems to be a badly sprained ankle, not, thank goodness, a broken one. But he'll take the boy to the hospital

10

and make sure. He raises him and tells two other players to come forward. They do, and he helps the boy get his arms over their shoulders.

"What happened?" says the fat kid, who's just come around the fence.

"Shut up," says Benjamin, following victim bearers and victim toward the field: two steps by the bearers, halt, a one-legged jump by the injured boy, two steps by the bearers, a jump, and so on, until they have him at the stands, where they sit him down.

The remaining players gather around and stare silently at the bare and swelling ankle.

"All right," says Benjamin. "I've got to take this— what's your name anyway?"

"Max Jennings," says the injured one, his face twisted in pain.

Oh oh. That's the name he forgot. The name of the pitcher. At the draft meeting one of the other coaches said, "That kid'll make the difference between a bad season and a mediocre one." How long does it take for a sprained ankle to heal? He's not sure. "All—all right, Max. I'll take you to the hospital. They'll wrap you up and you'll be okay in no time."

"I'll bet," says the grunter.

Strangulation will be too easy. I'll use a stiletto, an ice pick. He glares at Bobo, turns to a more tolerant face. "We'll call it quits for the day."

"Why?" says the one with the tolerant face. "We're not hurt. Only him."

The injured boy nods.

"Take Max," says tolerant face. "We can practice by ourselves."

Benjamin kicks dirt, says, "Listen, you little so and so's . . ." Bobo's head rises. "I was standing right there." He points toward the infield. "I was with you and this— this Max got injured. You're crazy if you think I'm going to leave you here by yourselves. I can't even turn my back." He's thinking of a more serious injury. Already he's probably earned a reprimand from Mr. Francis. What a start! In letting this accident happen, he may lose the team. A possibility. He's not sure he wants to keep this team, but he doesn't want it taken away. "We're quitting for the day. But you be back out here Monday after

11

school or—or I'm fining you each ten bucks! Be on time too!"

"Ten bucks!"

"Are you kidding?"

Bobo's eyes are tightly closed.

Benjamin looks around. "And tell your friends who didn't bother to show up it's their asses if they don't get here for that next practice."

They listen passively. What else can you do when a man is cracking up right in front of you?

"Good," he says, not knowing what's good.

He orders the victim bearers to take Max to the station wagon.

They bend until Max has his arms around their shoulders, then stand carefully.

He's waiting for someone, possibly Bobo, to say, "Why can't *you* carry him?" He wants to tell them it's better for someone with a sprained ankle to be guided by helpers who are approximately his own height. He wants to let them know he knows—well, something. But no one speaks. Some move toward their bikes, some to the Pee Wee Park entrance to wait for parents.

"Anyone need a ride?" he says.

No one answers.

He helps the bearers get Max into the front seat.

"You have a bike, Max?"

"I walked."

He tells Bobo to get in the back seat.

Bobo says, "I'll get someone to ride me on his bike."

"Get in," he says in a soft way that is supposed to signal Bobo that he means it.

Only after looking around, seeing that most of the bikers have gone, does Bobo get in.

On the way to the hospital none of them speaks.

Bobo is making hissing noises.

Max is watching his ankle get bigger.

They turn into the hospital entrance way. Calmer now, Benjamin glances at Max and says, "They'll tape it up. Maybe you can be back in two weeks." *More likely four,* he thinks, but he doesn't want Max to feel even worse. Which is why he doesn't ask the question that's been on his mind since he started running toward the right field fence: *Why did you sit on the fence?*

He pulls up at Emergency, goes in, gets a wheelchair, comes back, and orders Bobo to help get Max into the chair.

Sluggishly, Bobo does.

He'll make sure they call Max's doctor. He doesn't want to call the parents. He'll ask them to have Max's doctor do that too. Maybe the parents will call him later; he hopes not. After they leave he'll order Bobo not to make a big deal of the ankle when they arrive home.

It's not until they've wheeled Max to the X-ray room that Bobo says something.

"What was that?"

"I said, 'It was stupid.' "

"What are you talking about?" says Benjamin.

"They're gonna have *your* butt."

"Who?" says Benjamin, feeling a chill at the back of his neck.

"Everyone," says Bobo.

"Why?"

"It's not just him." He points to the X-ray room. "You want to fine kids ten bucks. You can't even fine us a penny. We're . . . we're kids."

"Is that right?" says Benjamin.

"That's right."

Of course it's right. Benjamin knew that before he asked the question. He asked because, with Bobo, talking is like a contest with paddles and ball. Bobo isn't an eager player. When he hits the ball at you, you'd better return it because he might not hit it again. It's Benjamin's chance to return. But he can't see the damned ball.

"Well, Dad?"

"I'll think about it and talk to you later."

"I'd better start by admitting I haven't been open about very much lately. That's my problem, not yours. And I know I'm going to have to do something about it. Soon, I'm afraid. I've got to keep that separate from this, but . . . well, damn it, Benjamin! Baseball!

"Small as it may seem to you it's going to wipe out our two-week family vacation at Traverse City. That's been like a . . . buoy I was swimming toward; it helped. Now we'll have only a few chilly days in September before the kids get back to school. Then we're locked in again 'til

13

their Christmas break. Last year we took Bobo off his team briefly. But he's only a player. You have to commit yourself from now 'til the end of August. I know you need the outlet or escape or whatever. I've thought of that, and I care that you're happy. But I've got to think of myself too. Now, I'm afraid, more than ever. I just don't like the feeling lately that everything is part of a misery that invades me. I'm no flaming feminist, as you know. I speak out of . . . of—oh, Christ, Benjamin!—weariness, I guess. I'm really not sure. Never mind. As I think about it, I know even a vacation on Lake Michigan isn't going to solve any of that. It's just that, having it cut off because of baseball season, I feel persecuted. It's not like a plot against me. It's like . . .

"Listen. I was going to keep my mouth shut about all of it, and then I heard about that first practice. I saw Mrs. Jennings at the A & P. I don't know her well, but she told me about Max's ankle, which may take months to heal. She didn't even hint at blaming you, and I'm not blaming you, even though you are the coach, the responsible one. That's important. No matter what that stupid form says that parents have to sign—"The Pee Wee League and coaches are not responsible for injuries' and such—the Jenningses could sue you, Benjamin. Lately I've been worried about Bobo breaking his leg or arm or running into a fence and having a concussion. I don't know why anyone lets their kids play certain sports. The risks are hardly worth it.

"Anyway, even if there are no injuries, you're going to be plagued with phone calls all the time from kids and parents. Remember how you used to call Harold Smith last year to ask why he wasn't playing Bobo more? Then tell me later an idiot could do a better job than him? Is that why you offered yourself? Never mind. Just remember: The parents and kids will be under your feet all the time, or will be unless you just turn them all against you, which would make it worse. I mean they'll be wanting to go to McDonald's for treats after the games and having team picnics and getting you to buy new mitts and gloves and balls.

"Something else. Bobo doesn't want you to coach. I mean, if he can't communicate with us at home except for a few questions and answers and grunts and groans, how *is he going to do it with you on a ball field? Nothing in those adolescent psych courses I took tells me why he's becoming more difficult by the day, for me as well as you. I, for one, can't stand all those four-letter words he's begun to use. And I* don't *understand why he wants to go out with a friend at nine o'clock at night and throw rocks into the reservoir, or have a walkie-talkie, or wear a certain kind of green socks you can get only by driving to some big department store in Toledo. I mean, there are enough oddities about him without us creating new ones. Which* you, *being his coach, will probably do, despite all your grand intentions.*

"I've never understood the Pee Wee thing anyway. You're supposed to teach the kids about the sport. Everyone is supposed to get into every game. There's not supposed to be all that competitive stuff like in regular baseball. But you name me a coach in the league last year who wasn't out to knock the stuffing out of every team he played. I heard of one of them—maybe it's the one who had the team they've given you—and he sent this poor kid who couldn't hit up to bat in the last inning, because the kid hadn't played yet so he had *to play him, and he told the boy to lean forward and get hit by the pitch, just so he would get to first base and make a run come home since there was a boy standing on every base at the time. Now if that's not trying to win instead of teaching kids I don't know what is.*

"Look. I realize I've said much more than I wanted to. Maybe it's just as well. It's shown me how much I've been trying to find in you the reasons for my own discomfort. That's not healthy, for me or you. At least I'm getting things out. I hope it hasn't brought you down or —fine time to say it—caused you to change your mind. Benjamin, if you do reconsider, do it because you've been moved to do it, for reasons that are your own.

"Strange. After all I've said I'm beginning to root for you to stick to your decision. At least it'd prove that one of us can fight against the monotonies in our lives. I probably should be inspired by the example you're giving me. But I'm not."

The second practice will be a lot more productive than the first.

Of that he's not at all certain.

He desperately wants it to be more productive.

He'll do something to make it so: He'll divide the team into sections, have some throwing, some hitting, some running laps. In effect, break up the mob, establish his authority, get them going in *his* direction.

No good. He's not dealing with prisoners out in the yard for an hour of recreation but, as Bobo painfully reminded him, kids.

How do you get kids to enjoy doing what you want them to do?

He doesn't know.

He begins to pick up pebbles on the infield. It's a boring job. He stops, puts his hand into his pocket, removes his strapless wrist watch: 3:30.

The schools have been out for twenty-five minutes. Where are they? Home, having Nestlé's Quik and bowls of sugary cereal, he supposes.

He accelerates his pebble picking. There are thousands of them. He's putting them into a paper bag. He'll never get to them all. One of the veteran Pee Wee coaches said at the draft meeting, "You'll never see a pro infielder who's come out of this part of the country. Kids can't trust balls to bounce right, and so they flinch. A true-bouncing ball, which you now and then get, ends up in their teeth 'cause they just don't believe it's going to bounce right." Benjamin thinks of the major league infielders whose places of origin he can remember. None are from this part of the country. Why, he wonders, can't someone come up with a broad-based broom with several handles and let the kids sweep it across the infield a few times before each practice and game? A mixture of sand and clay could be sprinkled over the swept part, at least before games. What a smooth infield that would make! He'll mention it at the next general meeting.

He removes the watch again: 3:41.

He scans the area around the park. No sign of them.

He stops picking up pebbles and sits in the stands behind home plate, from where he gazes out at the center field fence, wishing there were no baseball practice, no family to contend with, no guilty tugs about taking time away from his bookstore. Even before baseball season started he'd cut down on his time on the job. Some evenings he goes to the bookstore, but not to work. He takes a volume from his private bookshelf at the back, brings it to his cubicle office, and reads for a couple of hours. His collection, made up of books rescued from the shelves at the front, ranges from sports biographies to poetry and even philosophy: pleasure, not business.

He checks his watch again: 3:53.

After Marilyn's speech the other night he gave himself exactly forty-five days to meet certain self-imposed demands. That is, if, by June 30, he hasn't, one, heard from Bobo spontaneous and enthusiastic approval for his coaching of Gray's Cleaners Pee Wee League Senior Team and, two, received approval from the commissioners of a qualified assistant coach (unfound as yet) who agrees to replace him during vacationtime, he will, one day after said deadline, or on July 1, submit in writing to the commissioners his permanent resignation as coach of Gray's Cleaners Pee Wee Team.

All he told Marilyn about it was this: "If you and Bobo feel the same way you do six weeks from now, I'll quit then and there." She didn't exactly like the proposition ("You certainly give yourself a generous amount of time") but admitted that, given the strength of his baseball obsession, it was more than she expected.

What he said, casually, to Bobo was simply: "Let me know around the end of June how you think things are going." Bobo, he knows, will speak honestly and out of self-interest, as his immediate reply demonstrated: "I can tell you now, Dad." Benjamin had to repeat: "At the end of June."

"Hi, Mr. Dunne."

Sitting beside him after coming silently into the ball park is the fat kid, whose unfortunate name Benjamin knows from studying the application cards: Meryl Bagthorn. His card gave him away (Height: 5'2"; Weight: 151 lbs.).

"Hi, Meryl."

"You don't have to call me by my real name. The other kids call me Baggy."

"Do you like that better?"

"No. But I don't like 'Meryl' either, so it doesn't matter. Who's gonna pitch now that Max is out for the season?"

17

"Who says it's for the season?"

"My mom. She knows a nurse at the hospital. The nurse heard the doctors talking. His leg's not broken but they don't want him to play." He's now sitting arm-to-arm with Benjamin and, like a pet kitten, is looking straight up at him. He doesn't speak for a minute or so, then says:

"You don't want me to pitch, do you?"

"How can I know until I see you throw?"

"When are you gonna let me?"

"When we have a batting practice, I guess, which we'll have whenever the rest—"

An explosion of yells interrupts him. He turns to the Pee Wee Park entrance to see two sturdy-looking banana-seat bikes, each containing three boys, hurtling toward him. They seem to be racing, a red one and a yellow one, the yellow slightly ahead. As they get closer to the stands, they pick up speed. "Slow down!" he shouts. They don't. The yellow bike crashes into the stands, delivering the front rider across the stands and then down, tumbling, so that he ends up all twisted on the ground a few feet from Benjamin and Meryl. "Owwwwwwww!" he cries. The red bike meanwhile has crashed not into the stands but into the yellow bike, sending the boys on the red bike and those still on the yellow bike into a sprawl of flesh, bone, and metal. There are general moans and cries. Both bikes are clearly damaged. And so, it seems to Benjamin, must be the riders.

The boy who rolled down the stands is up, saying, "I've got splinters."

Turning from him, Benjamin watches as one boy, then another, and another, climbs out of the human pile, each slowly, very slowly. But they are moving, all of them, and soon each has made it to his feet. One is holding his shoulder, another rubbing his knee, all making pained sounds.

"Anyone hurt? Badly?"

Some embarrassed looks but no answers.

"Geez!" says Meryl. "That was something!"

They are moving about now, brushing dust from themselves, laughing.

Not hurt?

Maybe hurt.

Finally he doesn't care. *Let them carry their damaged spleens and other wounded parts through the rest of the afternoon,* he thinks.

"Run!" he says.

"Run?" says the blond who was driving the red bike. "Are you kidding?"

"Run where?" says the one who's been holding his shoulder, sounding as surprised as the blond.

"Run to the goddamned center field fence and then run back to goddamned home plate, and then back to center field, and then back to home, and don't stop until I tell you to!"

"We've got bruises," says the boy who was driving the yellow bike.

"Run," says Benjamin. "Run until you can't run any more."

It takes a few minutes but soon they are running, one with a pronounced limp and another with a slight limp, others holding parts of themselves.

He'll run them until they fall. Then he'll give them a short rest. Then he'll take a bat and smack ground balls at them for the remainder of the afternoon.

Now he tells them to go around the entire field.

Though they groan, they go.

Where, he thinks, *is that joker, Bobo?*

Meryl takes one lap to most of the others' two, puffing but hanging on, going as fast as he can.

Benjamin hears the comments they make as they approach for the turn at home plate.

"Twenty—*hfff*—bucks if you fall down."

"Yeah. Fifty—if you—break a leg."

"And uh hundred if you—*pwwwp*—die."

Not until some begin to stumble and fall does he tell them to quit.

One by one they come in and collapse in front of the screen behind home plate.

As the late arrivers appear, he makes them run too.

Soon all the ones who were at the first practice have arrived, all but two: Max Jennings, not expected, and Bobo.

By four ten they're huddled around the screen, shaded by the public announcer's booth, which is on a high platform behind the stands. They are puffing, exhausted.

Ignoring them, he turns the equipment bag upside down near the third base line, shoves the balls together, and fixes the bats against the fence, pushing the catcher's equipment to one side.

"Get up," he says, not looking at them, "and go to the positions you think you want to play."

He hears grumbles.

He takes the empty equipment bag to the dugout.

When he turns to come out, he sees all but one of them at the pitcher's mound. Some are standing, some sitting, one is lying down. The one who isn't there is Meryl, who's squatting on home plate.

Benjamin glares at the ones on the pitcher's mound, then, with deliberate slowness, turns, walks to the equipment pile, picks up one ball, says to Meryl, "Follow me," and heads toward the mound. The tallest of them all is the disheveled-looking blond boy who was pedaling the red bike. Benjamin points to him and says, "Go to first base."

"But I want—"

"Go." Now he's pointing to first base, or, since there are no actual bases, the place where first base should be.

By whim and instinct he puts the others at infield positions: a short, quick-moving boy with glasses on second; a squat boy with strong-looking arms on third; a lanky one with a large mitt at shortstop. As unscientifically, he directs the remaining boys to backup positions behind the others.

He hears a few muted curses, ignores them.

He turns to Meryl, still beside him. "You stay here."

Meryl is grinning up at him. "Thanks."

"You've got *him* at the pitcher's position?" says the shortstop.

"Yes," Benjamin replies brusquely.

"Shit," says either the third baseman or his backup.

Benjamin plays deaf to the remark. He goes to the equipment pile and picks up a bat and ball. He moves to the plate and starts hitting ground balls, low, hard, and clean. He begins at third, then moves the hits around the diamond. He is grateful that the bat connects with the ball every time he swings. Meryl takes each retrieved ball from the fielder and throws, not pitches, it back to Benjamin, who takes it bare-handed and hits again. The first time he hits around the diamond no one gets a glove on the grounders, not even the backup men. He tells the backup men to change positions with the ones they're backing up.

Before he can hit around again he hears a crunch, tire on dirt, and turns to see Bobo appear from behind a puff of dust, a candy bar sticking out of his mouth like a cigar. He drops his bike beside the wire fence, signals a greeting to one of the infielders, then turns to his father and says, "I want to play pitcher or short. Okay?"

He'll go over there, pull off one of Bobo's bike spokes and wrap it around his neck at least three times; it'll be a slow gurgling death. Despite the fury in his heart, Benjamin's instruction is soft: "Catch."

"Catch?"

Last year Bobo returned from his first practice saying, "If Smith makes me a catcher, I'm quitting." He dreads the position. "Catchers wreck their fingers," he said. "And, besides," he added, knowing that Benjamin had been a catcher in high school and college, "they're usually stupid."

"Catch!"

"What are *you* trying to prove?"

Benjamin looks around. For the first time in two practices every player on this so-called team is paying attention.

"Eh, Dad?" A probe, delivered from beside the low fence, where Bobo is now finishing his candy bar. Such challenges are designed to lead Benjamin to anger, often do. At home he doesn't do much more than send Bobo to his room. Sometimes he has to guide him by holding the back of his shirt. There are shouts, sometimes curses, from behind the bedroom door. Benjamin's fragile control has depended so far on calmly prescribed restrictions: no bike riding for a week, etc. Eventually conditions again become normal, or what he likes to consider normal, but shakily.

What now?

Benjamin isn't sure. An instinct tells him to turn his back on Bobo, pick up the ball and hit it to third, though the impulse to commit infanticide is still with him.

He makes the more civilized choice.

Amazingly, the backup at third fields the ball cleanly

and manages a good but looping throw to the first baseman, who, however, drops it.

"Nice throw."

He hits around the infield twice more. Few actually catch and hold the ball, but most of them, though clumsy, limping, uncertain, are somehow stopping it. No one is making clean throws to first. One problem is the lack of a base: Each time a ball is thrown, the first baseman must guess where he's supposed to stand. Benjamin decides to put the unused catcher's mitt down where the base ought to be. He turns for the mitt, is startled to see it on the hand of Bobo, who has moved part-way down the line toward home plate.

"This is a lot of crap," Bobo says; but he takes a step closer.

The ball is in Benjamin's hand. Quickly he underhands it to Bobo.

Bobo doesn't step aside, but catches it.

Though he knows nothing final has been settled, Benjamin feels a warmth in his belly.

He uses a folded chest protector as first base.

Soon he has an infield, tentative and leaky. He's sure it's the best now possible. Bobo, though sullen, is snapping up the balls the infielders are returning, handing them to Benjamin for the next hit, doing the job.

Meryl, chugging at the pitcher's mound, is at least slowing down every ball he can get his mitt on.

By the end of fielding practice, Benjamin is, in general, satisfied.

They're gathering around the bat pile when he tells them there won't be batting practice; it's now nearly five thirty, quitting time.

There are looks of disgust.

"What a robbery!" says the squat boy who was at third. "I don't like fielding. I just like hitting."

During infield practice Benjamin's doubts jelled to a kind of respect; they tried. So he's patient when he says, "Everything in its place. We'll have hitting tomorrow." No threat, no qualifying condition like *if you get here on time* or *if you don't come in crashing your bikes*. "Everyone will get a chance."

The squat boy's name is Nick. He has arms that remind Benjamin of a man's, including the hair. "So who gets to pitch batting practice tomorrow?" he says.

"We'll take turns. Meryl? You asked about pitching. I'd like everyone who wants to to have a chance. You can try first."

Meryl's cheeks are taking on the color of a boiled beet. Blinking, fidgeting, looking at the ground, he says, "I changed my mind. I don't want to."

There's no time to get to the *real* reason Meryl has backed off, though Benjamin is pretty sure he was intimidated by all the comments during fielding practice. ("Him a pitcher? Shee-*yit!*") The boy has, as of the moment, changed his mind. That's that. Benjamin is not a therapist. "All right. We'll go alphabetically and give everyone who wants to pitch a shot at it."

Stone-faced until now, Bobo winces.

Is it a reaction to Benjamin's democratic method? Or something else? Like his use of the word "shot"?

Benjamin doesn't know and, just now, doesn't care.

He goes to the dugout, gets the application/permission cards, which have the players' names. He finds "Adams, Timothy R.," and says, "Timothy or Tim Adams can pitch batting practice first. Where is he?"

"Not here," says Bobo.

This, he realizes, is the card of Bobo's friend, the one he was talking to on the front steps the other day. He hasn't been at either practice. "Sick?"

"Quit," Bobo tells him.

"Quit?" says Benjamin. "He—he hasn't even started."

A couple of players laugh.

"Doesn't want to play," says Bobo, knowing more than he's telling.

"Why not?"

Bobo gives the maddeningly indifferent shrug he's lately acquired. "Ask *him.*"

After the strangulation spoke is wrapped around Bobo's neck, several other spokes, stuck into the spaces between Bobo's ribs, will cause excruciating pain.

Benjamin puts the "Adams" card at the bottom of the pile. "Bagthorn. Wait. Meryl already said no."

"Muh—maybe I'll change my mind. But—not now. Maybe later."

23

"Sure." Benjamin goes to the next card: "de Oliviera, Anthony J."

"Geer and bresent, Meester Don."

Benjamin identifies a small slight boy peering up at him from behind oily black hair and above a toothy friendly grin. Maybe a son of one of the migrant workers who stay on the farms outside of town. He was backup second baseman. "Tomorrow you pitch batting practice."

"Hi like secon' base now, sor."

"What?"

"Porget thee peetching por me." He's able to speak and maintain the smile at the same time. "Hi have fon on secon' base an weel stay, eef heet's hokay." He doesn't seem at all bothered by the amused looks of the others. "Hokay?"

"Okay." Benjamin reads from another card: "Foxx, Harold." He looks about.

"I wrecked my arm throwing today." It's the lanky one who was at short. He's rubbing his arm between elbow and shoulder.

"You probably didn't 'wreck' it," says Benjamin nervously, remembering Max Jennings, "but possibly you strained it a little. No matter. We'll . . . we'll get someone else."

Next card. Next candidate.

This one, the first first baseman, has to see his dentist.

The next, one of the bike passengers who'd limpingly played backup at first, says he can't put weight on his right leg.

"All right. All right."

"You skipped me." It's Bobo.

For some reason, Bobo's card hasn't come up alphabetically. "Okay. I'll pick you up after school and get you here early to warm you up. You also owe me a bunch of laps around the field anyway."

"Wait. You didn't let me finish." It's his righteous tone. "I don't *want* to pitch."

"Why not?"

Bobo's making his eyes go back and forth, his way of insisting he doesn't want to talk about it. Benjamin feels insulted. It's late. He'll try to learn more when he and Bobo are at home.

He reaches the last card.

24

Not a single player offers to pitch batting practice to-morrow. Each has a reason that is at least partly credible.

Meryl's hand seems to be rising.

Benjamin, sensing Meryl will provide a complication, not a solution, ignores the wavering hand.

He knows there's something fishy about all the refusals and, for that reason, doesn't speak the thought. "Be on time" is all he says.

They seem to be waiting. It's like a contest, but he doesn't want to participate.

"That's all," he says.

Disappointed, they begin to drift off. All but Meryl. He stands beside Benjamin at the foot of the stands, gazing up at his coach with a cocker spaniel look. Benjamin waits, but Meryl says nothing. Benjamin doesn't feel like encouraging him. He starts toward first to recover the chest protector, then stops and looks back. Meryl is gone.

As he's stuffing the chest protector into the equipment bag, he glances toward the park entrance, sees Bobo with four or five others: a tight group, like a football huddle. He notices Nick, speaking with gestures. Then Bobo, leaning into the group, says something. There are nods from a few of the others.

Watching them he must remind himself: *They're kids, not the Mafia. Be calm.*

Still, he's uncomfortable.

He won't worry about it, not, at least, until after he and Bobo have spoken.

Having put the equipment into the station wagon, he sits alone near the bottom of the stands, closes his eyes to the empty field, and feels the last rays of spring's first warm sun soak his back.

"Mr. Dunne?"

He opens his eyes to a tall tanned woman in a well-tailored pale yellow dress, standing before him. He pulls himself up, noticing in the falling light that her hair is a delicate silver, sort of silvery blond. She's wearing large, undecorated sunglasses. She reminds him of a woman he's seen pictured on the dust jacket of a recent popular novel.

"Yes?"

"Do you have a few minutes?"

The shadows are long on the infield. He's slept. It must

be six thirty, maybe seven. Marilyn will be serving dinner, questioning Bobo about practice. He should go now. Instead he says, "Yes, I do," aware that his reason is like that of someone who examines a book simply because of the artwork on the dust jacket.

She lowers herself gracefully to a sidesaddle position, very close to him, and smiles.

He has no idea what the smile is all about but, as though he does, he smiles back.

"Big John Wayne American hero stuff. Right? Just hang in there and see it through. That's bullshit, Dad. I've got nothin' to hang in here for, except trouble. And I don't want any. Why don't you quit coachin' and start joggin'. You're really screwin' up my life, and those guys' too. You must be stupid if you don't see how. Listen to what you just asked me. About the others and what they think. You wouldn't go over to one of their houses, like that creepy Meryl's, and say, 'Hey, tell me what the rest of the team thinks about me.'

"I don't care if it gets you mad. I'm just going to tell you what I think.

"Like one thing is, I don't want you to be the coach because I have to be two people, the player and the son, and I don't like that. I wouldn't like it even if you were a good coach. Which I doubt you are 'cause you're so— you're so av-erage. It's like everything about you. You're not big or little, smart or dumb, thin or fat, crazy or not crazy. You're just—av-erage. I mean I can figure out everything you're gonna do before you do it. That's how av-erage you are. Nothin' is new.

"Like the way you get all shook up when someone gets his foot caught in the fence. Who cares? It wasn't broken or sprained, but then you came over just like an av-erage father and av-erage coach and did your av-erage thing, which was screw it up twice as much 'cause you twisted his ankle when you lifted him off the fence. More than twice as much. Max can't play at all, and he was a pitcher, the only one. Sheez! You screwed up the whole team in the first few minutes. Then you gave us all that crap about fines. Like that may be good for a laugh, not that you intended it to be funny, but it's also so av-erage it's embarrassing. I mean you just sound like someone in

26

one of those old black-and-white movies on TV. 'Hustle there, boys' and 'Give it your best shot.' I mean it's embarrassing how av-erage you are.

"I'll probably get some kind of punishment from you later, like demoting me from catcher to batboy. Or maybe you'll make me the kid to run the lineup changes to the announcer's booth. I don't care. You wanted to know what I think and I'm gonna tell you. Mom is just as av-erage as you too. She doesn't want you to coach because she wants a family vacation or something. I'll bet Suzie and Annie do too. I don't care about a family vacation. For me, playin' baseball is a vacation. I just don't want to play with you as my coach, even though, being av-erage, you're okay as a father. Just okay. Most of the time.

"Playin' baseball with you as coach will be like when we watch baseball games at the Mud Hens' park or on TV and you say, 'That guy's a good outfielder 'cause he can get a jump on the ball,' which I'll bet any kid ten years old, even Annie and Suzie, can figure out. But you have to be this big strategy guy sitting there knowing why this pitcher or that pitcher isn't going to complete a game 'cause of the way his arm is throwin'. Who cares? Like I don't look at a ball game to hear you. I want to figure that stuff out by myself. If I want to know, Dad, I'll ask. I don't want you to watch the ball game for me. Don't you know what the difference is? Never mind. I know you don't. But it kind of makes me sick.

"So you were a college player and then coached this army team. Maybe you were good and maybe you weren't. How do I know? It doesn't mean you have to end up being my av-erage coach. I can just about tell when anything happens what you're gonna do. With another coach I wouldn't know. He might be just as average as you but he wouldn't be my father and I wouldn't know at first. I could at least take a while to get sick of him.

"I don't want to bug you, Dad. I didn't even want to talk about anything. Now I'm just sayin' what I think. I hope you don't get all screwed up about it. Maybe if you would just not talk to me about baseball, or at least our team, I could think of you as an everyday Pee Wee coach. At least I could just sort of forget you being coach when we're home, or try to. If you weren't talkin' about it or whatever. But I don't know. Then, at the end of June, or whenever it is, I could tell you what you want to know. Like you said. So, between now and then, maybe you better not ask me anything. Like about why Tim isn't playing. I mean, you can ask him. I have his phone number.

"The thing is, I don't like father-and-son-buddies stuff. Not when you're my coach, anyway. I mean, what if I went to your bookstore with you and helped you sell pens and books and birthday cards? You'd probably get sick of me in one day.

"I'll admit you can probably teach me things I don't know about baseball. Despite what Mom says, you got me interested in it, by bringing a bat and ball whenever we went on picnics when I was little and taking me up to the park to show me how to hit and even throwing it around at home, at least once in a while. But now I'd rather learn mostly by myself. You can help me a little now. But not much. Like with the team. See?

"One other thing, if it's okay. After this, I don't want to talk about the team, but I think I should tell you this: It's worse now than after the first practice. What the team thinks. It's not my fault. It's not their fault. If it's anyone's fault, it's yours. That's my opinion. I mean, I think there's gonna be, well, trouble. Don't ask me what 'cause I don't know. And that's all I want to say."

TWO

May's weather is as uncertain as the team. Bright days are surprised by low gray winds, bringing mist, then rain. As quickly rain gives in to sunshine and fluffy clouds, but these are often violated by brief but heavy thundershowers. One afternoon, during a light but persistent rain, Benjamin sends his players home, then, too late, sees the sky quickly clear, leaving the abandoned field in nearly perfect playing condition. So it goes, with variations.

Having found no volunteers, Benjamin himself pitches batting practice. He throws like a catcher, bringing his arm behind his ear, then snapping it forward. The batters complain that he's throwing too hard. He slows his throws and, as a result, has trouble in getting the ball over the plate.

One afternoon Meryl hovers about as Benjamin unloads equipment from the car, finally speaks:

"I think now—I can try—puh-pitching. I mean, I'm not sure if you want me to, but—if it's okay . . ." He hesitates, then says, "Maybe—I shouldn't."

"Grab a ball," Benjamin says gratefully. "Go tell Bobo to warm you up."

In a few minutes Bobo is catching Meryl's pitches near the third base dugout. Benjamin looks over, gets rolled-up eyes from Bobo, ignores them.

On the mound Meryl is clumsy in his exaggerated windup, even ridiculous in the way he brings his front leg flappingly toward the plate. But he is able to do the two things Benjamin can't, at least simultaneously: pitch at the right speed and get the ball over the plate. In fact, Meryl rarely misses the strike zone. The result would be a nightmare in a real game, but is perfect for batting practice: Hitters meet the ball, deliver it over and through the infield, sometimes all the way to the outfield fence.

There's an unfamiliar enthusiasm:

"Hum on, Baggy. Give me another one like that!"

"He's better'n you, Mr. Dunne!"

"Watch me get the Pepsi sign on this one!"

After the practice Meryl apologizes to Benjamin for all the hits. Benjamin assures him that hits are just what are wanted. Meryl is doubtful. Benjamin proves it by appointing Meryl regular batting practice pitcher. There are no complaints from the others; Meryl has, after all, turned them into sluggers.

Meryl leaves the ball park alone as usual, but this time he's singing.

"Now you take my boy Fred there, for an example," says a stout, unshaven man in matching gray-green cotton pants and shirt. He's gesturing with a battered-looking yellow cap with a red-and-white Sperry Holland insignia. Fred Bostick, on first base, has just missed a good throw from one of the other infielders. "I don' take no lip from him. Fred's a good boy an' all, but now'n then I got to let him know which way's up. Hell, you jus' now see him miss that thing? Mus' be closin' his damn eyes. Hey, Fred!" As the man waves the hat at Fred, Benjamin notices "Karl" stitched in yellow thread over the left pocket of the shirt. "How many times you got to be told to keep your eyes on that thing 'til it's in your damn hand? Huh?" Fred squints across, replying with the tiniest of nods. "See. He can catch 'em if you ride his ass. Now you watch on this next one. Here it comes. Here it comes." The throw is good, as good as the last. This time, clamping his bare hand over the hand with the mitt, Fred holds the ball as if it were life itself. "S'all it takes," the man in green says to Benjamin. "Eh?"

Benjamin nods, not wanting to think about it.

Karl moves around the backstop and sits in the stands

30

near first base from where he continues to instruct his boy Fred.

Tim Adams shows up at a practice before Benjamin gets around to phoning him. He stands behind home plate, his fingers in the screen, watching the hitters. He has no mitt and his clean T-shirt suggests he hasn't come to play.

Benjamin is standing where he stands during most of each practice, outside the low fence in front of the stands along the third base line. He wonders, *Should I go over to him or wait until he comes to me?* He moves a short distance toward the backstop and glances over at Tim, hoping to catch his eye.

Tim, intensely watching the batter, doesn't see him.

The team has eleven players. It's supposed to have a minimum of thirteen. One boy has reportedly moved away because his father, a district manager for an auto company, was unexpectedly transferred to another state. Max is, of course, injured. Only Tim, or Tim's reason, is unknown.

Pwack! A foul smacks against the screen behind the plate.

Benjamin's eyes follow the ball to the dirt at the base of the screen. As Bobo retrieves it, Benjamin's eyes rise on the arc made by Bobo's hand, stop when they meet those of the visitor. "Hi, Tim," he says quickly.

Tim hesitates, abruptly says, "Hi," then looks off toward the cornfield beyond right field.

Benjamin has a hunch: Whatever's keeping Tim from practicing is also the source of the general grumpiness on the team, a grumpiness that, Benjamin is afraid, may soon turn to resistance. He hasn't sought and has not gotten any information from Bobo. He moves closer to the backstop, realizing he's not been keeping track of hits.

"Next batter," he calls out.

"Hey. I haven't had ten swings yet." It's Nick, turning, offended.

Benjamin's been forcing himself to respond calmly. Now he says, "You're meeting it so well, Nick, you don't need all your swings. We're running late anyway."

"Bull!" says Nick loudly. Like everyone else, he ends

31

with a bunt and a run to first base. It's a fine bunt, but the boy moves sluggishly to first, where he's thrown out easily.

Benjamin's eyes glide back to the screen behind home plate.

Tim is gone.

Tony de Oliviera, at second base, can cut swiftly sideways to stop balls flying toward the outfield between second and short. He snaps up ground balls that Fred misses and, often off balance, throws accurately either to puffing Meryl or to Fred, stumbling back to cover. He consistently gets the runners, even fast ones.

"Wot you theek ob that, Meester Don?"

"Just fine."

"Hi halso can fleep eet unnerhan or ober de top ob de head. Wan me do try?"

"Just straight throws, like you're doing."

"Hokay, Meester Don."

He waits. There were no hints or promises, but he thinks she'll return. He lingers after some practices, picking pebbles off the infield or just sitting in the stands. He looks up a few times at the sound of a car. It's never hers. He imagines finding a note on the seat of his own car; once he actually looks for one. There's no note.

The team begins to take Meryl and their hitting for granted. They are lethargic, indifferent. Their complaints increase:

"How come we have to stay 'til five thirty?" says Bobo. "Watson and Wills quits at five." Watson and Wills, sponsored by a real estate firm, uses the junior high school field on the other side of town. The team took second place in the league last year.

"And I don't see why we have to practice four times a week, instead of two, like a couple of teams do," says Nick.

Their tone stiffens him. "Three thirty," he replies. "Monday, Wednesday, and Friday. Ten on Saturday, as always."

"What difference will it make?"

Benjamin turns to the unfamiliar voice. Tag, so far

one of the least outspoken players, is slouched against the dugout wall. His demanding eyes don't match his posture; neither does his serious tone. "We practiced all the time last year and ended up in last place."

"I wasn't here last year," Benjamin replies quickly. "I wasn't . . . responsible."

Tag's eyes stay on Benjamin the way they've been staying on ground balls he's been picking up well in the outfield. "Then what difference will you make?"

He knows it's an honest question, but he hasn't got an answer. He struggles to find one. *A matter of believing in myself and you,* he tries silently. It won't do: a hazy response, not the sort Tag seems to be looking for, not the sort he himself wants. It's the kind of rah-rah response stupid coaches are likely to give; he imagines Block saying it. Turning away from Tag, he can do no better than mumble, "You'll see."

There's a low, multivoiced hum of disapproval.

He doesn't need to look at Bobo to know that his son's eyes are savagely closed.

See what? he wonders later. He has no formula. This is a team with angry eyes and flashing moods, a difficult team. Even an easy team would be made up of kids with varied personalities and uneven skills. What on paper seem simple and obvious approaches are turning out to be complicated.

Near the end of practice he discovers that he's had only one of the returning players, Tony de Oliviera, playing the position, second base, he played last year. Has there been a conspiracy of silence about positions? The boy called Speck asks with forced politeness, "Would you mind letting me go to center field, Mr. Dunne?" He explains that center field is the only position he played last year, the one he wants to play. That leads Benjamin to ask other returning players about their positions. He learns not only that Speck played center field, not backup at first base, but that Tag played shortstop, not left field; Lou Pera played left field, not third base; and Nick played third base, not one of the variety of positions Benjamin has had him at.

He makes changes.

At their new—or rather, old—positions, most of the players field smoothly and effectively. He keeps only

33

two, Tony and Bobo, at the positions he initially assigned them.

It soon looks like a different team, a better team, much better.

Why didn't he think of asking about positions sooner? Even today it was Speck, not he, who raised the question. What other questions isn't he asking? What other questions are they asking, *and* answering?

Every time he looks at Bobo he gets an I-told-you-so look.

By the time practice ends he's asking the question that started it all: *What difference do I make?* He won't pursue it, fearful not that the answer will be *no difference*, but worse: *a terrible difference*.

As he watches the players move toward their bikes, he hears mumbling. He thinks he hears, "That dumb jack-off," isn't sure.

"You've got about a month left," Marilyn says one afternoon as Benjamin is changing to go to practice. "Memorial Day is less than a week off."

"I'm aware," he replies.

"Then I don't have to say more."

"No."

She doesn't, and he's grateful.

He manages to get to his cubicle office at the back of the bookstore every morning at around seven thirty, there to go over the previous day's sales, new consignments, special orders, recent bills, and such. He must force himself to concentrate, not only because of his increasing interest in the team but because, in the past few months especially, he's felt an uncomfortable distance between himself and this, his chosen work.

While his own tastes would cause him to fill the shelves with works of literature and philosophy, what sells here are inspirational books; how-to books, especially on matters sexual; bestsellers, especially nonfiction; but, mostly, items that have as much to do with reading as, say, auto polish in a drugstore has to do with medicine: gift cards, posters, printed T-shirts, and the like. It's not hard for him to imagine the day when the store will offer everything *but* books.

34

By nine thirty his concentration begins to fade. Today, for example, he'll turn over to his young manager, Dan Schelling, the job of looking over some of the backlog of publishers' catalogues that lie at the side of his desk. That will free him to go home, lay the Gray's uniforms out in the garage, and make an accurate inventory.

"I'll be leaving early," he tells Dan, who's at the big desk outside the cubicle.

"Again?"

"The luxury of proprietorship," Benjamin says lightly.

He waits long enough to sign some papers Dan has been preparing—cancellations of some orders, the addition of others: *more damned comic greeting cards*. Signatures done, he checks through some long-standing orders, to be sure he doesn't want to cancel any of them, then urgently gets up to leave.

"Bet you've got a woman," Dan says as they walk to the door.

"The team. I have to check uniforms."

"You're just lucky you've got the best store manager in Ohio."

Since practices started, Dan's been patient with him, treating him as if he's a man with gout, or some other ailment that needs a lot of attention but will eventually heal.

He notices three inspirational books at the side of Dan's desk, hopes they aren't samples of books to be ordered. *Rather have a whole section of sports books or poetry,* he thinks. He says nothing about the samples.

As he heads for his car, he decides to spend the time between his uniform inventory and practice typing out the season's schedule. Tomorrow he'll take it to the Quick-Print Shop on South Main and have copies run off. No one will have an excuse for forgetting a practice or a game.

Before one practice Benjamin is in the men's bathroom in the small building a few yards behind the announcer's booth. From here he hears several players at the drinking fountain outside. Someone is addressing Tony. But Tony is not replying. Someone is replying, as if he were Tony:

"It's the way I stand when the ball's hit. On my toes,

35

leaning a little forward. Then, no matter which way it's coming, I've got the jump on it. If it's to the side, I kind of dart forward and to the side at the same time. Anyone can do it."

Benjamin opens the door a crack, sees that it *is* Tony speaking, an eloquent Tony, a Tony with the language of a national news commentator. Benjamin pulls the door quietly shut. He waits until the players at the drinking fountain have gone to the field, then slips out of the men's room and walks to his place by the low fence.

Why is he doing it?

Some instinct tells him not to press Tony or any of them. He'll have to guard against asking Bobo.

Are they all in on it? Or just the ones that were around the drinking fountain?

He watches them when Tony, during practice, talks in his Mexican voice; they act as if it's the real thing.

Why?

Later Tony is swinging two bats near the low fence, waiting his turn to hit.

"What hime tryeeng to do weeth thee bot, Meester Don, ees ponch thee boll to right feel, make eet jomp weeth a leedle loop ober de secun basemon's head."

"Keep doing it," says Benjamin, giving nothing away. "Get those hits any way you can."

"Guess who we are?" says a soft and muffled voice from somewhere in the living room.

Benjamin is standing beside the telephone stand near the front door. He's just come out of the living room, is about to call the bookstore and tell Dan, who's writing orders today, to be sure to get a couple of baseball biographies: they've received favorable notices in a magazine Benjamin's been reading.

A moment ago the living room was empty. He steps back into the room, eyes circling, sees no one.

"Guess!"

The voice—one of the girls? one of their friends?—seems to be coming from behind the big chair at the far corner. "I can't," he says finally.

A head pops up. It's encircled by fluffy blond curls. The mouth, wide and happy, moves slowly: "I am Annie." The voice is a robot voice.

36

For an instant, until she spoke, he didn't recognize her; it's the hairdo, wildly overdone the way kids Annie's age often want their permanents.

The head drops. Another, with dark brown hair neatly combed (no hairdo), takes the first head's place. They're unidentical twins. *More unidentical by the day,* he thinks. The thin lips move only slightly: "I am Suzie." The tone is similar but the words are spoken in a near whisper.

The fluffy head pops up as the dark one goes down. "We live here." Down goes the fluffy head.

There's mumbling from behind the chair; then the second head rises again. "We know who you are." The robot whisper somehow matches the staring eyes. Down goes Suzie.

Up comes Annie. "You are our dad. Hi, Dad!" Down.

He appreciates the game, the cleverness of it, but it's also making him uncomfortable. "All right," he says, advancing toward the sofa. "It's a great show. What's the message?"

The girls, laughing, jump out from behind the chair. "We were here for about five minutes, and you didn't even see us."

He had no idea they'd come in. "I was reading . . . a magazine."

"We know that," says Annie. *"We* saw *you."*

"We put up the volleyball net," Suzie says from behind her sister. "We bet you can't beat us."

"I *never* beat you."

"Try to this time," Suzie says.

He came up the back steps but didn't notice the net in the backyard. Having just returned from an exhausting practice, he doesn't want to play volleyball. *About the last thing I want to do,* he thinks. "Maybe after supper," he says.

"Maybe now." There's a bite to Annie's words.

Suzie's look is supplicating, Annie's insistent.

"Okay, okay." In the morning he'll tell Dan about the biographies. Dan can put them on a later order. "Don't cheat."

"We don't cheat," Annie says. "Maybe you do."

"How can you say that when I never beat you?"

"Maybe you're just so terrible you can't."

"Or maybe you cheat to lose," says Suzie.

He has. He smiles, asks where the volleyball is.

She giggles, says, "You almost tripped over it when you came up the back steps."

When he came in he was thinking about Tony and his accent, wondering if one day the boy might come to the ball park sounding German or Chinese. He remembers skirting a white blob of something.

Annie is now blocking the back door. "You can't go out until you say what you see that's new."

"That's dumb," Suzie says from behind Benjamin.

"Say it."

He hopes he's right: "The hairdo?"

"Did you notice it before I said that?"

"Yes. I did. I noticed it right away. I almost didn't know who you were."

"You don't know who we were anyway," Suzie says. "We were in the living room and you didn't even know it."

"I mean know who *she* was when I saw the hairdo." He tilts his head, studies the hair: "It's really fluffy and very nice. Who did it?"

"Marie and Mom. It took almost all afternoon." Annie opens the door, lets Benjamin go out first but cuts off Suzie by following right behind him. "The stuff they used stinks. Not *now*. When they put it on."

In the backyard he asks Suzie if she's going to have her hair done.

"I was but not now."

"Why not?"

She glances toward Annie, who's gone to one side of the makeshift court with the ball, preparing to serve, gives a sour look, and says, "She reminds me of one of those dumb dolls you have to put your hand inside to make it talk."

Annie's mouth breaks into a cool grin, almost a sneer. "*Your* hair can't even hold one single curl," she says icily. "*That's* why!"

All day Benjamin's been visited by thoughts and afterthoughts, things he should do, tasks forgotten, little worries, other such concerns; they've been like spikes knocked into his brain. The girls with their play and chatter have managed to drive out each and every one.

"I'm serving first," says Annie.

"She always hogs the serve."

"That's 'cause I can get it over good and you can't."

"More than you."

"Bull!"

"I'll serve," says Benjamin.

The game begins.

Waiting to hit, Bobo leans over to pick up a bat near his father and says quietly, "Are you ever gonna have a team meeting?"

Having a meeting hasn't occurred to Benjamin. "Why?"

"Just wondered. Some teams have meetings."

"We talk after practice sometimes."

"That's not what I mean."

"I don't see any reason to have a meeting."

A few minutes later, however, he thinks there may, after all, be reasons. Today, for example, four players haven't come to practice. Lately there has hardly been a day when two or three haven't shown up. One day five were missing. He might begin the meeting by asking, "What's bothering you?" He remembers failing to find out about last year's positions. What else has he forgotten?

Bobo, at bat now, is becoming a good singles hitter. Benjamin has been thinking he'll bat him second or third in the lineup after the season starts. The thought triggers another: *Have to start working on a batting order.* And that thought reminds him that the first game is a little more than a couple of weeks away.

Others bat.

Benjamin is now preoccupied with the lineup question: *de Oliviera first—no, second; Nick first; Bobo third.* That seems fine until the kid named Foxx bats, showing Benjamin that he has eyes like a good umpire, laying off pitches that are just barely out of the strike zone, hitting others well: a good leadoff man. So: *Harold Foxx first; Nick second; Tony third; Bobo fourth. Impossible, that last.* Bobo doesn't often hit long balls, and a team needs a slugger in the fourth slot. *Someone else fourth. Who?*

Practice ends before Benjamin has it figured out.

"How many practices do we get to miss?" Nick asks as he's picking up his bike.

"None," says Benjamin sharply.

"How about those guys who've been missing a lot?"

"I'll—do something about it. Just about everyone has

missed one or two. Maybe the ones who've missed a lot won't get to start."

There are groans from the field, the dugout, behind the stands. Everyone seems to have tuned in on the conversation.

Nick takes off without another word.

Benjamin has a second thought: *Not letting certain players start will screw up the lineup.*

Bobo pulls his bike up as Benjamin is about to leave in the station wagon and says, "What about the meeting?"

"I'm thinking about it."

But he hasn't been. He's been worrying about the batting lineup, still is. Maybe he'll have a meeting after he gets the lineup figured out. He tells Bobo that.

"I think you ought to have a meeting," says Bobo, riding off.

A couple of minutes later, as he's pulling up at the stop sign not far from the Pee Wee Park entrance, Benjamin shouts, "Damn it!" and hits the brake hard, sliding forward in his seat. He's realized he's overlooked the biggest problem of all. He, like everyone else, has been taking Meryl for granted. But Meryl's pitching won't do in games.

Who's going to pitch?

The lineup problem fades.

As he drives home he struggles to put the problems in a sort of order: 1. pitching, 2. lineup, 3. attendance, 4. attitude.

Before he pulls into the driveway he discovers yet another problem. Suppose no more players show up at the first game than show up at most practices. With fewer than nine players available, the team would have to forfeit.

He revises his list: 1. attendance, 2. pitching, 3. lineup, 4. attitude.

Immediately it occurs to him that no lineup will work if the team doesn't want to practice, play, and win.

He makes another revision before he goes into the house: 1. attitude, 2. attendance, 3. pitching, 4. lineup.

That, he thinks, *should do it.*

"Do you have an assistant yet?" Marilyn asks after supper.

An assistant?

Since he's presented her with his self-imposed conditions, she's not talked much about the team. There was only that one reminder, plus a few anxious looks, like those she gives him when he comes in late from practice.

"Not—not yet."

The problem of an assistant, in and out of his mind, vanished as the other problems arose. He did go so far as to jot down the phone numbers of some of the players' fathers, those who've watched at least parts of practices, seem interested in the team.

"When are you going to get one?"

"Very soon," he says, having at this moment made the decision.

"Good."

He goes to their bedroom, opens his desk drawer, removes a sheet of stationery, and writes:

1. assistant
2. attitude
3. attendance
4. pitching
5. lineup

After supper he calls three of the fathers, making his plea softly. "A few hours a week is all."

All are sympathetic; none is available.

In the night he awakens with a start, his heart beating rapidly. He struggles out of bed and gropes through the darkness toward his desk in a far corner of the room. He trips over a shoe, his or maybe Marilyn's, but puts his hands out and, with hardly a sound, breaks a fall by catching the edge of the desk. Straightening himself, he turns on the small lamp at the side of the desk, picks a sheet off the pile of papers on the right. With eyes focusing fuzzily, he sees that it is a letter to a book distributor. There are several piles of paper. He finally finds the one he wants. Feeling around in the middle drawer he finds a pen and makes an addition:

6. uniforms

He turns off the lamp and, with big careful steps—like someone climbing steep stairs—he starts back to bed. He sees the dial on the digital alarm on the dresser near the foot of the bed: 3:40. For at least a half-hour he lies awake, knowing there is yet another, a 7., or perhaps a 1. or a 4. He reviews the team in all its aspects.

It just won't come to him.

Thaddeus Gray, whose weathered cleaning establishment is at the north edge of town, has thick droopy eyebrows, reminding Benjamin of an old-time labor leader.

Benjamin introduces himself, says he owns Benjamin's Bookstore downtown.

"I know who you are," Gray says coldly.

Benjamin presents his list.

"What you mean, uniforms?" Gray says as he glances up from the list and straightens his bulky arms against the top of the counter. "I got 'em some last year."

Benjamin explains that Block has given him all the uniforms and equipment he had and that Benjamin has gotten a few other uniforms from last year's players. "Not nearly enough."

"Block's uh goddamn idiot," says Gray.

"The ones that are left are pretty ragged."

Fsssssssssssss . . .

Behind Gray a small woman about his age is operating a steam press. The steam seems to be rising out of the unkempt black curls on Gray's head.

"We coulda won that last game at least, one good stinkin' game for the year, only Block got mad at the umpire and started twitchin' and stutterin' like uh mad monkey an' they didn't give us uh break after that."

"I got the impression, from him I guess, that it was a pretty tough season."

"Yeah. On me."

Fsssssssssssssssssssssss . . . The steam rises, seeming to form an aura around Gray's head.

"I'm sure it'll be better this year," Benjamin says with unfounded hope.

"Better be. Or I'll be out there at the ball park myself, raisin' hell."

Benjamin waits for a laugh or smile to tell him that Gray doesn't really mean it. There is no smile. The man does not, in fact, seem capable of smiling.

Last winter Benjamin thought of requesting that his

bookstore be allowed to sponsor a team, mentioned the idea to Marilyn. It was like igniting a can of gasoline. When finally she calmed down he began talking, delicately, about managing someone else's team; this time it was like putting a match to a long fuse; there had followed a lot of fizzling, but despite her recent speech, no real explosion. He's still, somehow, on course.

"I understand from the players that the other teams all have a complete set of uniforms," he tells Gray.

"If those little crappers knew as much 'bout playin' baseball as they seem to know 'bout uniforms we'd win the damn trophy. I been waitin' for four years to stick it over there." He points.

Benjamin turns.

There's a stand on the wall inside the door, just right for a trophy of the size awarded to the Pee Wee champs.

Fsssssss . . . The steam glides forward and swirls about Gray's head and face. He emerges like an apparition.

The small woman gives Gray's back an apologetic look, as if the forward movement of the steam were her fault.

Gray's been talking, but Benjamin, watching the steam, has caught only the last of his words:

". . . payin' me off for not havin' niggers and wetbacks and females, I bet."

"Pardon me?"

"I said they're givin' me lousy teams every year cuz I'm not goin' along with the stupid rules. I don' want no creepo-weirdos on my team an' told 'em not to give me any. Girls either. That's just political. So they give me a lot of no-good little crappers to pay me back."

"They pick the teams by a draft," Benjamin says. "Names in a box."

"Ah, bullshit!"

That seems to be that.

"What about those uniforms? Is it possible you might . . ."

"I didn' even get a say 'bout *you*. You know anything about baseball?"

"I played in college and played and coached in the army."

"That so."

"Yes."

"Then maybe you can do somethin' with 'em, cuz that lunatic, Block, couldn't."

"I hope so. But I do need to know about uniforms."

"Tell you what, Mr.—Mr. Dunne."

Fsssssssssssssssssssssssssssssssss . . .

Much of Gray disappears, then reappears.

"Get that fuckin' back door open," he says over his shoulder. "You're gonna gas me to death."

The woman goes to the back of the shop and opens the door.

"You win two-three games in the first couple uh weeks," he says to Benjamin, "and I'll come up with some uniforms. Not uh whole new set. Replacements. I know where I can get 'em quick and all I got to do is have the wife stick on the numbers and the name of the place. But I ain't makin' the order 'til and 'less you win at least two games durin' the first three weeks. Meantime you find as many of those others as you can. Ain't gon' pay for another losin' season."

Fsssssssss . . . The woman has returned. This time the steam seems to rise from one of Gray's shoulders.

"I guess," says Benjamin, "that means we play the first games in"—he has trouble thinking of the term—"street clothes."

"You guessed right," says Gray, turning to examine the finished pile next to the press.

Karl Bostick drops off Fred, then joins Benjamin at the low fence, saying he's on his way to repair a friend's tractor. Benjamin tells him about the pitching problem. He removes his cap, studies its sweat-stained band, scratches the front of his scalp, and slaps the cap back on. After a few silent minutes he says:

"Hell, I'd just line 'em up 'long that fence there, half of 'em, facin' out, and put the other half—what's it for pitchin' in this league? forty-five, that's right—forty-five feet away, an' tell all of 'em to throw like they was pitchers. You gonna see who's puttin' some fire on the ball. Also who's gettin' it at least close to what figures to be the plate. Like you was sayin', it's awful late to be lookin' for a pitcher, an' you're right about that Murl. He's just fine for battin' practice but wouldn't be no damn good in a game. Now, if you get yourself a good one and he don't wanna pitch, just tell him he can go down City Park and play volluhboll with the girls. You gonna see him change quick."

Off comes the cap once more. This time he whacks it against the top of the fence as if there's a bug in it. He checks inside before flipping it on again.

"That's what I'd do."

"It gives me ideas." Benjamin starts toward the field, stops, turns and, on the heel of a thought, says, "I've got another question."

"Let 'er rip."

"I'm pretty sure I'm going to have a team meeting soon. The thing is, I'm worried, a little worried, that there are things I'm not thinking of, that I should be. Uh, problems, I guess." That isn't quite the word he wants to use, but it's close enough. "I was going to let them, well, state what they think the problems are and then respond to those before getting on to other matters." He hasn't even gotten to his question yet—something about how much leeway to give them with their questions and complaints —when he sees Karl shaping his mouth as if to blow out a candle. He stops, says, "What?"

Karl gives a little jerk of his head, looks thoughtfully to the bill of his cap, then to the ground between him and Benjamin. "Fred was on this team last year," he says. "It weren't only a poor team but a mean one. An' a lot of those mean players are playin' again." He frowns at Benjamin. "You give 'em a lot of room an' they're gonna push you right off the ball field."

The player who comes to Benjamin's mind isn't, oddly, one of last year's Gray's players but a new one, Bobo. *In fit company,* he thinks.

"Meetin's are fine," Karl goes on, "but with this bunch you wanna watch out that one or the other of 'em don't use it to try an' take over the whole danged team. Maybe the meanness comes from losin' so much. I don't know. Anyways, las' year, toward the end, they was jus' 'bout runnin' everything: tellin' ole Block when they was goin' in a game, and when they was comin' out. Things like that. He didn't hardly have no control at all."

Benjamin has already begun turning Karl's warning against his own impressions of the team. He's decided to

45

hold off on the meeting, not have it until they, *and* he, are sure about who's running this so-called team. Thin words fly through his mind: *leadership, discipline, authority, respect.* While they aren't words he likes, they aren't completely empty words. If they are to gain substance, however, it will be only when they derive from something acted out.

What something?

He turns, thinking to ask Karl. But the question is too deep and personal, too complicated.

He doesn't have an answer. He knows only that today, beginning today, he will try to fill in the words.

Karl is shuffling toward the parking area:

"Got to go."

And he does.

Benjamin calls the team together and says, "If you want to be considered for pitcher, line up about forty-five feet from the fence over there, facing it. If you don't, get next to the fence, crouch down and be a catcher, temporarily."

Conveniently, about half the team now thinks it wants to pitch.

Benjamin walks up and down behind the prospective pitchers. ("Don't throw hard until your arm is warmed up.") He sees a variety of windups, none quite as exaggerated as Meryl's but all with one eccentricity or another. ("Fred, your hand is nearly scraping the ground when you wind up. I don't think you have to bend that low.") After watching for a while he decides that two or three stand out: not surprisingly, Tony; also Nick; and the shortstop, the skinny boy whom the others have nicknamed Tag. After they've thrown for about twenty minutes, with many balls twanging against the steel fence, Benjamin calls a stop, then signals Nick to go to the mound.

Meryl now doesn't have a position. He sadly follows Benjamin toward the third base fence, sits down in front of the dugout opening, and watches Nick prepare to pitch to the first batter.

Noticing, Benjamin says, "Back up at first, will you?" He'll eventually explain to Meryl the need for another pitcher. His mind is on other things.

Meryl obediently chugs around the backstop and down the line, positioning himself behind Fred Bostick.

Nick is fast but terribly wild, hitting Paul Pulowski, one of the outfielders, three times. The first two just graze Paul but the third catches him under the ribs and knocks the wind out of him. After he's gotten Paul to his feet and sent him to right field, Benjamin turns to tell Nick he's going to make a change. Nick is already on third. "I know. I *know*."

Tag is less wild. He doesn't really pitch, however, but stands erect and wings the ball toward the plate, straight and inviting, and his pitches are smacked hard.

Tony, who's next, comes in with a quick and somewhat deceptive sidearm, not unlike a second baseman's throw to first. There's very little windup, which suggests to Benjamin that the boy is liable to strain his arm. But after throwing to five batters, with quite a few strikes, he seems as fresh as when he started.

"Meester Don, hi theenk hi got a new gareer on thee way, no?"

"Possibly."

"Hi halso hab a deepsy-doo wheech weegles on thee way to thee plate. Want to see eet?"

"All right."

Benjamin moves along the fence to position himself behind the screen for a good look at the dipsy-do, or whatever it is. He recalls the conversation outside the rest room. Several times, eyeing Tony, he thinks, *That little faker,* but has promised himself not to challenge the accent, and won't. Still, the old question persists: *Why?* No time to deal with it now. "Go ahead with your other pitch."

The dipsy-do is a kind of submarine pitch, not delivered like a softballer's but with a regular hardball windup, all the action under the belt. It hits the dirt in front of the plate the first few times. When he finally gets one up around the knees, the batter, Bobo, tees off and sends it against the left field fence with a crash. It's Bobo's longest hit in practices thus far.

"Thas eet por thee deepsy-doo," Tony says, bending for a handful of dirt.

"Try a few more," Benjamin tells him.

Tony does, a couple on Bobo and a few on the next three batters. It just doesn't work. It's the kind of pitch a kid can hold his bat out to, trusting the ball's speed to propel it back through the infield. With good swings the batters are putting it deep into the outfield.

"I hab one peetch now, thee sidearm fas'ball," says Tony resignedly.

"It'll do," Benjamin tells him.

There's been movement behind the right field fence: a head appearing, disappearing, part of a head. It's been distracting Benjamin; he moves from behind the backstop toward first base, trying to get a better look. He detects, behind one of the boards, a shock of blond hair, then an eye, a blue eye, which, on meeting his eyes, descends and vanishes. In a moment he hears a bike churning through the weeds behind the fence. Benjamin hurries toward the backstop for a better angle but can't catch sight of the visitor.

After the workout there are the usual grumbles and complaints. And some new ones:

"I didn't get a chance to throw to any batters. I can get the ball over when there's a batter."

"When are we gonna get uniforms?"

"The league owes us another player for that kid who moved away. When's he gonna get here?"

"How come you haven't given us the lineup for the first game?"

At least the attendance is good: all present, for once. If it continues, Benjamin can remove one item from his priority list.

Meryl, as he leaves, does not sing or, as he often does, gaze off at something in the distance: a tree, the near-by radio tower, an apartment building. His head is down and he's kicking a rock ahead of him, ignoring all else. By the time Benjamin thinks to call him back, say something encouraging, he's out of earshot.

Tony is one of the last to depart.

"Hey, Meester Don?" he says.

"What?"

"Whas good to rob on a sore harm?"

"Shit!" says Benjamin.

"Hue mus' be keeding, Meester Don. Sheet?"

"No, no," says Benjamin, blinking away his remark. "I

48

wasn't answering. Listen. Rub—rub Ben-Gay on it. Not too much. Let me know at next practice how it feels."

Marilyn is head of the crafts committee of the PTA. At the final meeting of the school year there will be a year-end raffle. In connection with it she has cut out a five-foot cardboard man and, in the evenings, has been painting on his face and clothes: a straw hat, bow tie, white shirt, blue-and-white striped jacket, blue pants. There are long sideburns and a walrus mustache over a broad smile.

Attached at the front of the stomach and between the hands is a small cardboard box. During the week before the raffle children and parents are to put the sold tickets into the box. "The principal thinks it will serve as a reminder," Marilyn has told Benjamin skeptically.

After supper he, and sometimes one or more of the children, watch her work at the side of the dining room, where the man stands (held upright by a block of wood nailed behind the feet).

She's working on the eyes now.

"Looks more real all the time," he says.

"Therapy," she answers without turning around.

From the bedroom last night he heard her telling Marie, the woman next door, that, since she'll probably never get to practice psychology on any but her own husband and children, she'd better take up a useful craft. "Know anyone in the market for life-sized cardboard figures?" she asked. They both had a laugh over that.

Now, at her request, he goes to the garage, finds a strip of wood to be used as backing for the cardboard box, returns. "Seems like a lot of work just for a raffle. What are you going to do with that guy afterwards?"

She leans back, regards the figure thoughtfully. Clearly the question hasn't occurred to her. Finally she turns with a smile: "He wouldn't look bad in your first base coaching box, would he?"

Her communications to him are often so abstruse they don't convey anything at all. This time, however, the message isn't lost. "I can find a better one than him. I think."

Later he makes phone calls to prospective assistants.

The replies are as polite as they were the first time, the answers the same: No.

The other day, before practice, Harold Foxx handed Benjamin a small sheet of stationery, folded in half and Scotch-taped closed. "Some lady came by and said give you this," Harold said. Benjamin slid the paper into his back pocket, thinking it was probably a note from one of the parents about a dentist appointment or something. He forgot to read it.

Now, changing out of his slacks and into his coaching khakis he finds the note, opens it, and reads in large symmetrical handwriting:

Benjamin Dunne:

Enjoyed our chat. Would "a man of solitude" care to have coffee some afternoon this week with an admirer?

Ellen J.
(352–1886)

Damn, he thinks, stuffing the letter back into the pocket of his khakis. He looks across at the phone on the bedroom desk. Theirs is a large bedroom, part of it serving as his office-at-home. Marilyn is puttering about in a nearby room. He'd best not call now.

But when?

There's no phone at the ball park.

If he calls from the bookstore, he'll have to be careful. Dan's been all too curious about his off-hours activities and might draw the wrong conclusion.

He checks the clock near the bed: 3:40.

He's already late for practice, so he won't stop at a pay phone.

On the way home? From the bookstore, after Dan and the clerks have gone?

Maybe.

It would anger him to discover a note like that, from a man, on Marilyn's dresser.

Would she tell him about it?

He thinks so.

Will he tell her? Show her the note?

There seem to be hints of intimacy or something, in

the note, the tone of it. How can he expect Marilyn to understand those?

There was only a moment. They walked to her car, she a bit ahead of him swishing in her yellow finery, the sun playing off that silvery blond hair—or did the sun only make it look silvery blond? She turned with the touch of a smile, said, "You seem to be a solitary man. Am I right?" It had been all businesslike up to then, she saying that a specialist in Toledo had informed her that Max might make it back by mid-season but that later her husband had called her—*called?*—wondering how the accident could have happened, finally that she herself knew the way kids horsed around and didn't hold him, Benjamin, responsible. *Solitary?* Maybe it was just that he'd been sitting alone. He said something flat, meaningless: "I guess I am." She got into her Gremlin, looked up, and gave him a warm smile. "I think I'm that way too," she said. There was nothing more, nothing but a little wave of her hand as she drove out of the ball park.

But there is something more: the note.

And there has been something more: his ongoing curiosity, causing him to turn and look up when he hears cars that might be hers.

More than curiosity?

Of course.

What?

He's not about to analyze it, isn't sure he can.

"Day after tomorrow is our first game, so I'm cutting practice short today to have a kind of official meeting right here in the stands. I'm pretty sure you'll have questions later, and I'm almost certain you'll have complaints. But first I want to go over a few matters. Maybe I'll answer some questions that way. Who knows?

"Before we get to the lineup for the first game, I want to thank someone for helping this team more than I've let him know. It's Meryl there. I doubt that most of you would be hitting as well as you are if it weren't for Meryl. And, even though he's not going to be our pitcher in the first game, he's contributed a lot. As far as I know, he's the only one who hasn't missed a practice so far.

"Now, about that lineup. I'll just give it to you and not

51

try to explain anything. If you have questions, save them for a few minutes.

"Batting first is Harold Foxx, playing center field. Second is Tony de Oliviera, pitcher. Third is Bobo Dunne, catcher. Fourth is Nick Luchessa, playing third. Fifth: Fred Bostick, first base. Sixth: Paul Pulowski, right field. Seventh: Tag Euler, shortstop. Eighth: Speck McGovern, left field. Ninth is Meryl Bagthorn, whom I've decided to start at second. The other three of you, Bobby Watson, Gerry Franks, and Lou Pera, will get in the game sooner or later. I'm not saying this is the permanent lineup. I'm just saying it's what we start with. Please put those groans and grumbles into words later when we have a discussion.

"Okay. We have some problems, which I'd like to share with you briefly:

"As you know, we're short of players. I was hoping Tim Adams would be on the team by now. If he doesn't decide to join in the next few days, we'll be getting a replacement when the commissioner evens out the teams. Two replacements, in fact, because they also owe us one for that boy who moved away. If Max Jennings comes back, which is a possibility, we'll have even another player. That'll make a total of fifteen. That's not bad, with the league maximum sixteen. Meanwhile we'll do the best we can.

"I was hoping I could tell you today that we have an assistant coach. I've been trying to get someone interested but haven't been able to so far. Yes, I'm disappointed too. You could help by asking your fathers or maybe older brothers who might have some baseball experience if they want to help. I mean it's at least slightly possible that I won't be the coach all season for—for personal reasons. So we need an assistant who can take over, just in case. Meanwhile I'll work on it. For now, I'll ask one of the players who isn't starting to serve as first base coach until he gets in the game. How about you, Gerry?

"No. Okay. Bobby?

"No. Lou?

"No.

"Look. It's your team, your game. I don't force things with you guys. Maybe I'll get someone from the stands to help. Let's go on to something else.

"Uniforms. I've spoken to Mr. Gray, the sponsor, and

he's not enthusiastic. Says he wants us to win a few ball games before he puts any money into uniforms. I realize that all the other teams have them and I don't look forward to playing in—street clothes. But, well, I can't do anything about it just now. I'm probably going to have to contribute some of my own money for equipment, but I think it'd be a mistake to try to buy uniforms. If I did that, I doubt that Gray would ever come through. Any of you that have shirts from last year, wear them. It's the best we can do, for the present. Maybe if Gray comes out and sees how sloppy his team appears compared to the others, he'll change his mind. Who knows?

"The next thing isn't easy to talk about, but I think I have to bring it up. One reason it's hard to talk about is that I can't put my finger right on the problem. I think of it as 'attitude.' I suppose I could just say, 'None of you seem pleased about anything,' but I don't think that would get me any closer to the problem. The thing is, I do get from you a feeling of dissatisfaction. It's not just the complaints but the silences that follow, the noises at other times, the disgruntled wisecracks, not just everyday horseplay and jokes. Bobo and I don't talk about the team at home—a deal we made—so I don't have a clue from him. I mean, it comes out all the time, with little things, like when I make a change in position during practice, and big things, like giving general fielding or batting instruction. I wish the grumbles would turn to words. There are exceptions. I don't want to make anyone stick out or be embarrassed by saying who. Anyway, here's a chance for the rest of you. I mean, when I end my talk, please speak up, let's have it out, with whatever's bothering you. It's obvious from your rumblings today that you—well, have things to say. So do it, please.

"I don't want to end on a down note like that. And there are a couple of positive things to say. I mean, despite the team's problems, the ones I know and the ones I don't, attendance at practices has picked up lately, which tells me, right or wrong, that you're willing to give out a bit and maybe win a few games, besides learning more about the sport, which is the main reason this league exists.

"And the playing itself has improved. I mean, we still have a leaky infield at times and the pitching has been,

53

and probably still is, a question. But the hitting has been good, exceptional. And it's not just due to Meryl. You all seem to be at ease at the plate now, and most of you have developed pretty good batting eyes. If this team does have a strength, it's the ability to hit the ball, score runs. A good offense. It's defense that we'll have to work on.

"Okay. That's enough. Now let's hear the questions, complaints, suggestions, anything.

"There must be something.

"Nick?

"No? Bobo?

"No one?

"You sure?

"I—I guess I can't force it out of you. I've got to admit: I don't know just how to handle this. I mean, I do want to know what's bothering you. What—what else?

"All right. There isn't anything more for me to say except—be here a half hour before game time tomorrow."

THREE

June has descended with a chill. No rain, few clouds, little wind. The unseasonable cold holds on today. Benjamin checks the time and temperature sign in front of the branch of the Mid-States National Bank at the turn-off two blocks from Pee Wee Park: 58 degrees at 4:27.

Swinging toward the park, he calculates the amount he has so far spent on equipment: new balls, $18.27; catcher's mask, $13.25; shin guards, $15.85; batting helmets, $16.40. He'd thought to go back and ask Gray for equipment money, but Gray's response to the request for uniforms stopped him. He doesn't like deceiving Marilyn, but he hasn't told her about equipment expense, and won't. She knows profits at the bookstore have been down for two years running (one reason he hired Dan, a solid accountant); she worries about money more than he. After Gray comes through with the uniforms, if he does, Benjamin will present the sponsor with a bill for equipment. *Intolerant son-of-a-bitch,* he thinks as he pulls into the parking area near left field.

Already there's a crowd. Parents and kids on both sides: about forty in and around the stands on the first base side. Fewer, about fifteen, around Gray's Cleaners' stands near third.

He gets out of the car and sees unfamiliar players in immaculate-looking pale green uniforms throwing balls in the outfield. Each baseball shirt has a first name sewn over the breast and the sponsor's name (Watson and

55

Wills Real Estate) and a number on the back. Underneath the shirts are turtleneck sweatshirts, forest green, a color that matches the color of their caps and of the thick stripes on their yellow socks. *Houses must be selling well this year,* he thinks.

He sees no sign of his own players as he removes the long cylindrical equipment bag from the back of the station wagon and drags it toward the third base dugout.

The infield has been raked and swept. Straight white lines extend from home plate to the foul poles. Two umpires, in light blue shirts and dark blue pants, stand near home plate and watch a workman with a rectangular wooden form make the white lines for the batter's box.

The Watson and Wills team is lined up in right field now, playing "pepper": Three players with mitts stand about twenty feet from one with a bat, who hits their throws back to them. Each of four sets of players stands about ten feet from the next set, all on an invisible straight line. No one's wisecracking. The balls are being thrown accurately, and the batters are tapping them back to each catcher/tosser in order, going left to right. They're like well-drilled troops. *All they need are swastika arm bands,* Benjamin thinks as he pushes through the gate near Gray's dugout.

The looks and movements of the Watson and Wills team send him deeper into a low mood that started after his meeting with the team. Sensing that Nick, Bobo, and the others, deliberately or not, had insulted him with their silences, he later replied sharply to a question Marilyn asked about the team, a harmless question ("How did it go today?") with something like "What do you care?" thereby creating a tension that carried through the evening.

In stupid frustration today he, quite impulsively, made a call to Mrs. Jennings after he left the bookstore, using the phone booth at a nearby gas station. There was no answer and that sent him deeper. He began to plunge even further when, driving home, he discovered that, after admitting that he was indeed a solitary person, he really wouldn't have had much to say to the woman. He imagined a conversation:

Yes. I am now and then a solitary person.

Oh, that's very nice. I like solitary people.

56

I got that impression from your note.

I hoped you would.

I did.

That's nice. How do you like this coffee?

Just fine. How do you?

The same.

Good. I'd like to ask you a question.

Oh, please do.

Do you cheat on your husband?

Isn't that a very personal question?

Yes, it is. But I don't like to beat around about such things.

Well (blushing), I haven't, but I'll have to admit that I've thought about it.

Oh, good. I've been thinking of cheating on my wife.

How interesting. Hah hah. It seems we have something in common. Shall we talk about it?

We could do that or—or—

—cheat together?

Why not?

Yes. Why not?

The conversation, though fanciful, has made him suspicious of his interest in Mrs. J.—it surprises him how much there is—and that has sent him even deeper.

He stands the equipment bag beside the low fence, looks into the dugout, finally sees his team. Several are squatting on the dirt floor. Others are crouched or slumped on the bench. One, Meryl, is standing at the chicken-wire screen, his fingers in the screen, watching the Watson and Wills players warm up. No one else is watching. They seem beaten, exhausted, like players who've just finished a game, not players about to begin one.

"Why aren't you all out there warming up?" he demands.

No answer.

"Well?"

"Screw off, Mr. Dunne."

The words sting him.

It's Nick, or sounds like Nick, someone at the back. Hard to tell. They're crowded together.

"Who? Who said that?"

No one bothers to look up.

He advances toward Nick. No one has admitted anything, but his hands are extended like claws. *What am I doing?* he thinks as he picks up Nick by the shoulders, the skin around the shoulders.

"Dad, you're actin' like a dummy!"

He starts toward the dugout entrance with passenger. He elbows and jostles the others as he half-carries, half-pushes his heavy load out, surprised at his own rage.

"Let me go!" Nick is saying for the second or third time.

Benjamin drags him past the chicken wire and into left field. *What am I doing?* He stops somewhere between third base and the foul pole, releases Nick, and says to the boy's shocked face in a violent but controlled tone, "Go over there to left field and wait for the others. Then throw baseballs back and forth until I signal you to stop. Understand?"

Nick, with the clamps off his shoulder, finds enough courage to say, "You had no goddamn right to do that!" Benjamin knows Nick could have said something else, a hundred other things, each of which would have left Benjamin with his throbbing question: *What am I doing?* But the question dissolves, though he still doesn't know quite what he's doing. It doesn't seem important. He ignores the boy's remark and goes right on talking: "If you don't do what I say, I'll kick you off this team and see that you don't play for any other." It's ridiculous, as impossible as levying a fine. More likely, properly complained about, the incident could lead to the removal of Benjamin, not Nick, from the Pee Wee League. He knows that, knows the risk, but is betting on Nick's ignorance. "Go."

Nick hesitates.

Benjamin now notices gawkers on both teams and, beyond them, gawkers in the stands.

Nick himself glares but doesn't budge.

Benjamin, envisioning fans and players coming out to rescue Nick, adds, "Now!"

And if Nick doesn't go, if he turns and leaves the ball park or goes running to an umpire, then what?

Benjamin waits.

Nick, slapping the glove, which has been on his wrist,

onto his hand, finally goes, slowly and with plenty of heat in his eyes. He mutters something, but he does go.

Benjamin knows he's just slid in under a catcher's tag with a go-ahead run. He turns for the dugout, aware that it's only a run.

Bobo meets him partway. "That's the stupidest thing you've ever done," he says fiercely.

"Move your ass," Benjamin replies as easily as he might say, "Please pick up that mitt."

"What?"

"I said, 'Move your ass.'" He passes the place from where his son has just jumped aside to keep from getting bumped.

"Dad?" Bobo calls from behind him.

"Go out to left with Nick," says Benjamin, now steaming toward the dugout.

He'll go into the dugout and pull them out one by one, like sacks of grain.

He doesn't have to.

Seeing Nick, then Bobo, they have picked up their mitts and some balls and are on the way. They pass Benjamin as they head for left, eyeing him uneasily, saying nothing.

He churns past the dugout. Nearing the plate he sees the coaches from the other team, three of them, standing between first and home, observing him with haughty looks. They're wearing light green slacks below dark green jackets, with names sewn in script on the jacket fronts: "Norm," "Doug," "Hal." He recalls a manager of the old Toledo Mud Hens who used to bring the lineup to home plate at Swayne Field with food stains all over his faded warmup jacket. He also had a wrinkled uniform and was often unshaven. *These guys look like mannequins in a sporting-goods-store window,* Benjamin thinks, giving each of them a mean eye.

One umpire, holding the chest protector and mask, is tall and stooped. He has a pocked face, crooked nose, protruding eyes, and straggly hair. He seems more nervous than his stocky partner. He doesn't fit Benjamin's picture of an umpire. Both umpires are in their early twenties.

"Who gets infield practice first?" Benjamin asks.

"Um," says the tall one. "Geez." He looks at the other. "The team that bats first."

"Which is that?" The tall one reaches into the back pocket of his pants, removes several scraps of paper, a couple of which fall to the ground, checks a scrap in his hand, bends and picks up the others, checks, finds something that seems to inform him: "You're the home team. So—so they go first."

"Thank you." Benjamin turns, walks toward left, and calls to Tony: "Take Bobo, then go over there beyond the dugout and start pitching to him."

Trying to ignore the buzzing in the stands that started when he pulled Nick to left field, he goes into the empty dugout and sits down, wanting to relax.

Practices are one thing, the season quite another. The pain of this truth is just beginning to reach him. A force has been released and seems to have a momentum, even a will, of its own. He knows he has to keep up with it the best he can, even if that means doing things he ordinarily wouldn't. Jumping on Nick, for example. Right or wrong, it seemed the only way to get the team to move. Later he'll probably think of several better ways he could have handled that, but, at that moment, it seemed the only way. Managers who are cool and glib in April throw locker room tantrums in June. The season, its momentum and rhythms, changes everything. Players with hitting averages as low as .200 in spring training have ended up winning batting championships. Pitchers who don't lose any games in the spring struggle to win a handful later in the season. That's how it goes.

"Hey, Dad! You gonna hit to us or not?"

Lost in thought, Benjamin has failed to see his team take the infield. He gets up, goes to the equipment bag, grabs a ball and bat, and heads toward home plate.

"Hey, coach," says someone with a gruff voice in the third base stands, "how many guys you gonna play at every position?"

Benjamin looks, sees that the players have lined up as they do at infield practices, regular infielders at their positions, outfielders and extra players just behind them. With no other coach to hit to outfielders, he's been keeping the team together by letting them all play infield. He looks to first. There are Fred Bostick (starter), Paul

60

Pulowski (right field), and Lou Pera (reserve). There are two or more at each position.

"He'll need all of 'em," replies a voice from the first base stands.

"Stay where you are," Benjamin says as a couple of the backup people, embarrassed, start to come off the field. "Do it the way we always do."

They return.

Right or wrong, he's sticking to multiple infielders. That's part of the momentum, like umpires sticking to decisions.

He decides to hit the ball sharply. If they miss they'll miss hard ones, and it won't be as embarrassing for them.

The first time around they hold the ball and throw well. Not until he hits a second one to Meryl, a tough chance, does it slip through. He gives Meryl another, nearly as tough. Meryl makes the play. Benjamin hopes the three dandies running the other team are watching. He goes around twice more. There is some fumbling, a couple of throws off the mark to first, nothing serious. He tries a couple of pop-ups, recalling that the coach named Norm, who hit infield for the other team, didn't try any of those. Nick calls for and gets one. Meryl calls for and gets the other. He glances toward the first base dugout: Norm and companions are watching. *Good.* The double plays don't go as well—Nick throws past second into right, though Gerry, backing up at second, stops the ball; and Tag, taking a toss from Meryl, throws one so high to Fred that it sails over the low screen beyond first and into the adjoining cornfield—but they end up completing about as many as their opponents did in their warm-up. All in all, they've looked as good as they have since practices started.

Signaling them to come back to the dugout, Benjamin feels satisfied. On the Love-Murder dial, lately in operation with Bobo, the needle edges toward Love. He feels something like it for all of them.

When they're in the dugout, he thinks of apologizing for his blowup with Nick, doesn't. He says instead: "Maybe they dress better but they're not better. If you make a mistake, try to forget it. They'll make some too." He sees nervousness in their faces. Meryl, Tony, Fred are actually shaking. "I honestly wouldn't care if they'd won the state Pee Wee championship last year. Which they didn't. You can take them. If you want to." Every expression he reads seems to contain a double message: *We want to believe you* and *We don't.* "It's in your heads, in your guts: if you want to win, you will." He doesn't know that. But he's also not lying. He's banking on the unseeable, the unpredictable. "We'll figure it out as the game goes on."

Only Bobo speaks, from the back of the dugout. He says in a flat and somber voice, "They *lost* one game last year, the championship. Gray's Cleaners *won* one, by default."

Benjamin responds quickly: "They're a different team. We're a different team. Forget it. It's a new season. Think of that."

Their troubled frowns tell him they're trying to.

And, for once, they're listening to him.

Benjamin knows that he himself is involved in two games, a game with Watson and Wills and a game with his own players. If the Gray's boys take his word about this game, act on it, come out feeling it is at least possible to win a game or two this season, he'll have a good lead in the game with them. It's an odd contest since he's on their side but must somehow play against them. As for the other game, he doesn't know if they'll beat Watson and Wills, yet he abides a thought that comes from feeling himself thrust into inevitable action: It doesn't, finally, matter.

Where was the wife/psychologist/friend, seeing through his foolish remark, patiently urging him to get at what really bothered him? ("You've obviously had a bad day. Let's talk about it.")

In fact, after his remark, she said nothing. She went from the dining room to the kitchen, where Annie and Suzie had been helping her prepare dinner.

He followed, aware of how foolish and unkind the remark had been. "Pressures," he said, hoping for an understanding response.

Both girls stopped what they were doing—Annie setting the table, Suzie nervously watching something simmer in the frying pan and watching her mother, waiting.

62

Words were always spoken here, even when there was trouble. Where, *Suzie's eyes asked,* are the words?

She seemed deaf to him, unaware of the girls.

He helped Annie with the table, poured Marilyn and himself a glass of wine, and headed for the living room, where usually they spent a few minutes before dinner, watching the news or sharing the day's pleasures and frustrations.

He waited, watching crossing rays of late afternoon sunlight deepen the wine in his glass from pink to red.

Was it so bad? he thought.

He heard clicking noises in the kitchen, knew the dinner needed only to simmer, wondered if he should go in there and admit, before she let him know it, that his sharp remark had been uncalled for, then apologize.

"Marilyn?"

She didn't answer.

Bobo had been in the garage, working on his bike. Now he came past the kitchen and into the living room, asking for the sports page.

Benjamin hadn't seen the paper, told Bobo so.

"Where's Mom?"

"In the kitchen, isn't she?"

"No."

"She went for a walk," Annie called. "She said we have to go ahead and eat. She'll be back later."

Noticing Bobo's look of concern, seeing an uneasiness in Suzie's eyes, he said, "She probably needs a little time to herself or something. Let's eat," then went with Bobo to the kitchen.

"Mom feels crummy," Annie said as Benjamin served up the hamburger steaks, French fries, and green beans.

"About what?" he asked.

"I don't know. I think she was crying when I got home from school." She imitated, making noises like someone with whooping cough—hee-yup, hee-yup—and added, "Kind of like that."

All three of the children began to pick at their food.

He wouldn't spill any more of his concern on them. "So how was it in school today?" he asked, looking from one to the other.

"Crappy," said Bobo.

"The same," said Annie.

"I can't wait 'til summer vacation starts," said Suzie.
That was that. At least they'd begun to eat.

About twenty minutes later he was alone in the kitchen, on his second glass of wine, when Marilyn walked in, red-eyed, said vaguely, "I went for cigarettes," and started to heat up her dinner.

Benjamin thought of saying, but did not say, "Neither of us smokes, Marilyn. Why did you buy cigarettes?" Instead he asked her if she wanted her wine, still in a glass beside the sink.

She said no.

She slowly ate her dinner.

He sipped his wine.

After eating only part of her dinner, she lit a cigarette, took a few puffs, made a face at the rising smoke, then put out the cigarette on her plate.

The girls came toward the back door, Annie calling out that they'd just found a big toad.

Marilyn looked directly at Benjamin for the first time since she'd come back, and, as if reading his latest thought, said, "Later, after they're all in bed. Okay?"

"Look, Dad, it's got white gooey stuff leaking out of it," Annie said after rushing in and holding the toad up to her father.

"Oh," said Benjamin, wanting to be interested.

"All right, coach," the shorter umpire calls, snapping him out of his thoughts, "let's get your team on the field."

He's been sitting with elbows on knees near the dugout opening. He straightens, says, "Let's go!" and leans back as his starting players move past him to their positions.

Against the surrounding order they are like a storm:

Fred at first base has his jeans' legs rolled up as if to go wading, and Benjamin now notices two different-colored socks, one a faded gray, the other a dirty green; like many of his teammates, he wears sneakers, not baseball shoes. The baseball shoes that are being worn by Nick, Tag, Bobo, and a couple of others are dusty and scarred, unlike the polished ones all the W. and W. players have. One exception to the raggedness is Tony. His dark blue shirt is open nearly to his navel, a religious medal hops around in the shirt opening; he's wearing clean light-blue cut-off pants; his sneakers appear to be new; but to Benjamin he's like someone dressed for polo, not baseball. Meryl's shirt, which must have been his father's or a big brother's, is striped and faded, an old dress shirt, and hangs all the way to his knees; when he lowers himself for ground balls, the shirt becomes an apron. Tag has, despite the cool weather, chosen not to wear a shirt and is so skinny—all ribs and two nipples—that he reminds Benjamin of an underfed orphan. Nick has on a tight black muscleman T-shirt, but faded oversized jeans; from the belt up he is like a fully developed man, from the belt down like a flabby unformed kid. Paul and a couple of others have on last year's Gray's Cleaners shirts, all well-worn, each with a single word, GRAY'S in scarlet, sewn on the back. The caps of those who have them aren't all baseball caps and show a variety of colors; none seems to fit.

"Hey, coach!"

He's been watching Bobo's T-shirt flap around as the boy catches Tony's warmup pitches.

"Hey!" The shorter umpire comes to the opening. "Who's gonna be your first base coach?"

He rises, says, "I'll—I'll let you know before we come to bat."

"We got to tell the commissioner up in the announcer's booth. He's going to keep the lineups and scoring record."

"*I'll* tell him."

He looks down the bench, thinking to put one of the reserves at first. But they seem terrified, barely able to play, let alone coach at first. *Who?* Anxiously he turns to the stands, sees Karl Bostick leaning against the top row of seats. *Why not?* He moves toward Karl, catches his attention, and makes the request, a desperate plea as it comes out.

"Hell, yes," Karl replies. "Just standin' here wonderin' when you was gonna ask. *Herff!*"

As Karl lumbers toward the field, Benjamin goes to the announcer's booth. He's about to call through the glassless window at the front when Mr. Francis, leaning down, signals him up the stairs at the side. Benjamin goes, opening the door at the top, seeing a high-school-aged boy at the microphone and Francis seated next to him. The commissioner turns from the window and says, "Give me the lineup. When you make changes, come over to the backstop and let me know." He glances toward the field, ponders something, then says, "I'd like to speak to you about another matter. But I'd better save it until after the game." *Save what?* Francis is nodding, assuring himself: "It can wait." Benjamin starts to back through the door, pauses. "You sure?" he says, worrying that it might have to do with the incident with Nick. Francis, studying the lineup Benjamin has handed him, gives a little fly-shooing wave and says, "Let's just save it." On the way back to the dugout Benjamin worries: *Haven't even played an inning and already there's some problem.*

He avoids looking at the people in the stands for the same reason he didn't insist on finding out what Francis wants to talk about: Just now any little disturbance will break his concentration. He wants no problems, no unnecessary ones, even reminders. He hopes Marilyn doesn't come, he hopes Mrs. Jennings doesn't come, he hopes Gray doesn't come, he hopes no one he knows is here. In truth, he wishes the stands were empty. *Ought to play the first game with no one around but the coaches and kids.* "Coaches" reminds him of something. He looks toward the first base dugout and sees the three dandies, who are side by side like a singing group. *Not even the coaches,* he thinks.

"Hi got pain een thee choulder," Tony says as Benjamin goes to the mound after the flag raising, intending to give Tony and Bobo opening instructions: Get signals straight and keep the pitches low.

"How bad?"

"Ees not too bad eef hi don' try an' poot too much on thee boll."

"Don't put anything on it. Just get it over the plate."

Benjamin returns shakily to the dugout, where he sees the reserves pressed against the screen, peering out, frightened, as if an out-of-control plane had just begun to plummet toward them.

Karl is outside the dugout at the far end, leaning against it with arms folded, frowning as he watches Tony's last warm-ups.

A whiskey-voiced fan in the W. and W. stands yells, "Les send these freaks back to the jungle!"

"Play ball!" says the tall umpire, sounding like a roos-ter being choked.

At this, the beginning moment, Benjamin can think of nothing more appropriate to do than close his eyes.

So he does.

In his self-created darkness he assures himself that, no matter what the ritual, what the rules, what the comic, foolish, or even heroic actions to come, no matter what the differences in the two teams' abilities, this game, like every other baseball game, will remain a mystery until the end, or very near the end. It's the ongoing moments, the in-between part, not the outcome, that matters.

His thoughts are violated by a rapid sequence of sounds:

a loud crack;
a chorus of shouts;
a distant thump.

His eyes remain closed until another sound punctuates the rest:

"Safe!"

On third base stands W. and W.'s leadoff batter, wiping a bit of dust from his pants as he takes a pat on the back from one of the dandies.

Next to the base, sitting down, is Nick, looking bewil-deredly at the baseball between his legs.

Benjamin effectively fights off a temptation to say, "What happened?" The question, he knows, would result only in the filling in of details: a solid hit, a dropped ball, a bad throw, a poor tag. What difference?

W. and W. finds its momentum quickly: There are two singles, then a double.

"Thee damn sky ees falleeng," Benjamin hears Tony say to Tag just before delivering a good fastball that the batter lifts to right field. It's an easy out, but Paul, turning this way, then that, lets it fall to the ground.

W. and W.'s fifth batter comes to the plate with no outs and the score 3–0.

Benjamin hears catcalls and laughter from the W. and W. stands as he walks to the pitcher's mound.

"Is it the arm?"

"Eet's no worse. Ees thee score thas bad?"

Benjamin, aware that at least a couple of balls hit off

67

Tony could have been caught, knows also that those balls were smacked hard. He's worried about the arm and decides to make a change. He tells Tony to go to second base and signals Meryl to come in.

Meryl's fat appearance and apron cause laughter from Gray's stands as well as from the W. and W. stands. His hand is shaking when he takes the ball. "Are you—are you sure, Mr. Dunne?"

Instead of speaking the cruel truth—"No"—Benjamin says with the blind hope of the doomed, "You can do it, Meryl."

Meryl needs nothing more. He turns and starts to warm up. He throws looping pitches, each of which enters the heart of the plate or comes very close. The waiting W. and W. batters observe and begin twisting about in delighted anticipation. One W. and W. fan, female, but with a voice as harsh as whiskey-voice's, shouts, "You better start runnin' after you throw them things, kid." Laughter from both sides follows. Benjamin looks about and sees a question in the uneasy eyes of his own players: *If they slugged Tony, what are they gonna do to Baggy?* It's Benjamin's question too.

"Gonna be a long afternoon," Karl says as Benjamin comes back to the dugout.

Benjamin nods.

By the end of the first inning, however, W. and W. has gotten only one additional run. There might have been more but for a couple of unusual plays:

After three weak singles, the first scoring the fourth run, the next batter slashed a drive toward the mound. While Meryl had no time to get his mitt down, his "apron," hanging low as he leaned forward in his follow-through, trapped the ball, forcing Meryl to fall forward. For a few moments no one knew where the ball was. When Meryl, fishing in his apron, got his hand on it, he looked up to see one runner standing a few feet off third. Quickly, from his knees, he threw the ball to Nick, who grabbed it, then lowered it in time to tag out the runner. With the ball now visible, Norm, the dandy coaching at third, started yelling to the runner on second: "Stay!" But the dandy coaching at first was as insistently saying to the runner standing between first and second, "Go!" Nick had the good sense to throw the ball to Tony at second in time to beat the runners crashing in. With two runners on the base one was called out.

"Damn," said Karl, "wasn't that somethin' to see?"

Not a single player on Gray's Cleaners seemed to know what had happened, including the ones involved in the double play. Even the umpires had to have a meeting with each other to verify the action.

The dandies, all three of them, complained loudly that the ball had been illegally captured by Meryl's shirt.

"They guh-got the guh-god-damned outs," said the umpire at home plate, though his face revealed that he still did not know quite how.

"This is a clown team," whiskey-voice shouted.

What difference? thought Benjamin. *We've got two outs.*

The final out was also unusual. Fred, at first base, chose an unfortunate moment to notice that one of his rolled-up pants legs had fallen. With Meryl going into his windup, Fred dropped his glove and bent down to roll up the pants leg. "What the hell is that kid of mine doin'?" Karl asked. "Hey! Fred!" Having had little action at first base, Fred may have decided there would be none at all. Whatever the reason, he was down when the batter delivered a line drive right at the place his stomach would have been, had he been standing. "On your damn feet, Fred!" Hearing his father's voice, Fred raised his head just in time to have it meet the ball and send the ball ricocheting upward, not toward the right field foul line, where it had been headed, but toward middle right, where Paul was standing. The ball delivered itself into Paul's mitt and stayed. Fred was dazed but uninjured.

"Sure is interestin' so far," Karl says as he begins his journey to the first base coaching box.

Benjamin, who, in spite of his theories, has begun to tempt himself with the possibility of a victory, grunts in agreement.

Their pitcher is fast but wild, and Gray's first batter, Harold Foxx, starts stepping back even before the ball is released. "Hang in there, kid!" Karl yells from the first base coaching box, but Harold, used to Meryl's gentlemanly pitches, keeps stepping out, until finally he is called out on strikes.

Tony, next up, ducks rather than steps out. At two balls

and no strikes Benjamin brings him to the third base box and says, "Stay in there until the last second, then turn your back on it, don't duck. He might put one over."

Tony isn't sure: "Hi try, Meester Don."

On the next pitch he takes a wild swing and pops the ball to the first baseman, who catches it easily. Going back to the dugout he says, "Thee nex' time hi keep thee highs hopen."

Bobo, apparently having decided to go after anything, takes a chopping swing at a very high pitch, luckily connects, and sends it over the shortstop's head. The left and center fielders, converging on it, stop, one for the other, allowing the ball to squirt through. Bobo ends up on third.

The remaining Gray's players are now on their feet, against the chicken wire.

Unnerved by Bobo's hit, the W. and W. pitcher throws four bad balls to Nick, who has the good sense not to swing at them.

"It's up to you, Fred," Karl calls to his son, now at bat.

The news causes Fred's upraised bat to tremble. On the first pitch, low and outside, he swings so hard that the bat ends up a few feet from Benjamin in the third base coaching box, causing laughter in the stands.

"You can do it, Fred!" says Karl.

Now Fred himself trembles. The second pitch hits him lightly on the back.

"Take your base," says the home plate umpire.

"Tole you!" Karl yells.

A moment later Benjamin accidentally gives the "steal" signal: pulling at his ear lobe. (Preoccupied, he simply reached up and scratched his ear.) Now, realizing it, he wonders if any of the three runners, Bobo (on third), Nick (on second), and Fred (on first) has seen it. He thinks of calling out, "Steal's off!" but the pitcher is going into his windup and Benjamin doesn't want to confuse either his batter or his runners. He'll wait until after the pitch.

Unfortunately Fred has caught the signal and, on the pitch, breaks for second.

"Get back here, you fool!" shouts Karl.

Fred freezes ten feet or so from first.

The catcher throws to the first baseman, who chases

down Fred and makes the tag before Bobo can get to home plate with a run.

"Where the hell you wearin' your danged brain these days?" Karl asks as he walks to the dugout, where Fred is coming to get his mitt.

"My fault," says Benjamin.

"Your fault?"

"I accidentally gave the steal signal. Only Fred caught it."

The announcement brings a look of relief to Fred's face, but it also stirs some familiar groaning among the other players:

"We're screwed," says someone from inside the dugout. There are mumbles of agreement.

Despite their doubts, the team moves briskly out of the dugout for the top of the second.

Karl has been leaning against the chicken wire, is saying to no one in particular, or perhaps to Benjamin through no one in particular, "We got to get our butts together 'roun' here."

Benjamin regrets the accidental signal. *It's all concentration,* he reminds himself. For the regular Pee Wee seven innings, or those plus any extra innings there might be, he must think solely about the game, reacting calmly to surprises, staying a thought or two ahead of the dandies, finding ways for his team to get runs, ways to keep the other team from getting them. He's in the dugout, not on the field. He has only a few decisions to make, but his own behavior will affect the team's: If he screws up or panics, they likely will too.

Meryl, after a couple of warm-ups, calls Benjamin to the mound and says, "Want me to throw my dropper?"

"Dropper?" Benjamin replies warily. "What's a dropper?"

"It's like the pitches I throw in batting practice, only a little straighter, but then it kind of falls down before it gets to the plate. I've been practicing it against the back of our garage. It's pretty good."

Meryl is not one for overstating things; Benjamin takes a chance: "Try a few. If you're not getting them to swing at it, go back to the regular pitch."

Meryl's first pitch sails to the plate, an inviting water-

71

melon, but, as the batter takes a fierce swing, it sinks like a periscope.

"What the hell?" says the dandy named Norm, rushing from the dugout to home plate. "Let's see that ball."

Benjamin follows. By the time he reaches the plate the umpire is handing the ball to Norm.

"What's the problem?" Benjamin says.

"No ball is supposed to do that sort of thing," says Norm, probing it with his fingers, searching with his eyes. "This ball's got to have somethin' on it."

"It's got strings on it," Benjamin replies flatly. "My pitcher probably just pulled one of them."

"That's not what I mean."

The umpire is smiling.

"Look at it," Norm says, handing it to the umpire. "See anything?"

"It's round like all the other ones in my pocket."

Norm examines it again, hands it back. "All right," he says, "but don't let the kid try any funny stuff," as if *now* Meryl will begin reaching into his pocket for pine tar or some other illegal substance.

As Benjamin returns to the dugout, he gives Meryl a flick of the thumb and a nod which say: Go on with the dropper.

The W. and W. batters, no doubt with memories of their first inning assault, swing ferociously. The dropper seems to have a sonar system that sends it into a dive as the bats approach. There are several fouls, but none of the W. and W. batters connect solidly. The first two batters, in fact, strike out, and the third grounds out weakly to first.

"We ain't doin' nothin' the way we're supposed to," Karl observes to Benjamin while heading to his first base coaching box, "but we're still in the doggone ball game."

She'd been talking about the man with the cigar box.

Benjamin closed the bedroom window against the evening chill and the air became close and musty. He thought of getting up, opening the window a crack, didn't.

"I had to look at him every evening, just standing there before me, and after a while I felt as though he were looking at me and asking what I was doing, which was—isn't it funny?—creating him."

72

She was turning uncomfortably, making the bed jiggle, all of which kept him uneasily awake. He couldn't concentrate on her words, couldn't understand what she meant.

"Well, I was. I mean, I'd cut him out of cardboard and made his clothes and things and finally his face, that mysterious face. I mean, I could see in the face whatever I wanted. That kind of face. Then it seemed to be saying, 'What are you doing?' Not, 'What are you doing by creating me?' just, 'What are you doing?' "

He felt a heaviness in his chest, finally got up and opened the window a crack. He thought of the action as ventilating not only the room but her thoughts and his own.

"You know, Benjamin, a person could go on, day after day, not asking that question. Isn't it incredible? I mean, we have minds that are meant to ask questions most of the time, but—but you get to the point where there are certain questions you never ask. 'Sublimate' is the word for it, but it doesn't really say what—what I'm trying to say."

He reached down to untangle the top sheet, which she'd twisted with her movements.

"I've begun to ask," she said. "Does that frighten you?"

"Why should it?" *he said, getting the sheet right, pulling it back over them.* "I'd say it's something good."

"Then—then why does it frighten me?"

He didn't know; it didn't seem she expected him to answer.

"God, it does. I went out tonight, hoping to leave the question somewhere, at the carry-out store, or on someone else's doorstep, in the gutter or in a garbage can. When I bought the cigarettes I thought of writing it down on the sales slip or the book of matches I got with the cigarettes: 'What are you doing?' Then, when I passed Marie's house, I'd walk up to her door and call her and hand it to her. 'Here,' I'd say, 'this is for you, not me.' "

He was caught in the music of her thoughts, began to sense rhythms of his own: uncertainties, swirling in upon him like the wisps of cool air now entering the room. He wished she'd stop.

"I didn't get rid of it, Benjamin. I got rid of that silly

73

cardboard man, but the question stays with me. That's why I can't sleep now."

"What does it come to?" he said, sensing his own anxiety.

"I don't know. I worry that it won't go away. It seems very momentous, like news of the unexpected death of someone you love. You must do something, but what can you do? It feels that way, and therefore I don't want to let myself take it any further. I want it to go away."

She cried then, and he held her, saying nothing, asking nothing.

She's asleep now.

He slides his arm from beneath her, gets up and closes the window. A chill remains in the room. He reaches down and pulls the spare blanket over them. He lies on his back, arms folded over his chest, unable to sleep.

At the top of the fifth, with the score still 4-0, their pitcher has found his groove. Except for allowing a couple of ground ball outs, he's struck out everyone he's faced.

Fortunately Meryl has been just about as successful, striking out four and getting others on weak ground balls and pop-fly balls. The W. and W. batters have been set off their timing by his unusual pitch.

Between the fourth and fifth innings, however, the dandies have had a dugout talk with their team and, in their half of the fifth, it's clear that they've given instructions as to how to deal with Meryl. Instead of slashing at the dropper, they now begin timing it and swinging more accurately. Meryl gives up two ground ball singles before he gets the side out.

"Mix your pitches," Benjamin tells Meryl when he comes off the mound. "You aren't throwing any of your old straight ones."

"Everyone can hit those," Meryl reminds him.

"Ain't the same pitch," says Karl.

"Huh?" Meryl says.

"Next to that slow one of yours that other one's gonna look like a fast one though it ain't that fast an' maybe is even slower, but it don't make no difference if it looks that way. So it ain't the same pitch it was in battin' practice. Know what I mean?"

"No, sir."

"Just mix 'em up," Benjamin says. "Then you'll see."

Meryl says he will.

Tag Euler, having hit some solid fouls, now straightens out the W. and W. pitcher's fastball for a single to center field.

Speck McGovern takes a normal swing at the ball, barely meeting it. It creeps toward third, where the third baseman can't decide whether to charge it or lay back. His indecision allows Speck to land safely on first and Tag to reach second.

Immediately Benjamin, wanting to disguise all accidental aspects of the hit, looks to first, where Speck is catching his breath, and says, "Nice swinging bunt, Speck!"

Speck frowns: *What's a swinging bunt?*

But Benjamin's intention is fulfilled: He notices the dandies conferring in the other dugout, making plans to counteract the "swinging bunt" and possibly other clever plays Gray's don't, in fact, have. He tells Meryl, the next batter, to choke up a little, as if he's going to try one kind of a bunt or other, but then to swing in his usual way if the ball is over the plate. Seeing Meryl fiddling with his bat, the W. and W. infielders move in and out uneasily. Will it be a regular bunt? A swinging bunt? What? They're still moving when Meryl takes one of his big slow swings at the first pitch, sends it hopping between third and shortstop. The shortstop, having made his third or fourth decision about positioning himself for Meryl, is caught backing up and can't get to the ball, which bounces into left center field. Tag scores and Speck ends up on second.

"Good *play!*" Benjamin calls out, wanting to maintain the illusion of strategy.

The misplayed ball or Benjamin's remark, perhaps both, brings Norm out of the W. and W. dugout for a meeting with his pitcher and infielders.

Seeing the other two dandies watching him, Benjamin calls Harold Foxx, the next batter, to the third base coaching box and asks, "What did you have for lunch?"

"For lunch?" Has his coach gone crazy? "You mean today?"

"Yes."

75

From the mound the dandy named Norm is now watching too.

"An apple and a tuna fish sandwich," he says nervously.

"That means you're going to hit a double."

"Huh?"

"Just go up there and swing. You'll hit a double."

The dandies' tilted heads and suspicious eyes follow Harold to the plate.

On the second pitch Harold swings hard and hits a ball that Benjamin thinks is actually going to be a double. But the W. and W. center fielder backs up and makes a good catch near the fence, then throws to hold Speck on second.

Returning to the dugout, Harold calls to Benjamin in the coaching box, "You were almost right. I nearly got a hit."

"Maybe you didn't eat enough of the apple," Benjamin tells him.

Harold gives him a puzzled smile.

Tony hits a fly ball to right. Though it's caught, it gives Speck time to tag up and score. Bobo hits a line drive, which the third baseman snags. At the end of the fifth inning the score is W. and W. 4, Gray's 2.

"An' they were nearly the *champs* last year," Nick is saying as the team leaves the dugout for the next inning.

"They was supposed to be better this year," Tag reminds him.

"They *ain't* better," says Nick.

"Maybe they *are*," Bobo says. "Maybe we're just better than we thought."

"We were supposed to be the worst team again this year," Tag remembers, "even with Max Jennings as pitcher. We can't be *that* much better."

"Ah, screw that," says Nick. "We can too."

His wish has somehow reached them and, at least temporarily, binds them. He knows that he in his paint-splattered T-shirt and dirty khakis and Karl in his overalls and washed-out farmer clothes are as much a part of this slovenly eccentricity called team as any of the players. The clothes belie the challenge. Like W. and W., Gray's uses baseballs, mitts, and bats, must function within certain boundaries, certain rules. Beyond that there seems to be no similarity. If Gray's wins this game, it will win in its own style.

Benjamin finds the notion both fascinating and complicated and wants to share it with someone. He thinks of Marilyn. Would she be interested or has her big question blocked out all else? He turns to the stands, searching for her, wanting, for the first time, to see her here.

She's nowhere in sight.

Had she come, she would have brought the girls and they would by now have come to the low fence to talk to him and Bobo. He pictures her in the old Volkswagen, their second car, driving through the town, searching for a trash can or incinerator in which to dump her question. Odd, but he knows now that his involvement in this game, in his thoughts about it as well, is somehow related to her uneasiness.

The wish has now traveled onto the diamond:

Nick makes an excellent diving stop of a ball that seemed a certain single and throws the runner out at first.

Tag matches Nick by making a leaping sideways catch of a line drive.

Alternating between his dropper and his straight pitch, Meryl strikes out the next batter.

It's the only inning in which no W. and W. player reaches first base; the Gray's players come off the field cheering.

The problem is runs. It's especially complicated because Benjamin hasn't played his reserves and, according to league rules, he must play everyone for at least one inning in each game. None of the reserves can hit as well as those now in the lineup. He decides to slip them in at less-than-crucial moments.

At the bottom of the sixth Nick, eager, pressing too hard, swings early on the first pitch and flies out to left field.

Fred, whose rolled-up jeans have now fallen and cover most of his shoes, looks uneasily to Karl after he steps to the plate.

"You're on your own, Fred," Karl shouts.

Unlike earlier comments from Karl, this one seems to free Fred. He begins wiggling the top of his bat as the pitcher goes into his windup. The first pitch is a wild one. What works works. Fred wiggles the bat during the second and third pitches, both of which are balls, far off the mark. As the pitcher winds up for the fourth pitch, Fred, for one reason or another, does not wiggle the bat and the pitcher, confused, hesitates in mid-delivery, then throws a pitch that goes over the top of the catcher's outstretched glove and hits the backstop.

"Take your base," says the home plate umpire.

Fred trudges to first behind delighted cries from his teammates.

Brilliant, Benjamin thinks, wanting to believe Fred planned the entire sequence.

Benjamin signals Lou Pera to bat for Paul, who's been playing an unsteady game. Before Lou, a poor hitter, goes to the plate, Benjamin calls him to the coaching box.

"Stand close to the plate," he whispers. "If the ball is inside let it graze you."

"Huh? You mean you *want* me to get hit?" says Lou, eyes widening.

"Not so loud." He glances guiltily about, then goes on. "It won't hurt you if you just turn your arm or leg into it a little. We need to get someone else on base."

Lou gives his coach an unhappy look and shuffles to the plate.

It can be a mean sport, Benjamin thinks as he sees the first ball shoot past Lou's chest for a strike. Tensely he watches as the second pitch bends in and grazes Lou just above the knee. There's no real damage, but Lou carries the play through by limping slightly on his way to first.

He shouts an encouragement to Tag, the next batter, sure now that in some gut-deep way he, Benjamin, more than the dandies, the players on both teams, the umpires, the rules themselves, is turning the events of this game. It brings a cold and malicious excitement of the kind he felt once in college just after he'd let his eyes scan the accounting test of the bright student beside him long enough to pick up a few crucial answers he himself didn't have. Before he has time to worry too much about his present motives, he hears Karl, who's been like a cattle prod these past few innings:

"They's two runs settin' on your bat, Tag!"

Tag nods to the challenge and, on the second pitch, singles to right, sending Fred to third.

From the dugout the Gray's players are cheering past Benjamin to the players on bases. They have regarded their coach from a safe distance throughout this game. With a couple of exceptions there has been no friendly kidding or small talk between Benjamin and them, them and him. He stands at a stoic distance from each, little more than a necessary presence.

Maybe that's the way it has to be, he thinks as he watches Speck move toward home plate.

He remembers reading about John McGraw of the old New York Giants, who won by stirring hatred toward him among his own players. He recalls stories about Johnny Evers and Joe Tinker of the old Cubs, who worked side by side for years, the best double-play combination in the game, and helped their team to championships and themselves into the Hall of Fame; through it all they despised each other and never conversed off the field. Ty Cobb, the game's greatest hitter, had few friends among his teammates. He finally remembers Leo Durocher's quote: "Nice guys finish last."

That's only part of it, he knows.

While he's been diverted by his thoughts, Speck has taken two balls and two strikes. Now he hits deep to short. Though he's thrown out at first, Fred comes home with the third run.

Meryl hits a solid one to the right of second base but is thrown out because of the second baseman's fine stop and his own lack of speed.

At the top of the seventh and final inning, the score is W. and W. 4, Gray's 3.

There is uneasy buzzing in the W. and W. stands. Whiskey-voice hasn't cried out during the past two innings.

The Gray's fans have remained apprehensively silent, perhaps disbelieving.

Karl is savoring the chunk of tobacco he has just stuck between teeth and gums. "What you think they're gonna do now?" he asks Benjamin.

"Don't know," says Benjamin, "but, whatever it is, we'll have to do 'em one better."

"You're sure right 'bout that," says Karl, going to his place outside the far end of the dugout.

Karl's question seems to be answered with Meryl's first pitch of the inning. The W. and W. batter bunts. It's too far in front of the plate for Bobo to reach, much to the right of Meryl, who stumbles going down for it and then can't make the play to first.

Though the score has closed, the odds against Gray's seem to have increased, for Gray's weak substitutes are now in the game: Lou Pera in right field, Bobby Watson in left, and Gerry Franks at second in place of Tony, who's now in center. The dandies have been making substitutions all through the game without noticeably changing the team's strength.

The next W. and W. batter hits a ball to second base, where Gerry juggles, then loses it, leaving runners on second and first. There are some grumbles from the Gray's starting players.

The next batter slashes the ball to center field, but Tony, rushing in, stops it for a single and manages to hold the lead runner on third.

The bases are loaded and there are no outs.

In each inning the opposing batters have been meeting Meryl's pitches with greater accuracy. However, Benjamin has noticed that, because the dropper is a low pitch, the batters have been hitting it on the ground. He goes to the mound and calls the infielders to him. "Play in," he says, "even closer than you'd play for a double-play ball, almost as close as you would for a bunt. About halfway in."

'S'pose they smash one?" says Fred.

"Keep your mitts ready. Meryl, throw only the dropper for a few pitches. They've been burying that ball. I think you'll have time to stop it. We can cut off runs that way."

Gerry Franks is tensely biting his lower lip.

"Stay calm," he tells all of them. "No one play is going to win or lose this game."

The next batter hits the ball on a low drive to Nick, who gets it before it hits the dirt. The runners scramble back to their bases.

After one more out he'll tell Meryl to return to his normal pattern of pitching and instruct the infielders to play back.

The next batter lunges at Meryl's first pitch, smacking it on the ground to Fred, who has his foot only an inch or so from first base as it comes down to him. The runner is out by twenty feet. Fred whips the ball to Bobo, but it's off target and W. and W.'s fifth run scores.

More a game of chance than poker, Benjamin thinks as he watches Bobo toss the ball back to Meryl.

The next batter, the cleanup man, approaches the plate calmly behind the final instruction of the dandy coaching at first: "No problem if you just meet it!"

Benjamin knows that for Meryl's pitching there could be no better instruction. He calls to the infielders to play deep and signals the outfielders to go back. His hope is for a high ball, easy to catch.

After Meryl makes one pitch, a ball, Benjamin notices that Lou Pera in left has not moved back far enough. He rushes toward left, along the foul line. He's only a few yards from Lou, still trying to get his attention, when he hears an ominous crack and turns to see the ball soaring past him. Lou backs up to the fence, mitt and free hand in the air, losing balance as he goes. He hits the fence, and the ball descends between hand and glove. No, only *seems* to, for when Lou lowers his mitt the ball is in it. He looks at the mitt, the ball, dizzily raises his hand.

"Out!" calls one of the umpires.

Benjamin catches a glimpse of something moving just beyond the fence.

"It bounced off the top!" one of the dandies shouts, running toward the field umpire, the one who made the call.

That, Benjamin is sure, it didn't.

Yet a home run has become an out.

The Gray's players are out of the dugout, cheering.

The field umpire, who was standing between Nick at third and Benjamin when he made the call, sticks to his decision. "He caught the damn thing!"

Lou is racing toward his joyful teammates, ball still in hand.

Benjamin turns toward the fence, wondering if he only imagined the moving object. Out of the corner of his eye he catches another movement, turns, sees a boy on a bike appear from the bushes beyond the fence and go racing down the street, away from the ball park, blond hair flying out behind him. The boy's head is turned the other way and he can't see the face.

A boy, that boy on the bike, caught the ball and flipped it into Lou's mitt. *Is that it?* For a moment Benjamin considers reporting the possibility to the umpires. He sees the dandies, all three of them gesticulating around the home plate umpire with righteousness in their voices, all of them knowing something strange has happened, not really knowing what. By the time he's reached the infield Benjamin has shucked his ethical urges and joins the Gray's players in congratulating Lou on a fine catch.

The dandies stamp about, kicking dust at the umpire, who folds his arms over his chest, closes his eyes, and raises his head to the sky. "Out," he keeps saying, "out, out, out, out."

Though they lose the argument, the dandies aren't finished.

In the last of the seventh they bring on the one player who has thus far seen no action: an oversized boy who's been sitting hunched at the far end of their dugout. He emerges and plods toward the pitcher's mound.

Benjamin takes his position in the third base coaching box and sees the three dandies looking out at him from their dugout, grinning.

Don't any of you ever walk in front of my car, he calls to them silently. But he doesn't give them even the satisfaction of a frown.

The pitcher probably is their executioner, their "hit man," saved for the last stages. He wastes little time: *Fwop! Fwop! Fwop!* Three quick strikes to Bobby Watson, all called.

Had W. and W. been behind at any time, the young giant would have been brought in. But the dandies waited, keeping it tense: good showmanship. The smash by the cleanup hitter didn't work. Now, with the score uncomfortably close, they've decided on a quick and painless death for Gray's.

Fwop! Tony, taking a sign from Benjamin, has tried to bunt, but the ball is so fast that his bat is still going down when the ball hits the catcher's mitt.

Baseball is partly entertainment, and the dandies are putting on a show. Fireworks go off at some major league parks when a home run is hit. There are singers and dancers before at some games and between innings at others. And some parks have organists, pep bands, and offbeat vendors. There are bat days, ball days, and jacket days, to say nothing of autograph days and two-for-the-price-of-one-hot-dog-and-Coke days. Contests are held for honorary batboys and batgirls, and there are drawings for autographed baseballs. Not long ago at one major league park, there was a fashion show before the playing of "The Star-Spangled Banner." It's all part of a modern tradition, which the dandies properly appreciate. So does Benjamin, at least when showmanship has something to do with winning games. The enormous pitcher oddly reminds Benjamin of the midget Bill Veeck, former owner of the St. Louis Browns, once brought to bat as a pinch hitter. The midget idea worked (he got himself a walk), just as this secret-pitcher gambit is working:

Fwop!

The kid's like an elephant flinging peas from its trunk.

With two strikes on Tony, Benjamin is now forced to withdraw the bunt sign. "Lay into it!" he calls ridiculously.

Tony strikes out.

So does Bobo, the next batter, ending the game.

No, Benjamin *won't* shake the dandies' hands or say something stupid like, "Nice game." On both sides it was anything *but* nice. Despite the loss, however, he feels something besides disappointment. *Damned if there wasn't something awfully impressive about the way those bastards won this ball game,* he thinks. The truth is, he can't wait to meet them again. He looks forward to nothing more than the chance to beat them into the dirt of an afternoon just like this.

The teams form two lines near the pitcher's mound and the players do shake each others' hands.

Karl says, "It wasn't as bad as I thought it'd be."

"Could have been a lot worse," says Benjamin, remembering Lou Pera's amazing "catch."

"If you need me, for practice 'n such, just don't hes'-tate to ask."

"I do. If you have time."

"Get the work on the farm done in the mornin's an'

do nothin' much but fix my friends' combines an' tractors an' such in the afternoons."

"I'd be grateful."

After Karl leaves, Benjamin goes to the dugout to pick up the equipment and sees pieces of white cardboard at the far end, under the bench. Curious, he drops the equipment bag and goes back for a look. As he's bending down, he sees long strips of wood against the wall behind the bench. He pulls out the cardboard cards and sees signs. He lifts them out one by one and reads the words, written with black marker pen:

THIS TEAM
IS
ON STRIKE!

WE WANT
UNIFORMS!

GET US A
PITCHER!

GET US A
COACH!!!

He lets the last card fall back to the dugout floor, grateful that he's only now come upon the messages they all bear, then turns to pick up the equipment bag. The cold wind sweeping in from right field seems to enter his bones.

They were made before the game, he tells himself as he carries the equipment bag to the car. *The game has changed all that.* He's not sure, not at all sure.

As he puts the equipment into the back of the station wagon he feels old and out of touch: a fool. *Damn them!* he thinks. *Damn their little asses!*

84

FOUR

Entering the house after the opening game, Benjamin finds the following handwritten letter on the dining room table:

Dear Benjamin,

Must I plead "forgive me"? That's how I feel like starting, but there's nothing I'm doing that needs my apology or your forgiveness. So I won't.

I need to get away for a while—maybe a week, or ten days at most. I called my mother this morning, didn't tell her about my "miseries," just asked how it would be if I and the girls went up to Minneapolis for a visit. I thought she might suggest some later time, but she said why not come now. Dad, it seems, is at a meeting in Chicago and she's alone on Minnetonka. (Seems they're thinking of abandoning the apartment in town, staying at the lake all year, since he's getting so close to retirement and needn't be at the office every day.) Anyway, it cheered me that she wanted us now and I decided to go.

I thought of calling you at the bookstore, but I knew you'd be hurrying to get out of there early because of the game so I decided not to stir up new problems for you. Bobo was with friends all day and doesn't know either. (*Do* explain to him that it's no "big deal.") I know he'll be disappointed to miss going to the lake but probably wouldn't have wanted to interrupt baseball anyway. If it turns out that we actually have a vacation at Traverse later, we might drive over to Minn. afterwards.

Wait. Don't suggest family vacation or anything to Bobo just yet. Am not sure whether I can handle a family vacation this year. I was pushing you to do something about it earlier, I guess, because, well, I'm not sure, I think I wanted you to take hold of things. Now I know *I've* got to. The thing is, I want to think. I mean forget what I said about the baseball, and other things I said that seem like complaints. Do what you have to do. I feel that lately I've been trying to force things with us. I'm not sure what I want. I've carried my "big question" around all day like a carcass. (Hope what I just said makes more sense to you than it does to me.)

Anyway, I finished packing Suzie and Annie's things a few minutes ago and will get to my own after I finish this letter (which, believe it or not, started out to be a note). We'll take a Greyhound, which will get us into Minneapolis at about 1 A.M. tomorrow morning. (Marie is driving us to the depot.) I'll put a collect call through to myself in the morning, before you leave for work, just to let you know we got here safely. Okay? Don't want to answer questions, etc. Try to understand.

Am sorry about the suddenness of all this but, you know, I could sit for hours trying to explain why I've got to get away and might never get to it (as I'm not doing here). Best to act quickly and come back (fingers crossed) renewed and happy, etc., with the BIG QUESTION buried deep in Minnetonka (I hope). I thought of leaving Suzie and Annie, by the way, but that would have left you with an unnecessary burden. (They are hopping around now with excitement about seeing Grandma and Grandpa, though Suzie has been a little nervous about leaving you and Bobo. Once they calm down, they'll be no problem.) I hope you guys win today. (Am envious about you and baseball, the way it seems to keep your mind off all else.) You were talking about you and Bobo getting to know each other better. Here's a chance, I guess. Anyway, have a good time together. I grocery-shopped yesterday. The refrig. is full. Water my plants. Don't forget to feed the cat. And now and then *pretend* I'm in bed with you.

Love,
Marilyn

He lowers the letter to the table and goes into the kitchen, repeating to himself the last phrase of the final sentence. Somehow, though it seems an afterthought, a way for her to finish the letter, it sticks in him like a fish-hook.

Pretend. Is the irony intended?

In loving, he and Marilyn close in upon each other in darkness and rarely speak. Though there may be conversations before or after they touch, the touching itself, especially lately, has seemed terribly anonymous and private. He's pictured others in her place: an imagined woman, or a woman he might have passed in the supermarket or on a sidewalk, someone he's never before seen. His fancies seem to grow out of his failure to perceive Marilyn exquisitely beside him. While he's discovered nothing of the origins of his fantasies, he now wonders if Marilyn has detected some visible sign of them—his moving toward her or away, his way of holding her. *Pretend.* Is she hoping that, by departing, she will become the partner those others have been?

He's fixing hamburgers when Bobo comes in, having stopped with his teammates at the Dairy Queen near the ball park.

Finally, he simply tells Bobo that Marilyn has taken the girls to Minnesota for a brief visit.

"Why'd she go and do that?" Bobo says, raising his head with a disappointed frown.

Benjamin hesitates, then says, "There's a letter on the dining room table. You might want to read it."

Benjamin hopes Bobo won't ask many questions about his mother's departure.

What answers does he have? How could he possibly share his guilt-born fears?

There are depths to Marilyn that neither he nor Bobo will ever understand. Of that he's sure. It occurs to him that when they've loved, images of others may have come to her as well. Indeed, that "big question" of hers may embody mysteries he has no right to share. Surely it's best that he not speculate about them. He *will* try to pretend she's in bed beside him, accept, if possible, whatever comes of that.

Later, entering the living room to read the paper and watch the evening news, he finds Bobo on the sofa reading Marilyn's letter. He doesn't turn on the news but picks up the paper and is soon eyeing his son over the top of it.

Bobo shakes his head a couple of times before putting down the letter. "She's got some hairy problem, doesn't she?"

"You mean the part about the 'big question' and her needing to get away?"

"Not just that. Not just the letter. It's the way she's been dragging around lately."

"I think she does. I don't know much about it."

Bobo, accepting that, rises from the sofa, asks Benjamin for the second half of the paper, the part with the sports pages, gets it, goes back to the sofa and plops down, legs out, head low on the sofa back, turns a couple of pages, and begins to read.

Benjamin turns on the news but doesn't watch. Only after Bobo has finished reading does he speak:

"Want to talk about the game?"

"Why?" Bobo's eyes don't rise from the paper.

"I have a couple of questions."

"We lost because they stuck that monster in at the end. Otherwise we would have won."

"I know about that. I want to ask you about some cards I found at the back of the dugout after the game was over."

Bobo's eyes glide away from Benjamin's. "We aren't supposed to be talking about the team, here at home. Remember?"

Benjamin also wants to ask about the mysterious catch. Did Bobo see it? Does he know anything about it? But he contains himself, having been reminded of the pledge he has thus far kept, will keep.

He waits for Bobo to mention the trip to Minnesota. Bobo doesn't.

On the Sunday evening following Marilyn's departure Benjamin leaves Bobo at home to study for a test and goes alone to a movie at the recently built shopping plaza at the edge of town.

The film is French and is about two relatives-by-marriage in their middle or late thirties who meet at a wedding reception and begin a platonic friendship which slowly develops into love. Increasingly oblivious to others, including their own spouses and children, they have an extended affair. At the end they spend most of a family Christmas celebration in a bedroom at the home of one of their mutual relatives, then ride off together as relatives watch, some in awe and admiration.

Benjamin isn't a student of films, can't decide whether it's a good movie or a poor one, but is moved tremendously by the easy way many of the characters—not only the lovers but their parents, their children, and others, including the lovers' spouses—begin to accept the relationship as it develops. *Love,* the film seems to say, *is a rare and sacred ritual, full of quiet ceremonies, which, when come upon, must never be avoided, never violated.* For some in the film, like the lovers' spouses, the ending is not a happy one, but for most, including the lovers' children, it is. Above all, it seems inevitable.

Wanting fully to understand the story, especially the two main characters' motives, Benjamin goes to his bookstore, turns on the lights, and searches both the hardback and paperback shelves for the novel from which, the film credits said, the movie was taken. He can't find it.

Afterwards he sits alone at a booth at McDonald's restaurant, having a cup of coffee, remembering the film, wondering at the possible connections between it and his own life. He's sure he'd be too uptight—not to fall in love and have an affair, but to let such a relationship develop naturally. That would be true even if Marilyn *were* as neurotic and unloving, as deserving of it, as the hero's wife seems to have been.

And Marilyn? Were she to find an admirer she admired, wouldn't she analyze to death her motives, the partner's, both, then take into account the effects on Benjamin, Bobo, and the girls? He's sure she would. She'd let nothing get out of hand. *Unless she's changing,* he thinks.

The restaurant is nearly empty. Four college-aged students, two girls and two boys, occupy a table near his booth, speaking lightly, laughing a lot. A family of five, including three small children haggling about who has the most French fries, are in a booth opposite him on the other side. A few others stand at the counter, waiting to pick up their food.

Ever since the film ended, he's wanted to call Mrs. Jennings. Suppose he invited her here. How easy, how safe, would it be to talk in a place like this? He shakes his head at the recurring impulse, knowing it results from the film, sure it has little to do with the realities of the moment: it's well after eleven o'clock; she's no doubt occupied with something, or in bed. *The French are different,* he tells himself, as if speaking an old and tested maxim, one that somehow applies.

He sees the umpire with the pock-marked face come in, watches him order a hamburger and Coke. Not wanting a conversation with him, Benjamin decides to leave. Before he can get out of the booth, however, the umpire has his order and is approaching. "Hi do, Mr. Dunne. Okay if I sit here?"

Benjamin forces a smile, eases back, then nods toward the seat opposite.

The umpire plops down. He's wearing faded black Big Ben trousers that are too large around the thin waist and a loose cotton shirt open partway down the front. He's grinning; Benjamin sees uneven teeth. "Damn near pulled it out the other day, didn't you?" He takes a bite, and half of the hamburger vanishes into his mouth. Again he grins. Benjamin sees bits of lettuce and relish on the teeth. "Wish you had. Hate the other mother-fuckers." He doesn't seem to notice the startled frown the epithet brings to Benjamin's face. "They're truly pigs."

The young man seems a weathered holdover from another time and place, and Benjamin doesn't know quite how to respond to him. So he says nothing.

"I was so zapped out at the end there I didn't know what was happenin'."

Zapped out?

The other half of the hamburger enters the umpire's mouth, followed by a swig of Coke. Chewing audibly, the young man closes his eyes and shakes his head slowly. "One of these days I'm gonna throw creeps like that out of a ball game the minute they stick their heads outa the dugout." He looks at Benjamin. "You aren't one of 'em. I can tell by the way you dressed for the ball game. Right?"

Benjamin wants to leave but feels that, before he does, he must say something. "I'm not big on Pee Wee coaches pretending they're major leaguers, if that's what you mean."

It's exactly what he meant, the umpire's nod tells Benjamin. "They're tryin' to turn kids into something they're not. Right? That's a goddamn crime."

Crime. Despite Benjamin's own grim feelings about the dandies, the word is too heavy, too harsh. He shrugs, trying to think of an excuse to leave.

There's no need. In a moment the umpire says, "Got to split," slides out of the booth, and heads quickly for the door, leaving wrapper, napkin, and empty paper cup on the table, along with several spots of ketchup.

Staring at the ketchup, Benjamin imagines blood. His? The umpire's? Whose? He gets up quickly but doesn't go for the door. Instead, he walks past the counter to the narrow hallway that leads to the lavatories at the back. There's a phone on the wall between the two lavatories. He fishes in his pocket, removes a dime, inserts it in the coin slot, and dials a number he memorized the first time he dialed it.

"Hello?" says a soft woman's voice.

"This is Benjamin Dunne, Mrs. Jennings. Max's coach, or, I guess, former coach. We spoke briefly a short time ago." He closes his eyes in preparation for his excuse: "I was wondering how Max is doing."

"How nice of you to call," she says, her tone gathering interest. "Max is doing much better. I left a little note for you not long ago. Did you get it?"

"Yes. Sorry I didn't mention that. I . . . appreciated it. And I *would* like to talk to you sometime." He pauses, trying to think of a casual, an appropriate, way to express his wish. "Funny thing," he says finally, "I'm having coffee right now, down at McDonald's." He remembers the time, so he tempers his near invitation until it's hardly an invitation at all. "It's probably too late for you to join me."

"I'd love to get out for a while," she replies, "and would if my husband weren't down from Toledo for the evening. Things to talk about and such. Why don't we, instead, have lunch during the week?"

"Lunch?"

"Do you like rolls and cheese and wine? I'm very good at that sort of thing, probably because it doesn't take much doing."

Benjamin remembers the lovers in the movie having a lunch much like the one she's described, as well as a plateful of delicate pastries. "French," he says, hoping it doesn't sound ridiculous.

"Yes," she says as if the observation is an obvious one. "Wednesday is best for me. How does Wednesday sound?"

Wednesday he's scheduled to work all day with Dan on their semiannual inventory. Instantly he redoes his schedule—Mrs. Jennings on Wednesday, begin inventory on Thursday—and says, "That'll be fine. Just fine."

After he hangs up he worries about everything: her seeming interest in him, his in her, that husband "down from Toledo." (Are they separated? or divorced? or just getting a divorce? Are they, in fact, happily married? No matter what the case, he senses danger.) And what of his acting behind Marilyn's back? (How uneasy he'd be to hear from Marilyn that she'd had lunch with—how would she put it?—an interesting man.) And isn't it odd that she'd ask him to lunch at her house? There's that husband. And what if Max sees him eating and drinking wine with his mother, then tells Bobo? (He might prepare Bobo by telling him he's going to drop in at the Jenningses' to check on Max.) The postponed inventory troubles him as much as anything else. He's dumped more and more of his work on Dan recently, mainly because of the team. Dan finally pinned him down to a specific day for the inventory; now he's going to back out of it. *I won't worry about anything,* he decides as he pulls into the driveway.

The house is dark.

He finds Bobo asleep in his room.

Nervous, he turns on the living room television set, searches the channels for a movie, preferably foreign, ideally French. He finds only a dated black-and-white film about an old baseball hero. He's seen it twice and it begins to bore him. He watches it until he's exhausted, then goes to bed, where he quickly falls asleep.

Tim Adams is waiting beside the dugout when Benjamin arrives early for practice the next day. "Can I talk to you about some things?" His eyes don't meet Benjamin's, so he doesn't see Benjamin nodding.

"Let's go into the dugout," Benjamin says finally.

All day he's been preoccupied with thoughts about Mrs. Jennings: What is it about him that really interests her? Its answer is no easier than its opposite: What interests him? He's grateful for Tim's interruption.

They sit several feet apart. Tim stares at the dirt floor, twisting his head, turning his shoulders this way, then that, finally speaking, but to the floor. "I think I should tell you why I'm not playing."

Though curious, Benjamin wants to say an explanation isn't necessary. He senses that the boy reached this moment painfully, but he also knows that in having reached it, Tim will complete the job.

"It's not you. After that first game I think you're a pretty good coach. It's—something else." Tim stands, steps to the chicken wire, looks out at the infield, finally lowers his eyes. "I don't know why it still bothers me."

"I don't know why a lot of things bother me either," Benjamin says truthfully, wanting to encourage the boy.

"But this is—over with. I think. But maybe not. That's why I'm scared."

"Scared?"

"It's Mr. Gray." He raises his eyes but can't keep them on Benjamin. This time they flee to the stands. "He kind of beat me up."

"He what?" The very mention of Gray's name has kicked up anger in Benjamin. Now, though Tim has given no circumstances or facts, the anger swirls hotly.

"It's hard to talk about it."

"You got this far. Go on."

"I went to his store to pick up some uniforms for Block one afternoon last year." He glances at Benjamin, then, seeming reassured, looks back to an invisible audience in the stands. "He was the only one there. He told me to go in this back room he's got. He said the uniforms were there. I went back. I didn't see any uniforms. Only

93

a chair, a wooden chair. Then he came in. He had a box, a uniform box, and he opened it. He said, 'Try this on.'" Each little statement seems to Benjamin a tale or chapter, terribly condensed, full of details unspoken. "He took out a uniform, a shirt and pants." He pauses at length now, studying Benjamin, making sure it's all right for him to go on. Something in Benjamin's look tells him it is. "The one he took out was small and didn't even have my number on it. I told him that, said it probably wouldn't fit. But he said, 'Put the uniform on.' He sat down in the chair. I said it wasn't my uniform. He said, 'Put it on.' I said I didn't want to. He said, 'Do what I say or I'll have you kicked off the team.' He looked like he was mad. His face was all red and he was panting. But he wasn't mad. It was something else. I kind of knew. I told him I had to go. Then he got up and grabbed me and shoved me against the wall and slapped me about three times. He said if I didn't put on the uniform he'd make sure I didn't get to play ball for *any* team. He said he could do that. I kind of thought he might be right but I wasn't sure." Benjamin is uneasily reminded of his threatening remarks to Nick. "Then he . . . I know it sounds crazy . . . he—he started to pull off—my pants." He checks Benjamin again, perhaps in search of a shocked or disapproving look. There is none. He goes on: "I pushed him hard and he went down and I ran out the door. I think I swore at him too." He's been standing stiffly, holding the chicken wire with both hands, having had awkwardly to turn back to check Benjamin's responses. But now, with the episode told, he falls back and sinks to the bench, like syrup that at any moment might spill all the way down, into the dirt.

"I never told anyone else," he says finally. "It was near the end of the season. I just quit the team."

Benjamin is fighting an impulse to drive to the cleaning shop and bludgeon Gray. He goes over, sits down beside Tim, and puts into words another feeling, one that has been building through his anger: "I'm really grateful, even honored, that you told me." The words aren't right, not strong enough, but they're close, the best he has just now. "You're a strong person to be able to tell me."

"I hate him, Mr. Dunne," Tim says, his eyes damp now. *Thank God,* Benjamin thinks.

"I didn't want to play for his team. But you're supposed to stay with the same team each year, unless your dad becomes the manager of another team or something like that. The only way I could have gotten off that is telling someone, like the commissioners. But they probably wouldn't have believed me. Anyway, I was scared of Gray. I still am."

"You want to play though."

"Yes. But not for his team. Ever. Even though I like you. I—I can't play for any team he—has anything to do with."

The temptation to kill has turned into a plan to report the incident to the commissioners, get them to drop Gray as a sponsor. There would be complications: the difficulty of proof, the revival of a scare Tim has already had a hard time dealing with, etc. Bobo comes to mind. He feels sure his son also would have struck back at Gray before running out. But then he would have told Benjamin or Marilyn.

"Why did you keep it to yourself, not tell your parents?"

"My mother would have gotten all panicky and not done anything right. My father got killed in Viet Nam when I was little, so I couldn't tell him. There was no one to tell, until I thought of you. I thought I'd forget about it, but I didn't. I dream about it a lot, stuff like that. I knew I had to tell someone. It makes me mad that I'm not playing baseball."

Benjamin explains that soon Mr. Francis will be making late assignments. Though Tim is already assigned to Gray's, Benjamin will find a way to have Tim's name put back into the pool. Then he'll make sure not to choose Tim. "I'll find a way."

"Everyone thinks I just don't want to play for you. That's the reason I gave to Bobo, after he said you didn't know much about baseball, even though I kind of knew he didn't mean it."

"I'll survive," Benjamin says.

Three times Tim thanks Benjamin for listening as they walk toward his bike. Finally he says, "Even though I haven't been on your team I've helped you too."

Benjamin smiles, guessing that Tim means he's been watching practices, giving moral support. Not until Tim, whizzing past the dugout, turns his good-bye wave into a grabbing motion, then points to the fence, does Benjamin figure it out.

"Christ!" he says loudly. Then: "Thanks!"

He goes back to the dugout to remove the equipment. What he now wants to do is put an anonymous note, made from cut-up letters from newspapers, under the door at Gray's Cleaners: OTHERS HAVE SEEN YOU! SOON THE WORLD WILL KNOW!

He won't do that. He won't do any of the things he's thought of doing, including trying to use the Gray incident to have Benjamin's Bookstore replace Gray's Cleaners as sponsor. The season has begun. There's that momentum that mustn't be broken. He'll think up other things to do. Hundreds of things perhaps. That, he hopes, will save him from doing what he mustn't.

In the second game Gray's Cleaners encounters V.F.W., which a year ago finished only one game higher than Gray's in the standings. The problem was pitching. Benjamin learns after two innings and two V.F.W. pitchers that the problem hasn't been solved. At the top of the third the score is Gray's 6, V.F.W.3.

The tall umpire is working the bases. Gray's players, when referring to him, use the name Daryl. Throughout the first two innings he's made a few jibing remarks to the V.F.W. coaches. Now Bobo, having hit a three-run double in the first, is up again in the second. Daryl looks over to the V.F.W. dugout, points to Bobo, and says, "Why don't you duds just shoot him this time?" He's addressing the head V.F.W. coach and speaks so loudly everyone on the field and in the stands can hear him.

Some of the Gray's players laugh, and one, Tag, shouts from the dugout, "You tell 'em, Daryl!"

Benjamin tells Tag to shut up.

"But he's on our side," Tag says.

Benjamin knows it; that's what makes him uncomfortable.

The V.F.W. coaches, despite their matching uniforms, don't seem nearly as pretentious as the Watson and Wills dandies. The opposite: Both are heavy and wear the

V.F.W. uniform, blue with red-and-white trim, including a kind of T-shirt, in a way that emphasizes their pot-bellies. On the back of each T-shirt is a name: BOB on one and LEWIS on the other.

Tony has again started as pitcher for Gray's. He does fairly well until the third inning when, facing his third batter—the first two having walked—he calls Benjamin to the mound and says, "Hi theenk hi hab rhoom-ee-tism."

Tony is full of design and deception. Today he's wearing a faded yellow basketball jersey with a torn green number 2 hanging off the back, oversized purple shorts that look like golf shorts, and sneakers without socks. Benjamin has been waiting to catch him slipping into his polished standard English so he can get to the bottom of the phony accent: Tony will just have to survive in the face of an exposé. The accent is thick now, as it always seems to be when the boy feels himself in a crisis.

"You want out?"

"Haftair thees heeneeng. *Whhffff.* Eef hi soorvive."

Benjamin follows his pitcher's advice. It's a mistake. By the end of the third the score is Gray's 6, V.F.W. 7.

Meryl comes in for Tony in the fourth.

The pock-faced umpire calls across to Lewis, coaching on first: "Bet you my pay for the game you don't take it, coach!"

It's an extraordinary remark. Benjamin can't understand why he has this unwanted ally.

Bob turns coldly to Benjamin in the Gray's dugout and says, "That yer brother er somethin'?"

Benjamin shakes his head.

"We're gonna be watchin' his calls. He better not bend 'em your way."

Benjamin sees Daryl, beyond Bob, winking at him, and turns quickly away, disgusted.

Gray's hits well and, by the end of the sixth, has scored a total of ten runs.

Unfortunately the opposing batters are timing Meryl's dropping pitch and, though they seem able to hit only singles, they hit them in batches and are ahead, 12-10, halfway through the seventh inning.

This is a sloppy game, the kind a team wins by luck or accident. Benjamin will be grateful when it ends.

"Two runs," he calls to his team as they return to the dugout. "Three to win. One more time at bat."

"You'll get 'em!" the tall umpire calls from second base. It's stark and certain, like a guarantee written in blood in an alley.

A few pitches later Nick punches a hit to right and tries to stretch it into a double. The play at second is a close one.

"Safe!" Daryl shouts.

Bob and Lewis rush from the V.F.W. dugout, not toward Daryl but toward the short umpire coaching at home plate. "We're playin' this game under protest," Lewis says. "The goddamn creep out there is their tenth player."

The home plate umpire doesn't seem to know what to do. After listening to more complaints from Bob, he reaches into his pants pocket, takes out a scrap of paper and stub of pencil, and writes something down.

Benjamin, now at home plate, doesn't know what to do either. He's sympathetic with the V.F.W. coaches: That crazy umpire certainly has been showing he's on Gray's side. On the other hand, the play at second might have been called either way. He doesn't want to lose the game or win it because of the umpire's bias.

He looks to second.

Daryl is grinning at him.

Wanting to slice out the troublemaker's eyes, he turns to Lewis, says, "I don't like what he's been saying and doing any more than you. Suppose we settle that call by appealing here." He indicates the home plate umpire, who's been making as many close calls against Gray's as he has for them. "It's, at least, less complicated than a protest."

Lewis and Bob step aside and talk it over. Lewis comes back to the plate and says, "All right."

All three coaches look at the home plate umpire, whose eyes begin to dart nervously back and forth.

"Did you get a good look at it?" asks Benjamin.

The umpire nods, setting his eyes on one of the steel posts holding up the backstop.

"Well?" says Bob.

The umpire mumbles something.

"What?" says Lewis.

"Thought he was out," the umpire replies.

Benjamin, though he regrets losing the possible run, is, all in all, relieved.

"He was out!" Lewis reports cheerfully to his players on the field.

"What!" Daryl is rushing in from second, pulling at his blue umpire's shirt, shouting obscenities. "I called the goddamned thing! I saw it! I *saw* it. What'd you change it for? You—you son-of-a-bitch!"

The Gray's players are up, screaming encouragement to Daryl.

The home plate umpire stumbles backward, away from Daryl, then looks up to the broadcast booth. Francis isn't at this game, so he's alone, standing still, eyes closed, as Daryl circles him, shouting more curses.

The Gray's fans have joined the players, are bellowing out their support for Daryl, causing the V.F.W. fans to shout warnings to them to shut up and stay in their seats.

A Gray's fan in suit and tie stands, points across to the V.F.W. stands, and says, "Go screw yourselves!"

Daryl now hits the home plate umpire on the side of the head. The other reels but doesn't go down. He shakes his head, drops his chest protector, and hits Daryl in the neck. Daryl grabs his arms, and they struggle to the ground, cursing.

A Gray's fan, possibly a player's father, bursts onto the field. He's dressed for tennis, all white, including cap with sunshade. He runs toward Lewis, who's been at the mound, motioning to his players to stay at their positions. Benjamin, at his dugout entrance, has been trying to keep his players inside. (Nick has stood a couple of feet from him, saying fearlessly, angrily, "You betrayed us! You're letting 'em have the game!") Turning now, catching a glimpse of the charging Gray's fan, Benjamin dashes after him.

The Gray's players follow him out of the dugout.

Benjamin sees the fan's fist rise in the air over Lewis. "Stop!" he calls.

No use. The fist comes down, catches Lewis behind the ear.

Lewis turns, swinging.

Bob rushes out of the V.F.W. dugout, toward Lewis, toward the crazy fan, toward Benjamin.

The opposing players are loose now, engaging each other. Soon wrestling matches are going on all over the field.

Bob tackles the Gray's fan as the fan is about to swing at him again. The two roll in the dust around the mound, pummeling each other.

"That's my husband!" a woman in the Gray's stands screams, pointing to the tennis player.

"He's a fag!" says a tough-looking V.F.W. fan in mechanic's overalls.

"That stupid umpire," says Lewis, rubbing his ear as he moves unsteadily toward home plate, where Daryl and the short umpire now stand a couple of feet apart, fists raised like fighters at the turn of the century. "Hit me, you fascist!" says Daryl. "Go ahead and hit me!"

Benjamin notices Meryl lying between the mound and second base, legs kicking the air above him, though no one is anywhere near him.

By quick estimate Benjamin concludes that this must be a standard riot. There is one exception. Two of his own players, Nick and Bobo, are fighting each other. He thinks of ordering them to stop but is sure it's pointless, given all else there is to stop. Those two fighting makes as much sense as anything else that's going on. He doesn't know why he himself hasn't been attacked.

The public address announcer has just thrown his microphone at someone from over the top of the backstop. It lies like a great silver stone a few feet from first base, where Fred, on the ground, has a leglock on the neck of the little V.F.W. batboy.

Benjamin, seeing the scope of this disaster, shouts, "Stop, everyone! Stop!" He raises his hands to the sky, turns to the left and right. "Stop!"

No one stops.

In fact, fans have entered the field from both sides and are pushing each other around on the infield.

In his changing field of vision Benjamin catches sight of Karl in the outfield. He lifts the V.F.W. center fielder and Speck McGovern, one in each arm, drops them on his big stomach, bouncing them to the ground. "Either of you touch the other one more time and I'll do it again!" They stare up, subdued but impressed, as he moves to left field, where Lou Pera and Tag have been ganging up on the V.F.W. left fielder. "C'mere, you li'l farts, so's I can ruin y'all!"

Benjamin turns back to the infield. "Stop it!" he cries, eyes reaching to spaces beyond the field.

No one stops anything.

"Please!"

They're all deaf to him.

Remembering something, he runs to his car, where a small girl is lying on the ground under his passenger door, looking through the stands and the fence with terrified eyes. "It'll stop pretty soon," he says to calm her; then he straddles the girl's head, opens the door, reaches into the glove compartment, pulls out a small object, and runs with it to the outside wall of the dugout, a place where no one on the field can see him. He puts the object in his mouth and blows hard.

The shouting subsides, but he hears some thumping.

He blows again.

Even the thumping stops.

He walks slowly to the end of the dugout, near the stands, and peers around. He sees many faces facing him, some near the ground, others above those, most flushed, a few with blood on nose and cheeks. Neat hairdos are twisted and askew. A few bodies are curled limply against the far fence, resting or defeated.

There is an uneasy stirring.

He raises the object to his mouth and blows again.

What? the waiting faces insist. *Tell us what that means.*

"Immediately!" he shouts at them. "Or else!" *Or else what?* he thinks.

Someone says, "It's just a goddamn whistle!"

"What do you think this whistle means?" he demands of the person who identified it.

The identifier is the man in the mechanic's outfit from the V.F.W. stands. He's standing over a boy about eighteen who looks like Speck and may be Speck's older brother. The mechanic, frowning, looks at the boy and then at Benjamin. "I dunno. What?"

"It means—it means all hell's going to break loose if you all don't get back in your places this very minute!" He raises the whistle and blows again, harder than ever.

A few fans and some players look toward the street as if awaiting the arrival of police cars. In fact, a helicopter happens to be flying nearby, and some have begun to look at it.

A few start back to the stands.

Benjamin blows the whistle again, this time with three short blasts.

A few players start for the dugouts. More fans move toward the stands. The public address announcer is out, picking up his microphone. He raises it, checks the plug.

A dark brown sedan turns off the street into the parking area. Everyone seems to be watching it, and some who haven't been moving toward the stands start moving. The driver pulls into the one open space behind Gray's stands. A man in a red-and-black-checkered hunting cap, gray windbreaker, and light blue dungarees gets out. Benjamin approaches him. The new man stares, put off by the odd sight of people walking from the field to the stands. "What's happening?" he says.

"Game interrupted because of—inclement behavior," Benjamin whispers.

"Huh?"

"Please stand just where you are and give a disapproving look to everyone who turns to look at you. In fact, shake your head and check your watch as if you're timing them."

"Pardon?"

"It's important. Please do what I say."

"What the hell's going on?" The man takes a step forward, only one. "I don't have a watch," he says.

"Stay," says Benjamin with all the authority he can muster. "Pretend you have a watch."

Benjamin's voice does it. The man freezes where he is. In a moment he's pulling back his sleeve, checking his bare wrist. It seems to be the thing he must do.

The players are in or close to their dugouts now. The fans are in or near their stands.

Only Daryl persists. He's beside home plate shoving the other umpire with his forearm, saying, "It was a good call, you asshole!"

Benjamin puts the whistle into his pocket, grateful that he left it in the glove compartment in the first place. Annie got it in the toy section at the supermarket, then marched around the house with it while he tried to work on the bookstore accounts. He told her to stop. She didn't, and he took it from her and hid it, intending to return it when he'd finished his work.

The game resumes within five minutes, all participants in their places, including Daryl.

Gray's bats are full of heat now. On two doubles, a single, and a walk, they pull it out, 13–12. No one, including the Gray's players, seems to care, maybe because the game itself was nothing compared to the brawl.

Lewis tells Benjamin afterward that it's the worst game he's ever been in or seen, but he assures Benjamin that he and Bob aren't going to protest. "You won her," he adds in a solemn voice. "That's what counts."

Though Benjamin doesn't believe anyone won this game, he nods.

Benjamin and Mrs. Jennings ("Ellen. Please") have been sitting at a white wrought-iron table on a screened-in porch at the back of the Jenningses' house. The porch overlooks a well-kept stretch of lawn with a scattering of pines, maples, and birches. Beyond the trees lie cornfields, farmhouses, barns, and, in the distance, patches of woods.

During his passage from the front door to porch Benjamin has learned that Max is spending the day in Toledo with his father. Sure now that he and Mrs. Jennings are alone, he's not relieved but acutely nervous. His one attempt to generate a conversation has been a flop: "It looks like the chill has finally gone out of the air." He found himself forcing a smile that in a moment seemed unconnected to the remark, to anything.

A whisper of old guilt is now taking shape in the realization that he and Marilyn have had few special moments like this—private, intimate even. It occurs to him, in fact, that he and Marilyn rarely eat together in a leisurely way like this, even when they go to the city to shop or see a movie. They stop at fast-food restaurants, often taking the food to the car and eating as they drive. Would Marilyn be happier if he'd thought to arrange such moments as this? The question takes a sharp edge when he realizes that he's willing to commit his entire afternoon to Mrs. Jennings, if that's what she wants.

She, too, is nervous. After his remark about the chill in the air her eyes flashed to the side, as if he'd just described the atmosphere between them. "Oh," she said finally, her eyes returning to his, "you mean the *weather*." They both laughed uncomfortably.

There's a bottle of chilled Rhine wine and two glasses on the table. With no more than a little fumbling, Benjamin has gotten a corkscrew from on top of the serving table next to the kitchen door, removed the cork, and poured wine for each of them.

"Well," he says, having at last come to something else, "we had quite a ball game yesterday."

"Oh?"

He describes the events of the game, concentrating on the small riot. He hasn't thought things through and spills out the incidents as they come to mind. As a result, his report, like the melee itself, is vaguely connected, a hodgepodge. She's soon trying to help him bring it all together with little connecting remarks: "What caused that?" "And then what?" "But isn't that terribly unusual?" They don't help. *This is awful*, he thinks as he looks into his glass and sees that—in one gulp? two?—he has emptied it. He quickly wraps his hand around the glass so as to conceal possible evidence of inordinate thirst, or worse.

But he doesn't deceive her. "Do have another," she says.

Clumsily he refills his glass.

The conversation goes on more or less the same flat way for fifteen or twenty minutes, Benjamin drinking too fast as he learns that Mr. Jennings is a lawyer in Toledo; that he and Mrs. J. have been separated from each other for more than a year; and that their conversation the other night, the night Benjamin called, concerned Max, who will be spending much of the summer at his father's apartment in the city. These are interesting facts, and Benjamin, hearing them, tries to piece together Ellen's relationship with her husband, or semihusband, as he holds off a wish to pour himself number three. She, not even halfway through number one, misreads his silence as boredom and says, "It's not important. Let me show you around the house."

Soon he's trailing her through the house: the kitchen with all its convenient built-ins; the dining area with its teak table, matching chairs, and the Oriental vase she says her husband brought back from New York; and Max's room, where an enormous color photograph of Pete Rose sliding faces an equally enormous photo of Hank Aaron batting. *A house is a house,* he thinks as they start back into the hall. What holds his attention is the liquid and inviting way Mrs. Jennings, Ellen, moves about. Watching her turn out of Max's room, he appreciates the way her light, off-white, somewhat transparent summer skirt clings to her lithe body through each move. Her parts are right, awfully right, with none of the early sag he's noticed in other women her age (thirty-two or -three, he's guessed). They are now standing before paintings in the hallway, he admiring a curve of breast beneath her tan sweater, as she, in her own dark tan, under her full blond hair, reaches up to point out something. Lowering her arm, she turns to him with a warm smile and says, "I did it myself."

He looks up and for the first time notices that the painting is of Max on a summer hill. "I like the rich colors," he says. The painting really does impress him. In its bright colors it seems to reveal something of her, much more than has been revealed in the conversation thus far. "I don't know much about paintings," he goes on, "but I like those colors. They assert themselves well, though the light in the hall is a little, you know, dim."

"That's very nice," she says, holding a grateful look. "Very."

In a moment she's reached the end of the hall and is pushing open the door to a large bedroom: hers, he presumes, though, perhaps out of some sense of discreetness, she doesn't say so. A couple of attractive landscapes (by her, he's sure) decorate the light blue walls. There's a large bed with an expensive looking mauve bedspread, and, in the corner, a small desk. Except for the bright and appealing paintings, it's just another master bedroom, and he can think of nothing more to say than, "Nice."

Not until they're back on the porch and he's poured himself that third glass of wine does he strike through to a matter more vital:

"Look. I've been looking forward to this, and I enjoy being here with you, but I'm a little uneasy for some reason. Nothing you've done or said. I just feel, well, sort of out of place."

"I can tell anyway," she says calmly. "Did you find it hard to call me the other night?"

"Not to call exactly. But when you were on the phone I felt a little awkward. No. More than a little. I mean you did say then that Max was okay, and—it kind of knocked out my reason for, well, seeing you. Though I wanted to."

"Still, *I* invited *you*, didn't I?"

"That's true."

"So maybe I'm the one who ought to be concerned."

"Are you?"

"No. I *wanted* to see you. I'm glad you're here. Lunch may even be an excuse."

He's losing his edgy feeling. Her frank remarks help, but there's also the way she tilts her head and reaches to him with her intense eyes. *Lunch might even be an excuse,* he repeats to himself as he takes a sip of wine.

"Are you hungry?"

"No," he replies definitely, feeling more able to get in touch with less visible purposes. "I enjoy the wine. I like talking to you."

"Good."

He pours more wine into her glass. As he returns the bottle to the table, she gently lays her hand on his wrist, keeps it there as he brings his own back to the table. It's not an empty gesture. Now, as before, her movements say more than her words. This last seems to challenge him to stiffen and pull away. He doesn't. There's no resistance in him at all.

"You're so unaware of your own presence," Marilyn had said one night. "It charms and irritates at the same time."

They'd just returned from a booksellers' meeting in Cleveland, which had ended with a cocktail party given by several publishers. After a couple of drinks Benjamin had relaxed and chatted easily with the executives and other store owners, not only about business matters like the improving prospects for sales in the area, and what the owners might do to exploit them, but about less momentous matters too, like baseball and some recent movies. A few wives had joined in during these conversations, and Marilyn had remarked on the drive home how unusually interested a couple of them had seemed in him. He showed surprise. She mentioned that the wife of one publisher had asked her how long Benjamin had owned his bookstore, was curious about how he felt about living in Centerville, and finally, with (Marilyn had said) the curiosity of an envious schoolgirl, even asked, "Where did you meet him?" That, it seemed to Benjamin, was flattering, and he said so, then suggested to Marilyn, jokingly, that it might result in Benjamin's Bookstore getting special discount rates from the publisher.

"We aren't chronic partygoers so I sometimes forget," she went on. *"But tonight reminded me that, without even seeking it or wanting to, you exude a kind of charm. More than that. Sexuality. When I see other women responding to it, I feel proud, but it also bothers me. I guess I can't help wondering what you'd be like if you were aware of it."*

"You mean I could be taking a lot of women to bed if I wanted to?" he said, raising his eyebrows à la Groucho Marx.

"Oh, be serious," she said. *"Did you notice that you were getting more attention than most of the men?"*

"No," he said truthfully.

"That's what I mean."

They were now in the kitchen having orange juice. She twisted her glass, nearly spilled the contents. "You're such a dummy. What happens—what happens to me when you find out?"

"I just now did find out, didn't I? And here I am, the same old Benjamin."

"Do you really believe *me?"*

"I believe you. I've just never thought about it. If you say it's true, it's probably true."

Yes, he remembered, there had been women at his side for much of the evening, one or two, including that publisher's wife, flirting a bit, or so it seemed. He hadn't given them much attention, hadn't wanted to, figuring that some people just become flirty after a couple of drinks. At such times he was too preoccupied with one thought or another to follow up. Follow up? What sort of following up was possible? Anyway, he felt pretty sure that women who'd aroused him were probably unattracted to him, just as overly attentive women usually didn't interest him.

"You don't know what's happening, Benjamin."

"Nothing's happening," he said uneasily.

"*Suppose you had the opportunity,* an *opportunity, with someone who attracted you.*"

"I'd grab her and run to the cheapest motel." He was desperate to keep it light.

"*Tell me!*"

"I don't know," he said, embarrassed by his apparent self-ignorance. "It hasn't happened. I don't think it will."

She got up and rinsed out the orange juice glasses.

"*What would it do to you if it did happen?*"

"Let's go to bed," she said.

In the bedroom he said, "*You didn't answer me.*"

She undressed quickly but didn't put on her nightgown. He knew what that meant; he didn't put on his pajama bottoms.

Their loving lasted for a long time. He thought of no one else.

Afterwards he reminded her that she still hadn't answered.

"*It's not for me to answer,*" she said firmly.

And in the silent touching that follows her first reaching out he wonders if this might be the beginning of an answer. He hopes it's not, but there is no way to tell. He waits for her to say something; she doesn't. He can think of nothing to tell her. The words that come to mind are for Marilyn:

It just happened. We were sitting on her porch having a glass of wine and, before I knew it, I was following her down the hall.

She flows, a swimmer, underwater, gliding toward a deep and hidden cave.

She entered the room, beckoning to me, as if it had all been settled and there was nothing to discuss, nothing but to—just do it.

She pulls a cord that closes the wispy drapes, then advances toward him, arms extended. Though she holds him tightly, she's soft and pliant in his arms. He feels a tremor, a chill, and releases her. Her arms fall and she steps back, whispering his name.

So, slowly, right in front of me, not the way you do it, by going into the closet, but right there in front of me, and so very slowly, as if to be sure I'd enjoy it, she began to take off her clothes. Not ashamed or anything. The opposite. She looked eager and lustful. How could this happen so fast? I kept thinking that. Pretty soon her clothes were all on the floor, sandals kicked off and everything, and she was reaching up to me again, this time with bare arms, all of her bare.

"Please undress," she says, her hands descending to the top of his shirt, playing over the hairs on his chest, opening the first button, moving quickly to the second, opening it, then, more urgently, the next and next, until she has the shirt completely open and is turning her softly scented face into his chest, feeling it with her face.

Wine or no wine, he can't relax, can't get with it. He stops explaining all this to Marilyn, thinks, instead, of his baseball team. Suppose they knew about it? Not just Max or Bobo, all of them. Then he actually imagines Meryl, innocent Meryl, at the bedroom doorway, looking in.

The vision doesn't quite numb him, for he's undone his belt and opened his pants. It's not the working of a passion; he's done it to save himself the odd sensation of watching her do it. He feels the pants fall to the floor and wishes she'd slow down. He hopes she won't reach down and remove his underwear. He'll grab the underwear, say, "I prefer to do that."

Now I don't want to make excuses, but I began to see her actions sort of like those of a nymphomaniac. I mean, I know you'll say that was just my stupidity again, me not knowing that I can turn a woman on, a normal woman, not knowing how I might make her want to do what Ellen was doing and all. And maybe I don't. That's possible. I mean here was a woman separated from her husband and maybe just horny because she hadn't had a man for a while. Normal, predictable, something I should have foreseen. But, still, there was something else, something unusual, by—by any standards, in that "full speed ahead" approach of hers.

He holds one hand against her shoulder and balances like an arthritic ostrich, trying to get his shoe off.

"God, I've wanted you!" he hears her say.

"I know what you mean," he says, falling against the bed as he struggles with his sock.

He wonders why he can't be truthful and say, "You are golden and lovely and flowing and I myself have had horny thoughts about you, but I had no idea it would come so quickly to this. I'm just not ready." It seemed impossible that the afternoon would end (begin?) this way. Lunch, a French lunch, is all he had in mind. French lunch! Was it some kind of joke or code? Is this what she thought he meant by French lunch?

He's sitting on the bed and she's taking off his other shoe and sock. His shorts are still on, but nothing else. She puts the shoe and sock on the floor and reaches around him at the waist. He thinks she may be going for the underwear. "I'll get those," he says, just in case.

Forgive me, but I felt I was being raped, if you can picture a woman raping a man, if you call it rape when a person has the power to get up, put his clothes back on, and get out. I thought of doing just that, in fact, but it seemed—I know this is going to sound stupid—impolite.

He's suddenly grateful that this conversation with Marilyn isn't real.

All right. It was happening. I was letting it happen. I had, I confess, had earlier had, thoughts about her. I'd even now and then thought something might come of them. But I didn't think she'd want to get in bed that afternoon. I thought I'd have time to—think it through. Maybe I'd get a sign from her that day that she wanted this sort of thing and then would go and think about it, possibly—no, probably—concluding that it would be unwise and that I'd better pull back. Certainly I'd have been tempted to talk to you about it, especially if you were clear of your big question by then. At least it's a good possibility. I doubt, Marilyn, I really doubt, that I'd have let myself get into that cozy situation if I'd known what it would lead to.

They're under the sheet and she's squirming against him, as if to let him discover how accommodating her body is for him. The thought that she'll soon be writhing beneath him excites him to an erection.

We reached a moment, I confess, when I couldn't pull back. Until then I was even having thoughts about how I'd explain it to you, actually was explaining it to you, in my mind at least. But after that moment I couldn't keep thinking about you. I was lost in—in, I guess, the passion

110

*of the moment as they say, though that doesn't quite ex-
plain it.*

She, too, seems compelled to explain something: "I
didn't plan this. It's just that your presence . . ." She
doesn't finish the thought but reaches around him, crab-
like, feeling, searching, biting at, then actually biting into,
the flesh above his belly. He lies back, taking it, wanting
it, knowing that, for a time at least, his pleasure is in
feeling himself the victim.

*I wanted it as much as she. If she'd stopped leading,
I'd have become the aggressor. I appreciated her knowing, sensing, that I couldn't lead. That became just another level of the excitement.*

He curls down, strokes her legs, presses his face between them, searches not with hands but with mouth and
tongue. She, for the first time, takes a cue from him,
lowering her head between his thighs.

*So we were both aggressors, both victims. Soon I felt
as though we were fighting each other. Near the end I
couldn't, it seemed, press myself against her hard enough.
When it happened we were like a poster for a movie I'd
seen where the woman's and man's bodies are superim-
posed on each other, the parts of one becoming the parts
of the other.*

Their bodies throb violently against each other.

She cries out.

When they're finished he realizes he hasn't even taken
off his shorts. He wants to say something about that,
make a joke of it, doesn't. There's no need to explain or
apologize for anything.

The sheet is off the bed, and she lies open-legged,
open-armed, lightly flushed. The sight of her beside him,
the sound of her breathing evenly but deeply, the sweet-
herbal scent she gives off, all gather to an urgency, and
to his own delight and surprise, he begins again.

This time she is the more submissive, moving only in
response to his moves. He invades her, too quickly he
thinks. But, as he moves fiercely against her, her eloquent groans reassure him. Soon they erupt into each
other, and he knows not only that he did not work too
fast, but that he couldn't have worked too slowly. *A
woman's supreme compliment,* he thinks, *a gift of im-*

mense freedom, immense power, deriving solely from her.

Minutes pass. (He may have dozed.) They do it yet again, this time quietly, with everything in slow motion: They close like petals at evening into the heart of the flower.

He sleeps.

When he awakens, she's beside the bed, dressed as she was when he arrived at the house, hair as full and fluffy as it was; and she is smiling as she was, all of her the same except for the reddish hue in her face. She's holding a cup of coffee and says lunch will be ready when he's dressed.

What struck me most, after the lovemaking and the lunch, when I was driving home, was how easily we'd done it. I don't mean just how easily we'd gotten to the bed and made love, but all of it, including the after part. We ate lunch as if nothing unusual had happened. Well, I mean her looks and moves might have been telling me how much she'd enjoyed it, but she didn't talk about it. Neither did I.

What they do talk about is Max and his father. Mr. Jennings, it seems, was "very upset" about the injury and scheduled an appointment with a specialist, suspecting that there might be permanent damage.

"I don't want you to worry about it, Benjamin," she says, reaching out to him. "Don is that way. The lawyer thing. Life for him is debts, contracts, personal injuries, and compensation. He does a lot of things one might call threatening. Usually nothing comes of them." Sensing Benjamin's nervousness over the matter, she adds, "I'll keep in touch and let you know the results of the specialist's tests."

He doesn't know how to reply. In remembering the accident, he's convinced himself that Bobo was right from the first: He, Benjamin, probably did cause damage to the ankle when he lifted Max off the fence. But permanent damage? For now at least, he's concerned more about the effects on Max than about a lawsuit, if that's what Ellen means by "threatening." No matter. He can find nothing to say about either.

What we have is deeply rooted, Marilyn, and that afternoon did nothing to threaten it. My God! It wasn't even an affair, just an—an encounter: Wham-bam, thank ya, ma'am. I seem to be making such a big thing of it. How can it possibly threaten—us? Things like that happen. Such is life. What would I do if you told me something happened in Minnesota? Would that erase for me the life we've lived together, the days we look forward to sharing? How could it?

Yet he says to Ellen at her door, "Even if you have no news about Max, I'd like to talk to you. Would it be okay to give you a call in a few days?" And why is he buoyed by her cheerful answer: "If you don't, *I'll* call *you*"? Why, when she rises on her toes to kiss him goodbye, is there a surge of the passion that should by now have been spent?

Dear Benjamin,

Hope you two are well, communicating, winning ball games, etc. We miss you both. It's been only a week but seems like months. I *think* we'll be home in six or seven days. Will call or write when I'm more certain. Have included separate note to Bobo.

I've been aching to tell you what I did Sunday. I know it's going to sound nutty but bear with me until I explain. Mother and Dad had to go to a party for one of his partners—cocktails, dinner, etc.—so the girls and I had the afternoon to ourselves. Mother had mentioned this crafts show, an annual thing. She went last year and said it was very impressive and thought we'd like to see it. I had *no* interest at all but knew I'd be bored sitting around the beach with their friends and neighbors and realized the girls hadn't really seen anything new since we've been here. Suzie, especially, has been all nerves. (I don't know why. She worried me sometimes. I think I know her less than the other children. Will talk to you about that later.) So, anyway, we went. Details, details. It's hard to describe, but I came away with such an odd feeling. How do I explain it?

First of all, there were just the three of us, wandering past all the displays in this park by a lake, knowing not a soul, free to stop and look as we felt like. I mean, Benjamin, there were hundreds! One woman makes opaque blue glass objects, animals and vases

113

and such, very original in shape and very attractive. Another, a man, sculpts things out of wood and he was chipping away at a squirrel he was making right there at the fair. There were, of course, a lot of people displaying paintings—charcoal, oils, water colors, all possible things. Captivating. Annie or Suzie would see a display she liked, we'd stop and look, then move on to the next. Some of the stuff was really pretty junky, a lot of it, but that's not important. I began to find in each something of the personality of the maker. I mean the man making the squirrel, for example. We watched him cutting and chipping for quite a while (Annie even picked up some of the bigger chips and saved them). Anyway, I noticed how, in the way he made his animals and lamps and such, he revealed something about himself. He had a peaceful face and was very calm in answering questions about things on his display table and about the squirrel, and so deliberate and sure in the way (even while he was talking) he removed bits and pieces from the block of wood he was using. I kept looking at the things he made, the objects on his table, and realized they'd seemed ordinary at first glance only because they were part of this enormous show where the things were sort of all jammed together at little booths or tables surrounded by other booths or tables. As part of the group they had little chance to assert themselves. I'm not saying the man was a great sculptor or any such thing. But I know that, after looking at his stuff for a long time, first the whole of it, then the individual pieces, at the same time watching him work and hearing him answer questions, I began to appreciate how really distinctive it was.

Later, because of what I'd appreciated about the sculptor, I took my time at other booths, where something especially interested me, and began to do the same—tried to relate a painting or whatever (in one case, toys made out of scrap metal) to the person who did it. I asked a few of the people how they started. There were all sorts of answers, but one thing that they all had in common was a sense of fascination—can't seem to find the right word. I mean they were all totally involved in what they were doing. One woman, who didn't seem to be selling much of what she'd made, spent about ten minutes telling me how she cut her artificial flowers out of pieces of metal and gold-leafed them. She not only didn't seem to mind sharing the "secrets" of her craft, but it was almost as though she hoped I'd get involved in it too. "You must begin with a very thin and pliable light aluminum or steel," etc. Meanwhile, as she spoke to me, people came up and looked at what she'd made, but she herself, while giving them greetings and such, seemed a lot more interested in talking about this craftsmanship of hers than in selling. Probably needed to talk and share something about it after so many hours in solitude making it, don't you think?

I hadn't put any of this together and was only just beginning to appreciate the show by the time I was driving the girls home in Mother's car. (Had planned to stay an hour or so and we stayed three and a half, and though it was a hot day, I almost literally had to drag Annie away.) I asked the girls what they liked most about the show, and they both, after mentioning favorite displays and such, said that everything was different. It's taking *me* hundreds of words to say what *I* liked. And they're right. Maybe what they said gets to the heart of it. Every person was somehow visible in what he or she did, and all were, are, so different. Even people who used similar materials turned out objects vastly different. Sometimes the materials themselves were strikingly original, like the sand one man used to make seascapes—a crude material, yes, but so what. Everyone there seemed to have found some way to make himself, herself, known to others through the craft and style he or she used.

As you can tell, I'm still "high" about it, and for the first time in a long time I haven't felt the drag of that old question of mine. Not that I've answered it. It's just that seeing those people and their work I have, all of a sudden, great hope that I will answer it. Remember when it started? How I was working on that ridiculous cardboard man for the school drawing? How he seemed to ask me the question? Well, you know, as bad as that cardboard man was, I was actually expressing something of myself while making it. I think it's possible

115

that in doing that—could have been making almost anything—I was detached enough from the rest of my life, at least temporarily, lost in something else, I could face the question he seemed to be asking. Only *seemed* to be, since it had to be me who was really asking it. Yes, I do think I need some kind of outlet, therapy, whatever. I can't picture myself sitting around making toys or rings and jewelry or, frankly, at this point, any of the things I saw at the crafts show. But I do need, well, something. I think I'd need it if I were not a so-called housewife or mother. I'm sure I would. Probably or possibly even need it more if I'd followed up on my degree work and had a job in a psych clinic or whatever. I know this is going to seem terribly anticlimactic, but I just don't have a clue as to what I'll want to do. Know only that I've got to get involved in what I'll have to call badly some kind of "creative work." Kites, anyone? Who knows? The possibility of doing it, even though I can't say what, is chewing away at the cable to which my big question is attached. I'm sure I'll know a lot more about it by the time we get home, since I think of hardly anything else.

Can you still love me after all this self-indulgence? I do dearly hope so. I love you very much and miss you more than my "problem" has allowed me to say. Miss my ever-changing Bobo too but don't want him cluttered with any of this, so just give him the cheerful (I hope) note I am including to him. Be good. No. Be happy. I know the house must be a mess. Am not worried about it, or anything else, even Suzie, just now.

All my love,
Marilyn

In less than two hours Gray's plays an evening game against opponent number three. Alone in the house Benjamin has forgotten the team Gray's is up against. He will, he's sure, soon remember. Bobo is having dinner at Tim Adams' and will go from there to the game. Bobo hasn't read the note Marilyn included; Benjamin will give it to him at the game. (Did Bobo remember to take his uniform? He'll check Bobo's bedroom and make sure.) He's not hungry but has decided to eat the contents of a small carton of yogurt before he leaves. Meanwhile he'll have a martini on the rocks and reread Marilyn's incredible letter.

He came home from work at three fifteen with a handful of work and spent two hours at his bedroom desk looking over outstanding bills for some of his regular customers. When he finished with the bills he called Ellen Jennings' number with nothing more specific on his mind than his wish to talk to her. As the phone rang he thought to say, "Just wanted to thank you for lunch the other day." He sensed the possible double meaning in it, as well as a lack of feeling, and decided on the more truthful, "I felt like talking." Sometime during the conversation, he'd tell her how very much he'd enjoyed the time they'd spent together. He'd think of a persuasive way to say it when the right moment came. He waited. The phone buzzed on. No answer.

Marvell's Auto Supply. That's it. He knows nothing about them except that last year they finished somewhere near the middle. Marvell's Auto Supply. Tag wants to pitch. There has been no practice since the last game, but Tag has been throwing pitches to Bobo. Benjamin asked Bobo how the pitches looked, apologizing for asking since talk about the team at home is still tabooed. Bobo gave him a completely unhelpful answer: "Okay, I guess." Benjamin didn't push it. He'll let Tag warm up as pitcher before the game, watch him closely, then make his decision.

Marilyn's letter left him tight and uncertain. The martini is loosening him. It's really a double, made from the last of a bottle that has been resting on top of the refrigerator for several weeks. He'd better reread the letter before the drink clouds his mind. Afterwards, he'll have that yogurt and some coffee, then find the little bottle of breath spray and use it before leaving for the game.

He spots the letter on the dining room table, along with a postcard from Dick Francis, which arrived along with it and several house bills. He looks again at the postcard:

Ben—
    See me after game. Have names of extra players. Since Gray's ended last last year, you get first choice. Maybe two additional players.
    Also, let's talk about that mess the other night.

Thanks for taking control. What do we do to keep things from getting out of hand like that again?

D. Francis

Put balls and chains on all the fans, Benjamin thinks, laying down the postcard and taking Marilyn's letter to the living room.

The letter, read very rapidly the first time, left him with thoughts seesawing. (Everything lately seems to leave him seesawing.) Wonderful that she seems to be floating free of the heavy question. But worrisome that she seems so obsessed by the crafts show. He doesn't know just where she'll land. He's searching the letter now, trying to find a clue. He can't; yet he's sure it's a real thing. She'll find some—there *is* no good word—outlet.

Escape?

From him maybe.

Is Ellen Jennings *his* craft, *his* escape?

Are Marilyn and he finding separate ways to flee from each other?

Oh, he regrets those protestations he spoke silently to her while he was preparing to make love to, yes, fuck, Ellen in her bed! How deeply rooted can his love for Marilyn be if he now spends nearly all of his few leisure moments thinking about Ellen? How easy it was for him to be himself with her! How un-easy it has been lately for him to be himself with Marilyn! They are, he and Marilyn, or seem to be, veering apart. She isn't the only one with a big question.

Questions.

Maybe the life he thinks he's living is not the life he's living. What a shock it would be to Marilyn, for example, to learn how little time he and Bobo have spent talking. "The best laid plans of mice and men . . ." How many days now has it been since they really talked? A week? Just about a week. Not a single damned conversation. Not after Marilyn's first letter? And that was hardly a conversation. Maybe Marilyn and he are growing apart, but no one is growing away more than Bobo.

They're all growing.

The girls too:

He recalls the comment in Marilyn's letter about Suzie's nervousness. Before they left for Minnesota he'd be-

118

gun to notice striking differences in the way each of the girls reacted to the same thing: Annie much calmer, almost detached; Suzie intense, insistent, often frightened. Too often he thinks of them as "the girls." There is Annie. And there is Suzie. And, of course, they too are growing, perhaps more rapidly if less noticeably than he, Marilyn, and Bobo, each in her own way, discernible if one takes the time to discern.

He now imagines a communication from Marilyn:

Am staying here and taking up crafts. Bottle painting. Feel free to come and see girls and me any time you want.

That triggers an imagined note from Bobo:

You tried to be a good dad but made no sense to me. Am leaving, hitchhiking across the country to find myself. Will see you again someday.

None of this is possible, he tries to convince himself.
Possible, he thinks, *but not probable.*
Possibly probable?
The martini has connected thoughts that might otherwise not be connected.
He pictures a sheet of paper with a note from Suzie:

Dear Mom and Dad,
   I cannot speak anymore. I cannot hear either. I will try to keep breathing. Please write on the other side of this paper if you have anything to tell me. I am scared. I wish you knew why. I don't know why. Please write something that will help me.

Have to write something, he thinks. *What should I write?*
Recognizing the absurdity of his thought, he forces himself to ignore it.
Finally there is this:
Mrs. Jennings. Let all else return to what it was or become what it might be: Bobo become his chum, Marilyn be his strong and devoted wife, Suzie calm and happy, both girls looking to him with pride and confidence. What-

ever. There is still Mrs. Jennings. Ellen. He can't deceive himself. Had Marilyn been in town he's pretty sure he'd have found his way to Ellen Jennings' bed. The parts of a life aren't doled out like playing cards, yet there now seems something fixed about his attachment to Ellen. He doesn't know what. Perhaps it begins with the lovely way she looks and moves, those compelling gestures. But what else?

He imagines a postcard, him to them:

I love you all but have found my fulfillment in a woman named Ellen Jennings. What else can I say? Good-bye, alas!

He grimaces at the composition, puts Marilyn's letter back into its envelope without rereading it, returns it to the dining room table, goes to the kitchen, eats two spoonfuls of yogurt, finds breath spray in the downstairs bathroom, uses it. He locates Bobo's spikes and takes them to the station wagon, where he makes a quick check of the rest of the equipment: all there.

Soon he's on his way to the ball park like a refugee fleeing toward a friendly border.

For information about their opponents, professional teams depend on a variety of sources like scouting reports, traded players, and magazines and newspapers. In Pee Wee baseball, Benjamin has quickly discovered, there are little more than rumors, delivered and distorted by one's own players and, more often than not, unreliable. Since the seasons are short, with no team facing another more than twice, a manager must rely on the rumors; see opponents playing, if possible; but, mostly, identify, on the very day of the game, the ways in which the other team is vulnerable. Benjamin has been learning to make quick evaluations.

Marvell's Auto Supply is, for example, a big slow team. One would think, watching them warm up, that this year's draft had been made by putting all the application cards of players who are over five feet seven and weigh more than 130 pounds in a pile and calling the team Marvell's Auto Supply.

In the dugout Benjamin tells his team, scheduled to bat

first, that they'll be bunting tonight. He's counting both on the heftiness of the Marvell's pitcher, catcher, and infielders and on his own players' speed, one of their strengths.

The fresh approach seems to appeal to his players. There are only a few questions (mainly about the bunt sign) and, strangely, no arguments.

"Play ball!"

Seeing that Daryl is not umpiring tonight, Benjamin wants to thank someone.

Harold soon heads for the batter's box and Tony takes his place in the on-deck circle.

Since the V.F.W. game there has been less grumbling, little arguing, almost no resistance. The victory may have a lot to do with it; he's not sure. He remembers the run-in with Nick, and the "strike" signs, knows there are still problems. From the coaching box he looks over, sees Nick tapping his bat against the concrete near the back of the dugout, appearing as sullen as ever. Nick is the touchstone, but the others, in their silences, are giving off glimmers too.

Harold has bunted for a single.

Tony now takes a fourth ball.

From the dugout the rest of the team yells in support. The game has started well.

Funny, he thinks, how a game plan can bring together a bunch of kids who might otherwise have nothing to do with each other. Few of these players pal around together when they're not playing. Some probably wouldn't say hello to him if they passed on the street. Bobo is most striking. Not only does he rarely converse with the coach, who is also his father, but the father's very purpose in choosing to coach—to get closer to his son—seems to have been lost. Though the boy has shown less tension and less sarcasm lately, in place of those he's offered silence punctuated by grunts and three-word sentences. And who, among these team members, are his friends? *The kid is a stranger,* Benjamin thinks as he watches him swing a couple of bats.

It's worse than that. Benjamin now realizes that if he were Bobo's age and living in the same neighborhood or playing on the same team, he wouldn't seek him out as a friend. Indeed, Bobo seems just the sort of boy Benjamin spent much of his early life avoiding: irritatingly self-reliant, aggressive, a maker of sharp-edged comments. Benjamin would have chosen, did choose, gentler friends.

Amazing! he thinks as he gives the steal sign.

The steal works and a run scores.

Later there's another run.

Tag takes the mound at the bottom of the first and is effective: a walk and three easy outs.

Gray's scores once more in the second.

By the bottom of the third Gray's has bunted itself to a 3–0 lead.

Made sleepy by the workings of the martini and bored by the effectiveness of his strategy, Benjamin is twice distracted:

First there comes his remembrance that after this, the third game, Bobo is to let him know how he feels about Benjamin's continuing to handle the team. Benjamin sees an opportunity for a real and long overdue conversation. Bobo's opinion about his managing matters: Benjamin wants to go on managing this team; it's become a vital urge, somehow; in view of his pledge he could end up in quite a crisis. Yet, in view of the distance Benjamin now senses between himself and his son, something else matters more. He's flat-out curious as to where the boy stands (sits or leans) on *any* subject, wants to hear him open up, wants to know whether or not they have anything, *anything,* to share about anything.

As Bobo puts on his catching equipment for the bottom of the third, Benjamin sidles up to him and says quietly, "Tonight's the night we're supposed to talk about me and the team. Remember?"

Snapping on his shin guard, not looking up, Bobo says indifferently, "I know. I've been waiting for you to say something about it," then, without another remark, hurries to his position behind home plate.

The second distraction occurs when, turning from Bobo to sit down in the dugout, Benjamin catches a fleck of light out of the corner of his eye, turns and focuses to find it coming off the tip of a car's radio aerial. He lowers his eyes, sees that it's Ellen's car and that Ellen is in the car, waving a greeting to him. There are a lot of objects catching sunlight at this predusk hour, yet his eye was drawn to Ellen's radio aerial. *A mystical thing,* he decides, and he waves back.

She's alone in the car. From the dugout entrance he checks the stands, does not see Max, and concludes she's driven here for her own reasons.

What else would you expect? he asks himself as he sits down. Had she not appeared, he would have tried to call her again tonight. Some of the implications of his afternoon at her house are just beginning to catch up with him. Much of his silent speech to Marilyn then seems now to have been evasion or self-deception. *How much farther am I willing to go with her?* he wonders as he rises, leans out of the dugout, catches her attention, and mouths, "Can you wait?"

She nods.

At the bottom of the fifth, the score is still 3–0, due to steady throwing by the Marvell pitcher and exceptional fielding by Gray's.

A Marvell's player finally makes it to third base on a low throw to second by Bobo on a steal. The manager, oafish in his too-small checkered red slacks and unmatching orange T-shirt (which has on the back a racing car crashing through the blue word MARVELL'S), steps out of his coaching box at third, puts his arm on the runner's shoulder, and says loudly, "This ain't but a dang rag-tag team an' we gonna beat 'em. Hear?" The manager has failed to call time out. Before he finishes, Tag alertly whips the ball to Nick, who puts it on the listening runner, standing a foot or so off the base.

"Kiss my ass!" says the manager.

And that's how the inning ends.

As close as the score is, this game doesn't challenge Benjamin, and he falls to other distractions:

Between the fifth and sixth innings he sees the florid face and cold eyes of Thaddeus Gray. The sponsor is standing beside the Gray's stands, looking out, his expression full of displeasure.

Benjamin can no longer think of Gray in any but disdainful terms: *When, you pervert, are you going to get us some uniforms?* When he finally catches Gray's unchanging eyes he returns a scowl, hoping it's full of the threatening knowledge he's gotten from Tim. *You seedy bastard!* he thinks.

Later, if Gray hangs around, he'll soften his question, but will ask it.

Every Marvell's player has been swinging for the fence. Tag hasn't been pitching an outstanding game, but the Marvell's players, overswinging on bad pitches, have made him and the infielders look good. After walking only two and giving up only three hits, Tag walks one batter at the bottom of the sixth. Then the Marvell's first baseman, taking a roundhouse cut at the ball, sends it over the left field fence, making the score 3–2.

A ball game at last, Benjamin thinks, not at all worried by the score. In fact, he's desperately wanted something to keep his attention on this contest.

The Marvell batters who follow, too eager to duplicate the first baseman's hit, go after everything. The first player pops up to Fred, the second and third strike out on bad pitches.

Before his team bats at the top of the seventh, Benjamin decides to go for insurance runs. "Their infielders have been playing in, cutting off some of our bunts. So let's forget the bunts. Just swing to meet the ball; try to send it over the infielders' heads."

No disagreement, not even a grunt from Nick.

After a few pitches there are two runners on base, on a walk, then a looping single that sends the front runner to third.

There is only one out, and Benjamin tells Nick to swing hard.

Nick sends the first pitch against the fence in left center for a double, scoring two runs.

It's 5–2, Gray's.

Too easy, Benjamin thinks.

There comes another distraction, a thought:

He'll ask Ellen to dinner. They'll go to a fine restaurant in Toledo. First he'll give Bobo hamburger money, then go home and get out of his grubby khakis and T-shirt and into sport coat and slacks.

In moments, however, he remembers that planned conversation with Bobo. Nothing is as important.

"Shit!" he says loudly, causing a turning of the heads of those players who are in the dugout.

Both the game and his thoughts have fallen on cold stone.

When the Marvell's manager arrives at the third base

124

coaching box for the last of the seventh inning, Benjamin calls from the dugout: "Know something?"

The sluggish man turns. "Yeah? What?"

"Your team is boring." He speaks it disgustedly, as if he might add, "You ought to be ashamed of yourself."

A couple of the Gray's infielders look over, startled.

"Pushovers," Benjamin goes on. "Where's your imagination? I don't like taking my kids out here to play dull games. You owe it to us, and your players too, to come up with something besides all that puff-puff swinging. The score could be a lot closer." He feels heat rising in his neck.

"We'll come up with somethin'. You jus' watch."

"It's sickening," Benjamin says, slumping down on the bench.

"At least we got uniforms," the Marvell's manager says. It seems to be the best he can do.

Toads, Benjamin thinks, *nothing but a pack of toads.*

He wishes another riot would start. He probably wouldn't be lucky enough to stop it this time. That would be just fine. Maybe he wouldn't even try to stop it.

As he could have predicted to anyone who asked, the game fizzles to an end, the final score 5–2, Gray's.

He goes quickly to Ellen's car.

She says she'd been sitting home, thinking about him, then checked the schedule and realized he had a game. Max was still with his father in Toledo. She came to the game without an alibi. Did he have time for that cup of coffee?

"Give me a few minutes," he says. "Business with the commissioner." He suggests they meet at the doughnut shop in the shopping center a few blocks away.

She presses her hand down on his, which rests on the window frame.

Aware that someone may be watching, he slowly pulls his hand away. "About fifteen minutes."

He hurries past the stands and up the stairs to the announcer's booth.

"Well, you got yourself a couple now," says Gray in anything but congratulatory tones. He's standing against the wall inside the cubicle, arms crossed.

Francis, at the small table overlooking the field, is making a final check of the official score sheet.

"When do we get the uniforms?" Benjamin asks Gray. "I want to see if you keep winnin'."

What bullshit! Benjamin thinks.

"Hear we get a couple of extra players," Gray goes on. "If we pick the right ones, maybe we'll win some more."

We? Why, suddenly, *we?* "I'll pick them," Benjamin says sharply. "League rules."

Before Gray can argue, Francis turns and hands Benjamin some application cards. "Pick two players," he says. "All the statistics are there."

Benjamin studies the cards one by one, keeping himself apart from Gray, saying nothing. Whether it's his feelings about Gray or some estimation he's made about the team, he finds himself especially attracted to two of these late applicants. He plucks their cards from the pile, hands them to Francis without showing them to Gray, then puts the remaining cards down on the announcer's table.

"Let me take a look at those," Gray says, edging toward Francis.

Benjamin is nearly back in the dugout, about to tell his team the date and time of the next game, when he hears Gray's bellow, then a string of vile curses. He thinks he hears the walls of the little booth being thumped, though it might be a distant thunderstorm.

"What's goin' on up there?" Speck asks.

Benjamin doesn't answer.

He makes sure Bobo is going home directly, says he'll be there to talk to him in a half hour or so, then picks up the equipment bag and takes it to the station wagon.

On the way to the doughnut shop he reviews his choices:

Name: Digby Wells
Age: 13
Sex: M
Experience: None
Comments: I am black. I hope you have other black players on your team. Digby.

and

Name: Pat Somerville
Age: 13
Sex: Female

Experience: I never played baseball before but softball with my brothers. I can't hit but I can throw like a boy. *Comments:* What I just said and I hope you give me a chance not just because I'm a girl.

Before he pulls up at the doughnut shop, he thinks of Gray, pictures him picking up one card, then the other, eyes widening, face reddening: then the explosion. The laughter in the car surely matches, decibel for decibel, the noise the sponsor was making in the announcer's booth.

Her hands do little ballet pastiches over her coffee cup as she admits that her going to the game resulted from something more than her desire to see him. Don has called to tell her that the orthopedic surgeon, after looking at Max's leg, found that the astragalus, a bone just below the tibia, was cracked badly and doesn't seem to be healing properly. If the boy's condition doesn't improve, Don will probably, through another lawyer, begin a suit, directed against Benjamin. "If he must sue," she says over the top of the narrow steeple her hands finally form, "why doesn't he sue the Pee Wee League directors or the city of Centerville, not you?"

"Did you ask him that?" says Benjamin.

"Yes. All he said was, 'This is the way to handle it.' He doesn't, of course, know that we've—seen each other. Otherwise he'd have told me nothing." The steeple breaks and behind the hands he sees her smiling oddly. "If he knew about the other afternoon, he might, in fact, be suing *me.*"

"I thought you were divorced."

"We don't live together. But, for reasons that are his, not mine, we're waiting a year before going through with the legal thing. I don't know his reasons."

"And you're not worried?"

"He's got his faults but he's not setting me up, if that's what you mean."

"The action he wants to take about Max's leg? Not vengeful?"

"He doesn't know you, has nothing against you. That's part of his way of dealing with things. If you can sue and get money, sue. God!" Her fingers close in a containing gesture. "That's one of his main faults surely. A fixation,

127

I'd say. Everyone is to some extent enslaved by his profession. Don has been devoured by his. Once, when I was tired and he wanted to make love, he said, 'You know, if you don't feel like doing this, you have a right to refuse.' After a while he became so—predictable. It's part of what bored me, part of what began to drive us apart."

Benjamin enviously wishes he had a simple way of dealing with the tugs and pushes of *his* life: Marilyn, Bobo, the girls, his job, baseball, and, lately, Ellen.

"Anyway," she goes on, "he probably won't make a decision about a lawsuit for a couple of weeks or more. He says the doctor wants to check that bone again. Funny, Max is up and around every day, despite the cast. He says the foot doesn't hurt. He wants to get back to baseball. I don't think there's a serious problem with that foot. But I'm not a doctor."

If Benjamin, hanging nearly halfway between ages thirty and forty, has learned any useful rule for survival, it's something like this: *Face problems only when you're sure they exist.* He's kept himself from speculating about the meaning of Marilyn's problem, hasn't analyzed the details of her letter. This fascination of hers with crafts very possibly is the first of a series of passing interests. He doesn't know. What happens will happen. It's a little like walking across busy streets. You can stay home and never go walking for fear of being hit by a car. Or you can go walking and look both ways *when it's time to cross.* So dangers exist. Some are real. Some aren't real but may become real. Some will never become real. There may be a lawsuit. Until he knows there will be one, what should he do? He must deal only with the existing realities. Like his attraction to a woman whose hands now descend to the table like a pair of gliding doves.

She says something about Max returning home tomorrow.

That reminds him that Marilyn, too, will soon return. Little time.

"Listen," he says. "I've got to go home for a talk with Bobo. Not this second but in a few minutes. I feel like spending the evening with you. Like to take you out somewhere, but that's impossible." Ignoring a fear that someone who knows one of them will look through the window or walk in to buy pastries, he lowers his hands, covers hers with them, says, "Maybe we can be together later tonight."

Her eyes, which have been dancing about, now hold him with a penetrating look.

"Unless there's some problem," he says.

"No." She glances around, to make sure that the girl behind the counter is out of earshot, then says, "I've never let go as I did with you, but I somehow knew before you got to the house that I'd take you to bed if I got the chance. I knew I'd let go. I've been with other men besides Don, before I married him and even, a few, since we split up. It's been awkward, at best. You've helped release something in me. Feel like saying some-*one*, a person who's been imprisoned and now is free. She's not someone like the prim and proper public me. Someone else. It's confusing."

"But you like that it's happened? I mean, it's not back-firing now?"

"The opposite. I get panicky when I think it'll all stop. It affects everything. When Don told me he'd probably go ahead with a lawsuit against you, my first fear was that it would drive us apart. I thought about that before I wondered about the real extent of the injury to Max's foot. *That's* how important! I don't want that other force in me, that other person, to be bottled up again." She sends her hands across the table, toward his. "Come by. But let's not have any heavy talk. Please."

"No heavy talk."

She's now taken one of his hands in both of hers, is squeezing it.

If Marilyn were to walk to the window behind him, see her holding his hands and looking at him the way she is. . . . The scene he imagines contains possibilities he's so far ignored. Sooner or later he'll have to face them. Sooner or later. "Eleven o'clock," he says. "Or not too long after that."

One of her hands finds its way to his face, touches it lightly, then dips to a closing gesture, full of apology.

It's like this, Bobo says:

He's done a good job of coaching, though not everyone on the team agrees. Bobo's not going to say who does and who doesn't. He's giving his own opinion, that's all.

129

Despite some ups and downs, he thinks Benjamin should stay on as coach. "And," he adds, "I'd prob'ly think that even if you had a better assistant to take over than Mr. Bostick."

Relieved, Benjamin finally takes off the windbreaker he's been wearing since the game ended. The coffee has left a bitter after-taste. He goes to the kitchen and gets himself a can of Coca-Cola, calls back to ask Bobo in the living room if he wants one.

"Do we have to talk anymore?"

"For a while. If you don't mind." Bobo has opened up, and Benjamin doesn't want to lose this chance. "Want that Coke?"

"Okay. If we have to talk."

Back in the living room Benjamin says, "I've tried not to anticipate what you were going to say. But, now that you've spoken, I'd like to go on." He sees Bobo make a sour-lemon face; it's probably the word "anticipate." *I need a translator,* he thinks. There is no translator; he must translate. "Look. What you said about me continuing really is a relief. I'm grateful. But I have other questions. Naturally. I mean, up to now we've ruled out talking about the one thing we do together. Fine. But now there are a lot of things I want to know about, a lot of things I want to say. I remember, for example, something you said about me being too normal. No. Average. Do you still—"

"Forget it, Dad," says Bobo over the top of his Coke can. "That doesn't matter. So you're a 'Mr. *Av*-erage.' So what? I mean those coaches on the other teams are such ducks. As far as managing goes, you look like Sparky Anderson in comparison."

It seems to be a compliment.

"Not that you're not *av*-erage. You're still real *av*-erage. But they're a lot more *av*-erage than you are. Know what I mean?"

Benjamin does and doesn't. "All right. Now there's something else." He's remembering questions that have been with him since the early practices; he feels that, if they aren't answered now, they may never be answered. "I've not been able to figure out why you took the catching job when you thought that was the worst position."

"I started figuring it was going to be a lousy season, so

I decided I might as well play in a lousy position. And I didn't want a big hassle with you."

The answer makes sense, at least in terms of Bobo's logic. The word "hassle" reminds Benjamin of something else. "What were those 'strike' signs all about?"

Bobo taps his Coke can against the heel of one hand, checking to see how much is left. He shrugs.

"Don't clam up now."

Bobo gives a vomity look.

It's "clam up." It might have been worse. He might have said "zip your lip" or "hold your fire," any number of other outdated yet useful terms—at times useful, except around Bobo. "What did they mean?"

"Mean?" It's a volatile word. "They didn't *mean* anything."

"Of course they did, or they wouldn't have been painted."

"Mean!" Bobo is saying the word in disbelief to his can. "God! They *meant* 'strike.' That's what they *meant*."

"I know that." Benjamin is defensive now, feeling himself as stupid as Bobo's eyes are telling him he is. "I —don't care who painted them. I just want to know why they were painted. I mean why someone had some notion to go so far as strike. That's pretty drastic."

"Someone was pissed off. That's why." Bobo tests the can again. It seems to be empty. He starts to get up, doesn't. "Are we almost finished?"

"I hope not," says Benjamin honestly. "All I want to know is whether the 'pissed off' person is still pissed off and—whether I should do something, or can, to—to—"

"Who said 'person'?"

"You said 'someone.' "

"It's just a way of saying it. Could mean a lot of people."

"How many?"

"Shee-*it*." Translated, it means the question does not deserve, and is not going to get, a serious answer.

Benjamin doesn't persist but does what he often does to sustain conversation with Bobo: leaps to another subject without making a connection back to the previous one. "How come you and Nick were fighting during the V.F.W. game?"

Bobo fields it the quick way he snaps up low pitches: "Everyone was fighting."

"You two are on the same team."

"A fight's a fight. We had a fight."

"About?"

"It's all over with, so why go into it?"

"No, it isn't over. *I'm* still interested."

"Forget it."

Benjamin won't. "Was the fight about the team?"

"Dad, you don't have to worry about it." Bobo has bent the can in half and is giving his father a pleading look that says, *Don't push me on this.*

"About me?"

"This is getting to be like a trial or something." Bobo turns the can over in his hand and looks toward the entrance to the living room, as if trying to decide whether or not he should go to the kitchen for another Coke, or just go.

The reference to a trial bothers Benjamin. It *is* like a trial, or an interrogation. Given Bobo's reticence, what other choices has he? "Being a father is sometimes being an interrogator," he tells Bobo. "You just stay there on the witness stand until I'm finished." Bobo's hands make the Coke can crack. "Well?"

Bobo gives his father an under-the-eyebrow look, glances away, then back. "Dad," he says in a calm and measured tone, "there are a lot of things you got to let me work out by myself."

"Of course," Benjamin snaps. "But what's that got to do with answering questions?"

"The signs. They aren't around anymore. I know why they were there and why they aren't there anymore. You don't need to know. If you did, I'd tell you. Believe me." The last statement is a plea.

"All right. Let's let the signs go, at least for now. What about you and Nick? Don't tell me that isn't of importance to me. You're my son, a player on my team, and you were fighting with another player. It *is* my business."

But it's not, Bobo's supplicating eyes say.

Benjamin waits.

Bobo, finally, wearily, says, "I know, at least now I do, that *you* know what you're doing with the team. Why

132

don't you trust me to know what *I'm* doing? You got to let me solve some problems by myself."

"What problems?" Benjamin says anxiously.

Bobo is shaking his head; he'll say no more; if necessary, he'll take the consequences, whatever they are.

The boy's pain has communicated itself, however, and Benjamin won't, for the present, force him. He doesn't understand Bobo's need to handle those problems, those mysterious problems, by himself. In fact, it seems to Benjamin *just* the time Bobo ought to share troubles (*my troubles too,* Benjamin is sure). Yet he won't create a crisis. Responding to something less (or more?) than his best judgment of the moment, Benjamin decides to end the interrogation: "Maybe I shouldn't unload my questions all at once," he admits. "But we *haven't* been talking."

Bobo nods an agreement.

After a long pause, Benjamin says, "Got anything *you* want to bring up? How about Mom and the girls? You miss them? You never say."

Bobo makes the can crack. "I miss them," he says, looking at his thumbs where they press in on the can. "Why do I have to say it?"

"You don't, I guess. But I wonder if it's caused you any extra burden."

Bobo wags his head, finally smiles. For once a question seems to make sense. "It's not been too bad, except you aren't a very good cook and you stuck some of the girls' clothes in with mine after you did the laundry."

Benjamin laughs at the screw-up and apologizes.

He's sitting at one side of the room and Bobo at the other. It's the way they always seem to be when they're in the living room together. He'd like to be closer, on the sofa beside his son. He'd go over now if he could do it without making it seem too chummy and forced. Bobo would probably say, "What is this, *The Waltons* or something?"

Bobo finally goes to the kitchen, saying almost absently, "I do have a question for you."

Benjamin hears the fizzing sound as the tab top is opened, then, barely, the question:

"What's going on between you and Mrs. Jennings?"

"Huh?" It's completely surprised him. "What are you talking about?"

Bobo doesn't say anything until he's back in the living room, standing by the sofa, looking calm across and down at Benjamin, waiting for his answer. "If questions are fair for me, they're fair for you."

Benjamin knows he's just made a diversionary comment, empty.

"So—what's up?"

"Does something have to be up?"

Bobo gives him an annoyed frown and says, "I'm not as blind or stupid as you must think."

"We're—friends."

"The way she was flapping her eyes at you at the ball park today, it seems like more than 'friends.' "

What *does* Bobo know? "Friends," he repeats.

Bobo gives him a mysterious smile that, as it lingers, becomes more mysterious.

Friends. If incomplete, it's at least not untrue.

"Are you and Mom having troubles?"

"Not that I know of." That's not really untrue either. Yet, on the heels of Bobo's question, it begins to seem untrue. He, Benjamin, has, after all, gone to bed with Ellen Jennings and now spends more time thinking about her than about his absent wife. Is that not a trouble? And is it not a trouble that Marilyn had to go elsewhere, away from him, to deal with her "big question"? He hasn't thought about these things, but it is, indeed, possible that he and Marilyn are having troubles in the way Bobo seems to mean. "Why did you ask that question?"

"Little things."

"Like?"

"Like the letters you get that are different than the ones I get."

"She had some hang-ups, about herself. I don't think she wanted to bother you with them. That last letter was all about a crafts show she saw. It seemed to cheer her up a lot. She probably wouldn't mind you seeing it, though she'll be home in a few days and you can ask her what you want to." Benjamin has done his best to relieve Bobo of unnecessary concerns about Marilyn. That's important. Bobo's relaxed nods signal that he's succeeded, but for some reason Benjamin adds, "I don't think you

134

ought to haul around concerns about your mother and me. Aren't the ones about yourself tough enough to handle?"

"I don't, Dad, haul around concerns," Bobo says, offended. "You'd prob'ly be surprised how little those things bother me. I just want to know about them."

Benjamin, had he spent time anticipating this conversation, would have seen himself as guide. At the moment he feels himself the one guided. Bobo is not frightened, mixed up, out of control, any of that. Nor is Benjamin. But, for once, for the first time, there is a clear sense that he is not talking to a child, a dependent; Bobo is more an equal. Almost. Were the sense of equality really here he might open up more about Ellen. It's possible that someday he will actually be able to talk about such things.

Bobo has finished his second can of Coke.

Benjamin thanks him for the honest talk, says he's only disappointed that they didn't spend more time talking about the team.

"There are still troubles, if that's what you want me to say," Bobo says.

"I don't want you to say anything, anything in particular. If I can do something about the troubles, maybe I should know about them."

"Well, they're pretty big."

"Do they have to do with winning or losing?"

"Not exactly. I just sort of know things are bothering some of them."

"What things?"

"I'm not all that sure anymore. The ones I'm thinking about don't talk to me much these days."

"For vagueness, that is a blue-ribbon answer."

"So?" Bobo shrugs. "It's the best I can do."

That, more or less, is where the conversation ends.

Bobo turns on one of his favorite television programs, and Benjamin uses the upstairs phone to call Ellen, having decided toward the end of the conversation with Bobo that tonight he can't sufficiently relax to enjoy being with her. In fact, he's exhausted. He apologizes, says he's been tied up unexpectedly. She's very disappointed and seems soothed only when he promises to call tomorrow.

FIVE

After an easy victory (8–0) over Mid-States National Bank, a team made up mainly of first-year players, Gray's is scheduled to face a tough opponent, Buck's Travel Agency, so far the only unbeaten team in the league besides Watson and Wills. If Gray's beats Buck's, the two will be tied for second place.

The Mid-States game wasn't even a good practice session. Tony started as pitcher, and by the fifth inning had allowed only three Mid-States players to reach base, two on errors and one on a pop-fly single. Wanting to enliven the game, Benjamin put in his substitutes early and let them play most of the game. He also replaced Tony in each of the last two innings with players who didn't normally pitch, Lou Pera in the sixth and Harold Foxx in the seventh. Both put runners on base with walks; Harold even hit a batter with a bad pitch; there was another Gray's error; still, Mid-States couldn't score.

Worried about the Buck's game, Benjamin decides to call a practice.

It's Bobo's job to initiate practices. He phones Nick, who phones Tag, who phones Meryl, who phones Speck, and so on, until all players have been called. The last person on the call list is to phone Bobo or Benjamin, letting him know that everyone has been informed.

The new last person is Digby Wells. Benjamin answers, and the boy says, "Thanks for letting me in the game."

"You'll get into every game," Benjamin tells him.

137

"I'm not very good, but Pop is a baseball fan and wants me to play. I didn't want to get on your team 'cause I heard they fight a lot and pick on people, but they were okay to me, even though none of them talked to me except the fat one."

"Meryl?"

"Yep. He even cried."

"Cried?"

"Yep. We were in the dugout and he was telling me about the pitchers and he said he used to be a pitcher. He went over and sat by himself and I saw him crying."

"He still is a pitcher. But not all the time."

"He's the kind of guy who thinks everything depends on him, Mr. Dunne. I know other kids like that. They bite their fingernails a lot. Like him."

He's right about Meryl's fingernails. Benjamin looks at his own: bitten, but not much. Has Digby noticed Benjamin's fingernails?

"Maybe I ought to use Meryl more often," Benjamin finds himself saying. "The thing is, I've got to develop a pitching staff, not just a pitcher."

"You don't have to tell me that, Mr. Dunne. I didn't say you should use him more. I'm the newest one on the team, except that girl, Pat. I don't know who you should use. I'm just telling you he talked to me and letting you know what he did. I hope I'm not squealing or anything."

"No," says Benjamin, realizing that, in moments, he's shared more with him than with all the other players combined. "Your impressions—matter to me. So just say what you want." Benjamin is grateful that Bobo is out bike riding.

"I don't have anything else to say. Not really. I wish some of those guys liked you better. But at least they do what you say. I wish that Meryl kid wouldn't be so worried about everything. I wish those other ones would talk to me more. It's a funny team. They don't talk to each other much. Pop taught me to speak up. We hardly ever lived where there were a lot of black people. He said I should talk when I want. I have this book about Jackie Robinson. They used to try to knock him out when he stole second and he couldn't hit back. I mean with his fists. He hit the baseball real good, and he was a really terrific base runner. His lifetime batting average is three eleven. I don't mean I'm like Jackie Robinson, even though he's my favorite old-time ballplayer. I'm just telling you what I'm telling you. I'll tell those guys the same thing if they start talking to me. Meryl is nice. I don't know, maybe the others are too."

Benjamin could listen to Digby all evening. It isn't the gossip. He knows most of what Digby is telling him. The only real news is about Meryl. He just likes the way the boy talks. "Listen, I put you in at second base. But you don't have to feel stuck there."

"I don't care where I play. I just want to play. Otherwise Pop'll give me a lecture about Jackie Robinson or Martin Luther King. Just so I get in. It'll keep the pressure off me."

Benjamin, sure he has wrung too much out of this chatty perceptive little player, thanks him for the conversation ("I really enjoy talking to you") and says he'll see him at practice the next day.

"Thank you too, Mr. Dunne," Digby says.

When they hang up, Benjamin thinks about Meryl, is sorry he's been taking him for granted lately, sorry he hasn't had more conversations with him. All of his conversations with Meryl have been pleasant.

When Bobo returns Benjamin says, "I hear Meryl's been in the dumps lately. You know anything about that?"

In the dumps? *Bluck!* says Bobo's face.

"Well?"

"Don't know. He looks all right to me."

"Ever talk to him? I mean other than during a game?"

"Hardly ever."

It's no surprise. *All strangers to each other.* He thinks about that through much of the rest of the evening, though soon he has changed it to a question: *Are we all strangers to each other?* He verifies his answer—*Yes*—with thoughts about himself and those closest to him: Bobo, Marilyn, the girls, the team, Dan. He recalls friends with whom he's lost contact, friends with whom he hasn't, his deceased parents, his own two daughters, finally himself, knowing even as he fingers through his memories that there is now one, only one, with whom intimate sharing is possible. The recognition frightens him, but it also gives him reason to find a way to see her at least once more before Marilyn returns.

The postcard has on the front a colored photograph of the Tyrone Guthrie Theater and on the back the following message, in Marilyn's long, symmetrical handwriting:

Benj. & Bobo—
We'll be home Sun. via Trailways bus to Toledo (5:47). Have enjoyed selves but can't wait to see you both. Girls and I saw a play here. I have "fantabulous" ideas about a new project, hobby, etc. Will say more later.

Love,
Marilyn

Within minutes he calls Ellen: "I wish I'd put aside my distractions the other night and gone to see you." He tells her about the card from Marilyn. "I'd like to see you tonight, if possible."

She explains that Max is now home but that he wants to see a new movie with a friend. "They'll be gone for a couple of hours. I don't care if you're here after he gets back, though I have a feeling that would make you uncomfortable."

"Yes. It would. What time does he leave?"

"Seven fifteen."

"I'll be there at seven thirty, if that's okay. A couple of hours."

"I can't be choosy."

His mouth tightens as he thinks of the time they won't have after Marilyn returns. "A *good* two hours," he says.

"See you at seven thirty."

He hangs up, knowing he'll have to lie to Bobo. It's *all* so secretive. Will there be a string of lies for Marilyn, later? He feels like a spy.

The feeling holds as he finds himself parking in front of a house a few doors from Ellen. Walking toward her house he wonders if eyes follow him from behind drawn curtains. He's sure it'll take him the whole two hours just to relax.

He's wrong. Though they speak few words and he has only a small drink of brandy, the darkened atmosphere of the house, her easy embrace, a general sense of familiarity help disarm him. By seven forty-five they are in Ellen's bed, where he's silently promising not to ask her or himself how it could have happened so fast.

In moments they're both completely naked.

He lies very still as she searches with her fingers.

He begins to work with both hands and mouth, finding the places clothed in daylight, sure that if those places were exposed and other places, say the face, were hidden, it would be the face he'd now be kissing, feeling, finding.

Abruptly he thinks of Marilyn, is on the verge of another silent speech to her, forces himself not to begin. Yet the thought of her clings. *How devastating it would be for her to see—this!* Did she foresee something like this when she talked about his attractiveness? Without a clue, at a great distance, will she yet have some idea? If not, will it show in his face, in his eyes, after she returns?

He pulls back, tense, admitting to Ellen that he can't relax. "My mind won't stop working," he says.

"What are you thinking about?"

"Marilyn. How I would explain it to her."

Her fingers fall away. "You're not thinking of *telling* her, are you?"

"No. It's—an imaginary thing. I can imagine myself saying things I know I'd never say. I can't explain it."

"Do you want to stop?"

"No." It's like a ball game that must be seen through to the end, no matter what the distractions.

Soon he's again entered the search, her very fragrances invading him. He presses his strength into her, locking and holding her, moving until their separate rhythms become one, then rise to a simultaneous and explosive ending. As he pulls away he says something that will later startle, then chill him: "I love you, Ellen."

"I love you too, Benjamin," she replies so quickly, so easily, so certainly, that he's sure that, for days, she felt it and could have spoken it.

Only after they're dressed does he make his first silent utterance to Marilyn. He's pictured her meet ~ Ellen in the supermarket: someone else's wife, known only through the League of Women Voters or last year's baseball games.

How, therefore, is it possible for you to know how she

ravages me? God, it's not even possible for me to know. What interest does she have in most of my life? The children. The bookstore. What interest do I have in hers? Do those things, in situations like this, finally matter? I remember you mentioning men, saying, "So-and-so is quite attractive, don't you think?" Well, I rarely did think so, though I'd usually shrug and say something uninformative like, "A woman's tastes and a man's are different." I don't know what you think of her. But I know I can't really tell you about her. I don't have the right to presume you'd understand. I myself would be swept up in a tornado of confusion if you said to me, about any man, even a man I liked, "Benjamin, I'm in love with him." It would loosen the foundations. Why, then, do I still think of telling you? Why, then, in a way, am I?

"Wake up, Benjamin."

"I'm not asleep."

"It's nine fifteen."

Dressed, they've been curled up together on her sofa, all the lights out but the one in the kitchen.

"I think too much," he says.

"Maybe I wouldn't love you if you didn't."

"Do you like baseball?" he says, grasping for something to put between himself and his thoughts about Marilyn.

"Baseball? Is that a test question?"

"No."

"Who do you think taught Max baseball in the first place?"

"Not Don?"

"Me. And do you want to know what Joe Morgan is hitting as of this week?"

"No." He laughs. "Are you just trying to impress me?"

"No. Are *you* trying to impress *me?*"

It *is* a strange question. From the moment he awakened to her, he's felt no need to hide, disguise, conceal, *or* impress. She's the farthest thing from a customer. Even in bed he hasn't tried to impress her. There hasn't seemed to be a need, as if, in some odd way, they've known each other for years. And in some ways not so odd, like baseball, which she's talking about now:

"It's full of order and disorder. Reminds me of painting. Fascinates me like painting, only from a distance. Incredible things can happen within those nine innings—or seven in Pee Wee—and between those foul lines. Marvelous and puzzling things. No game the same and all that. And, like a painting, no game ever seems to come out the way you think it will. That 'not-over-'til-the-last-out' saying has probably been overdone, but there's still a lot to it, isn't there?"

"What *is* Joe Morgan's batting average?"

"As of Monday, when the statistics appear in the paper, it was three thirteen, but he's raised it by at least five points since then."

"I *am* impressed."

She mentions Max, says, "He likes you, Benjamin," then gives an apologetic shrug. "I wasn't going to mention it, for fear you'd think I was something like the baseball equivalent of one of those overbearing stage mothers, trying to make points for her kid. But, well, he talks about you a lot. He knows the team has problems, but he thinks you're a good coach. His feeling comes out in funny ways. He knows we've seen each other, nothing more, and tonight he asked if you and Bobo could come over and have dinner with us some evening."

The compliment in her report falls before Benjamin's fear. He couldn't possibly hide his feelings for Ellen in front of Bobo and Max. Nor could he, later, effectively conceal from, or explain to, Marilyn his reasons for dinner. (He imagines himself saying to Bobo, "Now your mother mustn't learn anything about this.") He backs toward the door, saying, "I like Max too, but that's—impossible. You realize it's—impossible, don't you?"

"Yes," she says, looking disappointed. "I just wanted to let you know that he—" She shakes her head, shakes away the rest of her thought, looks up at Benjamin and says, "Listen. The boy hasn't had anything resembling a father. Try to understand that. I suppose you seem to be something like a father in his eyes. I'll bet that's true of at least some of the other players too." She pauses, her look full of curiosity. "You can accept that, can't you?"

He hadn't thought about it. Except for Bobo, he doesn't want to be a father to any of them—especially, under the circumstances, Max. She speaks about the "father" possibility as though he should be pleased. He's not; he's alarmed by it. Now it's late to talk about his feelings, so he hides them behind a quick nod.

A few minutes later, in his car, moving toward the corner of her street, he approaches a small station wagon. As it gets closer he sees Max at the near side of the back seat, looking toward him. He turns his head the other way, almost completely around, doesn't turn it forward until his car and the other have cleanly passed each other.

Hoping to find Meryl and have a morale-boosting talk with him, Benjamin arrives twenty minutes early for practice. No players are in sight, however, and he's taken by a worry that has recurred several times since he found the "strike" signs after the V.F.W. game:

They've all quit.

He removes the equipment from the wagon, takes it to the dugout, then, fighting off his worry, heads for the empty stands near third base, determined to devise an effective strategy for the game with Buck's.

By word of mouth he's learned that the next opponent has two first-rate pitchers. The manager alternates them throughout each game. One throws a jumping fastball and the other, unlike most pitchers his age, has developed a sharp curveball, which, amazingly, he can control. Each pitcher goes for one or two innings, then exchanges positions with the other. Benjamin is stimulated by the inventiveness of the Buck's manager. He sees the use of alternate pitchers as a kind of extension, if not perfection, of a method he's used: dividing a game between two pitchers. He's decided to turn Buck's strategy on itself. That is, he'll use alternating pitchers. He won't use two; he'll use three: Meryl, Tony, and Tag, all of whom have been effective, at least for short periods.

He's been hearing rustling sounds and laughter. No one seems to be in the ball park or the surrounding area. He checks the street beyond the parking entrance. No one. The sounds persist. Eventually he realizes that the sounds are coming from beyond the center field fence.

Beyond the right field fence there's a semicircle of tall grass. That's where the other players stood and watched as Max was caught in the fence. Beyond the grass are woods which curve inward toward the center field fence, bordering the fence until they're broken by the street, which lies a few feet beyond the left field fence and more or less parallels it. Someone is in the wooded area.

144

Benjamin goes out, stopping a few yards from the fence, listening to the voices beyond, boys' voices. But there is another, male, older, speaking low. Feeling like a spy, he moves to the fence, staying down so as not to be seen over the top:

"Sho I shez we gotta bust outa dish game cuz I got me a hot numbuh waitin' out in da limuhzheen." It's Humphrey Bogart, as good an imitation as Benjamin has heard in a long time. Only after it bends into the voice of Peter Lorre—"Myeee good mannnn, I ammm doinggg my vaireee best"—does Benjamin identify the mimic, who, before he completes his imagined conversation, adds the voice of Sidney Greenstreet: "Nn-gentlemen, we achieve nothing with all this nn-distasteful chatter."

It's Tony. As he goes on, Benjamin decides he's doing a wildly imaginative parody of a conversation among Benjamin (Lorre), Karl (Greenstreet), and Tony himself (Bogart). When he finishes he says, "That's from this terrific old movie I saw on TV about these guys who steal a statue of a bird."

There has been much laughter.

The next voice is unmistakably that of Daryl, the umpire: "I mean he dressed sloppy an' I thought, 'This dude's okay.' I had a hamburger with him one night. Don't let his loose clothes fool you, man. He's one of 'em. Don't be fooled."

"Who's fooled?" It's Tony in his own voice. "I give him that Mexican shit because it keeps me loose and that keeps him off my back." Pause. "Hue know what hi mean?"

The others laugh.

"I don't mind him." Benjamin recognizes Tag. "He kinda stays the same, except when he lost his temper with Nick. I mean, I know he's bossy and all that, but at least you know what you got to face every game."

"Crap. We're like puppets," says Tony. "He puts us where he wants. He doesn't ask. He says he's gonna do things, like get us uniforms, then he doesn't. We almost had a strike over him."

"A strike?" says Daryl. "That's wild, man!"

"Why not? The big leaguers strike. Know why it didn't work?"

"Why?"

"His kid talked us out of it. Bobo and him hardly ever talk, even though he's Bobo's old man. Bobo wasn't real strong against the strike 'cause he didn't want his father to coach in the first place. But he kind of screwed things up by sayin' we should first tell him what was botherin' us, before we had a strike. That swung a few players against the strike and made Nick real mad. He kept sayin' we should have one, so we voted and Nick won. We were gonna have it right in the middle of the W. and W. game, figurin' we'd be gettin' our asses whacked and that would be a good time. But the game got close and we almost won. That killed the idea of the strike, at least for a while. Nick and Bobo hate each other now. That's why they were fightin' each other at that other game. Bobo isn't big on his old man, but he doesn't want a strike. I'm not sure what Nick thinks about it now."

"That would've been somethin'," says Daryl. "A strike in the Pee Wee League!"

"We might do somethin' yet," says Tony. "Don't know what. Anyway he still pisses some of us off."

Benjamin has been getting the smell of something burning, a fragrant smell, one he first encountered during his days in the army. He wants to crawl closer to the fence and peek between a couple of boards but is afraid the other players, who'll soon be arriving for practice, might see him and report his snooping to those behind the fence.

"Know what the bus drivers did in Cleveland?" says Tag.

"What?" says Tony.

"They called in and said they had the flu. The buses didn't run."

"I'll tell Nick about that," says Tony. "That'd be a ball. 'Hey, Meester Donn, hi'm cougheeng op all sort ob jellow stoff.' "

"I wouldn't want to miss a game," says Tag.

"Your team ain't goin' anywhere," Daryl observes. "What do you care?"

"Up yours," says Tony. "We might."

"Fat chance," says Daryl, laughing.

"I like playin', that's all." It's Tag.

"Meantime we might try somethin'," says Tony. "Maybe not a strike."

146

"Want me to light another?" It's Daryl.

"No," says Tony. "We got to be able to see the damn ball. Anyway he'll be here pretty soon. We got to get movin'."

Benjamin scoots away from the fence on all fours, then stands and begins walking toward the dugout. No one else has yet arrived. He'll lay out the equipment. When Tony and Tag come around, no doubt through the parking area, he won't show a sign of having heard them.

Daryl was suspended after the near riot; the commissioners are thinking of permanently dropping him and the umpire who worked with him. Benjamin hopes they do. If they don't, he might just go to the next commissioner's meeting. "A dope dealer," he'd tell them and go on from that.

He's beside the low fence, watching batting practice.

Which of them were willing to join in a strike?

Speck, who's now at the plate?

He'd guess not. But how can he know?

There's Bobo catching.

Prior to the conversation behind the fence, he might have guessed yes.

He remembers the huddle of players after an early practice, Bobo among the others; it wouldn't surprise him to learn someday that Bobo, then and there, had planted the idea of a strike. Yet it did not surprise him to learn just minutes ago that Bobo, only a short time after the huddle, helped prevent a strike. The same Bobo? Yes. No. Benjamin doesn't know. An elusive Bobo. A moody Bobo. An uncertain Bobo. Benjamin wants to walk up, grab him by the front of his shirt, and say, "Who the hell are you, son? Spill it once and for all!" He won't, of course. He guesses there isn't a once-and-for-all. Maybe Bobo is like the season, full of whim and impulse, yet ever gathering momentum toward a singular destination, a completion of some sort. It's only a hunch, but he feels sure that if he ever puts together the puzzle called Bobo, it won't be by eavesdropping at a fence or conversing in the living room but watching and listening right here on the ball field.

Bobo is only the beginning.

What about the puzzle called Nick?

The puzzle called Tony?

The puzzle called Tag?

All the other puzzles?

He wants to forget the conversation behind the fence, concentrate on practice; he can't.

What, above all, about the puzzle called Benjamin?

Maybe it contains clues toward the solution of all the other puzzles.

Boys, he imagines himself saying, let's stop and confess ourselves to each other, finally and truly. Come over to the low fence here. . . . Good. My hope is that, in getting to know each other, really to know each other, we can eliminate the problems that now exist among us. Let me tell you something very personal. Recently I found myself attracted to a woman whom you may or may not know. She's the mother of a boy nearly all of you do know, Max Jennings. Now, while I am married to a woman I love, the mother of Bobo there, I find that, with increasing frequency, my time and thoughts are given over to this other woman. You may be asking yourselves, "What has this got to do with us?" All right. I'll tell you, or try to. To do so I'll have to share with you some of the ways this new—how shall I say it?—friendship in my life has affected me. Only then can you begin to see how it may have affected my attitude toward you. And yes, even yours toward me.

But his friendship with Ellen *hasn't* kept him from being closer to the members of his team.

Something or someone has.

Bobo?

His earlier caution with Bobo put a distance between himself and his son, not himself and the others.

How little he knows about all of them.

Tony, for example.

He can't stop worrying about that phony accent.

Why?

Pat Somerville comes to bat. The barrel of the bat rests on her shoulder. With Meryl's first pitch she raises the barrel from her shoulder. By the time she starts to swing, Bobo has the ball securely in his mitt.

"Hold it," says Benjamin, coming from behind the low fence.

She turns with a grateful look. Or is it grateful? Could

148

as well be embarrassed, frightened, resentful? Will she, later, as the result of the correction he's about to make, join his critics? Or not as a result. Will she join them out of some whim? She doesn't like his eyebrows. Whatever.

Who *are* those critics? Enemies really.

He pictures himself addressing them again:

That confession stuff I mentioned earlier is all off. It's impossible, the whole idea. My—friendship for Mrs. Jennings has nothing to do with you. Nothing has, except what we do with, to, for, each other. Nor can I become wise about you and your lives. We are individuals, thrown together in this sport called baseball. Due to circumstances over which we had no control, we find ourselves together. That is, as a team. Nothing that doesn't relate to that team playing really matters. Go over there behind the fence and smoke pot and talk about whatever you want. What do I care? Just come to practices, be at the games on time and, at all times, play your best. I have no right to ask anything more. I mustn't give a damn what you think of me. Can't afford to. Must, first and foremost, be myself: Benjamin Dunne, man, husband, lover, father, coach, the whole complication, which no one, not even I, can completely understand.

He changes Pat Somerville's bat, from the heavier wood to the lighter aluminum. He shows her how to "choke up." He lifts the bat from her shoulder and tells her to keep it in a cocked position above the shoulder. He says, "Try to watch the ball hit your bat."

She begins to meet the ball solidly, though none of her hit balls go past the infield.

Benjamin won't confuse her today by adding tips about footwork and twisting the body which will give her more power. That can wait. She has a gentle touch with the bat, is a fast runner, and will make a good bunter. Before long, he's sure, she'll be getting base hits.

Nick comes to the batting circle.

Benjamin, feeling sinister, greets him cheerfully. "How many runs you going to bat in against Buck's?"

"Don't know," he answers flatly.

"Any suggestions as to how we should handle their hotshot pitchers?"

Tag has moved in to pitch and is throwing his warm-ups, and Nick is beside the batter's box, swinging a couple of bats. His eyes are on Tag's pitches, not on Benjamin. "You're the coach," he says.

"That's why I'm asking about those pitchers. A good coach gets news about the opposition wherever he can." Nick watches the other teams play, knows about their pitchers and hitters. "Any special weakness you noticed in either of them?"

"Yeah."

"What?"

"The coaches switch them every inning, so the first few pitches each one throws are use'ly balls."

"That's helpful."

Nick shrugs and steps into the batter's box.

Very helpful. Later he will tell the other players to lay off the first two or three pitches each inning; maybe Gray's can get a man or two on base. He'll be sure to give Nick credit for the suggestion.

Nick's last hit goes fairly deep to left field. When he comes back to the low fence to pick up his glove, Benjamin tells him it was a good blow.

"If the left fielder was in the right place, he would have caught it."

It's true, but the ball was hit solidly. Why couldn't Nick take the compliment gracefully?

"Hey, Tony," he says, as the second baseman comes in to swing a couple of bats, "how's that ruptured arm of yours?"

"Ees marble-oos today, Meester Donn!"

This, he hears himself saying, *is the very last thing I have to tell you: I care. Never mind that other "what do I care?" remark. Rather, take it for what it really means. I do care, about Meryl and Digby, whom I've gotten to know a little, and of course my own son, Bobo, but also about those of you whom I haven't gotten to know, even Nick. I'll try to go out more to you, be a chum—sorry, Bobo. Pal. Friend—though that's not my natural way. And—*

Lou Pera has just hit one over the fence. It's the first ball he's gotten over, in practice or in a game. Mitts are off, and the other players are clapping. Lou, though it's only batting practice, decides to circle the bases, as if it were the real thing. The clapping continues. Benjamin

150

continues the ritual by going to home plate and shaking Lou's hand when he crosses. There is more applause for that.

In the dugout after practice Benjamin tells them he's planning to beat Buck's at its own game: Tag pitching for one inning, then Meryl for one, then Tony, then back through the cycle once more.

They're complacent.

"Can anyone think of a better way?"

Shrugs.

"Nick?"

"It might work," the boy says without enthusiasm.

Benjamin gives them a few tips, about hitting and fielding, and reminds them of how important base running will be against a team like Buck's, where the score is likely to be low. "Any questions?"

There are none.

He says he'll play the substitutes early so the regular players can be in at the end, when there are likely to be crucial plays. He'll put the faster players at the top of the lineup because of the base stealing. He's open to other suggestions.

He doesn't get any.

"Any final questions? About anything?"

Fred says, "What about our uniforms? Weren't we s'posed tuh have 'em by now?"

"Yep," says Benjamin, "but Gray hasn't come through, and I don't feel like begging him. Anyway, we're playing well without uniforms. Hate to be the only team without them, but that's the way it is."

Pat Somerville, who hasn't said much since she joined the team, raises her hand in a slow jerky movement, as though she might lower it at any moment.

Benjamin quickly nods at her to speak.

"Someone said you're going to play Digby and Paul and me only a little bit in the next game." She stops, looks around uneasily, apparently finding what she expected to: glares, frowns, a hand (Tag's) against a forehead. "My brothers said I would hardly ever get in a game, and—they're prob'ly right."

"You can't hit farther than I can spit," says Nick from the back of the dugout.

Some of the others laugh.

An instinct in Benjamin tells him to shut Nick and the others up, then give Pat an encouraging answer. Like many girls in Pee Wee League, she's the only one of her sex on her team. Coaches have tended to ignore the ritual practiced by the male players before games: catcalls to and about the opposing team's girl, usually when the girl takes the field or goes to the batter's box. Benjamin is sure Pat will take such blows. He'll be watchful, won't ignore the ritual. He can't rely on the Gray's players to talk back when their opponents make remarks; they've done little to ease the way for her during practices, giving her only a kind of teeth-gritting tolerance. He'll try not to overprotect her. At the same time he's moved by the courage she's shown in simply being on the team and coming to practices.

A new thought stirs. Nick, despite his rude tone, spoke a truth: Pat is a weak hitter, the team's weakest. At the beginning of the season Benjamin thought he'd play everyone an equal amount of time; he won't do that, is certain about it; and the certainty holds even as he answers her: "You did beautifully today, and I have no doubt you'll be banging singles and doubles soon, but we're going to play the Buck's game, like all of them, to win it. So I won't play you much, unless we get pretty far ahead." He kills off the temptation to add a little speech about her courage, figuring that, in this bunch, it might hurt her more than help.

Tears are rising in her eyes.

Beside her, Lou Pera, with a devilish look, leans over and mumbles something to her. She draws her arm back and jabs him sharply in the ribs with her elbow. "I'll be better than you," she replies to whatever Lou said.

"You'll play," Benjamin says to her. "More each game. I'm sure of it."

She nods, managing to hold back the tears, at least until the meeting ends.

As they're on their way out of the dugout Benjamin deliberately claps Tony's left shoulder and tells him he hopes his arm will feel good for the game against Buck's.

"Eet'll be wheezbong!" Tony says.

Is the word a takeoff on one of Benjamin's clichés? If so, how clever!

152

"A chameleon," Benjamin says softly as Tony leaves the dugout.

He hasn't noticed Bobo, behind him, stuffing the catching gear into the equipment bag. Benjamin turns to meet an approving smile, like one he got from a college instructor who handed him back a quiz with a score that was surprisingly high.

He meets them at the Trailways bus station in Toledo. He kisses and embraces each of them. Bobo isn't with him. It's a hot muggy day, and the girls want to get back to Centerville before the public swimming pool closes. "Let's go *now*," says Annie, tugging at her mother's slacks as Marilyn gives Benjamin a second lingering kiss. He takes the big suitcase and the girls their small ones, and they go to the station wagon.

She's changed, he thinks of Marilyn. There's a breezy look about her, a new vitality in her voice. In the station wagon she says she has many things to tell him, sounding as though she could talk into the night.

Bobo was going to drive with him to Toledo but has volunteered to stay home and take a phone call expected from Gray. The sponsor said he'd call this afternoon with information about the uniforms. Explaining Bobo's absence, Benjamin talks a little about Gray and the uniforms. "Maybe we're finally going to get them," he says. They're crossing the bridge over the Maumee River, and Marilyn, looking out at a pleasure boat moving toward the bridge, doesn't seem to be listening. Finally she turns and speaks:

"Do you want to hear about my fantastic new project?"

Her adjective has loaded the question. There *is* only one right answer: "Of course."

"I went back to that crafts show the next day without the girls. I mean, I don't know if I said so in the letter, but that first visit set something off in me. I wasn't sure what. That's why I went back again. I looked at everything. I thought, 'What sort of creativity—if that's the word—could occupy you (me, I mean) to the point where you could spend hours at a time doing it?' I wanted to be involved in something, as those people were, was desperate to find an outlet of my own."

Her narrative, like her recent letter, is smothered with

153

enthusiasm, like a steak with too many onions. He's going to have to fight through her enthusiasm to appreciate the rest.

They pass Exit signs for several towns between Toledo and Centerville, and finally he knows this:

She *has* found something, a project of her own. While the displays at the crafts show inspired her, her project is unlike any others she saw or has heard about. "The lucky inspiration of an amateur," she calls it. She's been reading crafts magazines and has looked into some library books on the subject. She thinks she's come up with something totally original. She doesn't yet know where to purchase the materials she needs or just how much equipment she'll need, but she'll take time to look into that. Already she's put some money aside: Her father offered to buy her and the girls airline tickets and she said no, they'd take the bus, use the saved money (nearly $100) to buy the first batch of materials. "I'm very serious about it, Benjamin. The idea has simply—captured me. Don't ask me why, because I don't know. I feel—I feel reckless."

The last is a word he's thought of when worrying over his assignations with Ellen. Perhaps for that reason, he appreciates it.

"Well, what do you think?" she says at last in a tone more insistent than curious.

"Can you tell me what the project is, specifically?"

"No, no," she says firmly. "I've promised myself not to talk about it until I'm sure it's possible." She explains that she hasn't spelled it out for her parents either. "I'll—finish something, then show it to you."

"Where will you work?"

"There's a little space in the basement, the storeroom. I'll make it into a workshop. Do you mind?"

"No. But it's going to be hard not to ask you questions."

"You'll know soon enough," she assures him.

He mentions that sales at the bookstore have been lower than expected. "I wish I had extra money to help with your project. We could take a loan."

"Maybe it's just as well we don't. I know the project is a gamble. I'm somehow going to have to get this thing going on my own." She's been looking thoughtfully out the side window but turns to him now and says, "Among other things, I'm aware that I can't lean on you as much as I used to. It's not just money. I've got to learn how to do my own things my own way."

The girls have been chatting to each other, but now Annie is leaning on the back of the front seat, asking about Bobo, wondering if any of their friends in the neighborhood are on vacation. Suzie is sitting back, gazing out at the farms they pass. Benjamin answers each of Annie's questions. Then there are more. Benjamin answers those too. He's waiting for Suzie to say something. She doesn't. Looking at her through the rearview mirror, Benjamin reads indifference. Finally Marilyn turns and says to Annie, "Be patient. We'll be home in five minutes or so, and you can find out all these things for yourself." Annie sits back and Marilyn turns and says, "Benjamin, you won't mind if I become a little freaky, will you?"

"Freaky?" He's never heard her use the word. Bobo and his friends use it, but Benjamin has never been sure quite what it meant.

"Maybe that's not the word. Maybe I don't even know how to say it." She laughs, flings her hands out. "Oh, what's the difference? I just feel I'm not going to let myself be dragged down by—by myself anymore."

Benjamin tilts the mirror down, sees Suzie staring at her mother. *What does* that *look mean?*

"So," says Marilyn as he turns into the exit lane for Centerville, "what's been happening with you?"

Something must be told. So much can't.

"Well?"

What *can* be told?

"Benjamin?"

"I've become . . . a winning coach."

"With *that* team?"

"Why not?" he says.

"Well, tell me about it."

He begins to, hoping her eyes will stay on or close to him, at least until he's finished.

Bobo reports Gray's message: There's been a dispute with the manufacturer, resulting in a delay in delivery of the uniforms.

155

"I don't believe it," Benjamin snaps, as if it might be Bobo he doesn't believe.

"That's what he *said*," Bobo insists.

Benjamin only partly hears his son's response.

For the next half hour he paces the house grumbling. He has fantasies about Gray, his demise: an explosion at the cleaning establishment, an arrest for the attempted rape of Tim Adams, wild obscenities scrawled on the cleaner's window. Only after he notices the odd looks he's getting from Annie and Suzie as they watch him plunge from room to room does he sit down and calm himself.

The news is so depressing, however, that he wants at least to call Gray, threaten to report the funny business about the uniforms to the newspaper unless Gray writes out a promise Benjamin can read to the team, the commissioner, everyone. Given his feelings, it's a temperate response. But he finally rejects even that, knowing *any* deal with Gray isn't going to be worth the dust a sliding base runner kicks up.

He thinks of the players, their wish for uniforms. Maybe, using some sort of argument, one he doesn't yet have, he can talk them out of the wish.

Annie is staying overnight with one of her and Suzie's friends. Suzie was invited but didn't go. That's not unusual; what strikes Benjamin as unusual is the way she's been curled up so quietly at the end of the sofa all evening. And he thinks it more unusual when Bobo comes into the living room and thoughtlessly flips the channel selector from the movie she's apparently been watching for nearly an hour to a detective mystery he wants to see. She doesn't budge, blink, or complain, though the movie just now seemed to be coming to a climax.

"Suzie?"

She turns listlessly. "Huh?"

"What's on your mind?"

"Nothing." A standard answer in this house. It's her vacant look that worries him.

He suggests they take a walk to the newly opened Friendly Ice Cream Parlor at the end of Main Street a few blocks away. "Let's see if their stuff is better than Baskin-Robbins," he adds lightly.

She thinks about the suggestion, then says, "Maybe you can just bring me something."

"I really want to take a walk with you. The ice cream, I admit, is just an excuse."

Though the television set blares with the sound of gunshots and shouting, Bobo says, "Will you two shut up? I can't hear anything."

Given the loudness of *all* the television Bobo watches, the loudness of the music he listens to, the loudness of him, his friends, players on the team, etc., Benjamin has recently concluded that his son's generation will all be deaf by the time they reach age thirty. "Come on," he says impatiently to Suzie. "We're going to get some ice cream."

Soon he's leading her through the streets of the neighborhood. She's dragging a bit, irritating him because she won't respond to his little efforts to get her to talk. ("Let's take a few stones and bet on who can hit that telephone pole the most times." She refuses.) He picks up speed, but she stays back.

They take a rear booth and end up ordering ice cream sodas. Everytime the door opens at the front she turns, nervously he thinks, as if she's expecting someone she doesn't want to see. She sips at her soda, spooning up very little ice cream. He asks her a few questions: about Minnesota, what she's missed most, what she'd like to do for the remainder of the summer. He gets one- or two-word answers or no answers at all.

Is there a change at all, or am I only imagining it?

She finishes less than half the soda. As they're about to leave, she raises her eyes apprehensively.

"What?" he says, but she turns away without answering.

He asks if she thinks he should get a half-gallon of ice cream to take home.

She gives a quick shake of the head. It's not an answer but a plea not to trouble her with such requests.

He pays, doesn't get the ice cream.

They're a block from the ice cream parlor when she rushes forward, saying frantically, "Dad! Dad!" then grabs one of his legs and twists back, pointing to something behind them.

"What?" His eyes follow her extended finger.

"In the sky! Look!"

He sees it, hovering and luminescent. *God!* he thinks. *What is that thing?*

It's above and beyond the Sunoco station. The night is misty. The floating light hangs unattached, seems now to be moving.

Not a flying saucer, he assures himself. But that's a conclusion based on his general skepticism about such phenomena, not on his observation; *that* tells him he is, in fact, looking at a flying saucer.

"Let's go," he says, starting across Main Street, toward the light.

"No!" She grips his legs with both arms; he feels her trembling.

"It's not what you think," he says, knowing it can't be, mustn't be.

"No!"

He's going to pick her up and carry her. She can't be left with this fright or with any uncertainty. He pulls her arms away, is about to lift her, when she takes his hand and says, shakily, "All—all right," as if she too has sensed she must go at her fear or it will control her.

Even as they cross the street it seems certainly to be a flying saucer. He half expects it to dart sideways or rise swiftly out of sight. They've reached the gas station before he notices something extending downward from the saucer. Quickly he leads her around the station. Only then, squinting, does he see that the light, about a hundred yards away, comes from an enormous lamp at the top of a narrow steel post in the parking lot of the supermarket. The lamp, recently installed, illuminates the lot.

"See," he says. "Can you tell?"

"What?" she whispers, still not certain.

He takes her closer, hurrying, until they're at the very edge of the parking lot.

She slowly loosens her hold on his hand, says finally, "Parking lot lights," and repeats it, "only the parking lot lights." He rests his hand on her shoulder as she gazes up, making sure.

On the way home they talk about how strange the light seemed at first, and he admits that he thought that it might have been a flying saucer. "We would have gotten our names in the paper if it had been."

She laughs at that and seems, finally, relieved.

After both Suzie and Bobo are asleep he reports the incident to Marilyn, who's spent much of the evening working in the storeroom. He ends by asking if she believes the hallucination, or whatever it was, means Suzie has some serious psychological problem.

"I don't know," she says after a few thoughtful moments. "You don't have to have serious problems to imagine something like that. I've felt on the verge of hallucinations myself lately. It's not the hallucinatory aspect of it that bothers me. You yourself thought 'flying saucer.' It must have looked like one."

"What then?"

"The reaction. It seems nearly hysterical, at least the way you describe it."

"I could have overdone—" He stops, recalling the incident. "No, she was hysterical. I'd call it that." He says he's noticed, since their return, other oddities in Suzie's behavior, mentions the television watching tonight.

Marilyn's nodding. "More than once in Minnesota I worried about her. She tended to draw away, especially toward the end of our stay. She stared at me a lot. It made me feel guilty about being so wrapped up in my new crafts thing. I don't think, though, that she was hostile. She seems to be caught up in thought a lot. She's never been expressive like Annie. I hope it's, well, just Suzie being Suzie."

"Are you worried?"

Marilyn looks at her hands, then tilts her head, nods. "A little." She pauses. "More than a little. For selfish reasons I haven't been dwelling on the changes I've seen in her. Maybe I should."

Benjamin is more uneasy than he was when the conversation began. Marilyn, because of her background in psychology, is not the sort to overstate one of her children's problems. Benjamin is certain she's more worried than she's admitted.

Marilyn suggests they make an appointment with an old friend of hers from college days, Marvin Keller, a psychologist who recently was made director of the Family Services Clinic at the state university (twenty miles from Centerville). "He's good," she says. "We may have to wait for an appointment."

"You think she'll be okay in the meantime?"

Marilyn closes her eyes, sits pensive for a few moments, then says, "There doesn't seem to be a crisis just now."

"Just now?"

"Benjamin," she says, her eyes opening under a frown, "I just don't know."

The game with Buck's turns out to be just the kind Benjamin would have ordered:

At the bottom of the fourth the score is still 0–0.

He's been chased all day by worries about Suzie. Now and then they've given way to thoughts about Ellen, whom he hasn't called since Marilyn's return. Seeking to flee those, he's run up against his anger toward Gray: when he arrived at the ball park he pictured his sponsor hanging by his neck from the top of the backstop. This is one day he doesn't need a lopsider. A tight ball game from first to last, one to challenge and engage, will do just fine.

Tim Adams, whose card was in the extra-player draft, is playing for Buck's. Tim so far has gotten the only hit of the game, a well-timed single off Tony in the first inning.

The manager of Buck's, like Benjamin, doesn't wear a team uniform. Unlike Benjamin, who keeps wearing his old T-shirts and khaki pants ("moldy," according to Marilyn), the Buck's manager seems elegant in his silky open-necked shirt with bright Oriental print (black on orange), his pajamalike slacks made of a material even finer than that in the shirt, and his Roman-style leather sandals. A final certification of his eccentricity is his full, black, neatly trimmed beard. He spoke to Benjamin before the game, actually shook hands with him, wishing him a good contest. His name is Edgar Wolfe, and he's an instructor in humanities at the little community college between Centerville and Toledo. He doesn't have an assistant coach; one of his players coaches at first base while he coaches at third. As he mingled among his players during pregame practice, his prancing movements reminded Benjamin of an exotic bird.

He's now in the third base coaching box, giving his batter elaborate signs: a tug at his beard, a stroke of his hand across the front of the shirt, a flapping hand against hip, and finally, oddly, impressively, a bow toward the batter. Sensing an attentive spectator, he turns to Benjamin in the Gray's dugout and says softly, "I like the ceremony of it all, don't you?"

"Not as much as winning," Benjamin replies flatly.

The sign was for a bunt, which the batter drops nicely between the mound and home plate. It catches Bobo and Meryl, Tony's replacement, off guard, and the batter reaches first base. The play was impressive enough, but it becomes more so when Benjamin notices that the next batter is Tim, the one Buck's player with a hit. The Buck's manager is clearly playing as if this is going to be a close game all the way—a sensible assumption. Another single by Tim likely would move the player on first over to third. Then nearly anything, including a bunt, a fly ball, even an error, would score him. One run in this game will be like five in some other.

Meryl gives Benjamin a frightened look.

Benjamin calls time out and goes to the mound.

The air is warm and damp, and Meryl is perspiring badly. "I'm worried, Mr. Dunne, that my hand's going to sweat too much and the ball will slip."

No rosin bags are provided, so Benjamin tells him to pick up loose dirt, wiggle it through his fingers until he's sure they're dry, then wipe his hand on a dry part of his shirt. He adds advice about Tim:

"He's going to do what he did with Tony: Time the pitch and try to hit a single to move the runner. Use your dropper and keep it inside, even if you risk walking him. But, when you get two strikes, if you do, fool him with that batting practice pitch of yours. He won't expect it and may swing too soon."

Benjamin returns to the dugout, watches Meryl throw two inside droppers, both balls, then another, just as inside, which too eagerly Tim swings at, fouling it toward his manager at third. Benjamin is now sure he's guessed right.

Edgar, however, calls time out and goes toward the plate for a conference with Tim.

Benjamin tries to guess at Edgar's instruction, can't.

The conference lasts only a few seconds; the advice, no doubt, wasn't elaborate, probably something basic like: "Swing only at the pitches you know you can hit."

Its effectiveness is surely in the delay, in getting Benjamin to wonder about it. Now Benjamin notices Edgar, on returning to third, give a complete set of signals.

That, thinks Benjamin, *is the tip-off.*

He calls time out for a second time (his limit in each inning) and heads for the mound, signaling Bobo and the infielders to follow.

"What the hell's going on?" Nick complains as he follows Benjamin to the mound. "We ain't even playin' ball."

"Pay attention," he says when they're all gathered beside Meryl. "I'm sure their manager just gave the runner a signal that Tim is going to try a bunt. All he said to Tim at the plate was, 'Bunt the next pitch.' They're not going to try to get the runner to third, only to second. Wait until Meryl goes into the windup, then rush in to take the bunt. We may get two outs."

"You're not supposed to bunt with two strikes on you," says Nick. "If it's foul, he's out."

"The value of surprise," Benjamin tells him. "They think you'll all be playing him deep. And he's a good bunter."

"Yuh steal a sign, Mr. Dunne?" Fred asks.

"I read a mind."

"Huh?"

"Never mind. Now, have you all got the idea?"

Their unruffled looks seem to say yes.

"Good, because I can't come out here again. If their manager calls his second conference with Tim, or gives a bunch of signals, that means they're changing plans once more. In that case, forget everything I just said and play back, as if Tim is going for a regular hit."

"This doesn't seem like baseball," Nick grumbles.

"Yeah," Tag adds. "It's more like checkers or chess."

"It's baseball," says Benjamin firmly.

"Just standin' aroun' bullshittin's what it seems like to me," says Nick.

Benjamin quells a strange impulse. "Any questions?"

The mumbles and grunts add up to a no.

On his way back to the dugout Benjamin remembers coming to a kind of second level of appreciation for this sport; that is, getting as much enjoyment out of watching managers maneuvering as, say, seeing a game-winning home run or a frantic slide into home plate. Joe Mc-

Carthy of the old New York Yankees hardly ever appeared on the field; he used to sit in the dugout in his street clothes and double-think his opponents. Other managers, like Eddie Stanky and Billy Martin, in uniform, hopping about, even playing, didn't seem to think at all, but suddenly delivered surprises: an unexpected pinch hitter, a double steal, a faked injury to give the relief pitcher more time to warm up. And it became even more enjoyable when both managers played the mental game: first manager brings in left-handed pinch hitter; second counters with left-handed reliever; first manager pulls out left-handed reliever for right-handed one. Given these givens, Benjamin feels a spurt of new interest, is grateful for Edgar and his challenges.

The reverie is broken when he glances into the stands and sees the scowling pink face of Gray. The sponsor doesn't usually attend games. As if his disapproving face weren't enough, Gray is now, for some reason, shaking his head. Benjamin doesn't know what Gray's current problem is. The conference with players? The low score? Maybe it's not just current. Maybe it's the very sport of baseball? Benjamin doesn't, finally, care. He does decide, however, that, in one way or another, he's going to bring the uniform issue to a head. That, in the few empty seconds that break this rich and compelling ball game, gives him as much diversion as he needs.

Edgar has guessed at Benjamin's instruction to pitcher and infielders and is now doing a whirling-dervish dance at third.

Gray's infielders, noticing, follow instructions and move back into their regular places.

Tim starts to take a swipe at Meryl's pitch, stops himself, and watches the pitch drop beautifully over the plate, just a trifle too low for a strike.

Will Meryl now remember to deliver his soft pitch, or will he, tempted by the effectiveness of that last dropper, try another?

Benjamin thinks of calling out a reminder from the bench: "Remember what we talked about!" But that would possibly unnerve Meryl and it might give the pitch away to Edgar, certainly nobody's fool.

Benjamin does the only intelligent thing he can think of doing at this moment: closes his eyes.

Cracko!

He opens one eye.

Nick is leaping, grabbing, holding.

It was a line drive, solidly hit, but now is only an out. Nick, landing perfectly, lets his throw go to first.

Benjamin watches Fred grab the ball to double off the runner, who'd confidently started for second.

Edgar flings both arms out dramatically and groans to the dank sky.

With such demands as this game is making, Benjamin can yet be drawn to other concerns. There have been bursts of worry about Suzie. Thinking he's seen Ellen's car, he moves out of his coaching box to check. It's her Gremlin. Now he sees that she's in the driver's seat, Max beside her. As Max offers a friendly wave, she raises her hand and gives Benjamin an approving thumb-and-forefinger circle. He points to the field and grimaces: *Tight game.* The tilt of her head says, *So? Be calm.*

Is Marilyn here? Did she see his gesture?

He checks.

She's not in the stands. Nor are the girls. Marilyn told Bobo she wanted to see some of the game. But there was doubt, something about fabrics to be sewn. Despite Ellen's presence, it would comfort him to have her here. Annie and Suzie too. Especially Suzie, whom the game might divert from her fears. He kicks aside a temptation to contrast Marilyn's indifference to baseball with Ellen's interest in it.

He sees Gray, expression unchanged, arms crossed. Though the stands are crowded, there's space on each side of him. He looks as though he might jostle anyone who sat close to him. His eyes cling to Benjamin. Benjamin goes behind the dugout, waits, comes back, looking. Gray's eyes pick him up again, instantly. Benjamin smiles and feels like saying "Boo." Gray doesn't smile back.

Thank God it's still close, Benjamin thinks, turning his attention back to the game, feeling too much the encroachment of forces beyond the diamond.

Speck gets to first on a walk with one out. There's hope. He steals second. Hope rises. The Buck's pitcher strikes out the next two batters. Hope departs.

Pitching now, Tag hits a batter. With the struck batter on first, Tag balks and the runner is sent to second. Benjamin goes out and tells him to concentrate on the hitter, not the runner. He does, getting out of the inning with the help of two fine fielding plays, one by Nick, one by Tony, and a pop-up to right field.

At the top of the last inning the score is unchanged: 0–0.

"I'm going to try and put one over the fence," Nick says in the dugout.

"No," says Benjamin. It would, he knows, be a big mistake, the common mistake of the inexperienced batter: blast the ball, end the tension, win the game. "Meet the ball," he says. "One run will probably win this one, but we aren't likely to get it with a single swing."

"What hue mean, Meester Don?" says Tony. "Neeck ees hable to poot eet out ob thee park like *no*-body."

"He's been up twice and he hasn't yet. Has he?"

"Maybe thees time."

"And maybe not. The way their pitcher is going, it's liable to be a strikeout."

"Whose ball game is this, Mr. Dunne?" It's Nick, complaining.

"What do you mean?"

"Yours or ours? If I think I'm able to put one over, why shouldn't I try? We're supposed to be out here learnin' things, tryin' things to see if we can do 'em. This isn't the goddamn major leagues. I want to find out if I can put one over."

"Aw, c'mon, Mr. Dunne," says Harold Foxx, "let him try to put one out."

"Listen," Benjamin replies, "this—this isn't a democratic sport." Though what he says is true, he knows as he speaks the thought that his timing is inappropriate.

"What's that s'posed to mean?" Nick asks.

Benjamin evades an impossible answer. "It means, and is supposed to mean, 'No.' "

The looks and sounds he gets amount to collective disapproval. But the momentum has picked up; there's no time for debate.

"Go."

Nick, grumbling, goes to bat and does his best to meet the ball, finally smacking a hard grounder that unfortunately finds its way to the shortstop's glove; Nick's thrown out at first base. He comes back, kicks a batting helmet from one end of the dugout to the other, sits down and curses. Benjamin ignores him and doesn't second-guess himself.

Fred, using a favorite tactic of his, crowds the plate, gets hit on the thigh, and goes to first.

Paul, however, strikes out.

Benjamin is down to his last card.

Tag, due to be up next, suggests to Benjamin that he be allowed to try to punch one to right field. He seems ready to argue, like Nick.

There's no need; it's a well-measured piece of advice; Tag is easily capable of hitting behind runners. "Try it," says Benjamin. "It might work."

He does it, looping the second pitch just over the first baseman's head.

Fred, though heavy-footed, ends up on third.

The Buck's pitcher, just now their curveballer, has been laboring a little, not bringing his arm fully back before the throw, not completing his follow-through. As the Gray's crowd becomes tensely silent, Benjamin tells the next batter, Speck, to take the first two pitches. "If both are balls, try to get the walk. That pitcher is tired."

Speck waits through six pitches, gets the walk.

Now all the bases are occupied, and Edgar is on his way to the pitcher's mound.

Meryl, up next, is trembling.

Edgar, perhaps missing the clues that his pitcher is tired, speaks to him but leaves him in.

"First, try to wait him out as Speck did," Benjamin tells Meryl. "If he gets a strike on you, swing at anything that looks good. Meet it. There's a good chance for a hit." It's a big gamble: Meryl's hitting has been poor. But Benjamin has used his reserves early, and there just isn't a pinch hitter. "You can do it."

After smartly taking two balls Meryl swings at a third, a bad pitch that hits the dirt. He looks to Benjamin, embarrassed.

"One strike only," Benjamin reminds him.

But a moment later there's another, called, on a close pitch.

Meryl comes out of the batter's box shuddering. He staggers toward Benjamin. He seems about to lose all his bones and collapse like an empty sack.

"You're doing fine." He's not, but what else is there to say? "If it looks good, hit it."

Meryl takes a massive swing at a good pitch and strikes out.

He's scheduled to pitch the last of the seventh but is such a wreck—eyes dancing, hands trembling, mouth moving wordlessly in some sort of silent apology—that Benjamin, with as little fanfare as possible, moves him to second, puts Tony at shortstop, and brings from shortstop the one among his three alternate pitchers who's been most effective today, Tag.

The more tense the game has become, the more Tag has relaxed. *Maybe it's pot,* Benjamin thinks.

He makes the changes, reports them to the scorer in the announcer's booth, returns to the dugout.

"I've had just about enough, haven't you?" says Edgar as he takes his place in the third base coaching box.

"I can take a little more," Benjamin replies from the dugout.

The Buck's manager gives an elaborate set of signals which translate into a running bunt, a beautiful bunt: It catches all Gray's infielders playing back, is too far out in front of the plate for Bobo to reach, and just swift enough to evade Tag coming off the mound.

A grin finds its way through Edgar's dark beard as he turns to the plate, where the batter is Tim Adams.

Tag's fastest fastball dives toward the strike zone. Tim takes a classic swing, but too soon, sending a drive, foul, over the low fence in front of the stands, out of sight of Benjamin in the dugout. There's an enormous roar, followed by a lot of people mumbling.

Benjamin rises and looks out.

The moment he sees what's happened Benjamin knows he will remember it for the rest of his life:

Bellowing, Gray is tilted to one side, holding his forehead, being helped from the stands by another man. "You rotten little son-of-a-bitch!" he shouts, shaking his free hand toward Tim. His face, not bleeding, is nevertheless lavishly scarlet.

It was only a glancing blow; if it had hit Gray straight-on, he might be dead. No one Benjamin has seen all year has pulled a foul ball that much. He looks to Tim. The boy's back is to the stands as, bending over his bat, he wipes dirt from his hands. He seems to be the only one in Pee Wee Park besides Benjamin who's not looking at Gray.

Gray is being guided to the announcer's booth, where Francis keeps a big first-aid kit.

Benjamin turns to Tim, quizzes him with his eyes: *An accident?* Tim steps into the batter's box, leans forward, and kisses the top of the bat.

Benjamin thinks he has his answer.

Despite Gray's constant rage and intolerance, Benjamin's feelings about him are diluted with sympathy. It grows out of a sense that in some way the sponsor is his own main victim. He remembers Tim's horror story, and for the first time imagines Gray's part in it, seeing now his face boil with frustration as Tim flees from him and the back room. How long had Gray prepared himself for that moment? How knotted in defeat he must have been when it came to so little! No matter, Benjamin reminds himself. Whatever the desperate underlying needs, no matter how human, how understandable they might have been, damage was done, perhaps lasting damage. Tim, not Gray, was the victim.

Gray is being repaired; the game resumes.

On Tag's next pitch, Tim hits a single, sending the lead runner to third.

Benjamin gets a time-out, goes to the mound, and gives standard instructions: infield in; pitch the ball low; hold or cut off the run. He doesn't need to say: "If the runner on third base scores, we lose."

The next batter hits a ground ball. Nick snaps it up, holds the runner on third, gets the out at first.

Tag strikes out the next batter.

Benjamin is confident now. The batter in the box is the weakest on the Buck's team. Tag need concentrate only on getting him out.

Waiting, looking over the runner on third, then the batter, Tag finally goes into his man-on-base windup.

Doesn't need to, Benjamin thinks.

Tag should use the full windup; with his speed and accuracy, he'll get the ball to the plate before any runner can steal home. Benjamin calms himself: *A man-on-base windup is okay, a way of playing it safe, keeping that runner close to third.*

But why is Tag now standing very, very still?

Pitch the ball! Benjamin calls out silently.

The longer Tag waits, *if* he's thinking of doing the jackass thing Benjamin suspects he's thinking of doing, the worse it's going to be.

Benjamin dares not shout out his instruction for fear of upsetting his pitcher.

Edgar leans forward in the coaching box and mumbles something to the runner leading off third.

The runner takes one more step toward the plate.

That does it: Tag flings the ball to third.

It's a stupid, a purposeless, and despite Nick's brilliant dive to the left in an attempt to save the bad throw, a disastrous move; above all, it's an unnecessary one. Even a good throw wouldn't have gotten the runner. Tag had a notion, was compelled by it, and threw.

"Damn!" cries Benjamin, smashing his open hands against the dugout screen so hard that the screen nearly comes loose.

Gray's players are crying out in pain and disgust.

Edgar comes to the dugout, waits for Benjamin to settle, then shakes his counterpart's hand.

Fuck you! Benjamin thinks, though he does take Edgar's handshake gracefully.

The whole team is soon in the dugout. Benjamin makes himself deaf to the moans, gripes, second-guesses, and tears.

He waits.

They quiet down.

A speech that might have been long comes to this: "It's over. You played a hell of a game. We have another next Tuesday."

They stare, waiting or not waiting for more.

He hopes they'll lose their tensions quickly, on the way home. He scrapes through his pockets, finds nearly four dollars, asks Bobo to take whoever wants to go to Dairy Queen and spend it.

"I wish I had a case of beer," says Lou Pera.

That brings the only laughs.

He hopes they all buy big shakes, spray what they can't drink over each other, go on laughing. He hopes they all sleep easily tonight, especially Tag.

Meryl is crying.

He takes Meryl by the back of his loose shirt, turns him around, pats his back, and hugs him.

The others seem to understand that, even Karl, who's at the dugout entrance, nodding.

Digby lingers after the others have gone and helps Benjamin with the equipment. Benjamin waits for, hopes for, a wisely perceptive tidbit of some sort from him, but there's nothing more than his comforting presence. What more can be said anyway?

He's lost track of his other concerns. Only as he's closing the station wagon's tailgate, does he notice Ellen at his side.

"You need a drink," she says, "whether I or someone else pours it for you. Anyway, that's an invitation."

"I accept."

"Bourbon?"

"Double."

He gets into the station wagon, exhales loudly against the windshield, blowing the dust of the game out of his lungs, wishing it were also the memory of it.

SIX

From middle to late July the air is constantly soggy and hot. Nights are no relief. The weather earns a small headline in the Centerville *Tribune* when, for one evening only, the temperature slips below 80 degrees. Faces hang and bodies sag.

At the practice following the Buck's game five players are missing, including Meryl, and those who attend move like slugs. Initially Benjamin thinks the problem is the heat, but he overhears grumbled bits of conversation about the Buck's game, a losers' lament. After practice he calls the players into the dugout, compliments several of them on recent fine efforts, and ends by reminding them, matter-of-factly, that the Buck's game is forever over with.

"So is the season," says Speck.

"What do you mean by that?" he asks.

"We can't make it to the championship, not with two losses."

He's heard none of them talking championship until now.

"Watson and Wills and Buck's haven't been beaten," says Lou.

"So?"

"You been playin' every game to win it. Right, Mr. Dunne?" It's Tag, who has nicely weathered his game-losing throw against Buck's.

"I don't know how else to play." Before the Buck's

game, Benjamin probably couldn't have admitted that to himself, let alone them.

"If it's true of a baseball game," Tag goes on, "it's also true of a season. Right?"

"I'd prefer to end up on top, if that's what you mean."

"That is what I mean. And we can't. See?"

But there's still a chance for the championship, Benjamin knows, a very slim chance. Though tempted, he's not going to describe for them this razor-thin possibility. He himself will be fueled by it. They must not. Individually or together, they may figure out their chances. He won't tell them, won't be the broker for their hopes; the chances are too thin. "Professional teams don't stop playing when they can no longer win a pennant," he tells them.

He gets a lot of responses to that:

"They get paid; we don't."

"Maybe they're trying things out for next year."

"That's their job; they got nothin' else to do."

He won't attempt an inspiring speech about playing the game for the sake of the game. All he can bring himself to say is: "I hope you keep coming out to practices and games. If I don't have nine players or more, I can't field a team."

That's obvious, their cynical eyes tell him. *What else is new?*

He gives them nothing else.

"I'll be here for the next game," Digby says.

No one else pledges anything.

"My world will not fall apart, my life will not become pointless, if you quit. Do what you want."

They don't like it; they want the inspiring speech.

He won't give it. "Game next Tuesday," he says, preceding them out of the dugout.

That night at home, furtively, under the light of his desk lamp, he works out the possibilities:

Both Buck's and Watson and Wills play four more games. If each loses two and Gray's wins its remaining games, the season will end in a three-way tie. The two contenders for the championship will then be decided by the difference between the total number of runs scored for and the total number of runs scored against:

172

Team X: runs for (45)—against (22)=23
Team Y: runs for (33)—against (15)=18
Team Z: runs for (50)—against (26)=24

Teams X and Z would play for the championship.

He adds up the runs scored for and against the three. The totals are very close: no more than five runs difference among them.

There are other factors:

Gray's plays weak teams from now until the end of the season.

Buck's and W. and W. play each other once, and each plays Marvell's, much improved.

Benjamin toys with some runs-scored possibilities, adding, subtracting, altering, adding again. The more he speculates, the more his hope grows. Finally he slips his calculations under other papers in his middle drawer, closes the drawer, turns off his lamp, and creeps out of the room, feeling about as malicious as he would if he'd just designed a bomb to blow up the Centerville courthouse.

There are several rolls of fabric under the living room window, all brightly colored. She comes up from the basement every so often, wielding her long scissors and trailing a measuring tape. "You won't believe it!" she said once, waving the open scissors at him. "You will just *not* believe what I'm doing."

"Maybe I will if you let me look."

"No! I want it to be a surprise." She drops to her knees, measures, marks (with the little piece of chalk she carried behind her ear), then, fiercely, cuts.

She begins working each evening at around eight thirty, moving to and from the dining room like a tornado. From the basement the sewing machine sounds like a distant jet in trouble. She's taken to wearing a sari and no shoes.

One night he heard the girls in their bedroom:

"Mom is gettin' real weird, isn't she?" Annie said.

"She hardly ever notices me."

"You don't have to take it personal."

Suzie is silent for a while, then asks, "What's she making?"

"She's got a whole bunch of masks."

"Masks?"

"Well, faces like, not whole big heads. I peeked. She got 'em when she went to Toledo last week. I wouldn't mind if we didn't have to stay with the yucky Andersons and eat *toooo*-na san'wiches. I hate *tooo*-na."

"I hate staying with . . . anyone."

After the conversation Benjamin began guessing: clown suits; cloth montages; Halloween costumes. He had no idea.

As she kneels to do more cutting, he mentions Suzie, wondering if both he and Marilyn should spend more time trying to get to the heart of her silences.

Marilyn stops working, says fretfully, "I know we should. I've been trying not to think about it. Marv will see her in a few days, then give us a report."

He thinks Marilyn indifferent until he remembers how little time he himself has spent with both girls since their return from Minnesota. Is she any worse than he?

She begins to talk about herself and Benjamin, not the girls: "At least we're both finding outlets."

"Expensive ones," he says, thinking of both the cost of baseball equipment and the cost of her materials.

Snip-snip. "I'm not in the least bit worried. I'm sure that what I'm doing, at least, will eventually make money."

He ignores the editorial, says, "In the meantime . . ."

"In the meantime I charge for a few pieces of material." *Snip-snip.* "The rest is my own free labor."

She hasn't wavered once. The bills for the fabric will arrive soon. He's not dared to ask her how much they'll come to. He guesses $150, will not be surprised at $200. He wishes he could be as confident about Suzie, the bookstore, his baseball team, and the other weights in his life as she seems to be about—whatever-it-is she's doing.

"Do you have to have a place to sell what you're making?"

"I have a plan for that. I'll let you know, soon."

"Can't talk about it?"

"Not yet, Benjamin. Please be patient."

While he's able to avoid thinking about Marilyn and her project, other anxieties persist like little misbeats of the heart after a strenuous day. They're too frequent to be ignored. Rising above all is his concern about Suzie.

He marks a difference between her tone and Annie's during the bedroom conversation: hers urgent, Annie's merely irritated. *A clue,* he thinks. *And what,* he wonders, *can this Marvin do for her?* A serious illness may take months, years, to explore, understand, cure. Perhaps she needs a psychiatrist who can offer extended treatment, not a psychologist working hastily at a clinic. His worries eventually bring him back to Marilyn, who's still in the dining room, still cutting. He says he wants to know more about Keller, mentions the possibility of psychiatry, then makes a suggestion: "Shouldn't we at least be making a list for Keller of the signs or symptoms we've seen?"

Abruptly, she flings her scissors across the floor, not in Benjamin's direction but toward the stairs, where it stops, a great silver X, lying open like a yawn. "Damn it," she demands, looking up to him, "don't you think I'm as worried about her as you!"

"That—isn't the question," he replies patiently. "I just wanted to know if you thought—"

"I don't know! I could pace around all evening, thinking the worst. What good would it do!" She's glaring now, arms wide like the scissors' arms, pleading between them: "I don't know how to put it to you except to say my daughter matters to me vitally, but nothing is more vital than my own survival. Right now, this!" She points to some swatches of cloth. "Do you—do you understand that?"

No, he doesn't understand it at all. Does her work matter more than Suzie's sanity? Were she to stop cutting those pieces of cloth would she fall over dead? "What do you mean?"

"I mean," she says more calmly as she crawls to retrieve the scissors, "I am worried about Suzie, but there's nothing I can do right now. There'd be nothing I could do if I were the world's most famous psychologist. Because she's—she's my daughter." She picks up the scissors, snaps it closed, reminding Benjamin of curtains being shut on an embarrassing sight. "I don't like waiting, but, like you, I *have* to wait. If I can't find a way to put up with the waiting, I *will* be in trouble."

He's sorry he touched something in her that he now knows shouldn't have been touched. Suppressing his anger at her uncharacteristic fiery response, he apologizes.

175

She soon goes back to the cutting. "Marvin is good," she assures him sounding more like her usual self. "Believe me."

He'll try to.

He goes to their bedroom. He'll attempt to sleep away his anxieties, keep them to himself tomorrow, after that too, until he can safely share them with her. They've always been able to share such things. It seems to him essential that they do. That, too, is a matter of survival.

W. and W. has defeated Buck's, 3-2.

Bobo, who's just come in from the game, reports the news: "The Watson and Wills coaches drove Edgar crazy with all their protests. The last one was on a squeeze bunt by Buck's that would have won the game. The ball rolled foul. Before the W. and W. third baseman could pick it up, it rolled fair again. The Buck's runner had crossed the plate. The umpire said the ball was fair."

"It *was*," says Benjamin.

"Nope. Those creepy coaches started stamping their feet and yelling the way they did at our game and got the umpire to change it. They said once the ball went foul it was foul for good. That's not right, is it?"

"No. Who umpired?"

"One of the new umpires and Daryl." The young man and his former umpiring partner were suspended following the near riot during the V.F.W. game. They have since been reinstated but are not allowed to work games together.

"Was Daryl in on the protest?"

"The W. and W. coaches appealed to him when the plate umpire said he wasn't sure of the rule. Daryl said the ball was dead when it went out."

"He's wrong," says Benjamin angrily. "So Edgar can appeal the game."

"I don't think he will. Do you?"

"I don't know."

"Edgar said afterwards that Daryl and the other umpire didn't know a baseball field from the Sea of China, or something like that."

Benjamin suspects collusion between Daryl and the W. and W. coaches. He sees Daryl as so whimsical and unrooted that he'd make a pact with the demons of his own life, including the dandies. He doesn't mention collusion to Bobo, fearing he might have to confess his eavesdropping at the fence.

"What a game!"

Bobo has been more animated than he's been during or after any of the Gray's games. For once he's had a chance to be a fan, a witness, not a participant. Being a fan can be hardest of all, Benjamin is sure. One has nothing to throw, nothing to hit, no one to give signals to, no one to call "out" or "safe." At times, as during the near riot, fans do let go. Bobo is letting go now:

"Would you protest the game if you were in Edgar's place?"

"Definitely."

That seems to satisfy Bobo, who goes to the kitchen to forage.

Edgar doesn't seem to be the sort to carry the game on after it's ended. Benjamin's secret hope is that he won't protest. Despite the odds against Gray's, there's still a chance for Gray's, and Benjamin would rather meet W. and W. in the championship than he would Buck's. He'd rather meet W. and W. than any team he can think of.

He's arranged for the drive in the country with Ellen, doing it in the way all cheaters and adulterers must arrange such things, surreptitiously, in this case by way of a phone call made just minutes after Marilyn had announced to him her intention to go to Cleveland and consult with some theatrical people about her project. (*Why theatrical people?* he didn't ask, sure she'd have answered the way she's answered most of his questions lately: "Be patient.") Marilyn's been very excited about the trip. Fortunately for Benjamin, she gave in to Annie's pleas that she and Suzie be allowed to go with her. Bobo is off fishing somewhere with Tim Adams and Max.

"Turn here," Ellen says.

He slows, sees a narrow dirt road going off to the left, follows it. About a half mile ahead are woods.

She's skittish today, saying she's taking him to a secret place, then urging him to guess where, laughing at his guesses: "Your parents' home." "The place where Max and Bobo are fishing."

177

"Did you bring your swimming suit?" she says as they near the woods.

"No."

"Good. Neither did I."

What does that mean?

The road enters the trees, becomes narrower, until there is barely enough room for the car. He slows nearly to a stop.

"Keep going," she says.

He gently presses the accelerator, squeezing between trees, following the barely visible road, no more than a wide path. Finally, turning, he sees a lake open before them. It's about five hundred yards long, about half as wide. There isn't a house or even a shack anywhere in sight. Stopping, he notices a gently sloping beach to the left, beyond a break in the tall grass. He gets out, opens the back door of the car. She's packed a picnic lunch, mainly sandwiches and beer, in a styrofoam container. He carries the container out. She removes a blanket and spreads it out near the center of the beach. He puts the container on the blanket, turns in a circle, searching:

"No one?"

"Hardly anyone knows it's here." She explains that the land belongs to Don, who got it cheaply in the settlement of an estate. They once shared dreams of a summer cottage here. Those faded with their love. "He never visits here now, says he has no interest in it."

They remove their outer clothes and go into the cool water. They swim to a tree stump jutting out about fifty yards away. They hold the stump, wrap their legs around each other, catching their breath, splashing water on each other. He paddles around the stump, goes under, comes up. "It's deep enough," he says. She climbs delicately to the end of the stump and dives in with a graceful swan. He follows with a clumsy jackknife. They swim back.

She's brought tanning oil. They undress completely and coat each other with the oil. They lie close, arm locked in arm, fingers in fingers. *Thousands of couples must be doing this,* he thinks, yet it feels as though they are the only two. *Our ceremony under the sun,* he thinks.

He sleeps briefly, awakens and, for a few moments, is sure that only they and this place exist.

He eases toward her and they hold each other, their movements becoming the movements of a single body. He swells into her tightly. The loving is long and full of hard and violent movements. Only when the sun's heat pries them apart do they rise and race together to the water.

Marilyn has taken a phone message from Gray. After hearing it, Benjamin rushes from the house, gets into the station wagon, and drives rapidly to the cleaner's.

Now, leaning far over the counter, he's gripping Gray's damp shirt, hissing out the only words he has:

"You call and say there won't be any uniforms for the rest of the season! You haven't bought a piece of equipment since last year. You haven't spent a cent!" Benjamin's fists come together on the shirt. He hears thread tearing. "The team has your name. You *seem* to be sponsoring a baseball team. People in the town think you are sponsoring it. What a lie that is!"

Gray, rigid, looking frightened, finally snorts back, "Get out of here or—I'll have you charged with assault."

Benjamin mentally steps back from himself, gets a sense of the crazy thing he's doing. *Why?* It's the impossible weather. It's Suzie and her problem. It's Marilyn and her obsessive project. It's Ellen and her growing needs. It's the baseball team. He doesn't know what it is. He's seen himself doing what he shouldn't be doing, but Gray's threat does not stop him. It's like a ball game. The action must be brought to a suitable conclusion.

"And I," he replies, "will have you charged with attempted sexual perversion." He has no idea as to whether or not such a crime exists.

Does Gray, his color deepening to blood red, know what he means?

"Get—out of here!"

Could Tim have made up that story? No, he must trust that Tim did not.

"You tried to rape a boy. Last year. I know about it."

"What!" Gray, mouth twitching, struggles to pull away.

Benjamin won't let go. "I want you to know I know about it. That may be enough to prevent you from trying something again." He *is* assaulting Gray. Whether he's right or wrong about Tim, he could be arrested. Yet,

179

going this far, he must go farther: "If you don't come through with the uniforms, I'll tell everyone. I won't mention the boy's name, but I'll mention yours. The boy may speak up. Others may speak up. Who knows what else is hidden under your rocks?"

Gray isn't struggling. His fury has etched new lines in his face, now turning purple.

Benjamin lets go.

Gray, puffing, says nothing.

Benjamin notices Mrs. Gray standing in the doorway at the back, leaning against the doorjamb, hair askew, eyes on him, speaking something. He can't read her message.

He looks back at Gray. "The uniforms," he says, calmer now.

He gets only a fiery stare.

Turning to go, he sees the woman, just where she was, still sending her mysterious message.

He's again had to talk Suzie into going for a walk with him. Though indifferent ("Oh, I don't care. If you want to"), she's less resistant this time. A few feet ahead of him now, she's holding a small dry branch she's picked up, flicking it against the trunks of the trees they pass.

Today she had her first meeting with Keller. "How'd it go?" he asks after they turn the corner onto the highway.

"Okay." *Swish.*

It'll take some cleverness to get more than one-word responses out of her; it always does. He waits until he has a question that might draw a more lengthy answer, then says, "What's the most interesting thing he told you?" He hopes she doesn't shrug or say she doesn't know.

Swish. Now she's going at the tall grass between sidewalk and curb. *Swish-swish.* "He gets scared too." *Swish.* She laughs. "He's kind of fat with a bald head and looks like he wouldn't get scared." *Swish-swish-swish.*

He senses a little breakthrough. Lately she's been less nervous but as silent as ever. Keller in the report he sent home with Marilyn said not to worry about the silences. "She's a bit solitary but not in any 'sick' way and seems to get a good deal of pleasure out of thinking things through."

All in all the report comforted Benjamin. Keller's

theme seemed to be that, even for normal children Suzie's age, anxious and even panicky reactions aren't unusual. They are sometimes brought about by changes, even small ones, in the family situation or some other aspect of the child's environment. "Whatever happens," Keller added, "it is important that you two (Benjamin and Marilyn) react in a calm and natural way." *What if*, Benjamin thought after reading the report, *the calm way isn't natural?*

But he is being calm now, ignoring the wish to ask Suzie if anything about his activities or Marilyn's has made her uneasy. Instead he picks up on her last remark and says, "What makes *him* scared?"

Swish. Whack. "Things happening you don't expect and stuff like that."

"Like what?"

"I can't think of anything right now."

She's a genius at bringing conversations to a dead end, as Annie is at getting off the subject. It takes Benjamin a few minutes to come up with another topic:

"Here's where we saw the strange light."

She's just made a whipping motion across the top of some tall grass in front of the used car lot. She stops, looks up, studies the parking lot light, which still hovers over the Sunoco station. But the air isn't misty tonight and the post is clearly visible. She turns stiffly to Benjamin. "Why did you have to remind me?"

He hesitates, wanting to conceal his true motive, doesn't: "I guess I wonder if you ever worry about—things like that. Anymore, I mean."

It takes Suzie's troubled eyes to let him know the depth of his mistake. He remembers Keller's words, *calm and natural*, however, and says, "It's nothing important. I mean, I'm not really worried about—about us seeing the light in a funny way again. Or anything like that."

She's started forward, toward the ice cream store. She mumbles something.

"What?" he says.

"Maybe *I* am," she replies, turning her head slightly.

He wouldn't have reminded her of the light if he'd been completely satisfied with Keller's report. At the end of it there'd been a kind of warning: "It's too early for me to know how extensive Suzie's fears are. While I'm

181

not at this time alarmed in any way, I want you both to watch for abrupt changes in her behavior." He gave examples: long periods of withdrawal, sudden outbursts of anger, marked changes in eating habits, a few others.

There's a telephone pole between the used car lot and the ice cream place. With a great sweeping motion Suzie smacks the branch against the pole, breaking the stick in half.

"I'm sorry," Benjamin says finally. "I'll stop talking about things that might be bothering you. Maybe I should say, 'bothering me.' How's that?"

Suzie goes ahead and opens the door at Friendly's, holding it, foot against the bottom, blocking his entry, facing him.

He stops before her.

"Promise," she says with pleading, troubled eyes.

"I do. I promise."

She hesitates, then pushes the door all the way open, letting him pass through.

Benjamin rescues books that don't sell at the front of the store and puts them in his private library, a small bookshelf outside his cubicle. Over the years he's painfully learned that (with exceptions like decorative editions of Shakespeare's plays) works of literature, philosophy, and such gather much dust and few customers.

While his tastes generally draw him to the contemporary, he's today chosen a collection of Walt Whitman's poetry, hoping it will lift him out of his gloom. The book rests on his legs, upraised on his desk, and he's reading "Song of Myself." He comes across a couple of lines that seem, amazingly, to have been drawn out of the events of his very own life:

I am the teacher of athletes,
He that by me spreads a wider breast than my own
  proves the width of my own.

He rereads the lines and decides to memorize them and recite them to his players at the start of the next practice: a way of showing them his function with them. He marks the lines with a pencil and is about to go on to those that follow when he senses the presence of another and looks up.

Dan is leaning against the doorjamb.

He guiltily closes the Whitman volume but keeps his thumb between his pages.

Dan has now and then interrupted his reading to remind him of work to be done. Usually the assistant is lighthearted, even makes jokes ("I hope that book of Camus"—which Dan pronounces Cam-muss—"is about profit-and-loss"). But today Dan appears serious, all too serious.

"What's up?" Benjamin says warily.

"I've decided to leave you. I'm—going to become a preacher."

"A what!" Benjamin is now aware he's sprung forward in his chair; he leans back. "A preacher. A preacher of what?"

"The Gospels of Jesus," says Dan calmly.

Benjamin, seeing Dan's dead-pan face, decides it's a joke. Dan is not going to become a preacher at all. This is his way of getting Benjamin's nose out of the book and onto business; the joke is a subtle one. "Smile now, Dan, and tell me what I should be doing. Inventorying the Hallmark cards. Right? I hate to, but I'll do it."

"I'm serious, Benjamin. I'm going to begin study at Waltham's Bible School in Cleveland to become an Evangelical minister."

"No, you're not." It isn't an order but a mundane statement of fact: Dan is a hard-nosed, efficient business manager, who only rarely goes to church (the First Episcopal). He'd never choose to be, of all things, an Evangelical preacher, hasn't.

"I've committed myself, Benjamin." There's no irony in the remark.

"Impossible!"

"Why?"

"It's a—a stupid profession." The thought popped into his mind and he spoke it.

"I'm sorry," Dan says patiently. He seems to mean, *I'm sorry for you, Benjamin.* "But I have."

"You wouldn't do such a thing." Benjamin's eyes fall to the Whitman poem. "Just wouldn't." He looks for the place where he left off. "We'll talk about it later." He uncharacteristically flicks his hand, signaling Dan to go away.

Benjamin's bookstore was sinking when Dan joined him. It's floating now; but, given the tugs and pressures in Benjamin's life, it might plummet like a lump of lead if Dan left. That's but another reason Dan isn't going off to be a preacher. Benjamin finds the "teacher of athletes" line, goes on to the next:

> He most honors my style who learns under it
>   to destroy the teacher.

Crap! He closes the book and tosses it to the corner of the cubicle, then sits silent, arms folded, forgetting the poem, trying not to believe Dan would make such a pointless, stupid, and above all, self-denying decision. "Don't you know that you have to work things out for yourself?" he calls loudly from the cubicle, unconcerned that customers or the clerks at the front might hear him. "Too many people put their marbles in their so-called God's bag and don't work things out for themselves which means they stop really being—alive!"

Is Dan not coming to the cubicle door to reply because it's the Christian thing to do?

"You hear me, Dan?"

Benjamin waits, but Dan doesn't reply or come back to the cubicle.

The work before Benjamin is an inventory of inspirational books, weekly increasing in popularity. He doesn't begin; it's a kind of protest. "Dan!" he finally shouts.

Dan finally comes into the doorway.

"Your life is your life," Benjamin says resentfully. "But, damn it, if you *are* crazy enough to want to be one of those ranting fools, you aren't leaving me until the end of baseball season. Hear?"

"I'm not sure that coincides with the start of my semester at Waltham's."

"I don't care whether it does or doesn't," says Benjamin firmly, pointing his finger at his assistant. "I've come to depend on you. Now you give me time to finish the baseball season and make a transition, time to— never mind." He's not going to recite a litany of his problems.

Another thought erupts: "Why are you doing such a thing?" he says in frustration.

"I've been alone," Dan replies, seeming to welcome the question. "Lately I've been watching Reverend Billy Lee Travers on television. Sunday morning he asked the television audience to kneel down while he prayed for them to receive the Holy Spirit. I was reading the paper. I hadn't been thinking about religion just then. But, for some reason, I knelt down. The Reverend Billy Lee prayed and" —Dan's eyes rise reverently, humbly, to the wall behind Benjamin's head— "the Holy Spirit *did* come into my heart!" Like his eyes, his voice rises too. "I'm not alone anymore."

What can Benjamin say to that? He turns away. When he finally looks back, the other seems to be in a trance.

"Dan?"

"Praise the Lord," says Dan softly. "Praise the Lord."

Preoccupied with worry over the impending loss of Dan, Benjamin doesn't remember until late afternoon that to-day's game is between Buck's and Marvell's.

He arrives at Pee Wee Park in the last of the seventh inning; the scoreboard in front of the announcer's booth shows Marvell's leading, 4–2.

Though his team is at bat, Edgar isn't in the coaching box. Benjamin looks around, sees him inside the first base dugout, feet up on the player's bench, hands wrapped tightly around stomach. Benjamin walks behind both stands to the low fence near the dugout, leans over, and asks, "How's it going?"

Edgar doesn't seem to hear him.

The crack of a bat sends Benjamin's eyes to the diamond.

A sluggish ball has been hit to third, is fumbled for a moment, then thrown in a weary loop to first. Any runner in the league would be able to beat it, but the Buck's runner trips and falls between home and first and is thrown out.

Benjamin glances back to the dugout.

Edgar shows no sign of having seen the play. His eyes seem, rather, to be fixed on a tree beyond the left field fence.

Benjamin repeats his question.

Without turning, Edgar replies. "Fate," he says. *"And* over-confidence." There's such a tone of doom in his voice. "My ulcer," he says. "The way it debilitates me. Also that." He stands slowly and carries himself out to the low fence, to a place near Benjamin. But he's not looking at Benjamin. He's not really looking at anything.

There's a pop-up. The third baseman circles clumsily under it. "I got it! I got it!" He weaves this way, that. Finally the ball finds its way to the edge of the mitt, almost topples off. The pitcher and shortstop grab the third baseman, squeezing him and the ball, saving the out.

"You nearly had a man on base," Benjamin says.

But Edgar, still not looking at the game, shakes his head, as if knowing the play was a close one. "What matter?" he says.

One more out and Buck's will have lost its chance to play for the championship—*if* Gray's wins its next and last regular game. Does Edgar know this? He hasn't watched the play just made. By the sounds, of course, he's certainly learned that a second out has been made, but he shows no sign of knowing it.

His desperate eyes reach to Benjamin's. "Forces are at work." He blinks, finally lets his eyes slide toward the diamond; they jump quickly back to Benjamin.

"There are two outs," Benjamin says, wanting Edgar to care.

"Tu-two," Edgar repeats like a man just learning the language. "I won't ask you which of my players is at bat."

"Strike one!" the umpire calls.

"Because it doesn't matter. We've peaked, as they say in this trade."

Benjamin, taking no pleasure in watching Edgar come apart, now reminds him that there's still a chance for a "two-out rally," a chance for him to win this game and get into the championship.

"Strike two!"

"Is there? Have you noticed the—the postures of the players on the bench beside me? Do you see victory on their faces? You're an acute observer of these—these children of Abner Doubleday. Have you been watching this game at all? What have you seen of the chances we've missed? Did you see how many men we had on base earlier? The other chances we had? These players are now gliding to a destiny I must have helped prepare during the first days of spring. There is a time for everything; today is our time to lose."

"Strike three!"

Edgar grimaces, says, "I will now hobble back to the dugout and praise them for the season, which ended for us a week ago. *That* was a good season. We've sunk ever since. It's—it's really that simple, Mr. Dunne."

"Simple?"

"Good luck, my friend. Good luck." Edgar turns, makes his way to the dugout, from where there already have arisen crying sounds. "Gentlemen," he says when the crying subsides, "please sit down. I have words of praise to speak to you."

She's rented a store.

From outside its window Benjamin sees a tall young man with golden locks dancing across the carpeted floor. He opens the door to hear the dancer singing, "Mari, it's the *per*-fect place. Mahhhgahhhddd, just *per*-fect!" The dancer wears a bright blue body-hugging shirt. His hands have been fluttering like sparrows. Now they pause, until one, like a dazed or drunken gull, sails outward, describing an arc that more or less parallels one of the bare side walls. "We'll hang our foo-foo's right along here!"

She's told him about Billy Sunrise. She met him on her recent trip to Cleveland, when she'd gone to purchase materials. They'd talked about her project, and now he's come to Centerville to consult with her, possibly even work with her. He's a costume designer by training, currently unemployed. "I know he'll be a partner," she said last night, "and I think we have a place."

It was startling news. Benjamin had guessed she'd continue working in the basement storeroom, figuring that, when she sold what she made it would be by taking it, them, whatever, to crafts shops or some such. But a shop of her own? *And* a partner? "My God," he said finally, "isn't it getting awfully complicated?" She reached out, took his arms, and with an intense yet remote look he's become used to, said into his eyes, "It doesn't *matter*, Benjamin! When you know what I'm doing, you'll realize that!" And she went on talking about the shop, on Main Street, only two blocks from the bookstore, then about Billy Sunrise, who, she said, was willing to work for nothing until they began to make money: "He'll be here early tomorrow. I want to be sure he approves of the location." She then begged Benjamin to take the morning off, come over to the store and meet her partner.

"Don't you think it's smashing?" Billy Sunrise asks as he pumps Benjamin's hand after Marilyn's introduction.

"I—don't know."

"It is," says Billy Sunrise petulantly. "It *is!*"

"Benjamin doesn't yet know what we're making," Marilyn explains.

"Oh, let's not tell him!" says Billy Sunrise, with several quick hand claps. "Let's keep it for a surprise!"

She's smiling, agreeing.

"We'll *have* to have little cards made," he says doing a half pirouette. "We *must* let the right people know where we are. They'll come from everywhere. My mother owned an expensive foreign glass place in Trumbull, Connecticut." (*Does he mean the rent was high,* Benjamin wonders, *or the glass was costly?*) "I mean, where *is* Trumbull? But they came, down from Boston, up from Long Island. They knew about her glass as they'll know about our—whoops!" In a great swooping gesture, Billy Sunrise raises his hands, clamps them to his temples, and says, "I very nearly let it slip out!" He winks at Marilyn and hops to the back of the store, chattering to himself as he goes.

"Isn't he something?" she whispers as her eyes follow Billy to the back. She means, of course, *something wonderful.*

"No," he whispers back.

"You haven't given him a chance. He's very talented. He's full of enthusiasm and he's been very supportive."

"We can work back here, darling!" Billy calls as, with one leg raised, he holds the doorjamb and looks into the darkened area beyond.

Benjamin notices Billy Sunrise's hand making circles over his head: a signal to Marilyn and Benjamin, or just Marilyn, to come and look. Benjamin doesn't want to look. He wants to trip his wife's partner to the floor and sit on him until he stops moving his limbs. He wants to

say blunt things like, "Her name is Marilyn, not Mari."
Hopping up and down in place, Billy Sunrise now slaps
his hand against the top of the doorway. "Hurry," he
says.

Benjamin wonders if he has to piss and is just holding
it in.

Marilyn goes forward, peers under Billy Sunrise's arm.
She agrees: It *is* an ideal place to work. "Benjamin," she
says, turning, "how much would it cost us to get a baby-
sitter for the girls?" Her eyes fall to the side. "Suzie," she
says flatly, giving Benjamin a worried glance. She fights
her way back from distraction. "I mean mornings until
September, when they'll be in school." Before he can answer, she says, "Billy, you *will* work late afternoons,
won't you?"

"Of course, darling. Despite my name, I hate to get
up early. Hah." He's dancing out into the store again.
"We're going to make it work. We *are!*"

What would Suzie think of him? Benjamin wonders.
(He knows what *he* thinks.) *What would she or Annie
or Bobo think of him? Of all of this?* If they only mildly
perceive the changes in their mother that he's perceived,
it's something short of miraculous that they're not disturbed. *If* they're not! Concerns about Suzie are like
quicksand. He's begun to have frantic thoughts about her,
about her possible reactions not only to the changes in
Marilyn but to those in himself, which he finds so much
less dramatic than those in his wife, so much less measur-
able. *Could I be affecting Suzie* even more *than she?*

He hears Billy Sunrise babbling on.

An old impulse overcomes Benjamin, but there are no
sharp-tipped instruments in sight. A closed fist on the back
of the neck might do it.

He watches as Marilyn, a woman he thought he knew,
and Billy Sunrise, a creature he wishes he didn't, grasp,
then embrace, each other. "We will," she says, uttering it.
"We will!"

Billy then says he's going to the restaurant on the corner to bring back coffee and sandwiches. Before he leaves
he asks for their orders. Marilyn wants Swiss cheese on
rye; Benjamin wants nothing. *"Spoil*-sport," Billy Sunrise
says to Benjamin as he goes out.

"I'm going to have to depend on him *so* much! You *must* like him!"

Benjamin's surprise at their embrace melts with his memory of himself and Ellen locked naked to each other at the hidden pond.

"He's *that* important?" he says finally.

"Yes."

"I don't like him as much as you do." The words are chosen carefully.

"That doesn't matter. But do like him enough not to —be bothered by him."

"Yes," he says, reaching out, touching her hand. "I'll try." The bottom line is not hurting Marilyn. That's why he won't share with her his present worry about Suzie. Finally, without urgency, he asks her when she's going to tell him what she and Billy Sunrise are making.

"In a few days," she says confidently. "I'll *show* you!"

Annie is striking Benjamin again and again with one of the sofa cushions.

It started playfully when she came into the living room and, as is her way, did something to get his attention: Sometimes she asks him to watch one of her self-made magic tricks, like putting an egg behind her back and making it disappear; at other times she simply plops down on his lap and says something like, "Guess who's the stupidest boy in my class?" This time she gave the newspaper a slap that nearly knocked it from his hands, then went across to the overstuffed chair. When he finished reading the daily UPI American League summary, he looked up, noticed her frowning at him. He plucked off a cushion and tossed it at her, saying, "What's bugging you?" The cushion rolled to her feet. She gave it a kick and it landed on his feet. "Don't ask what you already know," she said. In no mood to indulge her, he replied, "I don't know a thing," and began to read the National League summary, certain that she, being Annie, would sooner or later spill all. Then—*whacko!*—the sofa cushion came over the top of the paper and struck him on the head. He looked up to see her holding on to it.

Still holding it, she now starts swinging it from right to left, hitting him each time.

"Sit down!" he says. "That hurts."

But she keeps hitting, her eyes raging, upper lip tucked under lower. "What do *you* care?" she says.

"About what?"

"What do *you* care?"

He raises his forearms so that the cushion is now striking only those. "Annie. Please!"

Eventually she drops the cushion on the floor and hops back into her chair, where she raises her feet defiantly to the coffee table and starts moving the toes back and forth, like counteracting metronomes. "What if I turned into a creepo-weirdo too?"

"Who's a creepo-weirdo?"

"Who do you think?"

Me, he guesses. Then: *Marilyn.* Then: *Suzie.* Finally: *Bobo.* He doesn't know and says so.

"I could dig a hole in the backyard and climb in it like that stupid dog we once had used to do." (A small mongrel followed Bobo home from school three years ago and was the family pet until it was killed after being struck by a car last year. It had dug deep holes in the lawn and slept in them.) "You guys'd be lying down by my hole all the time asking me what was wrong. Wouldn't you?"

"I don't know." He's shoved the paper aside, is leaning toward her, trying not to smile. He often smiles when Annie becomes angry; there's something about that deep frown, the wonderful expressiveness of it, the vitality of her rages, that amuses him. "Probably not. It'd be so screwy maybe we'd just think, *Poor Annie went crazy and there's nothing we can do about it.*"

"Fun—*nee!*" But it's not, her eyes tell him, not in the least. "God, you're stupid!" she adds.

When Annie lets go like that Marilyn ignores her, waits until she speaks her feelings in what Marilyn calls "a civilized way," then deals with them. Not infrequently Marilyn ends up by reprimanding her for the initial outburst. Marilyn's method has always seemed roundabout to Benjamin. Impatiently he says, "Get to it now. What's got you all worked up?"

"You *know.*"

"I do *not.*"

"You prob'ly think it's Suzie, don't you?"

"I don't think any—"

"That's *just* what you'd think. It's not her. Even though she's getting crazier every day." The feet go more rapidly now: tick-tock, tick-tock.

"Then who?"

"I *told* you you were stupid!" She's rising in her seat, behind an accusing finger. "And you *are*." She falls back, her bright blue eyes seeming to want to eradicate him as they roll from his face to the ceiling, then back. "Mom's turned into a freak. She's prob'ly going to start taking dope or something. I can't even *look* at her anymore. She couldn't make me mad though, even if she tried."

"I'll bet it's—"

"Please shut up! I don't care if you *do* know." She smacks the toes of her sneakers together—*twack, twack* —as if there were a nut between them, or maybe a nose. "And don't make yourself even stupider by saying Bobo. It's not him either. Not that I like him one tiny bit." She holds out thumb and forefinger, an eighth of an inch apart from each other.

"Maybe it's you," he says, smiling.

"I can't *stand* you!" She flies out of the chair, grabs the cushion, begins beating him again, talking as she smacks. "How can you be *so* dumb! How can you!" *Whack, whack!* His arms are up again. "You and your stupid coaching made everything go wrong!" *Whack, whack, whack!* "I'll bet that's why Mom went to Minnesota and turned into a hippie. I bet hundreds of dollars it's why Suzie had to go to a psycho-lologist, and is getting crazier every minute. I *know* that's why Bobo is such an—an ass. And, most of all"—*whack, whack, whack, whack whack!*—"that's why you . . . are . . . so stupid!"

He gets up and wraps both arms around her, pulling her down, holding her firmly beside him.

She gives him a violent helpless look. "Let—me go."

He releases her. "What is wrong?" he says softly.

She stays, curled and exhausted, beside him. "I wanted to play baseball," she says, panting, pointing to herself. "*I* wanted to. I'm old enough for the beginner's league. You got wrapped up in everything else and you didn't know that." She's holding back tears now. "Why didn't you?"

"You didn't tell me."

"You could have asked," she whispers.

"Yes," he realizes, saying it: "I could have."

"You're the dumbest dad in the whole world." With that she rolls off the sofa and hurries out of the room, crying.

"Annie? Do you want to talk?"

"I just did!"

She's on her way up the stairs to her bedroom. He waits, hears the door slam and the lock click. In a few moments her and Suzie's radio will come on, loud. She'll stay for an hour, maybe more this time. No one else is in the house. By the time the others are here, near suppertime, she'll come down. Maybe she'll talk then. Maybe she'll talk about everything except what's been bothering her. Suzie is a slow fuse. Annie is a stick of dynamite: When she goes off, there's often nothing left.

He picks up the scattered parts of the newspaper. He wishes he'd insisted that *both* Suzie and Annie see Keller. He and Marilyn talked about sending both, decided that only Suzie needed help now. *God!* Should he make appointments for all of them? Himself? Marilyn? Bobo? He considers suggesting such to Marilyn.

She playing baseball? He *hadn't* guessed. It's too late now for her to join a team. All right. But he'll begin taking her to the park after the season, with Bobo, to learn the game and practice. Or maybe he won't. It's more than baseball she's been talking about. It's . . . He doesn't know quite what it is. Will there be time to know?

As he puts back the sofa cushion he faintly hears her tapping her foot to a monotonous rock beat: steady and angry.

The prechampionship practice has been going surprisingly well. Most players are taking the bad pitches, measuring and meeting the good ones; even Pat Somerville and Digby Wells have been hitting line drives. Only when the three pitchers—Tag, Meryl, and Tony—concentrate and throw as if they were in a game are the hitters mildly challenged. The infielders are turning into double plays balls that once would have been single outs or, as likely, errors; and the outfielders have at last learned to reach fly balls in time to position themselves for throws.

Baseball, Benjamin knows, is full of stories about teams

that reached peaks of performance too early, then collapsed. Recalling Buck's last game, he's worried that his team, so strong in this practice, will sputter and fall during the championship, still several days away. He's about to call an early stop to the session when he hears his name spoken and turns to see Max Jennings standing beside his bike near the dugout.

"My mom doesn't know I came out here," he says, lowering the bike to the ground. "Maybe I shouldn't have. But my leg is okay. I mean, the doctor says I can play on it now. Is it too late?"

Benjamin hesitates. Max is still officially a team member. "You're not in good shape, are you?"

"My mom's been catching me in the backyard. I asked her not to tell you or anyone until, you know, I was sort of sure I was okay."

Benjamin tries to picture Ellen in the undignified catcher's crouch, can't.

"She said she wouldn't interfere. I didn't want her to anyway. That's why I came by myself."

The other team members have been asking if and when Max would return; there won't be a problem with them if he allows the boy to play.

"If you think it's too late, I can be batboy or something. I don't care what. I'd like to help you."

Benjamin recalls Ellen's remark about Max liking him. He's even allowed himself to imagine becoming Max's stepfather or father-by-adoption. For the moment at least, he's not frightened or put off by the thought. Indeed, Max is the sort of boy Benjamin, when he was Max and Bobo's age, *did* seek out as friend: even-tempered, confident but not pushy, graceful in movement and manner. He thinks he may be betraying Bobo with thoughts such as these, yet he doesn't flee from them. Looking at Max, who's still waiting for his answer, he's struck by some physical similarities to himself: the narrow face, slightly long nose, full shoulders, long legs. Though broad-shouldered, Bobo has none of Benjamin's other features; is, rather, more sturdy throughout.

"Mr. Dunne?"

Such thoughts, he decides, can lead nowhere, or to a mad, cruel, purposeless conclusion: In some mystical way

194

Max is his spiritual son, Bobo only his biological son. He forces his full attention to the playing field.

Lou Pera has been hitting sharp line drives off Tony.

"Mr. Dunne?"

"Go out and pitch to the next batter," Benjamin says. "Let's see how you do."

No one complains when Max goes to the mound. In fact Nick, on third, gives him a friendly greeting and, during Max's warm-up, says good-naturedly, "The way we're blasting the ball you're gonna be the only pitcher who ever got knocked out of the box during batting practice."

No matter what Max does, the rhythms of this too perfect practice will be broken. Benjamin utters a silent thanks to Ellen as he watches Tag step into the batter's box.

After sending a line drive to right field, Tag is held to a few weak grounders. The more Max throws the bigger seems the hopping motion of his fastball. *Like a slippery minnow,* Benjamin thinks. He tells Tag to choke up on the bat; the result is a looping hit, not very impressive.

Max, obviously wanting to prove himself, goes at each batter the same way. To get any sort of hit the player must concentrate, swing evenly, meet the ball just as it snaps to the left or, as often, to the right. Few hit well.

Fielders soon begin to bend and concentrate. Few balls come to them, and those that do are hard to field.

A smooth practice becomes rough and uncertain. Benjamin is grateful.

Nick, who during his turn at bat, got only one solid hit, finally yells to his manager from third base, "How we supposed to win a championship when we can't hit a guy who's been sick on his ass for two months?"

Benjamin gives Nick a shrug he hopes is full of uncertainty. "Don't know," he says.

Nick smacks the pocket in his mitt, waiting for a ground ball he can chew up.

Benjamin hopes other players are asking Nick's question. He guesses they are. Whatever else happens, the championship game, not this practice, must be the season's climax.

Max pitches with easy motions; that heightens the others' frustrations. Between a couple of batters, he looks over to Benjamin, clearly seeking approval. Benjamin gives it in the most concealed and economical way: a flick of the hand.

When the practice ends everyone but Max seems nervous. They go into the dugout and wait for Benjamin to give them final instructions. He picks up some equipment, goes to the dugout entrance, and tells them nothing more than the time of the championship game, asking them to get to the ball park a half hour before it starts.

"What else?" someone says anxiously.

"Nothing else," Benjamin replies as he turns and starts toward the station wagon.

From the car radio, he's been learning there are countless ways to say "I can't live without you." It's the most constant theme in the popular, country, and rock songs he's been hearing.

If he's been a snob about anything, it's music. The radio has FM, and until recently, it's been tuned to either the classical music station in Toledo or the one in Ann Arbor. Now, often with head tilted toward the speaker on the dashboard, he attends to the words in the music he'd once have called trash. All of the songs bespeak the desperations of love: *his* desperations, he's sure.

He waits until Dan and the clerks have left the bookstore, then dials Ellen's number.

Since their day at the hidden pond they've seen each other twice, each briefly. Once they met at a coffee shop off the highway several miles from Centerville. Once, late at night, he stopped at her house after doing some last-minute shopping for Marilyn at the supermarket. Though each time Max was asleep, Benjamin was cautious. During the last visit, he nervously glanced at her living room clock and said abruptly, "I must go," right in the middle of a conversation.

Now, on the phone, she says something so pointed and unadorned that he's sure it's a distillation of the sentiments of many songs. "I want you to come here and be with me."

"I will," he says. "When I can find a little time."

"I mean now."

He's looking at the mouthpiece. An appropriate response might pass from his mouth through the mouthpiece: *Yes. I'll cancel everything.* Instead he says, "Is there some sort of problem?"

"No. I just want you with me. These stolen minutes just aren't enough, Benjamin."

Hasn't he felt as she does? Does he need a map with arrows all over it?

"Benjamin?"

Marilyn is at home, will or will not have dinner prepared, but will be waiting: a habit of years.

"Can you?"

Suzie has again seen Keller, whose second report has surely come.

"Benjamin?"

Reasons stir other reasons. Bobo has been talking lately, especially around dinnertime; Benjamin feels like talking to him today. And there's Annie; he wants to spend time with her.

"Benjamin?" His name is like a refrain out of a lover's song.

He has only reasons not to go; when he finally speaks, however, he says, "I'll be there in a little while." His words, he realizes, are the title and opening words of a popular song he heard on the car radio only yesterday.

SEVEN

Benjamin points to a stack of long, shallow cardboard boxes at the end of the dugout bench, says, "We have a few minutes. Make your own decisions about them," then leaves the dugout with his team's lineup card in hand.

He reads for the first time the words printed on a large sign hanging at the middle of the center field fence:

CENTERVILLE
SENIOR LEVEL PEE WEE LEAGUE CHAMPIONSHIP
GRAY'S CLEANERS
VS.
WATSON AND WILLS REAL ESTATE
DATE: AUG. 2   TIME: 7 P.M.

The sign isn't the only reminder of a big event. Temporary stands have been erected outside the low fences along the left and right field lines. The permanent stands are packed to the edges, and the temporary stands are filling rapidly. Kids are lined up at a concessionaire's truck, parked beside the public announcer's booth. There are no remaining spaces in the parking lot, and the street adjoining the ball park is a compression of cars.

As "The Star-Spangled Banner" comes scratchily out of the loudspeaker, Benjamin, standing a few yards from home plate, shifts his weight from one foot to the other and watches the W. and W. dandies whispering to each other on the opposite side of the plate, holding their green caps high on stomach or low on chest. They remind Benjamin of mischievous choirboys.

The umpires for this game were drawn at random by Dick Francis a couple of days ago. Benjamin learned only during warm-up that Daryl is to be one of them. From a few feet behind the dandies, Daryl has now caught Benjamin's eye and is challenging it with a stare. Benjamin turns quickly away.

Gray left a phone message with Marilyn this morning, telling her that manager and team should arrive at the ball park even before the time of its pregame practice. ("He said he had the uniforms.") With the help of Bobo, Benjamin was able to contact all of his players. When he and the players arrived, Gray was waiting in the dugout with the boxes, each with a first and last name scribbled on the side. Some players sat, some stood, and all looked indifferently at Gray. They listened to him say flatly, pointing to the boxes, "You all got time to go over in the toilets and change." No one spoke or moved. Gray squinted toward Benjamin, standing near the dugout entrance. "You gonna tell 'em to put 'em on?" Benjamin didn't answer at first, then said, "I'll take care of it." Gray waited for more, but Benjamin said only, "Thanks for your efforts," then led the players to the field for infield and batting practice. When he and the players returned, just minutes ago, he pointed to the uniforms and told them to make their own decisions.

Daryl is now offering Benjamin a surly look that somehow invites a response.

Benjamin glares right through it.

"Who's that new boy throwing pitches over by your dugout?" the head umpire asks.

"Max Jennings. He's been hurt but he's well enough to play now. Still on our roster. I'll be using him at pitcher, to start."

The umpire takes Benjamin's lineup card, looks. "But you've listed Meryl Bagthorn."

"I forgot to change the card." He takes the lineup card, removes a stub of pencil from his pocket, makes the change, reminding himself to explain to Meryl.

The head umpire is R. D. Falcone. He's umpired only one of Gray's games. There were no problems. He points out that W. and W. will be the home team since it was the last team to play in a championship game. He warns both managers that, because of the large crowd, children might wander onto the field. "Don't be surprised if I call time out without warning."

Benjamin wonders if any of his players have gone to put on the uniforms. He hasn't turned around since he left the dugout.

Earlier Karl yanked today's copy of the Centerville *Tribune* from his coat pocket and showed Benjamin a quarter page ad:

GRAY'S CLEANERS
SPONSOR
OF
GRAY'S PEE WEE BASEBALL TEAM

———

FAST & RELIABLE SERVICE

"Don't that take about all the gall a man can have?" he asked. "He ain't done a thing for us 'til now. Comes the big ball game and a chance for a lot of free advertisin' an' he buys an ad an' brings the danged uniforms."

"In character," Benjamin said.

"Gon' make 'em put 'em on?"

"No."

"Gon' tell 'em not to, huh?"

"No."

"What you gon' tell 'em to do?"

"Just what they want."

"Dang!"

Karl chose not to be in the dugout when Gray presented the uniforms.

Benjamin sees, out of the corner of his eye, the entrance to the boys' rest room, between the third base stands and the announcer's booth. He doesn't notice any of his players going in or out. As Norm, the chief W. and W. coach, starts complaining about a ground rule, which the head umpire has just described, Benjamin turns around to check the dugout.

The players are all at the entrance, crowded up into it,

like puppies in a pet shop window. None of them has on a uniform. They are, in fact, more ragged than ever. Many of the pants and shirts bear rips and stains only recently acquired. Even Karl, now lumbering across the diamond to the first base coaching box, has on his one and apparently only pair of overalls; it's splattered with newly acquired grease and food spots. Only Benjamin has made a compromise, a small one: He's exchanged his T-shirt for a short-sleeved plain white sports shirt. The shirt, however, is unpressed and one of the buttons is missing.

"I say let's not hold back," Norm is telling Benjamin. "If one team gets way ahead, let's just keep it alive and go for all the runs we can get. That's how we ought to do it in the championship games." He's sticking his hand out, to shake Benjamin's hand. "No hard feelings later. Okay?"

"We're going after your balls," Benjamin says, not offering his hand.

"Pardon me?" Norm replies in honest confusion.

"I want to acquire your testicles for my trophy room."

Benjamin did not plan to say what he's just said. He himself shares some of the surprise he sees in the eyes of the opposing coaches and the two umpires.

"Oh, yeah?" It's Doug, the W. and W. assistant.

"Definitely," says Benjamin, who has no inclination to take back anything.

"We'll see who *has* balls to begin with," Doug replies.

"We'd better get started," says the head umpire uneasily, bending down between the opposing managers to dust off home plate.

Returning to the dugout, Benjamin hears from the stands his sponsor's hostile voice: "They ain't changin'. Why ain't they changin'?"

He ignores it.

Finally Gray shouts, "Hey! Dunne!"

Benjamin stops, turns, sees Gray in the front row, hands on knees with fingers closed, the usual reddish hue of his face deepening toward crimson. The manager leans over the low fence, until he's face to face with his sponsor, and says, "It's too late." He whispers it, is heavy on each syllable.

"We'll see about that." Gray gets up now, kicks some

dust through the fence toward Benjamin, and moves toward the announcer's booth.

"Play ball!"

"He lied to me about the specialist, Benjamin," says Ellen, biting off every word. "I don't know what to do about it. I don't know his game."

Max has come out of his bedroom a couple of times and seen Benjamin in the living room with his mother. Has Ellen warned him not to mention Benjamin's visits? To Bobo? To anyone? The sight of Max, of Max seeing him, alerts him to the old need, now desire, to go home and confess to Marilyn all he can possibly confess.

"Do you have time to help me figure it out?" she asks.

"Yes," he says, forcing his attention back to her. "I had a lot of work at the bookstore, so I'm expected home late, but I've got to—should be home, well, fairly soon."

"You seem preoccupied."

"So do you."

"I am. Damn, he's up to something. I can usually read his hand. I can't now." She's speaking low. "Why did he lie about the specialist?" She's explained that she herself, hearing nothing final, called the doctor Max had seen. "There's nothing wrong, Benjamin. Nothing! He wants Max to play baseball. That's why I let him go to the practice. Don, in lying, has kept Max out most of the season!"

Her question is like that of someone pointing out a train window to a stranger and asking, "Why does that man wear high brown Oxfords?" Benjamin doesn't know, has no advice.

Ellen fumbles with a cigarette, lights it with a match before he can reach the lighter on the coffee table. He hasn't seen her smoking until now. She's doing it like someone who never smokes: the cigarette pinched between thumb and forefinger; an inhale that's too big, causing her to cough; scraping the ash off on the ashtray, rather than flicking it.

"When Max was staying there, Don talked to him about his going ahead with a divorce. That's really no surprise. It's dead between us. But I do want to know what the penalties are going to be. That lying about Max's leg is a bad sign. Christ, Benjamin!" She obliterates the remaining part of the cigarette, about three-fourths, in the ashtray.

"*Everything to him is a possession. He won't, if he can get away with it, leave me this house. He certainly doesn't want to leave Max to me. I mean, Benjamin, it would give him great pleasure to leave me with an empty sack and a tin cup.*"

"*Then,*" says Benjamin, "*you do know his game.*"

"*Meaning?*"

Benjamin's been here for at least a half hour, and neither of them has sat down. He now goes to the brown leather chair opposite the sofa, lowers himself to the edge of the seat. She stays up, pacing, five or six steps at a time. She's been turning, stopping in mid-move with a thought, going on. Now she listens.

"*If you're right about his—greedy motives, then you can figure the lie about Max grows out of those. Why would he say the specialist had told him the leg was bad when it wasn't?*"

"*It's possible,*" she says. "*He may have used the doctor as an excuse to keep Max in Toledo, away from me, close to him and to the woman he may or may not be thinking of marrying. She works for him. Max said he saw her several times. How smooth, how insidious, how—how damned ruthless he is!*"

"*What matters is what all that comes to.*" His statement strikes him as obvious, empty. He clarifies it: "*What do you do next?*"

"*I think I've got to find a lawyer dirtier than he, that's what. And I mustn't waste time about it. Oh, Benjamin . . .*" She advances to him, bending down, taking his face in her hands. "*I hate women who say what I'm going to say, but I'm still going to say it. Not, 'I want you with me.' I do. You know that. But for a while I'm—I'm going to have to lean on you. There's no one else for that, as there isn't for the wanting. I wish you didn't have to go home so soon tonight.*"

Max a few moments ago passed through the foyer on his way to the kitchen. He must have heard her words. Benjamin wants to warn her to be careful with Max here. Is she taking too much for granted? Worried that Max will soon be going back to his room and see them close, he raises his hands and slides hers from his face.

She backs off, stiffening, her mouth sagging a bit, as if she's sure his gesture was a reply to her appeal.

204

"Max," he says, assuring her. "That's all."

She turns about, seeming to be aware only now that Max is nearby, listening, possibly seeing. "Max?" she says.

In the kitchen the refrigerator door closes. Max comes into the foyer, stands at the two steps leading down to the living room. Wearing pajama bottoms and a blue T-shirt, he holds a fat sandwich, its lettuce hanging loosely out at the sides. "What you want?" He doesn't seem at all disturbed by Benjamin's presence.

Ellen turns from him, seeming to realize she didn't want anything more than to know just where in the house he was. "Uh—it's—it's way past your bedtime."

He shrugs. "I'm not going anyplace tomorrow." He gives Benjamin a smile, takes a large bite of the sandwich. It's as though he's waiting to be invited to join the conversation.

"Go to bed," she says pleasantly. "Mr. Dunne and I have—have to talk about some things."

He gives Benjamin another look, disappointed this time. What could they want to talk about that he can't share? After getting no encouragement from his mother and Benjamin, he turns and goes toward his bedroom.

Better, Benjamin thinks, if she'd let him go in his own time. Calling the boy was a trumpet blast. Now Max is sure to wonder about him and Ellen. He remembers the feeling he had about Max being his real son. Now he's cheated his son. But Max isn't his son, he reminds himself. He thinks of Bobo at home, possibly awake, willing, maybe wanting to converse. It's Bobo, the other son, his actual true son, he's cheating. Confused, irritated, more nervous than he was, he glances at the front door, wanting to escape.

She notices his uneasiness, says, "Have I been asking too much?"

He doesn't say: "I want to catch your needs." He has those words, can't get them out. He is willing, but it's a qualified willingness. How can he put it? Finally he says, "There are others to think of, and I must have time." Yes, he must see Marilyn through her recent change to—to something. And the children. One doesn't just stop appearing at home, for hours. Yet it's not, finally, the children. There are ways he could tell the children about her. It's he himself. He needs motive. Why can't he to-

night feel "burned out" about Marilyn, "swept up" by El-
len, caught in irrevocable movements?

He rarely remembers to wear his watch. "What time is
it?" he asks her.

"Ten twenty," she tells him.

Minutes have passed like seconds. "I must go. Marilyn
will wonder . . ." He backs away from her. "What you're
saying is important to me. But, under the circumstances"
—he looks toward the kitchen—"it will just have to wait.
Can it wait?"

Her eyes are lost in the shadow of something. He steps
closer, trying to read her look. When his eyes reach hers,
frightened, at the mercy of his it seems, he says, "Nothing
has changed. Understand that."

"Are you sure?"

He isn't. Something may have changed, here tonight, in
the recognition of just how much she needs him. He must
have time to think. He may have to find a way of talking
to Marilyn about her. Love's responsibilities are limitless,
he thinks. He holds her gently to him, kisses her softly,
feeling in her pliant response the surrenders already
made.

The big pitcher brought in at the end of the earlier game
with W. and W. is Bill Esterbrook, but his teammates,
now giving him encouragement from outfield, infield, and
dugout, use the name "Moose." For both speed and control he's the best pitcher Benjamin has seen in this league.
A machine, he thinks after watching Moose take his last
warmup throws.

The first pitch of the game, a rising fastball, sails in under Harold Foxx's jaw, nearly clipping it. Harold comes
out of the batter's box shaking.

During warm-ups Moose didn't throw anything but
strikes. Benjamin is suddenly suspicious; this first pitch
may have been a deliberate brushback. He sees the
pitcher look into the W. and W. dugout and nod.
He thinks he sees Norm nod back.

The next pitch is a curve. Harold backs away, but the
ball comes in for a strike.

"Stay in there!" Benjamin calls from his coaching box.

The next pitch is inside, way off the plate, and it sends
Harold to the dirt.

Benjamin is no longer doubtful.

On the next pitch Harold is ducking out of the batter's box even before Moose has released his pitch, another curve, a called strike.

"He's throwing at our players!" Benjamin calls to Falcone.

The head umpire's mask stays forward and fixed. Benjamin guesses Falcone doesn't think the inside throws are deliberate; otherwise he'd stop the game and warn Moose.

The final pitch to Harold cuts the inside corner for a called third strike.

Benjamin turns to his dugout. He's resolved to keep them informed of all he sees and to take advantage of any useful observations they might make. "He's trying to set up the batters with a brushback," he tells them.

"What're we s'posed to do?" says Speck.

"Wait for a pitch you can hit."

"We ought to threaten him or somethin'," says Nick.

"If the umpire doesn't catch on, I'm going to ask for time out and raise hell. Meantime you can do your threatening by getting hits."

"Why don't you tell Max to throw at *their* batters?"

The suggestion appeals. Max has enough control to do it. But today Benjamin feels himself tempted toward a limit of violence. While he doesn't know what the limit is, he fears what might happen if he allows himself beyond it. "I'll think about that," he says, turning toward home plate.

Tony leans away from a close-in strike, then pops out to the first baseman.

Benjamin senses the rippling effect of the brushback pitches: They upset not only the batter to whom thrown but the ones who bat after him. Indeed, the whole team may now spend the game waiting for the brushback. Extraordinary measures must be taken.

Bobo's up next.

Benjamin calls him from the batting circle to the coaching box, says, "We've got to do something to stop that pitch. Got any ideas?"

"Give them something as bad to deal with," says Bobo.

"What do you mean by that?"

Bobo points out that, during W. and W.'s fielding practice, the first baseman consistently caught throws with his foot at the center of the bag, instead of at the edge, where it should have been. "I can spike him if I get to first. Want me to?"

It's a brutal proposition; Benjamin is tempted.

"I'll cut him lightly, just to let them know *we* know they're throwing at us."

"No," says Benjamin finally, his reason now clear to him. It's not a matter of fair play but something more pertinent: Giving Bobo or any of the others such license might turn their attention from winning to retaliating.

"How about it?"

They'd be caught up in another kind of contest, vengeful and personal. The moment may come when he, they, will have to play dirty; but it's not here yet. "Forget it. Concentrate on trying to meet the pitch."

Disappointed, Bobo goes to the plate.

Moose throws an inside pitch for a ball, but it's not a brushback. The next pitch comes over the center of the plate, low, and Bobo, choking up, laces a drive to the pitcher's mound. It hits Moose's right foot and ricochets to second base. The second baseman gets it and throws to first for the out.

Moose limps slightly on his way to the dugout.

"Did you hit that thing at him deliberately?" Benjamin asks as Bobo, back in Gray's dugout, starts putting on his catcher's equipment.

"I didn't aim for his foot, if that's what you mean."

"But you did aim—for him?"

"Sort of. Anyway, maybe you're not going to have to worry about that brushback now."

Benjamin ignores an impulse to give Bobo a warning lecture.

The Gray's players move onto the field aggressively, whooping and yapping as they haven't in recent games. Benjamin's earlier announcement that Max will start has caused no grumbling. Meryl will later get his chance. So will Tony and Tag. Unless Max becomes indispensable.

"I won't have it!" he hears Gray shout from the announcer's booth. "Get them off the field until they put on my uniforms!"

"Time out!" calls the head umpire.

Benjamin, after reading Keller's second report on Suzie,

has made an appointment to see the psychologist. The report has made Marilyn curious too; she'll also speak to Marvin. "But not now. I've got a batch of materials coming in, so I'll talk to him when I take Suzie to her next appointment."

Marilyn's response ignited him; he had to leave the house to keep from her his volatile response. But as he meandered through the neighborhood, he gave it to her, silently: Is that damned cloth of yours more important than Suzie? Maybe you can wrap yourself in it so as not to see or hear her needs! Maybe you're already wrapping yourself in it, not because you need an outlet but because you don't want to pay attention to real things. It's an expensive mistake, Marilyn, at Suzie's expense. Passing through alleys that border backyards, seeking darkness, seeing no one, he ended with mutterings only to himself: Worthless project! Screwball assistant! Self-indulgent bullshit! He couldn't remember being this angry at her. Finding sidewalks and well-lit streets, he started home. Only then did he recognize that, for each accusation he'd issued to Marilyn, he could find a corresponding one for himself: for her "project," his baseball; for her Billy Sunrise, his Ellen; for her partial neglect of the house, his partial neglect of the bookstore. At least, he assured himself before reaching the front steps, I'm going out of my way to see Keller.

He has Keller's report with him in the psychologist's waiting room; he now reads the final paragraph:

There remain certain topics which cause Suzie to feel ill at ease, at times a bit panicky. I'm not referring to the "flying saucer" incident, which is less troublesome than other matters. For example, she perceives changes in your family life. Her impressions here aren't very clear, perhaps because the changes aren't clearly defined. Whatever the case, I want to recommend that you continue to send her to me for an indefinite period.

Entering the office, Benjamin finds a balding, stocky man whose rumpled sport coat hangs awkwardly from his shoulders. Keller rises briefly, gives Benjamin a quick

209

handshake, then plops back into his chair. Unsmiling, he watches Benjamin sit down, studies him.

After some small talk Benjamin says he thinks Suzie is right about the changes. He describes Marilyn's project, the little he knows of it, speaks briefly of his activities with the baseball team. For some reason, perhaps Keller's abrupt but interested nods, he wants to mention Ellen. The wish surprises him. He ignores it, ends with the observation that he and Marilyn have helped bring about the changes.

"Life itself is change," Keller says. "The point isn't to stop it but to deal with it."

"Pardon?"

"We get used to it, or learn how to."

Keller's reaction has been too quick, too general. Benjamin doesn't know how to respond to it, except to agree, more or less, by nodding. He wonders how Suzie manages to communicate with this man.

"You look uncomfortable, as though you've got something else on your mind."

"No," he lies. "Not really."

Keller and Marilyn are old classmates, old friends. Nothing Benjamin says here need be treated confidentially. He isn't, after all, Keller's patient, though he now feels as though he is. In truth, he'd like to talk about Ellen, to someone. Not Keller. Finally he says, "Suzie isn't the only one affected by the changes," and finds himself recounting Annie's action with the pillows.

When he's finished Keller says, "It seems she got her message across."

Message? Again Keller's response isn't clear. "I certainly regretted not getting her involved in baseball this season, if that's what you mean."

"That's not what I mean," Keller says firmly. "There was nothing you could do about this year. Did you talk to her about playing ball next year or playing some other sport in between?"

Benjamin says he isn't sure whether he did or didn't.

"That's important. She ought to have something to look forward to."

Benjamin finds himself nodding again. And again there's the impulse to mention Ellen.

210

Keller's eyes are marksman's eyes and Benjamin's nose the bull's-eye.

"I guess you see a lot of concerned parents," Benjamin says evasively.

"You're worried," Keller says.

"What?"

"How many of your kids' problems do you think you've caused?"

"Caused? Well, as I said, I've helped bring about some. In fact, I know—"

"That's your opinion. It might be none. I certainly don't know of any. It's something you can make yourself sick worrying about. So why worry?"

"I don't worry all that much," Benjamin replies quickly. "But with kids, the things you do—can—can sometimes cause them to, well, be uncomfortable."

"Not the same." *Keller's forefinger springs toward Benjamin.* "Live your own life, not theirs. Suzie has some problems that need attention. Annie might too. Neither seems to be in a crisis. I want you and Marilyn to pay attention to them, sympathize, but don't screw them up by adding your anxieties to theirs. Understand?"

Has Keller somehow read his mind, figured out that there's another woman?

"Guilt can be a killer."

Benjamin's mind is now leaping, confused. A Keller, he hears.

"So relax. Don't deny yourself the joys of your own life."

Has Benjamin traveled twenty miles just to hear such platitudes? What about specific solutions? Oddly, he didn't expect or want those. He did want something. Useful guidelines maybe. He's not sure what he's gotten.

"It's probably a good idea that I see Annie after I talk to Suzie once more. I'm not going to be able to change what they perceive. I can't. I can help get them used to it, if that's necessary. If either of them seems in very bad shape, I'll be in touch with you and Marilyn."

On the way home Benjamin is sure he could eventually have reached some of the conclusions Keller has reached. He would have considered them—Live your own life—selfish, perhaps even dangerous, however,

211

and ignored them. He can't be as cavalier about himself or his children as Keller seems to be.

Destinies, *he thinks as he nears Centerville.* The trouble with working out one's own, *he decides,* is that you don't really know what it is until you reach it.

Walking directly into the sunlight, he sees only the profiled silhouette of the home plate umpire, head raised to the glassless window of the announcer's booth.

"Order them to do it!"

He squints up, notices the shadowy figures of Gray and Francis framed in the wide rectangular opening at the front of the booth.

"Stop the game until they change!" Gray commands.

"Just a moment." It's Francis, raising one hand to Gray. With the other hand he signals Benjamin to come forward. He leans down, says, "Mr. Gray feels that his sponsorship of your team entitles him to insist that you wear the uniforms. I think he has a good point. After all . . ."

Benjamin takes advantage of the pause: "Have you seen us in uniforms so far this season?"

"No. No, I haven't, but . . ."

"That's because we haven't had them."

"I didn't have them to give you!" Gray interjects, hammering his fist on the scoring table. The sponsor's face must be rising to purple, but Benjamin can't be sure. With the sunlight against the manager's eyes, Gray's color is that of his name.

"We reached this game without the uniforms," Benjamin argues, aware now of the attentive silence of the fans on both sides. Is he turning a baseball game into a debate? It doesn't matter. "It seems only right that we get through it without them." He adds a notion he can't defend: "Maybe we wouldn't have made it this far if we'd had them."

"Bull!" says Gray.

"We're *his* team in name only," Benjamin says evenly.

There's a chorus of agreement from behind him. "Damn right," he hears Nick say. His players have closed in on home plate.

Encouraged, he stretches his hand out behind him. "Look at them. That's the way they are. That's the team.

If they wanted to be or look like something else, they—well, they'd have put on the uniforms."

"You ain't gettin' away with it, Dunne," Gray mutters. "Just ain't."

"Where was you when we *wanted* them fancy duds?" Karl calls up from behind Benjamin.

Gray doesn't give him an answer.

Francis has backed away from the opening, is turned around talking to someone, maybe more than one, possibly the other commissioners.

Fans on both sides begin to grumble. "Let's get this show on the road!" someone yells.

Benjamin turns, tells the players to go back to their positions.

"We gonna have to change?" Tag asks before they part.

"Not if I can help it," Benjamin tells him.

Francis has wasted little time conferring. Leaning down to Benjamin, he says, "There's no hard fast rule, Mr. Dunne, but we feel that, this being the championship game and you having the uniforms at your disposal, your team should wear them. Otherwise you might have to forfeit."

"What the hell you think uniforms are for anyway?" Gray adds.

Benjamin hesitates, then calls his team to the mound, including the substitutes in the dugout. He's sensed that carrying on an argument with Gray and Francis will do more harm to the team than wearing the uniforms. He's worried about a forfeit, yet can't bring himself to order the players to put on the uniforms. He summarizes the problem, trying not to editorialize, and ends by saying, "I think you ought to vote on it, right here and now. If you vote no, we might give W. and W. the game, but you might have the satisfaction of standing up for something important to you. If yes, we definitely play, maybe lose."

"What d'*you* think?" says Tag.

"I'm not going to tell you," Benjamin replies. "Not now, at least." He looks to Karl, hoping for some sign that his response to Tag's question is a good one.

Karl, a few feet from the mound, listening with arms folded, looks from Benjamin to Tag, giving no more guidance to Benjamin than he's giving to the team.

213

"Gray's an asshole," Nick says.

Bobo repeats what Karl earlier noted: Gray hasn't done any more for the team than give the name of his business to it.

Fred says, "I'd like to play ball. It's why I came out here."

"Me too," says Speck.

"But we're gonna have to eat Gray's shit to do it," Bobo adds, causing others to make disgusted faces.

"Look at it this way." It's Tony, for the first time speaking in his coaches' presence in more or less standard English. Benjamin notices Karl's head tilt back in surprise. Tony flicks his thumb toward the announcer's booth. "We take a bigger loss than he does if we don't put 'em on: We won't get to play and this is a game we all want. He just takes back his stinkin' uniforms and gives 'em to his team next year. No skin off him. So I say, 'Let's play.' But let's also think of how to get back at the bastard."

"We could hit a foul ball at his head like Tim Adams did that one time," says Speck.

"Or something," says Tony. "But meantime let's beat those dogs." He points to the W. and W. dugout, where managers and players have been smiling, making a few catcalls, enjoying the fix Gray's has found itself in.

"Let's vote," says Bobo.

"All right," says Benjamin. "A hand up if we play. Not up if we don't."

"If you lose on the vote, you got to go along with the others," Karl points out.

"That's right," says Benjamin, grateful that Karl has thought of unanimity. "Though there's not much anyone can do if you refuse. So how many want to—no, are willing to put on the uniforms and play?"

All hands go up except Nick's and Bobo's.

"You willing to stay and play?" he asks the two no voters.

"I'll play," says Nick, seeming almost pleased that the others have voted him down.

"I really want to play," Bobo replies. "I just don't want to give in to a goddamned dictator."

Not long ago Bobo's words might have served as a motto for his relationship with his father. In a queer way

Benjamin appreciates Gray. He hopes Bobo won't always need someone to react against.

"We'll get him, one way or another," says Tony with a roll of his eyes that causes Benjamin to believe he's already got something in mind. He turns to Benjamin. "So whee haff make thee de-cees-yon," another part of him reminds Benjamin.

Benjamin, irritated and curious, can't resist asking Tony, "What's the point of talking like that now, when Karl and I know it's faked?"

"Eet help me be loose, Meester Don. Hue know?"

He doesn't. Masks, disguises, role playing, and other poses have always seemed to Benjamin a puzzling escape from self. "No, I don't," he replies finally, "but I guess I have to believe you."

Benjamin goes to the stands, reports the team's decision.

Francis tells him the game will be postponed for five minutes, until the team puts on its uniforms.

Gray, sneering down, rubs his hands tightly together, as if ridding them of a stain.

It's late, nearly ten thirty, and she's not home. The girls, Bobo tells him, are next door at the neighbors'. "She was leaving when I came in around dinnertime," Bobo says. "She didn't say where she was going. I made myself a sandwich."

He calls the Andersons, asks them to send the girls home.

He's testy with Bobo, wondering if he hasn't something better to do than watch police programs with all the street shooting and car crashes.

"It's about a lot of real-life things," Bobo protests.

"But it's not," Benjamin replies, unable just now to say why. "Go to bed. It's late."

Not long ago Bobo would have given him the panther reaction, a low growl, a hiss or such, ending with the charge that he, Benjamin, didn't know anything about anything. Now, calmly, he asks if he can watch the program to its end, in twenty minutes or so.

"That's fine," Benjamin tells him.

He talks to the girls after they've had snacks and gotten themselves ready for bed. Suzie, though no less with-

drawn, has seemed calmer lately. Her eyes begin a nervous side-to-side search only after Benjamin asks if their mother happened to say where she was going. "No," Annie tells him, "but she said she might be late." He suggests she's at her shop, working. "Why don't you phone her?" Suzie asks. Benjamin tells her truthfully that the shop's phone hasn't yet been installed. "Quit being so jumpy," Annie says to her sister. Benjamin, after making sure there are no further signs of uneasiness, sees them to bed, then searches the house for a note or some other clue as to where Marilyn might be. There is none.

He conjures worries: Somehow she guessed that he was with Ellen, went to Ellen's house, saw his car, maybe even looked through a window and witnessed an embrace or intimate talk, and is now alone somewhere, weeping, distraught.

Bobo is soon in his own room; the girls are so far quiet in their beds.

The windows have been open against the heat. Now there's a warm breeze flowing through the rooms. It makes the house sound hollow, abandoned.

He turns on the television, searches for a movie, light, contemporary, fast-paced. He finds only noise and flashing movements: cars speeding, a frantic girl running down a San Francisco hill, a drain-opening liquid sucking the clog from a pipe. He stops at the educational channel, sees a figure in an old movie, standing alone, not moving. Benjamin focuses the channel, sees that the figure is that of Stanley Laurel. He's smiling his goofy unaware smile until a large sack flies at him from the side, knocks him down, then breaks open, spattering flour all over him. Oliver Hardy now appears, looking down, shaking his head, giving Stanley, then the camera, a wide-eyed disgusted look. Another sack falls from above and lands directly on Oliver's head, splashing open. Oliver vanishes from the camera's eye. When next seen he's on his back on the floor, open-legged, his clothes and face covered with flour. In his whiteness Oliver finds his tie, raises it, shaking off some of the flour, then begins helplessly to twist it. His eyes, like raisins in snow, find the camera, the audience, and he pleads his helplessness to them. Not until other sacks of flour begin to come, from above and the sides, knocking each of the characters down as soon as one or another tries to stand up, does Benjamin rise and turn off the television.

Now he hears sounds from outside: distant car horns, someone shouting a good-bye down the street or on the next block, the faint rustling of wind among the leaves outside the window. All these somehow combine to urge sleep upon him. He'd go upstairs to bed, wants to, but he knows he won't sleep until she returns.

He's managed to shed his fear that she's learned about Ellen. Indeed, she's shown almost no interest, certainly no alarm. If she's heard about one or another of his private visits to Ellen, say from Bobo through Max, she'd surely have questioned him about it, not gone out in the car on a hysterical spying mission, or worse.

He thinks he hears humming. The living room drapes are closed over both the big front window and the two adjoining side windows; only the side windows and the one at the back of the living room, beyond the television set, are open. The sounds seem to be coming from the front. Now he hears, is sure he hears, words being sung:

"Where arrrrr you?"

He hurries to the front door.

"Where arrrrr you?"

He opens the door just a crack. Something flits past on the lawn, a speck of something, green, pale green against the dark green grass of the lawn. He opens the door a bit more. Light from the two street-lamps on the left and right forms a kind of triangular stage between the evergreen trees at each side of the front yard. Another object, this one pink, darts out of, then back into, the shadow of the evergreen on the left. Just as his eyes adjust to the darkness around the trees the green object reappears, leaping, leaping and dancing across the triangle of light, its arms flapping in loose butterfly motions. It turns, spinning, twisting, its legs going up, twisting around its body, down and across. The face, caught full in the light as it turns, sends Benjamin back into the hallway, startled: There's a great leering mouth, froglike, and enormous staring animal eyes. But there's flatness where the nose and ears would be. The lack of nose and ears emphasize the size of the mouth and eyes. The green covering clings to all else: the skull, arms, legs, torso, and lower body.

"Ben-ju-minn?"

His name has not been spoken out of the mouth of the dancing green creature. It must be the other. One other? His eyes are drawn toward the sound. The pink figure appears from behind the tree, prancing toward the first figure. The body, like that of its companion, seems elastic as it shapes itself to the movements of the dance. But the face is different, the mouth more catlike than froglike, the eyes extremely slanted with very long lashes, only slightly open, little more than slits.

The figures dance together, bending and bowing toward each other and then, as if on some secret signal, gliding toward Benjamin. Together they come to rest near the bottom of the steps, the green one with legs and arms spread wide apart and the pink one in a kind of curtsy, arms extended forward, together, toward Benjamin:

"Do you like them?" says a voice from inside the rising pink head. Though muffled, the voice is unmistakably Marilyn's. Her hands rise, reaching to undo something at the back of the head.

Benjamin is too perplexed to speak.

The hands finally peel away the head mask and her hair bursts from its constraint. Her eyes laugh up at him as she twists her face this way and that, as if to restore its shape.

She's gone hopelessly mad, he thinks.

The other dancer has now peeled off the head mask and is saying, loudly enough for anyone still awake in the neighborhood to hear, "Gahhhddd! I felt like another beee-ing!"

Benjamin has moved onto the little landing outside the front door and is eyeing them cautiously.

"Body disguises," Marilyn says brightly. "A person doesn't have to be himself all the time. Isn't it—something?"

Benjamin is trying to nod.

"Think of what they can do for a party!" Billy Sunrise says. "You ought to try one on, Benjamin. You really ought to!" He has begun to unzip the back of the body part of Marilyn's disguise. "Think of all the creatures you can be! We've thought of at least fifty. We're going to make several for every kind of thing!" He's peeling off Marilyn's disguise now. "She's a true genius, Benjamin!"

he says, grinning up. "No one else could have thought of a thing like this."

"Body disguises," Benjamin repeats.

"I swear," Billy Sunrise goes on, "people will be wearing them around the house doing chores. You can't imagine how different they make you feel. Oh, please"—his arms are upraised to Benjamin's—"do try one on so you can feel like we did!"

"No. No—thanks," says Benjamin after he backs up a bit, studying Marilyn as, in her shorts and halter now, she ruffles her hair as she often does before combing it. "Are these the things you're going to sell . . . in that store?"

"Yes, oh yes," she says. "Don't you see?"

See what? he thinks.

"Each costume will cost a hundred and fifty dollars," says Billy Sunrise. "We'll be able to make two or three of them a week, until we can hire people. Then we'll design, and they'll sew and paint. We'll be able to make a lot more. Ohhhh . . . we'll be sooooo rich!" He's clapping his hands now and hopping in place, an oversized frog.

"Benjamin," she says, her tone full of wish, "what do you think?" Before he can answer—"It's crazy, impractical, won't make a cent!"—she continues: "Please approve of it. Please! I was so miserable before. It wasn't you or the children. It was me. I have to live with me. No. I have to not live with me. Don't you see?"

He is, he thinks, only beginning to. But he is nodding against the disgust he feels. He can't shake the feeling that approving of this will be like giving support to an alcoholic wanting to start a lifelong binge.

She's come up to the landing, is holding him tightly, gratefully, maybe desperately.

He wraps his arms around her and brings her closer to him. He's surprised by a tightness he feels in his throat, the wetness at the edges of his eyes.

"We can go back and begin another tonight!" Billy Sunrise says enthusiastically. "There is time, isn't there, Mari?"

"Not tonight, Billy," she tells him without raising her face from Benjamin's chest. "Go back to the motel. We'll start in the morning. Early."

Billy Sunrise has gotten himself out of his body disguise. He now picks it up, says, "In the morning. I can't

219

wait," and waves the empty costume at Benjamin before turning and hurrying toward a little MG, several years old, that's parked across the street.

Benjamin goes down the stairs, picks up Marilyn's body disguise, and leads her into the house.

"You don't know how it consumes me!" she says. "It's so maddeningly wonderful, but so frightening too."

"Maybe you're just not used to it."

"I hope that's it. When I'm not worrying about Suzie, about all of you, I think of nothing else. I think of how I feel when I put one on. I think of how others can flee from themselves. That's so important! I want everyone to be able to put on body disguises when they're feeling terrible."

Are you, *he asks her silently,* making one for Suzie?

Later she says, "It will take up more and more time. I know that. Do you think you can live with me? Do you think the children can?"

Without you, *he thinks. The sight of her and Billy Sunrise in those body disguises has overwhelmed him; he doesn't know what to say.* "It's not a question you ought to be asking just now," *he offers finally, hoping she won't argue.*

She doesn't.

Tony, the first to come out of the men's lavatory, wears a tucked-in shirt so large that the number on the back lies invisible below the belt line, leaving, just above his ass, only the name GRAY'S. The name is underlined by Tony's thick black belt.

Benjamin gave uniform sizes to Gray long ago; did Gray just ignore them?

Fred emerges, and his shirt, even more oversized than Tony's, is hanging out, so far out that it looks like a night-gown, an impression reinforced by the pants, which, if he's in fact now wearing pants, are either too short or pulled way up, above the bottom of the shirt. His long baseball socks with their thick red-and-white stripes rise to his knees, almost to the bottom of his shirt. He seems to need only a candle and a sleeping cap.

People in both stands are beginning to laugh and mumble. A couple of derisive remarks are flung from the W. and W. stands. A few of the W. and W. players, all now in front of their dugout, make mocking remarks, apparently with their coaches' approval.

Benjamin's impression that the uniforms are too large is broken with the appearance of Nick, whose shirt is so tight it won't button, leaving bare his dark muscular chest and stomach. The pants fit almost as tightly. There's a space of about two inches between the bottom of the pants and the top of the baseball socks.

A few people in the Gray's stands start clapping. Their eyes, everyone's eyes, are now curiously, expectantly, on the lavatory door.

Out comes Bobo, his baseball shirt on backwards, pants pulled way up over the knees and socks shoved down over the tops of the shoes. With the shirt turned around as it is, the name GRAY'S would be covered by his chest protector. The shirt is open in the rear, and, at the center of Bobo's back, the back that presumably will face up to the opening in the announcer's booth, directly into Gray's eyes if Gray remains there, is the word BOO! printed in red marking pen, or something similar.

Every player, it turns out, has created an original costume: Digby's shirt is so large it goes all the way to the ground, leaving visible only the toes of his very shiny baseball shoes; Speck's cap, shirt and pants are all on backwards; Tag, carrying his season-long style into uniform wearing, has kept his thin chest bare by bunching up his shirt and tucking it in at the back of his pants. Meryl has put his uniform on in the proper way, but, since it too is over-sized, the pants come nearly to his chest, hiding both the number and the word GRAY'S. The sleeves reach nearly to his wrists and the bottom of the pants covers most of his shoes.

An exception is, or seems to be, Pat Somerville. Having gone to the women's room, she emerges with a perfectly fitting uniform. *Looks tailored,* Benjamin thinks. She's pulled her hair up in back, put the cap on over it, but allowed neat curls to hang out all around. Her half-sleeved T-shirt shows just a touch of its bright yellow below the uniform arms, and the color is matched in the socks showing through at the heels of her baseball socks. She looks so good, so correct, that she appears to Benjamin to be a parody not only of her teammates' way of dressing but of the slightly disheveled way young ball players normally dress. Fans on both sides give her a separate and special applause.

Benjamin has been trying to ignore the sounds coming from the announcer's booth: Gray, thumping and cursing.

One of the players has now returned a uniform box to the dugout. Benjamin, seeing "Manager" printed on the top, opens it. Inside is a uniform. Benjamin starts to put the top back when he notices an invoice slip, picks it up, sees that it lists all the uniforms and their sizes and has stamped near the bottom, with spaces filled in:

RECEIVED BY <u>Thaddeus Gray</u>

DATE <u>5/28</u>

Benjamin shows the invoice slip to Karl outside the dugout.

"Son-of-a-bitch has had 'em for two months," Karl says, spitting a wet string of tobacco juice toward the announcer's booth.

Benjamin's been restless about the fashion show, now completed, was even beginning to feel sorry for Gray. The sponsor did, after all, finally come through. But the invoice, evidence of a sustained lie, brings back cold resentment. He takes the red baseball hat out of the manager's box, tightens to its fullest the adjustable strap on the back, and puts it on his head, where he hopes it'll look like a pea sitting on top of an apple.

"Let's play," he tells his team as, in the background, he hears Gray again, loudly complaining.

There's no rule about *how* uniforms must be worn. Benjamin hopes that Francis and the others won't produce an on-the-spot dictum. The uniforms are, after all, being worn.

The Gray's players take the field.

Benjamin looks into the tightly packed Gray's stands, sees Ellen near the announcer's booth, her amused eyes moving from announcer's booth to field to dugout. Benjamin averts his own eyes before hers find them. He locates Marilyn at the third base end; she's watching Bobo catch Max's warm-ups, but she soon lowers her head and begins, or continues, reading: her crafts manual, Benjamin guesses. Only on turning to her for the second time does

Benjamin notice that Billy Sunrise is seated beside her, staring distractedly toward left field. Beside him is Annie, giggling and chirping as she points to oddities in the Gray's players' uniforms. Billy Sunrise doesn't seem to care. Suzie is nowhere in view. Benjamin begins to worry about her, then remembers that last night she showed no interest in the game; he guesses that Marilyn has left her at the Andersons'.

There has been no announcement about the uniforms. Benjamin watches Max warm up—one of his own socks up, one down; cap on sideways; no baseball socks at all. The warmup pitches look good. He tells the infielders and outfielders to keep throwing the ball around. No guessing how long the debate, still going on in the announcer's booth, will last.

He's sorry to see that Daryl has been one of the most appreciative fans of the fashion show, ridiculously applauding as the players took the field. There's something as menacing about his appreciation as there was something innocent about the show itself. Benjamin remembers the icy response the base umpire gave him earlier.

"Mr. Dunne." It's Francis' voice, coming over the loudspeaker.

Benjamin steps out of the dugout.

"It seems possible that your players have put on the incorrect uniforms. (Laughter from the crowd.) "Do you wish to ask them to change with each other?"

"It's deliberate!" says Gray from behind Francis.

"No, sir!" Benjamin calls back. (More laughter and some applause.)

For a couple of minutes Francis doesn't reply, then says, "The other board members don't feel you should be ordered to have your players change." (Scattered applause.) "The game has been delayed long enough." (Loud applause and a "Damn right!" from the Gray's stands.) "You may resume if you wish."

"That's our wish!" (General applause.)

"You shouldn't let 'em get away with it!" It's Gray again.

"Play ball!" says the home plate umpire.

The bottom half of the innings begins at last.

Max, having had extra warm-ups, strikes out the lead-off batter on four pitches.

The second batter lines one on a high bounce that seems certain to go over second base, but Tony, moving quickly, leaps and, in a single movement, snags the ball, spins and throws to Fred at first. It's a low throw but, remarkably, one that is perfectly on line. Fred, stretching as far as he can, snaps it out of the dirt, getting the runner by a half step.

The dandies are up, grousing at Daryl, but there's really no basis for argument and they soon file back to their places—two in the coaching boxes, one in the dugout.

Moose is the next batter. He slashes a ground ball to third which Nick deflects, sending it into the glove of Tag, coming in from short to back him up. Tag whips the ball underhanded to first and they get Moose by a step.

The infield play has never been better, Benjamin thinks. The players' movements have been natural; they've shown little nervousness, despite the large crowd and the importance of the game.

As the W. and W. pitcher heads for the dugout to get his mitt, Benjamin notices he's limping ever so slightly. Moose didn't seem to sprain anything on the way to first. It must have been that hit by Bobo at the top of the inning. It's slowed him, maybe just enough.

Benjamin is soon watching Moose warm up, waiting for, hoping for, a sign that the pitcher is favoring his bad leg. If the sign appears, Benjamin will call his team together and give cunning instructions.

The air conditioner in the station wagon is broken and from the vent come summer's clashing blends: the sweet green aroma of growing corn, the acrid odor of chemical fertilizer, the biting stench of a dead animal rotting in a ditch or field.

He's left town almost by accident. From the bookstore he drove to the ball park out of habit, then realized there was neither a game nor a practice scheduled today. He continued on, however, and soon found himself turning onto the entrance ramp to the thruway.

He's a few miles from Centerville, headed toward Toledo. As the traffic thickens, he opens his window all the way to get the fullest possible circulation of air. He feels as though he's going on a long trip, though he has

224

no destination. When he grows tired of driving, he supposes, he'll turn back.

He'd been reading de Tocqueville this morning, Democracy in America, *which he'd plucked from his private shelf after the morning work had eased up. He was impressed, particularly by one of the author's remarks about the results of democracy, where the author says it* ".... throws him [man] back forever upon himself and in the end confines him entirely within the solitude of his own heart." *He hadn't paid much attention to de Tocqueville's reasons for making the statement; it was the words themselves that attracted him, the sentiment they expressed; that seemed awfully right, though he couldn't be sure even of his own reasons for thinking so. Finally he called to Dan at the big desk outside the cubicle, said,* "Listen to this," *and read the line. Dan didn't do what he often does when Benjamin reads him something—shuffle papers, make a friendly but sardonic remark, give a reluctant grunt of appreciation. Instead he came to the cubicle's entrance and said,* "You're not completely alone, Benjamin. No one is." *Benjamin hadn't intended de Tocqueville's words as a way of talking about himself.* "You didn't need to make a remark like that," *he said.* "What's that got to do with . . . anything?" *Dan gave him a knowing shrug, then said,* "You've been feeling low lately. You can't hide it. It's no surprise to me that you'd pick out a statement like that." *Damn him, Benjamin thought. He got up, pushed past the desk of this man whose interest had so quickly turned from dollars-and-cents to personal salvation, went out into the bookstore, stopped, turned back, and without planning to, spoke one of Dan's typical lines:* "There's work to be done."

Dan's remark stayed with him, however, and led not only to resentment but to a gush of afterthoughts. For much of the rest of the day, as if he were his own psychiatrist, Benjamin slowly identified a kind of theme in his life: It had to do with parting or separating from those he knew and loved. It was an impulse that, until now, he'd felt but hadn't quite accepted. Yes, he was now able to admit for the first time, he and Marilyn might eventually part from each other. Divorce or separation had become a kind of modern solution; who was he to think he, or she for that matter, was somehow immune?

Now he pictures himself living alone, not in Centerville but in a city, in an apartment there, without Marilyn, without the children. Bobo soon comes to mind. He's sure he could survive well enough without Bobo, as Bobo could survive without him. Odd, he thinks, especially since he and his son are now closer to each other than they have been in months, maybe as close as they've ever been.

Abruptly he cuts across two lanes and goes onto the exit ramp at a turnoff about halfway between Centerville and Toledo. He'll cross the overpass, get back onto the highway, return to town.

He tries to imagine living apart from Suzie and Annie, can't. But he does begin vicariously to remove from his life others he cares about: friends, including Karl and Dan; the players on the team, even Meryl; the few neighbors and friends to whom he's felt close; and finally, surprisingly, even Ellen. He again tries to picture his life apart from the girls. He sees unbearable results: Suzie cracking up; Annie becoming uncontrollable, a delinquent. Yet the thought of leaving persists.

When he's only a few miles from Centerville he's able to press past his anxieties about the girls and face the ultimate, a complete uprooting.

It is possible, he thinks.

He recalls a recent article from the Centerville newspaper that fascinated him: A man named Elmer Jackbar, mayor of Boise, Idaho, and a retired lumberman, regretting the demise of minor league baseball in America, had a plan to revive the old Class C Pioneer League of the Northwest. The league would be independent of the major leagues, self-supporting. Jackbar admitted the odds were heavily against him, but he apparently had money and some support from the city fathers whose towns would make up the proposed league. "What I need most," he concluded, "is the assistance of someone who loves baseball as much as I do and has a little business sense, kind of a general manager."

Benjamin wonders if he would qualify to be Jackbar's general manager. The thought doesn't seem ridiculous. He loves baseball and has business experience. Why couldn't he contact Jackbar, go west, work something out, sort of piggyback on Jackbar's dream until it became a dream of his own?

Only when Centerville comes into view does his fantasy subside. Boise, he thinks, realizing how far away Jackbar's city is, for God's sake! He's sure that de Tocqueville is at least as much to blame for getting it started as was Dan. By the time he's on the exit ramp he knows he can blame neither. It's he himself, something hidden, hungry, and unsatisfied within him. An urge? An impulse?

He can't identify it.

Benjamin calls Nick to the third base coaching box. He knows what he wants his third baseman to do, but he hasn't gotten his best results by giving him orders. Nick tends to resist, to argue. This is no time for an argument. "The pitcher hurt his foot on the last play at first," Benjamin tells him. "It's probably going to affect his throwing. What do you think you ought to do?"

Nick replies without an instant's thought: "I can prob'ly get around on his fastball now. Bet I can put it out of the park."

It's a wild conclusion, which Benjamin seeks to tame by saying, "Take a look at his warm-ups."

Nick turns, watches Moose deliver a pitch into the dirt in front of his catcher, waits, sees him throw another outside the strike zone, then limp a little as he steps back to the mound after taking the return throw from the catcher. Twisting up his mouth, Nick turns to Benjamin and says: "I prob'ly ought to wait and see if he can get the ball over first. Right?"

"And if he can't?"

"Wait him out for the walk."

"Right."

Nick swaggers to the batter's box as if he'd known just what to do all along.

Moose throws two low pitches. The pitcher obviously can't put all his weight on his front foot. Finally there's a strike, barely over, then two more balls for the walk.

Fred, the next batter, has become a master at getting walks and needs no instructions: He crowds the plate, wiggles his butt, shakes the top of his bat and, on four straight pitches, gets his walk.

Norm asks for time out and rushes from the dugout to talk to Moose.

Guessing that the W. and W. pitcher won't be removed just yet, Benjamin calls Digby Wells, the next batter, to the coaching box at third. "You know what to do?"

"Yes, sir. Get a walk." He looks nervously to the mound. "But suppose they change pitchers?"

"Same thing." Digby is a poor hitter. Under all circumstances the walk attempt is advisable. Benjamin is using Digby, Pat Somerville, and his other weak hitters early so that the better hitters can be in at the end. Though Digby doesn't know it, this will be the one and only time Benjamin is going to allow him to go to bat.

Norm returns to the dugout without removing Moose.

The W. and W. manager isn't stupid, Benjamin knows; he must have given Moose advice that will help him through the inning. What advice? Benjamin looks into the W. and W. dugout, searching for a clue in the eyes of Norm and the other coaches; there isn't one. He looks to the W. and W. outfield: no changes in the player's positions. The infielders show no movement. *Good poker playing,* he tells the W. and W. coaches silently.

"Move around a little," he calls before Digby gets back into the batter's box. He's hoping that, among other things, the flapping-nightgown uniform will distract Moose.

Without changing his pitching motion, Moose puts one strike over on Digby. Then another. Moose's pitches are slower now.

Benjamin calls time out, meets Digby partway between home plate and the coaching box, and asks, "What's he doing?"

"I don't know, Mr. Dunne. The pitch looks like a banana."

"Must be a curve, an easy overhand curve," says Benjamin, thinking aloud. "He doesn't need to put so much weight on his foot for that. And if it looks like a banana, he's not snapping it off well. In fact, from the coaching box I can't see it breaking. But he's getting it over."

"So what should I do, Mr. Dunne?"

228

"Bend down as low as you can. Make him work for that third strike."

"Whoo," says Digby, looking relieved. "I thought you were going to ask me to put one up against the fence." Digby smiles at his own joke, then goes back to the plate, where, on the next pitch, a near strike, he not only bends low but smartly brings his bat forward and fakes a bunt.

That stirs all sorts of movement in the W. and W. infield, movement that tells Benjamin what will happen if one of his players should bunt.

The next pitch is a called strike, and Digby is out.

Benjamin reviews the action of the W. and W. infield on the faked bunt: third baseman charging, pitcher covering third (because of the runner on second), shortstop covering second, and second baseman backing up at first. The first baseman didn't charge in. No one, therefore, covered the space between pitcher's mound and first.

Benjamin instructs Tag to take a hard swing at the first good pitch. "If you don't get a hit, I'm giving the bunt-and-run signal. Be sure to bunt down the first base line. Shove it about halfway to the base, if you can. Then go like hell to beat it out."

Walking back to his coaching box, Benjamin notices that the crowd, unlike crowds at other games with a lot of interruptions, is patiently tuned in to the mental moves that are being made, probably second-guessing him and the W. and W. dandies.

Daryl has now positioned himself between second and third. Benjamin is sorry that he didn't, earlier, give Daryl a sign of recognition. It's tactics, not affection. He looks to the shaggy umpire, gives him a little nod.

Daryl's mouth moves stiffly into a smile.

In the distance a siren sounds. It seems to be approaching the ball park. Benjamin remembers the melee at the earlier game. Maybe word has gotten to the police that another hot contest is under way, one that's liable to result in a brawl. Yet this is a different sort of game. Not only is the crowd attentive but so far there's been little trouble on the field. That siren finally reminds him only that there's a lot of locked-up energy wanting release. Even the pressures of a good close ball game do not quite explain it. Whatever it is, it's building on itself, seems bound to explode.

Tag knocks the first "banana" pitch foul into the dirt near home plate.

Benjamin gives the bunt-and-run signal. He notices Fred, on first, yank up his pants. An acute observer, seeing Fred, would now be able to figure out the plan. Benjamin quickly checks the W. and W. dugout. The dandies have their heads together, are clucking about something.

Is it Fred's move?

He can't tell.

Tag crouches as the pitch approaches, then pushes a good bunt toward first. The W. and W. infielders dart to their preassigned positions. No one is covering that triangle formed by the pitcher's mound, first base, and home plate. Finally the catcher chases the bunt, leaving home plate uncovered. Benjamin waves his hand toward Nick roaring down from second. But Nick isn't watching his manager; he's hungrily eyeing the third base bag, getting ready for a slide. Benjamin must now shout: "Go all the way in!" Everyone hears, including the W. and W. catcher, who's between home plate and first base, grabbing at the ball. Tag crosses first base safely. Now there's only one thing for the catcher to do: race Nick to the plate. As Nick churns in from third, the catcher turns and starts his sprint. Benjamin yells a thought that comes out like a bloody spurt: "Knock him down!" As the catcher, heavy and lumbering, and Nick, a rolling boulder, reach the plate, Nick extends his head and puts it into the catcher's stomach. For an instant the ball touches Nick's shoulder, but then the catcher's arms fly upward and the ball shoots backward, against the screen.

"Safe!" calls R.D. Falcone, leaping away from the collision with both arms flying out.

The first baseman now races in, picks up the ball, and raises it threateningly above his head to hold Fred on third base.

Tag has landed safely on second.

Nick, on his feet, is running, arms up, to the Gray's dugout, where his teammates are applauding.

The W. and W. catcher rises slowly, woozily, like a boxer after a solid knockdown.

The dandies, Norm in front, Doug and Hal trailing, approach the plate.

The home plate umpire signals time out.

The dandies, stamping their feet and gesturing, claim that their catcher held the ball long enough for the out. As they're speaking, the catcher staggers to the low fence near first base, searches for the ball, finally sees it in the hand of the first baseman. He then collapses to one knee, still feeling the effects of the crash.

The coaches ignore him, go on with their complaint.

They haven't noticed their third baseman, who's been hovering around them. The boy finally catches the sleeve of Doug and whispers something to him.

"Yeah?" says Doug, surprised. He grabs the sleeve of Norm, who's still bellowing, finally pulls him back, and relays the third baseman's message.

"Good," says Norm, who steps past Doug, puts his arm around the third baseman's shoulder, and gives him a rapid instruction, to which the player nods.

Norm then goes to the catcher, now shaking his limbs to see if they still work, and whispers. The catcher also nods.

Benjamin sidles to the dugout and asks Nick whether or not he touched third going around.

"Sure I did," says Nick defensively.

But when play resumes, the catcher quickly tosses the ball to the third baseman, who steps on the bag.

Daryl floats in from behind the base, faintly grinning. He stops, sends his right fist down, toward the base, holding it low for a few long seconds, then shooting it upward, thumb extended. "Out!" he shouts.

It's a punishing sound.

When Daryl raises his face, eyes on Benjamin, the grin is no longer there.

In a dismal aftermath Fred is picked off third base to end the top of the second inning.

A boardwalk passes the back entrances of several stores, from which extend the shadows of late afternoon. There are no identifying signs at the back. Benjamin has taken a shortcut from his bookstore. Unaccustomed to approaching the Main Street stores from the rear, he passes several windows, peering in. One of the last has a film of dust.

He uses the side of his fist to wipe away dust and make a peephole. Through it he sees a partition that partially blocks his view of a long table. Hanging over the end of the table is a body suit. He hears the voices of Marilyn and Billy Sunrise coming faintly through the window and guesses the two of them are behind the partition. He moves from the window to the door, a couple of feet away, and opens it.

"It does you no good to sit there glumly sewing your troubles away," *Billy Sunrise is saying.*

"But don't you see?" *Marilyn replies.* "It does do me good. I can at least lose myself in this. I'd be a mess if I were at home, say, doing homemaker things, and trying to work it out."

"You're just avoiding the real thing."

"I have to find myself before I—well—get the strength to face 'the real thing,' as you put it."

Lose? Find? And what "real thing"? Holding the door partly open, Benjamin stands half in and half out of the store.

"Why don't you talk to him about it?"

"I . . . can't."

"I don't know him well, but he does seem to be a sensitive person. You know?"

"Maybe that's why I can't tell him."

The subsequent silence provides an invitation to break in; but the conversation, like an organism with a birth, existence, and death, seems to be only in mid-life. He is curious, especially about the reference to himself, but is sure he will learn nothing unless he stays back, allows the talk to reach its own natural end.

"I would tell him, darling, whatever the cost. Meanwhile you have me for whatever you need me for. You know that."

Sobbing? Is she sobbing?

"How do you . . . tell a person who's already done his best . . ."

"You tell him that your very identity, your very life, depends on it. If it does."

"I don't know that it does."

"Well, something does. You aren't happy, Mari."

"I am when I'm here, working on these. But . . . oh, God! The implications! I mean, if I trust in my feelings,

232

how far will they take me? It's one thing to do something creative, but it's quite another—frightening—to realize you no longer want to be with the only man you've loved. And when will the children begin seeming . . . extraneous? They don't now. The opposite. You'll never know how much I worry about Suzie. I can't let him know. But, if I were really to let go, I could slip away from my responsibilities even to her."

There's a pause.

"Yet I . . . I must trust in my instincts, mustn't I? If I've learned anything, it's that. I mustn't deny them."

"So?"

"Maybe they won't possess me. I've worried about that. On the other hand, maybe it's all just a fling. I don't feel the need to run, exactly. Maybe, when I finally do find myself . . . Oh, Billy—I just don't know." Now she is crying.

"I wish I could—do more, Mari."

"No. Please. Your . . . your company is enough. Thanks for that."

There's a long silence, during which Benjamin pictures Billy Sunrise, with a fretful expression, holding her by the hand and gazing at the blank inner side of the partition, the outer side of which Benjamin himself now faces.

"I've become so much like a child," she says, recovering a bit. *"It's not all bad."*

It has ended, this conversation. Benjamin feels its age, its exhaustion. He backs out of the doorway, having decided to save Marilyn and Billy Sunrise the embarrassment of his appearance, to save himself the embarrassment of their explanations.

The children, *he thinks as he tiptoes along the board-walk toward the parking lot.* The thought repeats itself: the children. *It doesn't extend itself.* He remembers, of all things, their expressions in the close-up photos he and Marilyn took just after buying a special lens for their old Polaroid a couple of years ago: Annie surprised and mimicking, Suzie sad and pouting, Bobo pensive, indifferent, defiant. For the moment the memories of those photographed expressions, are more vivid than the memories of their real faces. If he and Marilyn hadn't taken the photographs, would he now be able to picture any of them? Searching, he sees Bobo in his catcher's mask, his face

*mysterious behind it; he can't make the real face appear
outside the mask. It seems a great joke on his memory.*

Pat Somerville opens the third inning with a single between
first and second. Her cap flies off as she reaches the base,
starts blowing toward right field. Without calling time
out, she starts chasing it, holding her loose hair as she
goes.

"Come back here, girl!" Karl says from the coaching
box.

The right fielder, not seeing she's badly overrun the
base instead of making the proper turn, throws the ball
slowly to second.

Pat stops, turns to Karl, pointing ahead of her: *I have
to get my hat.*

"Time out!" shouts Karl, waving both hands, turning to
Falcone.

"Time out!" repeats Benjamin from the third base
coaching box.

And finally the phrase is issued in chorus from the
Gray's dugout.

Falcone, without seeming to know just why, calls time
out.

Pat gets her hat, which she was determined to do anyway, then returns to first.

The dandies stir in their dugout.

Daryl has shuffled toward first base.

Benjamin holds his breath, waiting for a complication,
like Pat being called out for going out of the base path.

But apparently Falcone has called time out soon
enough; there's no protest.

Benjamin lets out a long exhale as he watches Max
move into the batter's box. Max has a good sense of the
strike zone and works Moose to a three-ball-two-strike
count. Benjamin is confident that Pat will make it to third
base on a single, come home on anything more. On the
next pitch, however, Max laces the ball to short for an
easy double play.

Pat, knowing she did all she could, comes off the field
in a proud prance. After Benjamin congratulates her
on the hit, she goes into the dugout, where he hears her
say, "I could have made it all the way to second if I
didn't lose my hat." Benjamin turns, sees that she's ad-

dressing little Lou Pera, hunched over and looking guilty.

Harold walks, but in his eagerness to get the jump on the pitcher is caught leaning toward second; Moose picks him off before throwing the next pitch.

At the bottom of the third, W. and W.'s first hitter takes a fierce swing at Max's first pitch, twisting his body as he follows through, then releasing one hand so that the bat strikes Bobo at the side of the head just behind the mask.

Bobo falls to the ground and lies still.

Benjamin rushes to home plate.

The umpire removes the catcher's mask as the two of them bend over the boy.

Benjamin reaches down, touches his son's limp hand: "Bobo?"

He doesn't reply.

Falcone gently turns Bobo onto his back.

The boy's eyes open slowly, circle Benjamin's head uncertainly, finally find his face.

Francis has come down from the announcer's booth with a first-aid kit. There is some clapping from both stands as he and Benjamin help Bobo to his feet. Francis tells Bobo to walk slowly toward first base for a few yards, then come back. Bobo does so; there's little stagger in his gait. "I'm okay," he says, his eyes confidently on his father's.

Benjamin nods, then notices that, beyond Bobo, Doug is with the hitter, who's back at the dugout now. The coach jabs him, says something, then smiles. That crack on the head was deliberate, planned; Benjamin is sure of it. They're paying Bobo back for hitting Moose on the foot.

Francis raises his fingers in front of Bobo's eyes, two fingers, then three, then one, asking how many he sees.

Bobo answers correctly.

"He's okay," Francis says, sounding as though he knows what he's talking about.

"I can take you out," Benjamin tells his son. "It might be best."

"No," says Bobo, eyeing the hitter whose bat struck him. "I'm okay. I want to stay in." He begins taking practice throws from Max.

Sensing something, Benjamin turns to the announcer's booth.

Gray's cold eyes are on him. He swings about, sees

235

Doug watching Gray watching him. The web of vision connecting the three of them, his awareness of it, makes his back muscles tighten. He breaks the web by turning to the stands, where he finds Marilyn's worried face. She's standing, peering over the heads of others. He raises his hand, signaling to her that Bobo is all right, hoping it's true. She settles back, looking relieved. Though tempted, he doesn't look back at Gray or at Doug.

Max pitches well, getting the hitter on a fly ball to center field and the following two batters on strikeouts.

Bobo has held onto Max's pitches easily and shows no effects from the blow. When he returns to the dugout he says, "I'm going to get that bastard." He's looking out at the third baseman, the player whose bat struck him.

Benjamin senses danger, not to the W. and W. third baseman, not to Bobo, but to his team: Revenge will pull their attention from the game. Such a diversion, the W. and W. coaches' smiles now remind him, can be as useful to the opposing team as home runs.

Benjamin turns, thinking to warn Bobo and the others not to let their attention be drawn from the game. He hesitates, says nothing, knowing that they, not he, must finally shape the outcome of this afternoon.

There come moments when he's sure that speaking to her candidly about Ellen will free her to open herself to him, as she opened herself to Billy Sunrise:

Does one need to explain such things, even to oneself? Something began, that's all: in my case when I opened my eyes at the ball park to see Ellen standing in the afternoon sunlight; for you, I guess, when you went to that crafts show in Minneapolis. Anyway, maybe neither of those moments were real beginnings. Strange, but at times I think there was no beginning at all with Ellen. She became part of something taking place in me already. Was I, without knowing it, looking for another woman? And had I begun to sense that you . . . Never mind. I'm getting off the subject. I've said Ellen has become a friend. I want now to admit to you that she is, has been, more than a friend.

Is Billy Sunrise more than a friend?
A lover?
He doubts it and decides not to distort the uniqueness

of his relationship with Ellen by making the comparison.

How then can he describe to her his feelings for Ellen?

If you can accept, Marilyn, that it's not unnatural, and may even be healthy in some way, to feel strong affection for more than one person, to be intimate with more . . . than . . .

How self-serving that is! How cruel!

I have felt for Ellen love or something closely akin to it. Now, before you draw any firm conclusions, I must tell you that my love, or whatever it is, has limits, may not in fact be love in—in the ways you, or others, even she, might expect.

Is it so?

What kind of oddball, then, does that make him?

I do love her, in a way. I mean, in her presence, I have been able to—to contact forces in myself that . . .

Forces in self?

I'll start again. There is an easiness between Ellen and me, a certain natural relaxed sort of thing which . . . allows both of us, has, except for short periods, to release, well, feelings which, for . . . a lot of reasons, we weren't able to, before that.

That makes it seem as though he's blaming Marilyn, her weighty problem, her work, something. Then there is that awful implied comparison: Life is easy with Ellen, not with Marilyn.

Scratch what I've been saying. I'll try to bring it all down to the nuggety bottom. I feel strongly enough about her to—to, now and then, imagine myself living with her, apart from you, though with a close, I hope trusting, friendship continuing between you and me. I've even thought about how we'd work out our lives with the children. That trusting friendship would be important for their sakes as well as for ours. It could work out. Take Bobo. Same age as Max, similar interests and such. They could live with Ellen and me. I pull back at the thought of leaving the girls, just as you may at the thought of leaving Bobo. So, if we were to look upon it not as leaving, not as parting, but more as living apart . . .

It's as if he's arranging a puppet show.

What does he know about what the children would want, given the possible choices?

How dare he presume . . . anything?

237

Even about himself. He hasn't spent much time imag-
ining a life with Ellen. If anything, he's imagined doing
as he does now: seeing her at times of need and want.

Maybe I'm overstating all this. For example, lately I've
found myself pulling back from Ellen somewhat. That's
what I meant when I said "except for moments." There
are times when I just don't want to see her. I suppose
that's expected in any relationship.

But why the extremes? At times he can all but lose
himself in Ellen's presence; at others, he sinks to a numb-
ing ennui.

Does he not love her?

Yes, he assures himself, he does love her.

Why, then, the hesitation?

Marilyn, there are some things about all this I just
can't explain.

Between the bottom of the third and top of the fourth,
Benjamin announces substitutions: Pat and Digby out,
Lou Pera and Bobby Watson in. He scans the faces in
the dugout, looking for Meryl, wanting to tell him he'll
soon be in the game, if not at pitcher, at another position.
But Meryl isn't there.

"Where's Meryl?" he asks.

Several players look around, seem as surprised as Benjamin at his absence.

"He went out of the dugout last inning," says Digby.
"I thought he was going to the bathroom."

Benjamin leans out of the dugout, looks toward the
lavatories, sees the men's room door open. There's no
sign of him. "Was he—all right?"

Digby looks at some of the other players, as if hesitat-
ing to answer, then turns to Benjamin, his troubled eyes
saying more than his uncertain words: "I don't really
know."

Benjamin doesn't dare allow himself to be distracted
for too long by his worry over Meryl, though the worry
will hold until he knows where the boy has gone. He
asks Digby to take a look around the ball park and surrounding area. As Digby hurries out of the dugout, Benjamin calls after him: "Tell him he's going to get in.
Soon."

Benjamin forces his attention back to the game.

Tony, speaking to Moose in his Spanish-American dialect ("Jure banana ees makeeng me hongry, beeg boy. Why don' ju poot wan een close so hi can bite eet?"), distracts the pitcher and gets Tony a walk.

Tony reaches second when Bobo manages to bounce a hit past third base.

From first base Bobo calls across to the third baseman: "I'm gonna carve your initials on your legs when I get over there!"

"You're gonna be doin' it with a baseball in one of your eyes," the third baseman calls back.

The clash between Bobo and the W. and W. third baseman is avoided, at least temporarily, when Moose, despite his gimpy leg, mixes fastballs with the banana and gets the next three batters easily, Nick on an infield out, Fred on a strikeout, and Bobby Watson on another infield out.

Digby can't find Meryl. "Maybe he went home," he suggests. "Is there a phone in the announcer's booth, Mr. Dunne?"

"Yes," Benjamin tells him.

Digby rushes off.

During the last of the fourth inning only one W. and W. batter comes close to reaching base. It's the third baseman. Though Max strikes him out, Bobo uncharacteristically drops the third strike, allowing the batter to make a run for the base. Bobo snaps up the ball and chases him, sending the ball against his back with a right-jab motion that knocks him to the ground. As the third baseman groans, rubbing the place behind his shoulder where he's been struck, Bobo wheels and flips the ball to Nick for tosses around the infield. He then turns to his victim and says, "Just a good clean play in a good clean ball game."

Benjamin, angry, wants to call for time out and remind his son of the risk he's just taken: Had he lost that third-strike pitch, the runner would have been on first, might later have scored. Yet, he realizes, Bobo measured his move well. One certain result is that the W. and W. third baseman, the other W. and W. players and coaches, now know their tricks won't go unnoticed, unpaid for.

After standing with his hands on his hips for a few moments, glaring into the W. and W. dugout, Bobo turns and gives his father a curious look.

Benjamin won't allow his eyes to comment: no approval; no disapproval.

It's a mean sport, he thinks later, remembering that Ty Cobb played constantly with spikes high and fists moving. He wonders if Bobo has a better fix than he on the risks that can be taken.

Digby returns from the announcer's booth. "I let the phone ring for a long time, but there was no answer."

"Maybe he's on his way home." Benjamin pictures Meryl, in his oversized uniform, stopping under a tree, just sitting there. "Keep calling."

"Suppose no one answers. Should I go and look for him?"

"No. Come back and tell me."

Digby flies off.

Benjamin can't stop for Meryl. Unseen forces are in motion here. Strange that the game should be more important than Meryl, even Bobo. But it has, in a way, become so. *Understand that, Meryl,* he pleads silently to his absent player. He himself doesn't understand it at all.

He drives them swiftly into the dark promise of a storm. The wind pulls weeds and small debris is being pulled across the highway. After he turns onto the dirt road the dust rises against the windshield, causing him at moments to raise his foot from the gas pedal and steer blindly.

It is, *he thinks, our place.* It'll seem a different place on a day like this, but, still, it's our only place.

There's such darkness when they pass through the woods. He imagines himself driving into the night and out of it again.

"Maybe we'll have time to swim," she says.

Yesterday, after Dan and the clerks had left the bookstore, he tempted himself by scanning his bookshelf, then deciding he was too nervous to concentrate on reading, went into his office and called her. He asked if she'd found a lawyer. She said she had, one she trusted, and that he'd advised a divorce. She then invited Benjamin to the house for a drink. "No," he said, surprising himself, "not today." She told him that Max wasn't at home; they'd be alone. He said again, "No," and didn't explain.

He didn't have an explanation. He pictured a balloon inside himself, its skin flaccid, and he thought that if something would touch it, it would break and spill out a powdery substance, dark and leaden, inert. "Are you sure?" she said. "Yes," he replied. But he suggested a ride to the pond tomorrow, sure he would then feel different about seeing her.

Though the water on the lake is choppy, the wind that stirs it up is warm. She takes a blanket out of the car as he stands at the edge of the beach, looking out. The other side isn't visible. He imagines the pond a great sea.

He turns.

She's undressed herself on the blanket.

He watches her run naked into the water, hears her cry out as she stretches into it, sees her go into an elongated dive, sink, then rise again a few yards beyond where she went under.

"Come in, Benjamin," she calls.

He shakes his head, smiling at the childlike way she thrashes about, turning, wagging her head.

There was a time when he wrote down reasons, arguments pro and con. Were he to take long sheets of paper and write down on the left side his reasons for a life with Ellen and on the right his reasons against, he would, he is sure, need several pages. Yet, when he finished, there would be very few on the right side.

He's wrapped the blanket around her, is drying her as she shivers against him. He lowers his hands and tightens the blanket, pulling her closer. The slight movements of their heads, his downward, hers upward, remind him of branches reaching as if to touch.

At other times when he was with Ellen, his silent words were for Marilyn, but now, oddly (insanely, he thinks), they are for Ellen herself:

I think you would leave everything, even Max. I was for a time stopped by the fear that you wouldn't. But you would, wouldn't you?

She's sunk away from his hold and is spreading the blanket out. "Lie down on top of me," she says. "I want to feel your weight against me. I want you to press me to the sand."

Soon his bones find soft places, fitting like tongues into

241

grooves. He twists her down. His upper arms cradle her shoulders and his hands, upraised, enclose her skull. Their open mouths meet, their tongues stiffly connect.

Today I'll be your rapist, tomorrow your child. There's only one way with Marilyn. A husbandly way. With you the ways are countless.

He pounds against her. His penis seems thicker, harder, than it's ever been.

She emits a cry of pleasure.

We could both be other people, in dress, talk, loving, as many as we'd want. But we'd always come back to being ourselves.

The rain, falling lightly, makes cold pinpricks on his back.

They're tightly locked. She moves one leg slightly, as much as she's able to. He presses his own leg against the moving leg, feels her trying to make it move again, keeps pressing until she can't.

I want to become mindless, a kind of beast. It might be a way of survival, escape, and . . . His thought won't finish itself.

He hasn't bothered to remove his pants. He presses hard, feels cloth against skin, hairs grating, bone knocking bone. Before they finish her fingernails are tearing through the back of his shirt. Though he's pushed her deep into the sand, it now resists them. When he comes he feels a burning sensation, and the explosion brings her up, throbbing against him.

This is no ceremony, *he thinks,* no celebration.

Later, in the car on the way back, she laughs, says she's been wounded in battle. "Take me to the emergency room at the hospital."

The rain beats against the windows on the driver's side. He's conscious of its tappings. He wants to speak, but even the silent words won't come.

She reaches across, pokes him below the ribs. "I'm not a tragic woman," *she says.*

"What does that mean?" *He's watching the road, not her.*

"Mean? It means I'm just not." *She slides closer, puts her hands on his shoulders, rests against him.* "Remember that, Benjamin."

242

She's asleep before he feels he's gotten the gist of it, too late for him to speak a grateful response.

At the top of the sixth inning Tag doesn't move on an inside pitch and is struck beneath the shoulder. He wiggles the skinny body as he moves to first, is checking the parts. He's apparently bruised but not badly hurt.

As Benjamin is trying to decide what instruction to give Gerry Franks with the runner on first base, Daryl approaches the coaching box and says, "Remember that play at third base?"

Puzzled, Benjamin nods.

"You realize it could have gone either way, don't you?"

"What do you mean?" Either Nick touched third base or he didn't. "Was he out or wasn't he?"

"Just want you to know," says Daryl, almost smiling.

Benjamin is making guesses at the reason for Daryl's puzzling and uncalled-for interruption when it occurs to him that the field umpire has distracted him from important thoughts about Gerry, who's already stepping into the batter's box. Did Daryl plan the remark to distract him? He's beginning to suspect a plot (W. and W. coaches suggesting Daryl interrupt him at critical moments) when he realizes that his suspicion is itself a distraction. The only pertinent question just now is: What does he tell Gerry?

The first pitch is thrown for a ball before he has his answer.

He calls Gerry out of the batter's box. The boy is a weak hitter but makes consistent contact with pitches. Benjamin instructs him to begin by holding out for a walk. "But if there's a called strike, then swing at the next good pitch."

Gerry, a pensive, curly-haired boy, has rarely spoken to Benjamin; he doesn't speak now but goes to the batter's box and waits through two more balls; then comes a strike, which he swings at like a robot and punches sharply to right field for a single, moving Tag to second.

Moose, with shoulders hanging, climbs wearily to the mound.

Norm has his second-best pitcher, a left-handed sidearmer, warming up behind the W. and W. dugout.

Benjamin asks for time out, gets it, signals Karl to come to the home plate area. When they meet there he says, "I'm thinking of putting on the steal signal and telling Max to swing at the first pitch. After this inning we've got only two more at-bats."

Karl is perspiring profusely though the sun has already dipped behind the trees at the back of the announcer's booth and a soft breeze has begun to float across the diamond. "Shit, Ben," he says, raising his cap a little, "it's a tough damn game and has me tenser than a bull in heat!"

"Be sure to send Max to second if he gets a hit and there's any possibility he'll make the extra base. I'll do the signaling after he gets there. We've got to try to come up with at least one more run this inning, maybe more. We've got to take chances."

"That's fine with me, Ben."

Taking chances has reminded Benjamin that it's Gerry who's on first. He looks out, sees the boy standing at stiff attention, his small puzzled eyes on his manager: *What's happening?* Does Gerry even remember the steal signal? Benjamin will give his plan away by going out to speak instructions. There's another way: As he nears the coaching box, he furtively flips the steal signal to Gerry, then waits. Only Gerry's head moves: tick, tick, tick, down; tick, tick, tick, up. He's apparently gotten the signal, though the expression that now crosses his face says it gives him no comfort at all.

Benjamin calls Max aside and says, "Swing at the first pitch if it's anywhere close. Get what you can."

Max, rubbing dirt on his bat handle, nods. He follows instructions well, is as calm at the plate as he is on the mound.

On the way back to the coaching box Benjamin sees Daryl, near third, watching him with a surly expression.

"Who needs you?" Benjamin says.

"Huh?"

Benjamin goes to the coaching box, where he turns his back, letting the umpire's curious response fall to the dirt behind him.

Max laces a high banana pitch, one that might have been called a ball, over second base and into center.

Tag is on his way to third.

244

"Go all the way in!" shouts Benjamin as he sees the ball take an odd bounce in front of the center fielder.

Daryl is bending eagerly over third, but he's not going to get to make a call, for the center fielder, having to get down on one knee to block the ball, comes up slowly and is going to make a late throw.

Tag goes chopping around third, makes an upright run to the plate.

Benjamin sees that Daryl is now even closer to third, crouching, eyes fixed on the bag. *Why?* Benjamin glances up to see that there may be a play there after all: Gerry has made the turn at second and begun a sprint to third.

"Go back!" Benjamin yells.

Gerry digs his heels in, goes down, spins quickly around and pops up, half-running, half-diving, back to second. The third baseman, who's gotten the center fielder's throw, flings the ball to the second baseman.

Daryl is now hurrying to second.

It's a good throw but Gerry is in, head first, under it. Benjamin waits.

Daryl doesn't make a call.

"Hey!" shouts Lou Pera from the Gray's dugout. "Call him safe!"

You bastard! Benjamin thinks as he watches Daryl saunter toward home plate.

Several Gray's players have come out of the dugout and are standing beside Benjamin, yelling, some cursing, at Daryl.

"I didn't see it too well," Daryl says to Falcone, "but I think he was out."

"He *was* out," Norm calls from the W. and W. dugout, as if on cue. "We could see it clearly from here."

"Out," echoes the W. and W. second baseman, who failed to make the tag on Gerry.

"I was safe!" Gerry is shouting from second.

Benjamin had a good angle on the play. There was no doubt about Gerry's being safe. Daryl couldn't have missed it. Benjamin, lacing up his fury, heads for the plate. Before he gets there, however, Falcone, having called time out, addresses Daryl:

"You don't need to make the call."

"What are you talking about?"

"I saw it."

Daryl stops, surprised. "You were supposed to be watching the runner coming to the plate," he says.

"That runner had already scored. I had a good look at the play at second. The runner's safe."

"You—sure?" says Daryl, seeming to swallow each word.

"I'm sure," Falcone responds calmly. He signals Daryl to go back to his position in the field.

"Just a minute!" Norm and his look-alikes are now marching toward the plate.

The call has been made. Falcone won't change it. Benjamin has nothing left to deal with but his own rage. He finds himself following Daryl back across the infield. He's walking close, threateningly close. Out of the corner of his eye he sees Nick, traveling with him like a destroyer escort. "Hey, you!" he says to Daryl.

Daryl turns.

Benjamin feels heat rising in his neck. "What are you trying to do to us?"

"I'm not tryin' to do nothin'." He pulls his shoulders back as though Benjamin has grabbed at them, then turns and continues walking.

Benjamin follows. "Don't pull that stuff anymore."

There's a grunt of approval from Nick, still beside him.

"What stuff?" says Daryl.

"Any stuff," says Benjamin definitely. He knows he should leave it at that, lead his pugnacious sidekick back to the dugout. In a moment or so Falcone will have shooed the dandies back to their dugout, will then tell him to get into the coaching box and Nick to go to the Gray's dugout. But the anger sizzles in his pores. "If we get any more of it we're gonna tear you apart before you leave this ball park!"

Nick is delighted. "He's fuckin' right," he adds.

"Are *you* on his side?" Daryl asks Nick like a child who's just been shunned by a playmate.

"It's my game the same as his," Nick replies firmly. "We're with the same team, in case you never noticed."

Daryl turns from Nick to Falcone, who's just gotten the dandies back to the W. and W. dugout. "Call time out!" he snaps.

246

"What for?" asks Falcone, puzzled; he's just called time in.

Daryl is shuffling toward the plate, his hand dangling behind him, forefinger out. "That manager just threatened me! Forfeit the game to W. and W.!"

There's a buzz of interest from the stands, then movement:

Gray rises from his chair behind the scoring table, grin breaking, hands moving together as if for slow-motion applause.

Ellen stands too, giving Benjamin a surprised look that seems to say, "You wouldn't do a stupid thing like that, would you?"

Not far from her, Marilyn's head has come up from her crafts book and she's looking around, wondering what all the fuss is about; beside her, Billy Sunrise, hunched forward, is fast asleep.

Daryl, at the plate, speaks so loudly he can be heard at every corner of the field: "They're going to attack me after this game!"

Benjamin and Nick remain where they've been, in shallow left field, alone, apart from all others.

Benjamin looks down at Nick, says quietly, "Did you hear me say anything to that gentleman?"

Nick is smiling up at him, smiling at him for the first time all season. "Yes, I did."

"You *did?* What?"

"I heard you say, 'You're sure doin' a nice job, Daryl. Keep up the good work.'"

Benjamin laughs and puts his arm on Nick's shoulder. They start toward the dugout. "I'm happy you heard me say that, Nick. You know why?"

"No. Why?"

"Mr. Dunne!" It's Falcone.

"Because it occurs to me that there was no one else who witnessed the conversation."

"Heh," says Nick. "That's good. No one else. Right!"

They've reached the coaching box. The other Gray's players are standing against the dugout screen. In their crazy uniforms they remind Benjamin of figures behind a fence at a lunatic asylum. Their mouths hang in surprise as they watch Benjamin and Nick behaving in such a

247

chummy way. *Maybe,* the expressions seem to say, *we've been missing something.* Finally Tag cheers, and the others follow with applause.

"Mr. Dunne!" Falcone again.

"Let's acknowledge the clapping," Benjamin says impulsively.

"Sure."

Like a couple of vaudeville comics after a performance, the two instinctively turn to the Gray's dugout and bend from the waist simultaneously: It's exaggerated as each tries to get himself lower than the other. When they rise Benjamin says to his partner, "Would you care to join me for a chat at home plate, Mr. Luchessa?"

"Not at all, Mr. Dunne."

As they move off, approving laughter follows from the dugout.

Possibly because he's riding this new wave of good fellowship, Benjamin doesn't see the frantic figure of Digby Wells stumbling down the steps of the announcer's booth.

On the kitchen table he finds a note from Bobo:

Mrs. Jennings called. Wanted to talk to you. About Max. Says please call her back.

It's nearly suppertime. He stuffs the note into his back pocket, opens the refrigerator, and begins to remove ingredients for a salad. Marilyn has been leaving the girls with a sitter across town, picking them up soon after work at the store, getting home in time for supper.

Today he didn't stop by to see Ellen and didn't call her. They've spoken only once since their recent trip to the hidden pond, briefly by phone, about Max's eligibility for the championship game. Though Benjamin said he was sure Max could play, Ellen wanted him to make it official so that Max wouldn't be surprised or hurt. Benjamin has verified with Francis that the boy is eligible, wishes she'd taken his word.

He's put the cutting board on the kitchen counter and is now slicing tomatoes on it. In a large bowl next to the board there are green onions, cucumbers, and lettuce. After he's arranged the ingredients in the big wooden bowl, he'll make a dressing, his own recipe: apple vinegar and olive oil with brown sugar, bits of garlic, lemon juice, powdered seasoning, table salt and pepper. He'll fuss with it until he thinks the taste is right, then test it on Marilyn and the children and follow their advice: a touch more of this or that. Rarely does it please everyone. He doesn't care, likes having them all participate.

After the ingredients are in the mixing bottle he goes to the phone in the hallway between living room and kitchen, dials the first four digits of Ellen's number, then abruptly puts the phone down and returns to the kitchen, where he shakes the bottle and tastes the dressing. Later, he thinks. He adds a little more oil, shakes the bottle, and tastes again. Now he adds a pinch more of the seasoning, shakes and tastes once more. He puts the lid on the dressing bottle and watches as the layers of oil and vinegar blend to a murky substance spotted with bits of seasoning and pepper. The layers re-form, each less distinct than it was before he shook the bottle. He's always careful to pour the dressing onto the salad the instant he stops shaking the bottle, wanting the blend to be as complete as possible.

The back door opens and Bobo tromps in, grunts a greeting, and seeing the salad bowl and the bottle of dressing beside it, takes a teaspoon from the kitchen drawer, shakes the bottle, pours some dressing onto his spoon, and tastes. "Good but too salty," he says.

They'll ruin it, Benjamin thinks. Yet he adds a little more oil. Before they eat, he will, on the suggestions of Marilyn and the girls, have added at least a touch of every other ingredient. Numerous times he's promised himself to leave the salad dressing just the way it was, his way.

Bobo takes the evening newspaper off the kitchen table and starts for the living room.

"Want to do me a favor?" Benjamin says.

Bobo replies without enthusiasm: "What?"

"Call Max. Tell him Francis said it's okay for him to play in the championship. I've checked on it."

"That's great. Him playing. Yeah. I'll call." He again starts for the phone, stops, and adds, "How come you don't call Mrs. Jennings like she wanted? Thought you were kind of friendly with her."

Benjamin puts the top back on the dressing bottle, glances over to see Bobo standing beside the phone, paper

249

under one arm. Looking into the kitchen, he's waiting for his answer.

"A favor. Okay?"
Mercifully Bobo picks up the receiver and begins to dial.

After Marilyn and the girls come home, Annie and Marilyn taste the dressing, suggest other changes. He makes them, waits for Suzie to taste the dressing. She doesn't come to the kitchen. He thinks of calling her in but recalls Keller's advice about not spilling anxieties on the children. He'll wait until she makes an opening, then try to work toward a conversation. Finally he gives the bottle several vigorous shakes, then pours the contents over the salad. As he picks up the big wooden fork and spoon and begins tossing the ingredients, he resolves to call Ellen later. He'll admit his recent reluctance to call her, will try to explain it.

"Dad," *says Annie, bouncing into the kitchen,* "is it okay if I put these peanuts our baby-sitter gave us into the salad?"

"No," *he says softly, eyeing her to make sure she doesn't drop in a few.*

"Well," *she says, looking over the salad,* "it still needs something."

First, of course, he's going to have to explain it to himself.

Digby waits near the dugout, apart from the other players, as Benjamin speaks his case to Falcone:

Why would he and his player want to make a threatening remark to the field umpire? They got the call they wanted on the play at second base, didn't they? Aren't they winning this game? Daryl, feeling the pressure of the game, must have misunderstood.

"That's bullshit!" Daryl shouts.

Falcone, blinking as he listens, finally takes advantage of a pause in the exchange and says to Daryl, "Go back to your position."

"If anything happens to me, Falcone, you're going to pay for it!"

"Sure," says Falcone, putting on his mask. "Play ball!"

Returning to the coaching box, Benjamin spots Digby

beside the low fence, sees that he's crying, stops, bends down, says, "What's happened?"

"I . . . called his house. Nobody answered at first. Then a man came from next door and answered and . . ." He rubs his eyes with the back of the sleeve of his sweatshirt. "He said Mrs. Bagthorn went to the hospital 'cause someone phoned her and said Meryl got hit by a car."

"Jesus!"

"He left here without us knowing he did," Digby goes on. "He must've got hit walking home."

"How bad is he?"

Digby raises his left sleeve and, holding part of it with his right hand, blows his nose into it. "That man didn't know . . . so I called the hospital. I have a high voice so I pretended I was his aunt. I knew they wouldn't tell me anything unless I pretended. They said he was unconscious at first. But then he woke up. He broke his leg and some ribs."

"Digby?"

"What?"

Benjamin puts his hand on the boy's shoulder and grips it tightly. "You going to be okay?"

"Yes. I'm pretty sure." Digby unashamedly presses the side of his face against Benjamin.

"Want to go to the hospital to see him?"

He feels Digby nodding.

"I'll get someone to drive you."

"My dad and mom are here," Digby says, raising his head. "One of them will take me."

He and Benjamin turn and look toward the stands where, out of a mass of white faces, a black face has risen, a man's face, eyes frowning, apprehensive.

I won't tell the rest of them, Benjamin decides as Digby hurries toward his father, *not until after the game.*

He turns, sees his players in the dugout bending forward and concentrating.

He'll stay here with them. After the game he'll go to the hospital, take any of them who want to join him.

Damn you, Meryl! he thinks. *Damn you!*

He looks out and notices that the shadow of the announcer's booth has reached past second. Before it gets to the outfield fence it will fade into larger shadows, and then there will be no shadows, only the shallow light

251

that precedes nightfall. There's about another good hour of ball time. *It won't take that long,* he assures himself. *We can do it quickly.*

He's alone on the landing at the top of the stairs, gazing into the dark hallway below, listening to the soft night sounds around him. In the girls' bedroom Annie has just murmured in her sleep. Bobo, still awake, is shuffling about behind his bedroom door, a step up and a few feet from where he stands. From behind the door to his left, the door to his and Marilyn's bedroom, come the faint sounds of Charles Ives's Symphony Number One, which has been playing on the Toledo classical music station for the past few minutes. He leans back, feels the cool plaster wall against him. The night is humid and warm. He turns the palms of his hands against the wall, slides them, lightly perspiring, from side to side until they begin to dry, then holds them there flatly, letting the coolness enter them.

Bobo's door opens and the boy emerges with a towel wrapped around his middle. From behind him shines the dim light from his desk lamp. He leans forward, starts to open the bathroom door, then stops abruptly, jumping sideways, smacking his back against the bedroom door.

"Damn!" he says, peering down.

"Didn't mean to scare you."

"You look like a statue or something. How come you're standing there?"

"Just sort of relaxing," he says.

"Mmm," says Bobo, sounding puzzled. "Well, I'm going to take a shower." *He hesitates, then closes the bedroom door, enters the bathroom and closes that door before putting on the light, as if sensing that light shining on the landing will somehow be an intrusion on his father.*

In a few moments the shower is on, its swishing sounds soon broken by the movements of Bobo's body underneath. The interplay of body and water soon create a kind of music that works in counterpoint to the notes of the Ives symphony.

It's near midnight. Marilyn isn't home yet. She called during the first hour of darkness, apologizing, saying they'd had good news: A contact Billy Sunrise had in

New York, a distributor of costumes or party knick-knacks or something, wanted to see samples of the body disguises. "Nothing definite," she said. They'd be working late tonight, however, possibly tomorrow and the day after. Billy, not wanting to delay, would then drive to New York with samples.

For several days the girls had been begging him to tell them a story. After the phone call he urged them to bed early with a promise that they'd get the story later.

"Are you sure?" Annie said.

"I'm certain," he replied.

Had Marilyn noticed, as he had, how silent Suzie was lately? Though her eyes showed anticipation when he promised the story, she said nothing at all. Often she didn't seem to hear the questions he asked her about her activities, friends, the baby-sitter. He planned to make the story a good one, full of elements that would cause her and Annie to comment and ask questions; he'd get her to open up.

On the way to the girls' room he identified the source of a recent resentment toward Marilyn. It wasn't her obsessive work with the body disguises; it was her silence about Suzie. Yes, he knew she too worried; but didn't she share her concerns with him, not just with Keller or Billy Sunrise? That silence, above all, seemed proof that something important had been lost between them.

The story was about a family of coins who lived in the money box of a candy machine: two quarters (parents), a nickel and a dime (children). They were pushed around a lot, particularly by fat and bossy fifty-cent pieces. ("I didn't think fifty-cent pieces could fit into candy machines," Annie said. "In this one they could," he answered.) One fifty-cent piece sat on their heads a lot, lording it over them, making sure to remind them all the time how very much more important it was than they. They managed to survive the fifty-cent piece's bullying and other problems until, one day, in giving out change, the machine sucked one of the quarters down the change slot and it vanished. "A very sad moment for the family," Benjamin said, stopping, watching his daughters react, Suzie with a troubled frown and Annie with a couple of fierce sniffles.

"But of course," he went on, "the quarter eventually

returned. A small boy who'd received it as change came back to buy something else with it later." He was about to close the story with a more-or-less-happily-ever-after ending when Annie spoke:

"Maybe someone else came along later and took one of the other persons in the family. But maybe that one wouldn't get put back in that machine."

"No, no," Suzie reminded her sister, wanting to hold on to what had happened and not be troubled by other, gloomier, possibilities.

"The quarter came back," Benjamin said. "And I think the others probably would too, though I can't prove it."

"If you keep the story going, we can find out," Annie said.

Suzie now stared at the curtain that covered one of the two bedroom windows.

"Right now I just don't want to keep the story going."

"You mean it's boring to you?"

"No. Not that. Suzie?"

She didn't respond.

He reached out, nudged her shoulder, which rested just below her pillow on the big double bed.

She turned, found Benjamin, then Annie. "Maybe you don't want to hear more," she said with a warning look.

"Why not?" Annie insisted.

Suzie didn't answer.

"Let's just let it stay where it is," Benjamin said to Annie.

"Are you sure that quarter came back?" Annie wanted to know. "Are you really sure?"

"I'm certain. Aren't you, Suzie?"

Though it took her a few seconds, Suzie finally nodded.

"Bull," said Annie.

The swishing sounds have stopped. Except for the Ives symphony, its notes fading, rising, falling, there's a general silence. The darkness seems to heighten the odors and aromas of the house: the soapy fragrance coming from under the bathroom door, the lingering smell of the spaghetti sauce he made for their dinner, the sweet scent of the cherry woodwork itself.

Bobo opens the bathroom door, seems surprised to see

254

Benjamin still standing at the top of the stairs. "Something wrong?" he says.

"Nothing wrong. Feel like talking?"

"Anything serious?" Bobo is put off by "serious" conversations, meaning those that include lectures, advice, all such that give off even the faintest whiff of instruction.

But Benjamin doesn't want to deceive him. "Yes," he admits, "serious."

"Oh oh."

When Bobo goes to change Benjamin enters his own bedroom and goes to the work area and his desk, pausing long enough to scan its face, now cleared of papers, pencils, pens. He wheels the chair out and turns it so that it faces the bed.

Bobo, in bright red gym shorts and clashing orange tank top (the sort of outfit he's lately adopted in place of regular pajamas), comes in and lowers himself to the side of the bed, looking bothered.

Benjamin sits relaxed, a foot up on the chair's seat, arm wrapped around his leg. "I'll just say, without explanation, what I've been thinking I might do, then answer any questions you have, if any. The reason I'm not going to explain is that, right now at least, I haven't got any explanation."

More interested than bothered now, Bobo leans forward and, without even a touch of sarcasm, speaks one of Benjamin's clichés, as if it were the only possible word for the moment: "Shoot."

The Ives piece creeps through its closing notes as Benjamin begins to speak.

It's time to break their resistance, he decides after he watches Moose, possibly unnerved by the delays and arguments, deliver four consecutive balls to Harold, loading the bases.

The first pitch to Tony is wild, allowing another run to score.

Benjamin calls Tony to the coaching box and tells him to move around before setting himself for each pitch. "We can finish off Moose right now."

Soon the second baseman is following instructions: flapping legs, arms, and bat. The count on him is soon three balls, no strikes.

Norm finally comes out of the dugout, waving in his relief pitcher.

Benjamin calls Tony to the coaching box as the new pitcher approaches: "He's got to get the very first one over. Otherwise you've got yourself a walk." The new pitcher has heard the remark; it'll be an additional pressure on him.

Tony adds more pressure by saying loudly, "Hi am geeveeng ten-to-whon odds he don' even get eet een thee catcher's meet."

The new pitcher's warm-ups show a dipping fastball and a sharp-breaking curve. He's putting most of his throws into the strike zone.

"Play ball!" calls Falcone.

Coming down the stairs, Benjamin plays back his son's last words, spoken softly from the doorway: "The thing is you've got to do it if you believe it's the right thing." He paused for a moment, his eyes reaching sideways, finally coming back with a question: "Do you know if you're going to?"

The question repeats itself even as Benjamin seeks to flee from his answer to it by flipping through a volume of the encyclopedia the children sometimes use for homework assignments. Both question and answer fade only after he finds the article he's been looking for.

What first catches his eye is an aerial photograph showing the state capitol building and other, smaller, buildings, each surrounded by tall and rugged trees. "Boise," the caption says in part, "is a town with wide streets and many open spaces." He goes on, reads the entire article, then looks at the photograph again. Again he goes back to the article, picking out details: ". . . western slope of the Rocky Mountains . . . crop farming . . . dairying, livestock, lumbering . . . settled in 1863 . . . administered by full-time mayor and six councilmen . . . several parks." He turns from the book, marveling at how, on the spur of that small newspaper report about the man named Jackbar, he's been stirred to a fascination for this distant and unexceptional place.

He puts aside the encyclopedia but remains immobile on the sofa for a long time, a captive of small and feeble impulses: to lie out on the back lawn under the murky night sky; to exhaust himself with a long and aimless walk through the streets of the town. The impulses seem to conflict with his interest in Boise, even with each other. Yet all, he's sure, come from fixed and persistent sources within himself. He began by confessing to Bobo that he'd been full of a strange nervous electricity that somehow demanded release through action. Bobo suggested he might just have jitters about the upcoming championship. "Jitters about what happens afterwards, I'm afraid." He was going to add more, but said only, "I may leave, at least for a while, go to another town, pretty far from here." He mentioned the Jackbar story, said how, if nothing else, it at least had allowed him to admit to himself how strong was the desire to go. Bobo now sat on the bed, was leaning back on his elbows, watching his father with worried attention. "I wouldn't go until I was sure everything was all right with Suzie."

"Will it be?" Bobo wanted to know.

"I think so."

Benjamin gets up, crosses the room, pulls back the drape over the big window, and looks out, hoping for some sort of distraction. A person, perhaps a stranger, will pass, glance over at him, and nod a greeting. No one passes. He lets the drape fall closed, returns to the sofa.

Speaking evenly, Bobo said that, no, of course he wouldn't like it and he knew the others wouldn't either. He agreed with Benjamin that it would be very hard on the girls, especially Suzie, even if she did improve. "If they knew they could see you sometimes, if they knew you'd come back, they'd get used to it, I guess." Bobo seemed to be speaking for himself as well when, after a moment's thought, he added, "They'd just have to."

Believing he'd made a cruel mistake in saying so much to Bobo, Benjamin thought about making up for it by reporting that he'd spoken to Dan about staying on at the bookstore temporarily and turning all profits over to Marilyn; but remembering that brief conversation with Dan, in which he'd deliberately exploited his assistant's new Christian spirit, begging him to postpone by at least six months his entry into Bible school, Benjamin felt even more cruel. All he could say to Bobo was, "Money matters and other such things would be taken care of."

Standing, giving his father a look that was more sympathetic than resentful, Bobo asked his last question.

Benjamin, who'd entered the bedroom thinking he had an answer, finally knew he didn't and could only reply with, "No. I don't. It's a very powerful impulse, despite the arguments I put up against it, but . . . I don't know."

Raising his feet to the coffee table, resting the encyclopedia against his upper legs, he once more rereads the article. This time, however, he uses details from the narrative to expand the aerial photograph out into the town itself: its business district, parks, museum, neighborhoods with redwood Victorian houses, the rugged hills beyond. He then begins adding details that don't come from the article: a lake, hidden pathways, the faces of children, a baseball stadium, more, much more. Soon he's creating a Boise of his own, a Boise of the mind.

As the new pitcher watches Falcone dust off home plate, Bobby Watson calls to him from the Gray's dugout: "Remember, Shorty, this pitch has *got* to be a strike."

The pitcher Bobby has both christened and warned stops, looks (pleadingly Benjamin thinks) toward Gray's dugout, then drops the ball to the ground.

"That your pitch?" Nick bellows.

Shorty actually shakes his head in a serious response.

"Don't forget," Bobby says in the tone of a friend giving advice, "it's all on *your* shoulders."

After picking up the ball, the new pitcher turns stiffly to face Tony.

"Good haftairnoon," Tony says as Shorty bends into his windup. Tony's come out of his batting stance, is facing Shorty with bat on hip. As Shorty shakily raises his arm to prepare his throw, Tony continues: "Hi whish to whelcome hue do thee chomp-peen-sheep game ob thee Centerveel Pee Wee League. Hue may conseeder hureself locky to be joe-sen do feeneesh dees *mose* him-*por*-tant game por jure team, Whatson an' Wheels. . . ."

Shorty has stopped in mid-windup: a balk.

Falcone waves, signaling the runner to advance; Max scores and Harold is on third base.

Norm erupts from the W. and W. dugout, complaining about dirty tactics.

Tony turns, gives Benjamin a masterful stare.

Benjamin winks at him, then calls Bobo, his next batter, to the coaching box, and says, "Tony's probably going to get a walk. You can fool around like him and try for the same. But we need as many runs as we can get. So I'd suggest going after whatever your bat can reach."

"Nick's going to be pissed off if I bat a bunch of runs in." He looks at the Gray's dugout thoughtfully, then adds, "But that's his problem, isn't it?"

Benjamin nods. "One more thing. In warming up, this pitcher threw a curve, then a strike, a curve, then a strike. That seems to be his pattern. Watch for it. If he alternates like that on the first two pitches, figure the third pitch to be the opposite of the second. Be ready for it. Understand?"

"Yep." Bobo, eyeing the pitcher, eagerly taps his bat against the side of his shoe. "Maybe I won't have to wait for two pitches."

"Maybe."

Daryl has gone to home plate, is actually helping Norm argue his groundless case with Falcone. The dandies were once Daryl's enemies; now they're his chums. Benjamin takes strange pleasure in the recognition. He's even more pleased to see that Falcone has begun to lose patience: "A balk is a goddamned balk!" Though he's standing no more than a foot from Daryl, Falcone is shouting: "The batter was in the batter's box! He could have stuck the bat up his ass! No difference!" Daryl says something about "delay of game" tactics and suggests, amazingly, that Tony be thrown out of the contest. Falcone yells, "Baseball is full of delays! You don't even know the rules! And you can't make a simple call right in front of your nose! I ought to throw *you* out!" There are a few more whines from Daryl, but Falcone doesn't back off.

"Play ball!" he commands finally.

Tony gets into the batter's box, straightens his arms, and holds his bat directly above his head like a flagstaff. He's turned around, facing Shorty. He looks as though he's going to continue his speech; he doesn't. He simply watches the pitcher.

Shorty, biting the side of his lower lip, trying to ignore Tony, perhaps waiting for him to say something, goes into his windup by the numbers—one: bend down; two: straighten up; three: raise leg; etc. The resulting pitch is so low that the W. and W. catcher has to block it with his legs to prevent it from reaching the backstop.

With Tony's walk there are two runners on base.

Benjamin tries not to build his hopes, yet he has faith in all of them, especially Bobo and Nick; they don't collapse under heavy pressure.

Benjamin looks about:

Norm is kicking at the concrete blocks outside his dugout.

Daryl is back at his infield position, talking to himself.

Behind home plate Falcone is cursing off steam built up during the argument.

Shorty, after closing his eyes for several seconds, steps to the pitching rubber and starts his windup.

The Gray's players in the dugout begin rattling the chicken wire.

Shorty, numb to distractions now, goes through with his pitch, a fastball for a strike.

Bobo kicks away dirt, plants his feet more firmly in the batter's box.

Shorty takes an easy windup and throws a good curve that just misses the strike zone.

On the next pitch, a fastball, Bobo's swing is level and clean with no nervous extra effort; the ball bursts toward left field: a line-drive single.

One run scores.

The left fielder, who charged forward an instant after Bobo hit the ball, snatches it up on the first hop and sends a low throw to home plate.

"Go back!" Benjamin calls to Tony, who's come around third and is racing for the plate.

Churning up dust, Tony skids to a halt, turns, and in three leaps is back on third, easily beating the throw from the catcher.

"Safe," Daryl says in a depressed tone that's almost a whisper. Only Benjamin and the Gray's players in the dugout can hear him.

"Safe!" Benjamin repeats for the benefit of all others.

Cheers rise from the Gray's stands.

Nick approaches home plate like a hungry man who's late for lunch. He eyes Bobo at first base and Tony at third. Benjamin can't see his face now but guesses his tongue is circling his lips. He bends down and hits the top of the plate so hard with the head of his bat that it's not necessary for Falcone to come forward and brush off the dust left when Bobo took off for first base. He turns around and gives Benjamin a smile that is full of complicity.

The first pitch is a smart-looking curve that breaks over the plate belt high. Nick is surveying the fence between left and center fields when it passes, like someone still looking at a menu though the meal is being served.

There are groans from the Gray's stands.

But Benjamin knows, and probably so do his other players, what the W. and W. coaches and pitchers should by now have learned: Nick doesn't like curveballs. *Thank you,* his nodding gesture seems to say, *but I'll wait for the next course.*

Benjamin has broken the W. and W. pitcher's code: curveball, then fastball. There's no reason to believe that this mechanical pitcher or his unimaginative coaches will change the pattern. However, he doesn't want to risk awakening them to such a possibility by calling Nick over and assuring him that the next pitch will be a fastball. Nick's bravado at home plate—he's now indicating to someone in Gray's dugout the general area in which he intends to send his hit—suggests he knows he's going to get a fastball.

Shorty, every limb strung tightly, delivers the fastball low and inside, such a bad pitch that Benjamin glances away before it reaches the plate. The solid crack of bat against ball shocks him back:

Nick is standing in the batter's box.

A foul?

But Nick's eyes are moving, upward.

Benjamin looks up in time to see the ball cross between two branches of a tall elm just beyond the left center field fence.

Finally Nick drops his bat. He doesn't run to first base; he struts.

A single cheer, rising from both Gray's stands and the dugout, now turns to a sustained roar.

Nick stops at first base and shakes Karl's hand. He dances to second, crosses it backwards with a little wave for the W. and W. second baseman, goes sideways to third, doing a bow-and-handshake for Benjamin. He removes his cap and waves it at the Gray's crowd as he walks very slowly amid sustained applause toward home plate. Standing on the plate, he turns around and aims a little wiggle of his butt at Gray in the announcer's booth.

The sponsor closes his eyes, then turns abruptly away. The score is Gray's 7, W. and W. 0.

Benjamin calls Max to the coaching box and asks him two questions:

The first: "How does your arm feel?"

Answer: "Better than when the game started."

The second: "And your nerves?"

Answer: "Very loose, Mr. Dunne, especially now."

We've got it, Benjamin thinks, *unless we give it away.*

He stands before Ellen's front door, leans around and glances at Max and Bobo, who wait in his car in the driveway, looks back:

"Are you coming to the game?"

"Of course," she says as if she's been insulted.

"I just told Max I'm thinking about starting him, letting him go as far as he can." The decision, he doesn't tell her, will be made after he watches Max practice with Bobo today at Pee Wee Park. He's already begun to worry about his other pitchers' reactions. "I'm not sure yet."

"It'll make his summer." She considers something for a moment and adds, "You're not doing it for me, are you?"

"No," he says truthfully. "I want to win the thing. I feel ruthless about it. I want to do whatever it takes. I've turned around that old saying about sportsmanship. For me, now, it doesn't seem to matter how you play the game, but whether you win or lose."

"Abner Doubleday didn't invent a sport you're supposed to go out and lose. I never trusted those coaches of Max's who used to say they didn't care if their team won, so long as everyone played and learned something about baseball. They can all play and learn, and sometimes win. Can't they?"

"I hope so."

He leans away from the door again, looks to the driveway, notices that Bobo and Max are gazing out of op-

262

posite windows. Where's the strategy talk between pitcher and catcher about how to handle the W. and W. batters? The expressions of enthusiasm about being in the championship game? Maybe Max has said something to Bobo about Ellen and him. Have they already shared their disgust, even contempt?

He pulls back, out of the boys' line of sight, watches her step toward him.

"It wouldn't do me any good to ask about us, I suppose."

"I wish I had something to say," he replies.

"All right." She seems about to reach out and touch him. Finally she stretches past him to the honeysuckle vine near the doorway and plucks a flower; it still holds its colors, is not as curled or dried as some of the others. She hands it to him. "I don't know why I'm doing this. I hate sentimental gestures."

"So do I." But he takes it, puts it carefully into the pocket of his windbreaker.

She gives his hand a tight squeeze and says, "I'd like to spend at least a few minutes with you after the game."

He looks at her, waiting to feel powerfully the tug of an old desire; he doesn't.

She also waits.

Even the simplest words won't come.

"Something has changed," she says finally, softly. "Hasn't it?"

"I can't explain it." As he searches for words to add, some kind of explanation, he notices her nodding.

It's a precise and eloquent gesture that tells him his answer can stand as it is.

Yet there must be a reason: selfish, guilty, caring, reckless, an honest reason; he can't get to it.

Her hand has started toward him, then stopped.

He thinks to say, "I'm sorry," but only shakes his head weakly.

No other words are spoken.

He hurries to the car.

On the way to the ball park he escapes from the conversation by telling Max he wants him to throw his best pitches to Bobo, as hard as he would in a game. "If your arm and ankle feel right and if you have the kind of control you had the other day, you'll definitely start."

The announcement doesn't cause talk at first. Not until they turn at the bank for the last short stretch to the ball field does Bob break the silence:

"There's prob'ly gonna be a big crowd for the game. That bother you?"

"I'll tell you after the first inning," Max says with a laugh.

They go on, anticipating the game.

The light exchange somehow assures Benjamin that they haven't been sitting back there chewing themselves apart with questions about him and Ellen.

Would it matter now? *he thinks as he pulls into the parking area.*

EIGHT

The light has slipped away almost imperceptibly. Benjamin noticed the darkness only when, holding the big gold-plated trophy that Francis presented to him near the pitcher's mound, he led his team in single file through a limp handshaking ritual with the W. and W. players and coaches.

He's sitting cross-legged behind second base, looking in at the diamond, thinking what an odd perspective he has. From nowhere else would all the action of a ball game be more visible, more intimate. Yet no player ever positions himself here.

The concessionaire's truck, with parking lights on, pulls slowly away, the last vehicle to leave. The only remaining light comes from the raging flames in trash containers, a pair of oil drums, one standing between the announcer's booth and the Gray's stands and the other between the booth and the W. and W. stands. It's an eerie light, a changing light.

A small boy runs from behind the drum on the W. and W. side, pauses beside the drum, looking out, perhaps trying to identify the figure seated beyond second base, then retreats behind the drum, disappearing into the darkness of the parking area. When the flames caught his face in full light, it appeared to Benjamin to grow older.

Someone is taking care of the fires. Someone, maybe the same person, will close the gates to the park. He, or one of them, will soon tell Benjamin and those wandering about that they must leave. Meanwhile he'll remain in this private and peaceful place.

Just before Francis came down from the announcer's booth to present the team trophy, Marilyn stopped at the gate in the low fence and said, "I've got to pick up Suzie at the Andersons', get the girls ready for bed, and put aside some material for tomorrow's sewing. So I'll rush off and see you at home."

He nodded, then bent down and kissed Annie, who'd been bubbling to him about Nick's home run.

"Marvin called."

"What?" Why had she left this news until now, given it as an afterthought?

Seeing his concern, she quickly said, "Nothing about Suzie, except to remind me of her next appointment. I think—" She checked Annie, saw that she was watching some of the Gray's players nearby, not listening. Her mouth worked its way into a little smile. "I think he was calling about us. I think he wonders if *we're* falling apart. He asked about my project and said he hoped you guys win the ball game. Passing-the-time-of-day sort of talk."

Prepared for a bolt of bad news about Suzie, he was happy to get something else. "So . . . how are you doing?"

She gave a little sigh, said, "The game reminded me that there's another world out here. Nice to get a break from mine."

He nodded to that, the tone of it more than its meaning, which he didn't quite grasp.

She took Annie's hand and hurried off to her car or to Billy Sunrise's, whichever they'd taken.

A few minutes ago Ellen appeared between the two drums and looked out to him. She did nothing more than raise her hand in a little wave.

He thought of signaling her to come out and sit down, knowing he could now speak to her more clearly, more certainly, about his intentions. The wave seemed to tell him an explanation wasn't necessary; he simply returned it. Amid the leaping flames she too seemed to change, not so much in age as in expression: sad, joyous, puzzled, joyous again, indifferent. Soon she was gone.

Gray didn't stay for the final ceremonies. A couple of

Benjamin's players, hovering near the announcer's booth, reported that he'd argued with Francis that the presentation of the trophy should be to him, but lost. They said he then went off angry.

Benjamin leans back, feels the sturdy trophy against him. He's had it with him ever since he passed it among the Gray's players after the handshaking. Each of them fingered one or another of the three golden figures: hitter at top, fielder on one side, pitcher on the other; some ran their hands over all of it. "It's a big mother, isn't it?" Nick said.

They kept asking about Meryl.

He talked about the game first, said little moves as well as big ones had helped them get the victory (final score: Gray's 7, W. and W. 0), and used as example Digby's fake bunt that had let Benjamin know how the W. and W. infielders would play bunts. He mentioned every player and something each had contributed, even players who'd helped when not in the game (like Bobby Watson, who, in reminding the W. and W. pitcher of how much depended on him, helped cause the balk). He gave much praise to Nick, Max, and Bobo, those who'd done the heavy work.

But where, they wanted to know, was Meryl?

He then told them what he knew about the accident. Digby, whose father had brought him back in time for the final ceremonies, had reported that Meryl, after deciding to go home, had been struck by a car and suffered two cracked ribs and a broken ankle. Benjamin explained why he hadn't mentioned the accident earlier. "It seemed important that you *not* play this thing because of him."

They gave him surprised looks.

"It's got something to do with having to do it for yourselves. Don't ask me to say any more because I can't."

They didn't ask him to say more. But after expressions of concern, some asked if they could go over to the hospital. Digby said that visitors would be allowed, briefly.

"Why did he leave?"

Benjamin said he didn't know.

"Let's show him the trophy," Nick said. There was unanimous agreement.

Benjamin and Bobo will soon meet the others in the hospital lobby.

Daryl came up behind Benjamin as Benjamin was walking to the place he'd spotted behind second base. "Nice game," he said. "I got to admit it now that it's over."

"Go away," said Benjamin, not bothering to turn.

Daryl took the remark as though it had been the opposite, a request to stay, and kept following. "What you got against me?" he said.

It struck Benjamin as an enormous question, an honest one. Stopping, turning, he saw Daryl's torso curled against the light, his head twisted expectantly to one side. For an instant Benjamin felt he was looking at a distorted shadow of himself. The impression, though momentary, troubled him. He glanced away, said only, "I don't know."

Daryl moved partly around Benjamin, as though to block his way. "What do you mean, 'don't know'?"

The flames, their reflection, now wiggled into, then out of, Daryl's eyes. "I want to be alone," Benjamin said finally. "Can you understand that?"

"No. Why should I?"

Even that seemed an important question. Benjamin watched the other's eyes trying to hold the flames. He groped for something conclusive, something penetrating, to say. Nothing he thought of made sense to him. The best he could come up with was "Please."

"You're sick, man. You know that? You're really sick." Daryl stamped his foot for an emphasis his voice couldn't quite convey, then turned and started toward the low fence, hurrying as if to an appointment for which he was very late.

Bobo has emerged from behind the raging drums, shrinking a little as he moves out of the reach of the light. He crosses behind the backstop, toward the low fence on the first base side, then moves to the gate near the W. and W. dugout, opens the gate, and approaches Benjamin.

"You look like an old Indian chief," he says as he comes near.

"A man weary in his years."

"Time to go, isn't it?"

"I guess so."

Bobo reaches down, takes his father's hand, and pulls steadily, carrying most of the weight as Benjamin rises.

He then picks up the trophy, glances at it, and hands it to his father.

They pass the first base coaching box, near where Benjamin gave Karl a tight hug at the end of the game, getting in return an enthusiastic handshake ("It was a real great season, Ben. Sure did enjoy helpin'. Hope we can do 'er again next year").

Now, passing between the oil drums, Bobo creates a draft that makes the flames reach inward toward Benjamin, following. The orange tongues seem to be hands grabbing for him. He hesitates for a moment, watching one of the hands reach and recede. He stands between the drums, welcoming the heat they give off. As with the darkness, it's taken him time to feel the damp invading chill of evening.

Bobo holds open the back door of the station wagon. "You gonna say anything to him about runnin' off?"

"Yes." Benjamin leans in, slides the trophy across the seat.

"I thought so."

Benjamin sets the trophy firmly against the back of the seat and comes out of the car. "All right with you?"

"Sure," says Bobo, his tone letting Benjamin know the question needn't have been asked.

There'll be a celebration later. The team, except for Meryl, will go to Dairy Queen or another of its favorite stopping places. Karl has already contributed five dollars for treats, to which Benjamin, through Bobo, will add another five. He himself won't join them.

The trip to the hospital is a silent one, even more silent than was the drive to the ball park.

"I don't know how to take it," she says, reporting that Billy Sunrise has been to New York, has been given qualified encouragement, no promises. *"All of the potential distributors want to see a variety of samples and then do some kind of study on their marketability. Why can't they just know people will want to wear the disguises?"* She pauses, thinking, then says, *"I suppose that's how businesses have to work."* Another pause, then: *"It may take time to produce a lot of them, but I think we'll prove ourselves and be making good money, within a year. Don't you?"*

269

He doesn't. Of nothing is he more certain than the risk and foolishness of her and Billy Sunrise's project. He's accepted the body disguises as essential therapy for Marilyn, even briefly thought they might make a little money. Her practical question, however, has forced him to a practical rock-bottom reaction: the body disguises are most likely a bad investment. He, the businessman in him, might have known that all along; it's taken those potential distributors to bring him to an honest answer, for himself, for her. They're in bed, where they've had their best talks. He turns toward her, is about to tell her that no respectable company would make a full-scale commitment to anything as uncertain as the disguises.

She's still talking, however, gushing on about the possibility, within two years, of several little body disguise factories being opened at various places throughout the country. "We can train supervisors and they can train their staffs."

Suppose he's wrong. He can't, after all, measure the effects of her wish to succeed. That matters as much in business as, say, in baseball. He recalls teams that were picked for last place and won pennants, even World Series. Wasn't it the Boston Braves who were in last place with less than two months remaining in a season long ago, then ended up in first? Statistics and other practical criteria are one thing, but . . .

"Don't you agree?"

Agree to what? *He hasn't heard the lead-in to the question. Rather than admit he wasn't listening, he closes his eyes, tries to guess at the question. Before he comes up with anything, however, she begins talking again, this time about an instruction booklet she's thought of which will describe the various ways the body disguises might be used at parties, carnivals, fund-raising events, and such.*

Suppose, even, that he's right and that the business fails: soon, a year from now, whenever. Can he be sure that the time, energy, and money she puts into it in the meantime will go for little or nothing? She is, isn't she, finding a way to express something original in herself. Won't that continue until . . .

"Benjamin?"

In the end it seems impossible for him to give her solid

270

advice. There are too many unseeable factors, too many variables.

He flees from her last question, his thoughts about the project, imagines himself floating in a dark space between two enormous and equidistant planets. He sees his body roll upward in the darkness, taking the tug of one, then the other planet. The body goes this way and that until finally he sees it drifting toward one of the planets, and away from the other. As it drifts his body grows, becoming flat and flexible like one of Bobo's favorite comic-strip characters, Plastic Man. The planet from which it's drifting is getting smaller now and seems, somehow, to be falling into its own shadow. The other planet grows larger, brighter.

"I don't want to complain, but you've said nearly nothing useful."

In his drowsy state he momentarily thinks the words have come from the bright planet. He's watching his body spread before it like a soft and pliable film. The body now appears larger than the bright planet. Soon it has wrapped itself around the planet, completely around it, covering it like a protective layer. He waits to see more, but the vision begins to fade.

"Why haven't you been saying what you think?"

He finds himself with an answer now, a kind of answer.

"Maybe I seem sure of myself, but I'm not," she goes on, "I mean I want to believe certain things will happen, but . . . I don't know. Those responses Billy got make me wonder if I've built my hopes too high." He feels the bed quiver as she turns uneasily toward him. "Have I?"

"Go on with what you're doing," he says calmly.

"That's not really an answer."

"I'm not finished. Don't expect the project to succeed and don't expect it to collapse. Just . . . just keep doing what you're doing: making the disguises, believing in them, trying to attract the distributors, all the rest. Sooner or later you'll be sure that it'll work, or sure that it won't."

In her silence she seems to be waiting, as if again he'll say, "I'm not finished," and go on.

But he is finished.

Tears have come unexpectedly into his eyes. In his surprise he blinks against them, causing one of them to fall away. It begins to wind down the side of his head, wig-

271

gling as it goes. He follows its slow movement over his temple, past the highest part of his cheekbone, across the flat place in front of his ear, finally into the ear itself.

She's said something. He thinks she's said, "You must tell me what you really think," but the tear has plugged the ear nearer her and he isn't sure. He moves his jaw several times, unplugging his ear. He knows now that her question, no matter what it was, can bring only one answer. He speaks it softly:

"I've said all I can honestly say about the project." His words, too, come to him muffled.

The jerky movement of the mattress bespeaks her disappointment.

But he's certain: he can't honestly or usefully say more than he has.

Again he flees. This time to a letter, composed a few days ago, to Jackbar, the man from Boise. In it he emphasized his love of baseball and his possible interest in working on the Pioneer League project. Near the end he made a small apology for having had experience only with a boys' team. Yet he added that he did have business experience ("on the managerial level") and ended by reminding Jackbar of his own recognition that enthusiasm is what matters most. Though he thinks it's, all in all, a good letter, he hasn't yet mailed it.

"I can be realistic, Benjamin, if that's the message behind your last remark. It's just easier to get the work done when you believe something will come of it. I mean I am going to allow myself to look forward to the day when all Billy and I will have to do is design. I can do that and still, as you seem to be suggesting, take things as they come."

A phone call to Jackbar might even be better. At least he'd save a lot of time. Maybe Jackbar has already found a general manager, for example. The phone call would allow Benjamin, Jackbar too, to get the answers they might want quickly.

"Before Billy went to New York we talked about moving to a bigger place. We even saw ourselves eventually working out of Toledo or Cleveland. That plan will have to wait, I guess. It's not going to be as easy as I'd hoped. Any of it. Still . . ."

Bobo is old enough to travel, even to a town as

far away as Boise. When settled, Benjamin could invite Bobo to visit. Maybe Bobo would want to stay with him for good. But what about the girls? It'd be such a long distance. He wouldn't want Marilyn to put them on a bus or plane. How, then, would he see them, they him?

"Do give me more than you have, Benjamin, at least a general response. Don't you think, everything considered, it's worth all the time we've been putting into it?"

Her question stirs the memory of the conversation he overheard between her and Billy Sunrise at their shop. Ignoring that, ignoring his strong doubts about the practicability of the project, he says, "Yes. I do." He doesn't feel at all hypocritical.

She gets up, feels her way to the door, opens it, turns on the light at the top of the stairs, and says, "I'm going to get some orange juice. Want some?"

"No, thanks."

She goes down the stairs.

It would be best for him to leave without fanfare. He'd write Marilyn a letter, explaining the move as best he could. He'd phone the girls and Bobo frequently. He'd write to all of them each day. What else?

She comes back with a tall glass of orange juice, sits at the edge of the bed, facing the light she's left on at the top of the stairs, sipping. Her short nightgown shimmers in the light, and the strong features of her face—chin, nose, brow—seem very pronounced. He knows from the way she sits, from the way she regards the light, even from the deliberate way she raises the glass to her lips that she's riding a troublesome thought.

"Why has it become so hard for us to speak easily to each other?" she says at last, turning.

Replies come too quickly: We've changed. Or: It's just too painful. Or: We don't know, so can't talk about, the real reasons for our actions. Each would take hours to explore. Best to say nothing.

She drinks some of the juice, offers him the glass.

"No, thanks."

Finally she says, "Though I can't tell you just how I feel, I won't try to write it out, though that might get me closer to it. And I won't grab at some currently fashionable explanation—say, a feminist line—because, if I did, it would cloud my own reasons, the personal part." She

273

turns. "You don't owe me anything, Benjamin," she says, searching out his face. "Don't feel you do."

"Suppose, for some reason, I found it important to leave."

"Leave?"

"Made appropriate arrangements, the best I could, and then . . . just left. For, well, an indefinite time, maybe for as long as a year."

"Alone?"

"Yes."

"God! Are you serious?"

"Yes."

Having turned back toward the light, she now twists around again, frowning. "So often lately I've thought of just the opposite: me leaving. Now you say . . . I mean, you seem to be saying . . ." She stops, raises the glass toward the light, sees there's a little juice left, offers it to him; the gesture seems a substitute for the words she can't find.

He takes it, finishes what's there.

She reaches down and takes the empty glass, then gets up and goes softly out of the room.

"Marilyn?"

She doesn't answer.

He hears her in the kitchen, waits for a sign: the glass clattering in the sink, a cupboard door being slammed, a sob. There's nothing. She comes up the stairs, puts out the hall light, moves swiftly across the room, and gets into bed, swinging the sheet and blanket over her, wiggling easily toward him.

Will there be a delayed reaction? Later in the night? Tomorrow? Next week?

She's turned and is facing him, her hand on his bare shoulder. "How certain are you about going?" she asks.

"The feeling, the wish, stays with me. I guess I hope that talking about it will in some way kill it."

"If it's real, talking won't stop you."

"Would you be able to forgive me if I went?"

"I wouldn't have to forgive you."

"Sure?"

"Yes. I'm sure," she says in a convincing tone that tells Benjamin she's somehow had time to think about the question, its answer. She puts her arm around his shoul-

274

der, holds him close, not tightly, bringing her face to his.
"I don't want to discuss it anymore," she tells him. "Do
you?"

"No."

The night sounds have subsided: no children groaning
in their sleep, no creaking in the walls and floorboards,
not even a hushed swaying of trees outside their window.
The silence seems a kind of courtesy.

Lying very still, they separately, silently, part into
sleep.

Passing from the hospital's side entrance to the nearly
empty parking lot, he senses the air colder than it was
when he went in, the night darker. The darkness presses
in on the bluish light coming from the several facing lamp
posts, as if tightly to contain it. Aware that all the lamps
but those in the emergency area will soon be turned off,
he reaches into his pocket, pulls out his key ring,
searches, finds the right key, and moves quickly toward
the station wagon.

Only after the other players had gone did Meryl
turn his wounded eyes to Benjamin and say, "I knew you
weren't going to let me play. That's why I left." Benjamin
held his anger and forced himself to listen to the boy
stumblingly say he was sure his coach had decided he'd
let the team down and would do so again today:
"It didn't surprise me when I found out I wasn't starting
at pitcher or . . . anywhere. I didn't deserve to." Benjamin hadn't planned to chide or reprimand, but now the
anger broke and he said impatiently, "Do you have any
idea what was going on out there?" Only Meryl's eyes
answered, sliding apologetically from side to side, searching, not finding, eventually creeping back: *What?* In controlled tones Benjamin explained why he'd used some of
his weaker players first and kept his more reliable ones
until later. He said he'd started Max at pitcher both because the boy was throwing well and because he offered
the weapon of surprise: W. and W. hadn't faced him all
season. He said that Meryl would have played, in the
last, the most important part, of the game. "Having you
in the lineup then would also have allowed me to use you
at pitcher, if we'd needed you there." Meryl stared, wanting to believe. "You had no reason to go," Benjamin

added firmly. He had other words, urgent sharp-edged words: *You ran away out of fear or suspicion or both.* And: *You ran only from yourself, not from me or the team or the game.* And: *That you must never do since it's impossible to run from yourself.* He was looking for a way to soften what he had to say when Meryl's eyes stopped him; they reached out, not pleading or needful but damp with some small recognition. His hand followed, weakly, yet certainly. Benjamin stopped trying to find the right words, responded instead to the feeling Meryl's look had ignited: He went over to the bed, bent down, and took the boy's hand gently in his own. Meryl squeezed back tightly. In a moment or so Benjamin lowered himself and, careful not to put pressure on the taped ribs, embraced him. They held each other for several minutes. He could faintly feel Meryl crying. Finally he spoke a thought that had been washing away at his anger: "You have some idea of what I was going to say, don't you?" He felt Meryl nodding, heard him whisper, "I think so." Backing off, Benjamin knew that the boy couldn't, in these few moments, have grasped all the subtleties and complications behind the unspoken remarks, even if he somehow had gotten the gist of them. Yet there was a belief, soon hardening to certainty, that it didn't matter just now, that Meryl would search in his own time and own way, would eventually find out. *Soon enough,* Benjamin hoped.

He's driving along dark and unfamiliar streets, feeling free for once from the grip of forces outside himself, being guided only by small impulses—to stop, slow, speed up—going nowhere in particular. He hasn't reached to turn on the car radio, preferring the rhythms of silence and thought. A thought now shapes itself to an unspoken statement: *Imagine me almost giving* him *a lecture about running off.* But the statement doesn't lead to another, and he has no specific listener in mind, though he's sure that any of several—Marilyn, Ellen, Bobo—might appreciate the irony of his recognition.

To fill in time, he begins matching houses he passes to team members. (He's seen few of their homes.) He picks a wooden Victorian, run down but sturdy, for Nick; a low ranch with yellowed overgrown lawn for Tag; a cottagelike place with flowers around the windows for Meryl.

He finds himself approaching Ellen's street. He can think of no good reason to turn onto it, yet he does so, experiencing as he nears her house a faint sweet ache. Her living room light is on, a warm bright rectangle illuminating both lawn and street, the only bright light in the neighborhood. Slowing, he peers in, wanting to see her, only to see her; he's relieved when he doesn't. He goes to the end of the street, around the cul-de-sac, then returns, this time not turning to the window. The ache has sunk to a kind of embarrassment; he hopes she isn't looking out. He makes a quick turn at the head of the street and starts toward the center of town.

He goes past his own street and heads down Main, slowing when he reaches the store Marilyn and Billy Sunrise have rented. The display case is bare, and the store's only sign of life is a small rectangular card in the window: OPEN SOON. There's smaller lettering below that, but he can't read it. *Like a prayer card*, he thinks.

After a couple of turns he's in front of his own store. The light above the window has been left on, and now, for the first time, he notices that the book display has been changed. Spread out behind the glass in fan shape are inspirational and religious books with gaudily illustrated covers. He can't remember Dan asking him about making the change. He'd never have approved; the window should have variety; a searcher after literature might pass and think the place a Christian bookstore. Sure his assistant has become a blind subversive, he waits to feel anger; there isn't any.

He's saved the ball park until last, wanting to be sure everyone is gone, hoping even that the fires, which might attract passersby, have burned down. Having parked the car outside the closed gate, he's climbed over the gate and is standing at the screen behind home plate. In the first few minutes the field seemed clothed in impenetrable darkness, but his eyes have adjusted, and he can make out the base paths and even the outfield fence. He waits, looking out, expecting to relive some of the game's crucial plays, is surprised when he doesn't. Even his memories of them have begun to fade. Nothing moves but a couple of hot dog wrappers, hopping lethargically, one, then the other, in no certain direction. The whiff of something burning causes him to turn, see a wisp of smoke rising out of the nearer oil drum: a last remnant smoldering. He turns back to the field. Though bare and clean now, it will soon be allowed to grow over; even the infield will sprout weeds and tall grass. By the beginning of winter, this place will look like any other uncultivated field. He closes his eyes, until both the field and his thoughts about it are blotted out. After opening them he turns and starts back to his car.

He's at the stop light near the bank. It was yellow when he approached, but he made no attempt to accelerate through it. As he waits a thought begins to sustain itself. Letting his hands fall from the steering wheel, he indulges it:

When the signal changes he can go left and drive through town to Ellen's house. He is able to; it is a power he has. He can go inside and tell her truthfully about the light she has brought to his days. He can tell her there is still in him a desire to exist in her light. It is a power he has had for a long time; but now he is acutely aware of it. He can also speak the commitment that would follow from his words. He is aware that he has that power too.

He has other powers:

He can turn right when the light changes, drive the short distance to the thruway, then north to Toledo, then west to the turnpike. He has a few credit cards, some money in his wallet. In three days at most, hours really, he can be in Boise with Mr. Jackbar. He has the power to do that. He could eventually send for what little else he needed. Dan would handle the store until Benjamin made permanent arrangements, turn over the profits to Marilyn. Those he leaves would not be destroyed without him—Marilyn; Bobo; even the girls—as they would not be destroyed were his car, say, to be struck and he to be killed after pulling away from this stop light. Even Suzie would not be destroyed by his death or his going. It is conceivable that she'd find her bearings sooner, if more urgently, without him. He has faith in her. After leaving he would, of course, write them, call them, stay in touch. He could go, now, by turning the wheel left when the light changes.

The light has changed. He remains.

There are combinations among the possibilities. Ellen might be willing to leave Max in his father's care and travel west with him. He has the power to ask her to do that. And, ignoring Ellen, he can go home, get one or both of the girls, take her or them west with him. He can do that with or without making arrangements with Marilyn. He has such power. There are so many things he can do; he knows he's reached only the outer edge of possibilities, some more likely than others, some probably ridiculous, all possibilities just the same.

He has another, more obvious, power. He can go straight from the stop sign to the road at the far end of town, the quickest route home, put the station wagon in the garage, and remain. He guesses the girls are still awake. He'd probably end up answering Annie's questions about the ball game: finding out what Suzie did today at the Andersons'; listening to Marilyn talk about the fabrics she's been working on; waiting up to talk to Bobo. None of that would be unusual, yet in his power he knows that none of it would be quite usual either. He's reminded of the way a certain hit or pitch can turn the course of a ball game, always a matter of inches and small angles. The championship game, played yesterday or tomorrow, might have ended differently. Even played today it might have. Suppose, he thinks, Moose had thrown a pitch just a few inches higher than the one Bobo sent back against his foot. . . . But the speculation is pointless and could lead to others, as pointless. The game has ended; he has seen it through. Elsewhere nothing has ended.

The light has again turned green.

Seeing it, he raises his hands to the steering wheel and presses his foot softly against the accelerator.

Tonight, at least, there is only one place to be.

The best
in modern fiction from
BALLANTINE

G-3

The most fascinating people and events of World War II